Elle Laga'aia was born to US Navy Samoan parents. She grew up between California and American Samoa. Elle lives in Southern California and is the mother of three daughters and a Siamese cat. In her waking hours, she supports and advocates for animal charities.

Elle enjoys traveling to circumnavigate the world, one country at a time.

In loving memoriam to my great-grandmother, Vaotaua Laga'aia, born and raised in Vailoa, Palauli, Savai'i, and by marriage to my great-grandfather, of Afega, Samoa. Without her, we would not be this literate or as variegated and ambitious descendants vis-à-vis her grandsons. She was the embodiment of grace, love, and patience for these young souls who learned at her fingers and feet how to read the Bible and master their primers before they started primary school at Marist St. Joseph. Literacy was that important to her, and this carried forward to her seventh living generation today.

I hope to give her memory great honor. I ask this of Our Good Father. *Ma le alofa tele ma le 'ava tatau iai auā o lo'u tua'ā fa'apelepeleina!*

– Elle, great-granddaughter.

Elle A. Laga'aia

Tepatasi: Le Au'alumā

AUSTIN MACAULEY PUBLISHERS™

LONDON • CAMBRIDGE • NEW YORK • SHARJAH

Ordering Information
Quantity sales: Special discounts are available on quantity purchases by corporations, associations, and others. For details, contact the publisher at the address below.

Publisher's Cataloging-in-Publication data
Laga'aia, Elle A.
Tepatasi: Le Au'alumā

ISBN 9798889103523 (Paperback)
ISBN 9798889103530 (ePub e-book)

Library of Congress Control Number: 2024902964

www.austinmacauley.com/us

First Published 2024
Austin Macauley Publishers LLC
40 Wall Street, 33rd Floor, Suite 3302
New York, NY 10005
USA

mail-usa@austinmacauley.com
+1 (646) 5125767

Table of Contents

Tepa tasi: (to) look over something (often an event, point in history, a memory) to recollect, to remember once more.

Le Au'alumā: a group of women, often related, who are the soul of a family in the Samoas. They gather for the purpose of organizing events ranging from church inaugurations and funerals to weddings, bestowals of titles, etc. They are the capable hands that deftly move a family through its rigors.

Book One

I. 1905

Le Tumutumua'i Le Lalolagi
The Top of the World

Oh, the loud rattles of the kingfisher over the dawn! The fierce noisemaker startled several chickens as its powerful beak swooped down Kamikaze-formation upon the feathered congregation. A ruffled hen reared with its wings spanned as cover for her chicks turned and confronted the criminal culprit. Thinking wiser of the moment, the kingfisher fluttered its shiny blue feathers mid-flight and flew off to a safer perch on the beach hibiscus tree far above the terra firma collectivist farmed beasts.

The aching heartbeat of life began here on her mountaintop.

Better luck next time. I have all day, socialist sheep! With a wicked caw, he was off to find other victims to torture this morning. Breakfast may be in the offing as well. An *iao* heard the commotion and sounded the morning alarm.

The climbing sun's rays slowly gravitated over the thatched roof of the hillside cabin as morning called the day to order. The cleft on the verdant hillside and the humble patchwork of the roughly hewed, open-faced timber cabin was flanked by mottled mango tree trunks. Papaya grew abundantly around the four corners of the structure, sun-ripened fruit still in laden clusters. Starlings, in their waking hours, have helped themselves to a leisurely breakfast. Their leavings attracted fruit flies in droves daily and sugar bandit fruit bats at sundown. Coconut trees lined the property, carving a meandering dirt road from the cabin to the creek below.

Mother's variegated garden bobbed around the front steps into the cabin, a menagerie of tropical scents mixed in with the life-giving earth. White gingers and begonias with peppermint bluebells were vibrant bevies in the soft breeze. Overhead, silver trumpet trees offered shade with the sweet smell of blossoms. On the last day of November in the islands, they lent time to a new tropical summer on this draft side of the island. Thankfully, the boys were home from boarding school.

Under her threadbare, soft-washed muslin sleeping gown, sun-kissed legs had found their way onto the back of one sleeping soul. Turned onto her left hip sometimes late at night, she slept on with unruly cropped dark brown curls nestled against the bare chest beneath her cheek. Her tiny arm against his clavicle, one fist locked on a corner of a homespun pillowcase, the other clamped on her brother's forefinger.

The sun's rays gradually splayed over the upright side of her face, tickling her nostrils. Wakefulness touched her young body with a cat-like stretch, her bare foot jerking against the shoulder blade of the other slumbering soul. She peeled her head from its comfortable cradle and sat up, rubbing the sleep out of her eyes. A shiver worked out of her body through her shoulders to the tips of her toes. She peered about her, her translucent almond-shaped brown eyes unhurriedly taking in her settings. Her older brothers flanked her out in the living area on their shared sleep mat, while in the corner of the cabin, a long tapa screen afforded their parents a modicum of privacy from their young children.

Pele's cradle, Sama, was the eldest of the Stafford children. Long-limbed, he was taller and limber than most boys of his age. Sinewy muscles in his upper arms had begun to bulge in his prepubescent biceps. His long frame is in a floral *lavalava*, green and white wrap tied around his waist, the flowing fabric tucked between his legs. Arm flung over his eyes; his aquiline nose was prominent above slightly parted warm lips. God smiled upon their parents when they conceived Sama. Their mother knew this was so.

Pele's footrest was the quiescent Fano at eight. He was the cantankerous fellow with a clear complexion and a shock of dark black hair. Even at that young age, his features were reminders of foreign presences in Samoa, now two generations removed. His obsidian eyes were slightly upturned in the corners; mischief abounded when they were wide awake. Whereas Sama was proportionate to his height and weight at fourteen, Fano was bone thin but was more robust than an ox and about as bullheaded as one.

Eli, Sama's twin, did not live with them as he was adopted by their paternal grandparents, who lived in Savai'i. Eli came home during holidays, but she was too young to recall him ever being home. He lived with a few of their cousins under their grandparents' cloister. It all seemed challenging to grasp for Pele, but this is how things were long before she came along.

Turning towards his ear, Pele leaned into Sama and whispered, "I *must* go. Can I go? Please, Sama?"

He stirred towards her voice and dropped his left arm. Without opening his eyes, he reached for her head and pushed it down on his arm. "Sleep, Pele. You have all day to roam." He reached down for the corners of their shared *'ie 'afu* and pulled it playfully over his sister's head. Pele settled back into the crook of his arm, counting the minutes hopefully before rousing Sama up again.

She pulled the threadbare floral sheet off her face, careful not to disturb her brother, whose breathing slipped into its deep, slumberous rhythm. Sunshine banked on their bare tiptoes as the rays settled over them as a blanket against the morning's cool. The hours were witling away! *Oh, how can the boys not understand this?* How could they not want to be out there basking in the rising sunrise now that they were home to stay for the break? The chortling kingfisher, a fickle resident of the canopied skies above the cabin, now perched upon the kapok tree, mocked her like the wattled honeyeater from its hideaway upon a papaya tree.

Pele rolled onto her back as thoughts of the day's plans unfurled furiously. Her city needed another road, another house on the grid. Her pigs must be corralled, she fretted. Before Mother found her out this morning, flowers had to be gathered for the tea table. And yes, she had to tend to her toiletry before she forgot. Mother often scolded her for not minding her constitution. She was a girl.

Without waiting for Sama to come to his senses, she sat up from her middle tuck, unraveling herself from his proffered arm, careful not to disturb Fano, the kingdom's tattler. Pele dropped on all fours, wiggling between her dear brothers, who were still unconscious to the world. Once detangled from their sheet, she hurried on her tush so her footsteps would not reverberate onto the floor planks. Not much stirred from her parents' side of the *pupugi* either. All was well; she smiled, utterly pleased as pie at her church mouse stealth. Mother can't possibly mind now that her sons are home, and she, Pele, the family goat she is in her mother's eyes, is free to do as she wishes without the misery of being the only child at home. Summer's freedom never felt more liberating.

Pele! Pele! Peletumuaotamali'i, e te va'ai iai pea a'u mauaina oe e! Her mother can declare a 'Pele' moratorium and rest comfortably. When she remembers her manners, Pele can be the picture-perfect fit for her namesake, "the utmost beloved of the genteel." With their sons home, Mother's exasperated calls, the spankings, and the battle of wits with her daughter's obstinate silences came to a brief moratorium.

A cedar chest stood in the corner as storage for clothes sat in the far corner of the room. Pele lifted her threadbare nightgown and neatly folded it into a corner. Pele neatly pulled a lavalava from the stack and tied it around her chest, as Sama had often knotted for her. This once, she admitted that it was a messy affair, but that couldn't be helped. She must get to her pigs and flowers, and she had so many things she couldn't wait on sleeping, exhausted brothers. When they woke, there was always time to ask permission.

Mother's prized kitchen possession was the clear glass armoire where she stowed the sweets. She popped its glass door as quietly as she could and reached for a digestive biscuit, the tin one shelf higher than she was tall. Pulling out a wrinkle in her lavalava, she slipped the contraband treats into it. It was breakfast, she justified to herself, which should justify the cause. Mother would never let her go without a meal, no way. Why, not on *this* morning when she'd feel generous on account of her sons.

She slipped into the world via the open doorway, sweeping aside the lavalava sheet strewn from the wood beam. Once on the last step fashioned from river rocks, the relief of feeling the dirt beneath her bare feet was astounding. This haven was a heaven above the world below that took her brothers away to boarding schools, and she was stuck at home, one so lonely without them. There were enough other children like her who saw their siblings off to lands they were too young yet to see and discover. However, when her brothers were home on their breaks, she enjoyed all her time with them. Better yet, her Sama was here now.

Sole is the family dog. He wiggled out from the crawl space with his ears piped up. He looked up at his mischievous miss and yawned despite himself. She was up to something bound to get them both in trouble with the elders. He barked loudly, trying to alert the brothers.

Someone get her, please! She's running away again!

"Stop that, Sole," Pele hissed with a finger over her lips. "Go back to bed if you'll tell on me." Sole winced. He crouched down obediently against his better judgment, out of habit when told by his humans, with his nose between his front paws. Pele knew the look all too well. "Stay here, okay? Love you, but you're such a *faikala*." Tattler! Sole hung his head. A *town crier*, she accused him of being.

That hurts, Pele! Sole's tail sank a bit.

She stopped when she turned away and walked a few steps beyond the garden. Without turning around, she whispered conspiratorially, "Oh, okay! You can come with me, but you so bark a hiccup, I'll send you back." Sole popped upright, wagged his tail happily, and followed her. If only to look after the adventurer; he was doing his due diligence.

Traipsing through Mother's garden, Pele plucked some white gingers for her morning bouquet for her little haven from home. Careful not to leave the spike bare, or her mother would have her head for the morning repast, she moved on and clipped a crown or three of the fragrant *sugi* flower. These grew low to the ground when not fully developed and bore bevies of blossoms that rivaled the jasmines' blooms.

Pele had a bouquet of white, pale peach, and fuchsia red. Pele walked around the corner of the cabin and hopped onto the walking stones that cut through the watercress growing in the little creek that Father dug out of the ground after watching an eel wiggling back and forth, stranded in the murky eddies. Father fashioned a larger pool for the living eels out of the trickling watering hole as they swam from the river below. This pool became the eels' refuge upstream in shallower eddies. A quarter-acre of watercress grew abundantly on the verdant hill, away from the worries of the lowlands.

Balancing on her hunches, Pele picked a few leafy tendrils and chewed on them before she jumped onto the last rock on the path to the little knoll on the other side of the greens. She walked farther down the hill, out of sight of the cabin, and squatted down to relieve herself in the foliage, sheltered from the sun's rays and any curious eyes. Mother told her that a *girl* must always be careful not to wet her feet or ankles.

A rustle in the dried leaves sounded Sole's presence, which meant he was waiting there. She looked up and through the leafy thicket and at the besieged protector. He stared back at her, undeterred by the rebellious imp's disdain.

She clambered onto the grassy patch before her; the morning's breeze blew at her curls, delightfully relaxed and welcomed. The source of her great pride was up here; this was her castle. Before her, giant red torch gingers stood in a majestic cluster. They were taller than their father, and he was not short. Spikes with blood-red blossoms bobbed gently as the breeze whimsically danced through the stalks. Oh, how amazing their scents are!

Pele dropped to her knees to squeeze through the stalks. The center of the patch was a comfortable circle in which she had set up her village. Stone houses were set up neatly in a small semi-circle around the base of a stalk. Her dolls, which Mother had fashioned out of dried papaya stalks, were much like cornsilk and had been lovingly covered by blankets of sectioned *lausalui*.

This enclave was a private sanctuary where Pele's possibilities were infinite. Her dolls, Sina and Tasi, were her best friends. *They* understood her even if Father and Mother did not—well, not *most* times. She built the girls their homes and perfect flat stones gathered from the falls below. Like Father, who provided a good living for them, it was only fitting that she was here for her loves and to be their bastion against wayward weather, bugs, and one cranky brother. Or *two*.

The porcine roly-polies clambered out her hands, searching for freedom from the determined five-year-old. Almost six! She rearranged ferns for their comfort and placed her morning bouquet on the top of a flat river rock. At long last, the home was finally home. Pele sank contentedly upon her hunches, began playing with her dolls, and ate her contraband biscuit.

Sama woke up as the sun's rays danced over his face. He blinked against the harsh light and stretched out his full length languorously. On his own, Fano was still unconscious of the world. Sama stifled the temptation to kick his brother as that has never bore out well. He turned on his side away from the morning light, and Sama rolled over. He rolled *over*. No little body next to him. He blinked again. *Pele!*

Pele was not next to him. That girl! She will be the end of him yet. Wiping the sleep from his eyes, he stifled a yawn and wearily rolled cricks from his weary shoulders. *That girl*, he swore softly under his breath! He had to find her before Mother found out she had snuck out of the cabin before any of them were awake.

Footsteps crushed dried banana trees in the underbrush. These trees had fallen from a previous storm near the ginger patch. Sole wagged his tail, happy to see a responsible human rise from home to come and get his ward. He was guilty by association, Sole thought shamefully. Sama reached down and patted him on the head, empathetic. "You're not alone, boy." Sole looked down at his empty belly.

Dropping to his knees, he spied her back between the stalks. She was chatting up a storm with her dolls. Smiling to himself, he shimmied between stalks. Sama bent his shoulders to better sidle through the long green stalks so closely wound together.

"Please don't say it. I *know*. But you wouldn't get up with me." Pele quickly charged without looking up. Rushing on before Sama could interject a scolding, "So, in a way, it's your fault for not getting up when I *asked* you." That is the most porous argument if Sama has ever heard one.

"How is it you don't listen to me, and it's *my* fault?" he chided gently. "I don't know why you're up so early anyhow. What couldn't possibly wait, Pele?"

"My dolls have to be looked after!" She looked at him with those translucent brown eyes as if he had no clue. And that he needed to find one now. "Sina and Tasi have lives, too, as do my pigs." She pointed him to the corral of five roly-polies curled up tight. The early morning wake-up offended even the sow bugs. Sama had to laugh at the upturned face of sheer outrage.

He helped deliver his sister into this world and watched her take her first cleansing breath. Father had traveled to town that morning to fetch the doctor. It was clear Pele had other plans and pushed her way into the world before her parents and brothers were ready for her. When Mother delivered her right into his young arms, Sama fell in love with her the instant she looked up at him from the crook of his arms as though she expected him to be waiting for her.

Now, that same expressive face looked at him as though he had no sense in his noggin. He guffawed out loud. "Don't think I will forget this disappearance, Pele." He scowled meaningfully, although it was hard to convince her when a smile tugged at the corners of his mouth.

"I won't," Pele vowed eagerly. "So, you won't tell Mother?" She had to ensure that her brother was devoted entirely to their secret. It isn't a secret when it saves their mother from any distress. It is more of a child's gift back to her parent. She flashed a toothy smile at him, punctuating the act by blinking back a few crocodile tears.

"You're something else, Pele." He chucked her chin playfully. "C'mon, before they wake up and find that we're both missing." Sama parted the long-stemmed gingers, careful not to break the flowering spikes. He held the stalks apart so she could walk out before him, out of the safety of her playhouse.

Crouching down to her level, he motioned her to his back. "Get on." She squealed delightedly and clambered onto his back, clamping her arms around his neck. "Not so tight!" She ignored him. Standing up, he chuckled as he loosened her vice-like grip so he could breathe. Sama secured her spindly legs for the piggyback ride.

"Where are we going? To the falls?" Her exultant squeal resonated in the still of the morning. "Go faster, Piggy!"

The humidity settled over them as quickly as the morning broke. Finding some breeze was a godsend on the steep descent to the falls. Thus, Sama carefully navigated the path to the waterfall with Pele on his back. The whipping vines lined the underbrush and wound their way around under the floor of the large leaves of the aged beach hibiscus trees that lined the path. Careful not to slip, given the soft dirt beneath his bare feet, he held Pele a little tighter. The path was steep and challenging in parts as the road gave way to a few cut notches into the hillside with only enough leeway for one hiker at a time. Sole bounded to the front of them and disappeared around the bend in the hillside, chasing after an unseen interloper. It was not long before they heard an angry squeal in response to Sole's barking.

Pele recited her Samoan alphabet, phonetically sounding out each of the fourteen letters as she was jolted to and from on his back. Sama was pleasantly happy to hear that his tutoring was stuck in her stubborn head. "How about your numbers?"

She counted with emphasis, "Tasi, lua… *lua sefulu*!" From her Pi to her numbers, he bridged into her biblical primers. *"O ai na tāina le papa? O le a mea na oso mai iai? Fia aso ma po na folo ai Iona le i'a? O ai na a'e le sukamoru?"* All of which she answered ably. *Who struck the rock? What came from that rock? How many days was Jonah in the belly of the whale? Who climbed the sycamore tree?* She answered all of them correctly.

"Excellent, Pele." She beamed with glee into his bare shoulder. "I have a notebook for you to start writing out Pi and your bible scriptures."

"A notebook for *me*? I don't have to share it with Fano?" Pleased as the honeybees in her mother's garden, she could not wait to see this notebook when they returned to the cabin.

Sama stopped to think about this. "Well, maybe Sole needs to learn his Pi, too. Who knows? He might learn how to write me a letter to you."

Pele pinched his upper arm. Sama yelped in exaggerated pain. "I don't have time to write. And I know that Sole doesn't care about letters. He's a *dog*." She rolled her eyes at such a silly idea.

"You'd be surprised, Sister." He chuckled. With her vice-grip locked around his neck, he steadily made his way down by holding on to the mammoth guiding root of a nearby *futu* tree, used as a poisonous option in fishing. Contrarily, its red and white blossoms were so pleasing to the eye. Leaves and woody seed pods littered the narrow path as they carefully turned around the bend.

They were now standing over the rim of the waterfall. Below, a clear, cerulean pool promised relief from the arduous morning hike down from the cabin. The thunderous stream poured the pillowing water into the catchment pool. Sama let Pele down onto the massive rock face so he could walk her down to the pool without both pitching head-on forward. The base rock was smooth after years of water falling over its outer face. Sama cautiously maneuvered his way down before holding his arms up to his sister. She walked into his arms, careful not to knock him over. Sister and brother have done this often enough to know how treacherous the waterfall can be.

They made their way around the pool before letting her slip out of his arms. A loud, sudden splash hit the water around them as someone from behind them cannonballed into the pool from above the craggy face of the waterfall. *Fano!*

The younger brother exploded to the water's surface, breaking the plane of the rippling waves. He grinned at his siblings, unconcerned, as Sama flashed him a displeased look with a fiery admonishment bubbling to the top of his throat.

"Stop it! You're not Mother *or* Father, Sama," Fano yelled from behind the sheer curtain of the waterfall. He slipped under the cascade to avoid his older brother coming after him. "Just my stinkin' brother, that's all!" Fano laughed gleefully, seeing Sama stand with his feet apart on the far side of the pool, annoyed by Fano's daredevil antics and childish taunts.

Sama felt the itch to clobber Fano imminently. "Your stinkin' *older* brother, mind you!"

After he sat Pele down upon a rock, Sama quickly disappeared into the water without a ripple as he dove towards the cascading water flow. He resurfaced under Fano. The younger had been holding on to the face of the boulder, reveling in the pummeling downpour. Sama grabbed his brother's ankle and yanked him away from his watery perch, hurling Fano into the pool, bottom first.

Fano shot back up, sputtering water out of his nose and mouth. He glared up at his older brother. "You didn't have to do that!"

"Well, the next time you want to kill yourself, don't do it in front of us, *fiapoto*." Sama wasn't keen on letting his smart-aleck brother off this time. To cannonball from the top of the waterfall was extremely dangerous. Fano's foolhardy dive could have gone very wrong. *"Ke fia oki?"*

This tomfoolery wasn't the first time Fano had plowed and dove mindlessly into the pool below. The runt of the litter had filled in, and he could not afford to be so reckless, no less agile than the year before.

Fano bit back a retort as the thought crossed his mind. Sama cared about *him* and not just the Brat. He cracked an unrepentant smile floating on his back. "You left without even asking whether I wanted to come along. That hurts like a festering blister, *uso!*"

Sama slipped back into the water below. He sidled up to the floating daredevil and flipped him over, face first, this time into the water. Sama laughed merrily as his brother struggled to surface. He quickly swam over to Pele, sitting with her back to the boys, slapping off mosquitoes hovering over the little eddies as the waterfall flowed into moving rivulets.

Sama grabbed Pele around the middle and hauled her, wriggling, protesting. "I don't want to go in, Sama!" She tried to kick her way out of his vice grip. Her protests were brushed aside as Sama dropped her into the pool's shallow end with about a four-foot drop.

Pele glared up at him. "I could have walked in by myself, Sama. Why did you do that?" A wet cat could not have been more peeved.

Sama shrugged his shoulders. "We didn't come this far down here, and you do not *kaele*."

"Maka fefe! Maka fefe!" Fano taunted unmercifully. Scaredy cat! "I don't know why Sama even bothers with you. Nothing but a useless, ugly girl, that's what you are. I don't know why you were born! We should have kept Eli and sent *you* away."

Pele recoiled at Fano's rancor. "I wouldn't talk, *makagaga!*" Sama immediately blocked Fano as he treaded toward her menacingly. "Pele!" He sighed. She's overheard enough of Mother's rebukes when Fano refuses to mind and repeats them at will.

There is much to be said about Mother's patience, as Father would not have wasted his breath. Father was not a man to be tarried with—not by his peers and, least of all, his children. These two would have been on a burning death pyre if they even imagined stepping out of line with him or if he heard them right now.

She waded out of the water and hopped onto the smooth, dry rocks that served as stepping stones. Some feet away from the pool, a grassy pool served as a little pool where she fit without any issues. She floated on her back and stared at the clear blue skies—what a relief from the humidity and her backwater sibling.

Sama turned to Fano, swearing up a storm, and splashed his brother angrily. "Shut up and grow up. *E leai a se mea ete so'ona fai ai fua le teine!*"

"She'll live." Fano splashed Sama's back. "Why don't *we* play? Without *her*?"

Sama looked at him, paused for a minute, then with barely veiled anger. "She is your sister, whether you like it or not. Be kind to her!" Fano shrugged his shoulders, seemingly unaffected by Sama's admonishment. "Otherwise, don't bother."

Sama trod the water toward the pool's shallow end, hiked his lavalava, and walked out toward Pele. He grabbed the *tauaga* and a bit of soap he had taken from Mother's collection. Squatting next to the waterhole, he called Pele toward him to the edge of her pool.

Pele swam over to Sama. He lathered the scant soap into the stringy loofah. Standing on a nearby rock beside him, Sama scrubbed her head to toe. "Thank you, Sama," Pele said quietly. "You don't have to protect me *all* the time." She raised her arms obediently. "Soon enough, I'll fight my own battles."

"Soon enough, *tama'i monti*." Sama rewrapped her into her lavalava securely and neater than the mess he found her in earlier. "Until then, I am your brother, and no one, not even Fano, can hurt you."

Pele hung her head. "I don't know why he hates me so much." Sama pulled her into his arms and hugged her tightly. "He doesn't *hate* you, Pele. Give him some time to come around, okay?" Sama hoped that this was a mere phase that Fano was going through. *It's been almost six years*, he thought. It will be a long school break if Fano does not quit his pettiness.

There's been enough of that surliness as of late, and his school chums certainly didn't help. It didn't help Fano when his friends were primarily the second sons of chiefs. Fano did not favor himself by limiting his circle of friends, the careless and the rootless rebels. If the Schoolmaster reported some of the shenanigans that Fano and his '*usos*' got into, his father would pull him out of school and most likely banish him after a good beating. It wasn't his place to snitch on Fano. He will come into his own with Father by his telling and actions. In the meantime, Sama can only hope for that day.

Sitting down on a nearby rock, he motioned Pele over. She clambered onto his back without hesitation, wrapping her arms around his neck while he secured her legs securely into her customary piggyback. They had to ascend the hillside from the falls as their parents were already well into the day's work. Giant *olioli*, the majestic tree ferns that lined the banks, offered the much-needed shade for the streaming waters to remain nestled in their side of the hills even though the rains were scarce. Pele stared at the underside of these immense leaves and imagined herself the monarch of the river. Sama would be her trusted advisor. If the role of the *umu kavige* were available, she would nominate Fano.

Sama expertly maneuvered through the canopied forest's underbrush, the intertwining ravine, grabbing onto sturdy climbers and thick undulating roots to propel them forward. Fano followed comfortably, knowing that Sama was none too pleased with him.

As they reached the plateau, Sama sank to one knee to let Pele off his back. She slipped off and started to walk onto the time-worn path bordered by a field of wild ferns for as far as her young eyes could see. Banana trees sprouted all over this hill, complete cycles of untold seasons. Along the ridge, a divergent mango grove peppered the hillside. Lime trees bursting with fruit from their branches wove around and grow wildly in the shade offered by the colossal banyan tree. Their paternal grandfather cultivated this land before Father brought Mother home.

The insular isolation was not unbearable if Fiso was nearby, she often told herself on good days. Leata often thought about walking to town on bad ones, but the road was long and arduous by land. She would have to go by canoe, but even then, the ocean between their home and her father's home in town was unpredictable.

With the children born and raised here in the hinterlands, she struck a bargain with her husband. Their sons were to be educated as he was in boarding school in Upolu. They could not afford to send their sons out into the world ignorant and uneducated. Sama and Fano would not grow up without contact with the world outside this cloistered back hill. One day, she hoped, they would move beyond the provincial world politics of the village. Leata was not bound to this land as much as her husband. She had to think beyond this outlying village's politics.

What to do about Pele? She mused. She would have to cross that road when her daughter was of age. In the meantime, Leata could only wait and hope. She hoped her daughter would become more biddable over time. She wants to ensure that Pele is matched with a good marriage and that stubbornness.

Knowing that the boys were following in her wake, Pele broke out into the run, laughing and snorting with such abandonment as Sama vowed to catch her and give her a hiding. She dodged under guava and cacao tree branches as they leaned over the path, dragging Chinese mile-a-minute weed strings as her feet wandered by and moved around the dragon ferns. Her giggles echoed through the clammy morning, with a carefree, racing heartbeat in her ears.

"Pele! Hold on!" Sama called out to her. He had skimmed the path and detoured through the hip-high gooseberries. Ripe ones were wonderful treats; this *vi vao* grew randomly among the ground ferns. Sama pulled some lavalava at the waist, fashioning it into a pocket, and dropped the heaping handful he had plucked from the vines.

He straightened to his height and saw his little sister edging back toward him.

Laughing heartedly at her sass, he waved her over. He chuckled as she sidled up to him. "Open up, *kama'i monti*."

"Why?" She shifted from foot to foot, ready to race towards the cabin if her brother had any ideas. Sama grabbed her hand and dropped some of the fruit into her palm. Sole preened forward to see if he would get one. Sama gave him two, which the faithful stead swallowed and soon regretted.

"*Now* eat." Pele saw the berries and chuckled. She palmed all into her mouth, munching away. Sama chortled with merriment at her expression of sheer pleasure painted all over her cherubic face. As she finished her cheeks full of fruit, Sama urged her forward. "Run along—I'll give you a head start." She smiled back at him with so much love for her brother. Pele ran along the almost nonexistent path, with Sama trailing leisurely behind her as she was determined to make it to their parents before the boys.

She rounded the last bends, where a breadfruit tree leaned forward like an archway into the cabin's yard. Smoke was streaming over the corner of the cabin. Their parents were out and moving around. Her shoulders were hunched over as she knew the morning's fun was over.

Mother was outside by the fire pit. Without turning, Leata called out to her. "*Matuā leva na outou kaele!* Where are your brothers? Go tell them to get some coconuts." She pointed toward Sama, whom she spotted coming around the bend.

"Sama's coming, Mother. How many coconuts do you want?" Pele shifted her lavalava before Mother noted that this, too, was wrong.

"As many as you can gather." Leata stood up and gazed at her daughter. "Hurry along. Your father is already working and will soon break for the afternoon meal."

Pele ran along, knowing the urgency of the time as Father would expect their afternoon repast layout.

Coconut trees peppered the cabin's yard, so she had nowhere to go. Plenty of brown coconuts, the *popo*, were strewn on the ground. Pele grabbed two and then kicked two others with her foot to move all four. Gathering enough into a pile, she threw each as far as she could to get closer to the work yard without making numerous trips back and forth. She dropped two in her arms, which she hurriedly grabbed before Mother spotted her.

Sole had found an excellent spot under the mammoth elephant vine leaves, the roots of which clung to an ancient breadfruit tree. The harried soul had turned himself upside down as he nestled into his bed of ferns, the air cool under the shading leaves. It was hard work watching after Pele. He had earned his dog nap.

Fano came up next to her and took some of the coconuts. A stake leaned up again, an embedded lava rock. He leaned forward on one to steady his footing while the other braced the rock. He quickly husked Pele's gaggle of coconuts, throwing the nuts over to Sama, who was already sitting on the scraper.

Sama motioned Pele over to sit by him on the work-horse-like creation. She sat down with her back leaning against Sama's, adding her little weight to help balance the *asoalo*. He turned the nut on its slide and broke it with the edge of a flat volcanic stone, cracking it in perfect symmetry. The lower half caught part of the coconut juice, which he handed Pele.

She quenched her thirst noisily. Sama gave her several of these halves filled with juice and handed several to Fano, who stood nearby waiting. Then Sama poured some liquid into a shallow gourd and handed this over to Fano to take over to their mother, who was now clipping taro leaves from a few plants that Father had grown into the bottom edge of the watercress rows.

Leaning forward, Sama scraped the coconut meal into a wooden *tanoa*. In one of the coconut halves, he found the spongy 'candy', the sweet *o'o,* over to Pele, who was expecting these. She ate them, relishing their sweetness with each bite. He scraped on as they had to start the *umu* soon. Pele slipped off her perch on the back of the asoalo as Sama moved over to the makeshift table and folded the tauaga, the fibrous strings peeled from the stalks of the heliconia plant, he draped over the scraped coconut meal and wrung milk out of the coconut flakes. He dropped the residue onto the ground for the chickens that had gathered. They happily scratched and pecked at their morning meal.

Sama set aside the tanoa once filled with coconut milk and covered it with a banana leaf cut in half. He shooed the chickens at his feet so he could walk toward his mother, who was still working in the nearby taro patch.

"Mother, we're going up now. Do you need anything before we leave?" He grinned at his mother. "Do you want me to leave Fano here with you?" Weeding the watercress plots was not a chore for one soul. It is much work for Mother alone, even with Pele's help.

"No, take him and go to your father. There's still much up there that needs doing before nightfall." Her benevolent features browned from the blistering humid summers spent on the plantation. "Hurry on before he calls for you boys. And take some water up to him."

Sama and Fano followed the trail their father had shown them when they were in the mountains. As the path narrowed, Sama took the lead and cut the foliage away from over as they made their way further into the hillside, where their father's ax pounded as he cleared the underbrush and overgrowth. The brothers each used their machetes, cleaning the banana trees of dried leaves and cutting off the inflorescences on those that had sprouted on bunches of bananas so the fruit could mature on their spikes. Sama cut down some of the apple bananas that had ripened perfectly on the tree. Setting these aside, he chopped down the tree trunk to its midpoint to allow another to sprout. Then, he methodically traversed his way through the assortment of fruit trees.

On the adjacent end of the clearing, Fano purged the area of male papaya trees that only served to pollinate the fruiting trees. He reached up and harvested the mature fruits as hordes of birds had already devoured sun-ripened ones in the same bunch. Hummingbirds were not happy with this intrusion into their platter of easy pickings. Neither were the starlings, the *fuia* and *mitivao,* as they flew off, loudly heralding their displeasure by this unsolicited foray in their space by this impertinent boy, this inconsequential little human being.

Their father was still out of sight. The rhythmic sounds of his ax pounded down on the branches of trees that had fallen to the covered ground and arched into twining, cumbersome obstacles in the path toward the pinnacle of the hillside overlooking their village below miles of the Pacific Ocean before them.

Lauolefiso was a willow of a man. Standing six feet tall when he stood up to his length, graced with robust, sharp features, prominent brows, and amber eyes, a startling compliment to his sunburnt complexion. His dark hair was slicked back and neatly cropped at the collar.

The man moved about handsomely with the grace of a native dancer. Sweat beaded and flowed from his brow to his back, an untapped sea of salty water as the humid air hung throughout the morning. His lavalava was soaked at the waist. Father labored on as his goal was to reach the apex of the hillside by early noon. It was evident to Sama why their mother left home to follow him this far from town and her family.

Fano was nearby but out of sight. Swearing under his breath, Fano worked his way adjacent to their father, where the lime groves grew wildly. Brambles with dead branches had poked through his slippers, scraped his bare shoulders, and clawed at his face. Determined to get through this on his own, Fano swung his machete at the dead branches, carefully extricating them and throwing them into a burn pile. The lime tree had fallen on its front quarters some time ago.

Sama called out to his father, "We're here, Father!" He walked on toward the sounds of the ax falling. Careful not to startle his father, he called out again.

"Pull those branches and cut them down to size. Start a fire and burn them," Father instructed, calling out at him in his tenor sing-song voice. Sama approached him with the gourd of calm waters from the brook. Father took it from him appreciatively.

Sama moved adeptly through the maze of felled dried branches from the *poumuli, lagaali, maota,* and the bountiful beach hibiscus trees. He cut them into halves before moving them into piles for burning, neatly clearing the leaf-covered ground of the kindling. The sun burned through the gap between the blue skies and the earth beneath their feet. Gathering some dried coconut husks and fronds, Sama built a fire, slowly adding the felled branches to the fire. The fire hissed, crackled, and sparked as it burned through the green stems.

Fano had his fires incinerating the brambles of the lime trees on the adjacent knoll. His face was beet red from his efforts to start the fire. He was relieved that he did not have to call over his older brother to help him. Lord knows he would never live down the jibing bound to come about. He stood back and surveyed his work, satisfied that he had cleared enough to pass his father's exacting inspection.

Fano picked the limes into his lavalava, then tied the lot so the limes did not fall out of the satchel-like pouch. He walked to the clearing to wait for his father and Sama to come down from the incline.

Sama came through the banana trees with an *amoga* of bananas cut into bunches and placed in woven baskets, balancing weights on the end of the long sturdy stick. Father followed on his heels, carrying the machetes, ax, and whetstone. Both were sweaty from work on the crest.

Father inspected Fano's work and nodded, wiping the sweat at his brow with a corner of his lavalava. "Good work, son. Make your way to the next knoll over this afternoon." Gathering the papayas he plucked earlier, Fano placed them into Sama's baskets before they worked their way down companionably toward the cabin to Mother and Pele. He jostled along with the limes in his.

Mother was near the outside kitchen, gently washing the taro leaves on the shady bank of the trickling creek. She broke the center of the greens and set them aside. Sama dropped a load of ripe apple bananas near Mother, offering them to her. "Put them on the table, Sama." She smiled at him; her eyes warmed with love for her son.

As Sama laid out the bunches, Fano plucked a few plump morsels and went to sit down below the ancient breadfruit tree next to Sole, who was left behind to watch his mistress and the young miss, watching over them as the men worked the morning away. If truth be told, Sole could not move in this sweltering humidity. He preferred his bed under the cool *fuesaiga* shaded by a colossal elephant vine leaf.

There needed to be more wind up here. The sun had traveled across the clear, azure, cloudless skies. The rays, glittering and waning, bore down without promise of a respite from the scorching humidity past noon. During the evening, there was a south-easterly breeze that kept them calm. There is so much hope.

Sama strolled over to the watercress plot, where he saw Pele's small frame bobbing as she attentively weeded undergrowth in the irrigated fields. He dropped to his knees next to her. He pressed down on the soft mud so pockets of the trickling water bobbed into his cupped hands. Drinking a little, Sama splashed his face with the rest of the refreshingly cool water. His sister's nape presented a superb target. He poured the water down her neck with another handful, watching it trickle down her back.

Pele giggled despite herself and her standoff. She was determined to work on it right through high noon and not let her mother see her wilt under the sun. She vowed she wouldn't wander into the shade unless Mother called her over. Before then, she will keep on weeding.

She surveyed her work, and she was satisfied with her efforts. Her mother should see this in time. Meanwhile, she was no quitter.

Until her brother came along and dismantled her resolve. "Rebelling *again*?" Sama sat on one of the stepping stones. A well-lined brow was creased. "What if you get so burned that you can't enjoy my gift?" he groaned mournfully. "I guess Sole *will* get the notebook after all."

"No! You can't do that." Pele looked hurt enough at the thought. Does Sama give the notebook to *Sole*? Mother has not seen a reason to buy her one yet. Pele deserved her brother's regard, and besides, she *needed* the notebook. Sole would eat it like he does everything else. She had letters to write, the Pi to expound upon, and pictures to draw! This tomfoolery cannot be!

"Then you must mind Mother, Pele, and get out of the sun right now." Sama bent over for another drink before standing and holding his hand out to Pele. "C'mon, there's more work to do elsewhere." Pele took her brother's hand, effectively ending her boycott.

Fano and Father were stacking the lagolago of the umu together. These logs gave the *umu* its four-cornered foundation. At the bottom of the heap were creek rocks. Dry coconut husks were stacked in a pyramid, and the *losoloso* the children gathered and stockpiled near the umu for ready-to-use kindling. Father rubbed two sticks together for embers to help light up the dry husk. Once the ember came to the bed of kindling, he blew on it until there was a flame. Once the umu fire started in earnest, Sama helped Fano place more creek rocks on top and around the pyramid of husks.

The chores of the umu began in earnest. Mother handed over the taro leaves to Father as he picked up the tanoa of coconut milk. He added a pinch of sea salt they brought yesterday from home, squeezed in a few hot chili peppers and wild scallions, and stirred. Grabbing the taro leaves, Fiso expertly formed a funnel with the leaves and then poured in the coconut milk mixture before sealing the taro leaves with coconut frond veins that snapped into a small toothpick-sized skewer. After wrapping a dozen of these bundles, he placed the individual servings into the middle of green breadfruit leaves that he used as outer wraps and secured in place by snapping the stem into the leaf, unlike the simple mechanics of a barrette.

Father stoked the fire and threw some of the rocks that had fallen back on the heap. Cracking a green banana leaf in half, he dusted the ashes off the sides to ensure that dusty embers would be minimal when they broke the fire down.

Sama cut down a bunch of bananas slung with the sinewy rib of a dried banana leaf on one of the outer beams of the cabin. A hardier eat, this was a ripe cluster of the *paka* banana, which he handed over to Pele, who was waiting for them at his feet. It was easier for her to peel half-ripened bananas than to try and beat Fano in a race over the green bananas.

Tending to her chore earnestly, she carefully peeled each sun-ripened banana, others more so than those at the bottom of the spike, and placed them onto a clean banana leaf. Banana soufflé with coconut milk was a rare treat but a delicacy the children looked forward to when Father felt up to the chore— sliced along the natural groves in the bananas before pouring coconut milk over them with a bit of sea salt to flavor the pan of bananas.

Green banana leaves from nearby trees were cut and halved. The sturdier stem was cut off; Sama ripped the stiff ribs from the undersides with his teeth to render the leaf malleable. He prepared a dozen. Fano took these gently to glide both sides over the top of the umu quickly. Handing these over to Pele, she walked them over to their parents.

Mother took a couple of these banana sheets and folded fish and coconut milk before folding these up into the waiting *ti* leaves, which she tied into a bundle. Father put together banana soufflé before standing.

"Pele, gather everything together," he told his youngest. "Put everything next to your brothers." *Palusami* were placed in a small basket, as were the two fish bundles. Careful not to jostle the basket too hard, she walked these over to the boys and placed them against one of the nearby rocks. She returned to get the peeled green bananas while her father carried the banana soufflé, which was too heavy for her thin arms to support.

As her father grabbed the long stick, the boys dusted the sides of the umu with a handful of old banana leaves. Sama grasped the outer side of one of the *lagolago* and rolled it off. Fano did the same for another side log, thus breaking the quadrant of red-hot lava rocks as they crackled and fell to the base of the umu. Sama walked around and kicked another record to the side, careful to keep the embers from flying. His brother ably moved the last out of the way. Father moved in and stoked the rocks into the base, flattening the lot before the boys started to dust off the broken coals that had fallen into the middle with the stones. Laying down some bananas in their peels, the boys circled the rocks with bananas, a couple of breadfruit, and a few taros.

With several green banana leaves covering a section of the stones, Sama carefully situated the fish bundles. Father moved in with the green tongs, handing others to the boys, and they started to place hot dusted rocks onto the foodstuffs, building up layers. Into the upper layer of stones, he put the soufflé and covered it to keep it from boiling over.

The umu was covered with the new banana and yam leaves, and then with the old covering from previous cookouts, the *fa'avevela*. Pele struggled but managed to drag up a bucket of water. Sama dipped granary sacks into the water. He handed one over to Father, who dropped it onto the umu, flattened to help keep the steam in the bed of food and rocks. The entire umu is sealed with another leaf to cook all its foodstuffs.

Pele walked over to her brothers and father with a keg of fresh water. Fano cupped a handful and washed his face, as did Father. Sama fetched water to wet down the corners of the logs of the umu. These will be used again in another. When done, he poured the rest of the water over his head.

Under the shade of the nearby breadfruit tree, Mother wove baskets for the umu, which she set aside for when they would break the umu and bring out the cooked food. Pele sidled up next to her, ready to nap. She turned her face into her mother's arm and closed her eyes.

"Pele, scoot over to the shade so you don't burn out here." Mother gently pushed her over toward the cavernous roots. "Take a nap until we open the *umu*." Pele nodded, too exhausted to protest.

Damp curls stuck to her forehead, and a streak of dirt ran down one reddened cheek when she moved from Mother and dragged her feet over to the bed of green ferns. Falling to the soft perch, she curled up as tight as a land crab to a coconut husk and closed her eyes.

Father looked grim but resolved. "She needs to go, Leata. We cannot hold onto her. She is growing up and needs to be in school."

Mother cried, "But does she need to leave this young?" She fretted with Fiso. "She is so young, and her brothers will not be nearby to look after her."

Father batted off her hand. Leata grasped his upper hand again. "Please reconsider. She is our only daughter. How can you be so cold and let her go?"

Let me go. Where am I going? Why will Father not listen to Mother, to her pleas? Shouldn't I go away from them? Who would look after me?

Pele started to cry soundlessly, lest her parents discover she was listening to their discussion. Why didn't Sama tell her this? Of all the things that he had chosen to keep from her, he decided this. Her imminent departure for a place so seemingly far away from home and no one had told her. Betrayal, she sobbed. Away from all that she has known. From the comforts of home to somewhere that even Sama hasn't been. And not even a hint that he knew.

"Pele—*suga!* Wake up!" Her eyes fluttered open, sooty lashes wet from crying in her sleep. Startled, she looked about her as the day's events flooded back. Still, under the breadfruit tree, she remembered Mother urged her to shelter from the sun ages ago.

She stared at Sama, not seeing her brother but another untrustworthy adult in her life. An *almost* adult he was. An annoyed pout took over her better judgment. How could he not have told her? Did anyone ever love her enough to tell her the truth? Even Fano's heckling seemed bearable now that she saw how honest he was with his feelings toward her. Sama was already as distant as the northern star that Father often spoke of reverently.

Foodstuffs from the umu were now on the *lalaga*. Everyone had gathered to get ready to break the meal together. Pele wiped her tears with her hand to wipe away the hurt that had banked hard in her heart. Everything was so lost to her. Now that all knew that she was about to depart, her family, her heaven here in these hills. Everyone knew but her.

"Pele." Sama extended his hand to her to pull her up. Smile as sunny as the giant orb behind him beamed down at her. "Come on, let's go eat." She got up and walked on, leaving Sama's hand in mid-air. "What's wrong with you now?"

Pele didn't turn back. "I'm just warm." She just wanted to bawl her eyes out.

With a hand on her shoulder, Sama turned her toward him. His kind eyes searched his sister's face when he noticed she was more flushed than usual. "Whatever it is, you better tell me. No sense sulking about it."

"Why didn't you tell me?" She whirled around to glare at him. "Why did you not tell me, Sama? That they were going to send me away."

"What are you talking about now? No one's said anything about you leaving!" Sama's amber eyes grew dark. "*No* one, Pele! Come to your senses!"

Her heart in the pits of the earth beneath her feet, she yelled her heart out. "I heard voices, and Mom and Dad were talking about me going away, and you didn't tell me. You!" She turned her back to him, wiping her tears with her hand. The smudge on her cheek worsened, but she didn't care if she looked like she had just rolled out in the pigsty mud.

Sama turned her around. Upon seeing her tear-streaked dirty face, he guffawed at her anger. Pele went on full mutiny, which made Sama laugh even more complexly. "Stop it!"

"Pele, no one's conspiring to take you away. It was all a dream. Just a foolish dream!"

Sama pointed to their parents and Fano nearby. "Nothing has happened since we did the umu." She blinked, trying to recall the day back before her nap. In the shade of the cabin, her parents sat with Fano as they broke the staples and started portioning their meal onto the banana leaf. Her shoulders drooped a bit as Sama's declaration rang a truthfulness that is her brother. How silly and stupid could she be? A bad *dream,* that is all it was.

"Sama, I'm so sorry!" Repentent, she turned to look up at Sama. "You're right—so silly and stupid I believed Mother would ever let me go. Or you."

Wiping her tears away with the back of her hand, Pele reached for Sama's hand. "I'm sorry."

Sama looked down at her dirty, tear-streaked face. "Hey, not so serious, you." He took her to the brook. With the gourd, she used earlier to irrigate the greens, he scooped up some cool water and offered the gourd to her. She cupped some water and cleaned her face off. "There. I can't see you beyond the dirt." A smile broke the plain of his handsome face. He flipped a dampened curl on her forehead before pushing her forward to walk on and join their parents at the meal.

"*Ua lou moe?*" Mother asked, smiling at them. "*Omai loa o lea fai tatou mea'ai.*" Urging them to take their places next to her and Father, she motioned for Father to bless the food.

Sweat beading on his forehead, the family bowed their heads in synchronicity as they listened as he blessed their meal.

"Fa'afetai tatou Tama o ile Lagi, mo lenei mea tausami ua ou matou mauaina i aso ta'itasi. Fa'afetai fo'i i lou agalelei aua le tamaoaiga o lo'o matou mauaina aso uma. O lo matou 'oli atu lea. Ile suafa paia lo tatou Tamā o ile lagi. Amene."

Mother and the children echoed 'Amen' at the end of Father's simple prayer. Gratitude was expressed out loud for the bounty before them. As they passed the staples and the main course of their meal, there was a lot to be thankful for, Pele mused. She never wanted to change how life was to her above all the village noise. There were no reminders that her brothers had to leave or that her father would sail off with them for a spell. Those were the loneliest times through which she had ever lived. These times were her world, the cocoon from the sadness that was always that ocean out there.

Sama and Fano were jostling back and forth, a mouthful of taro with *palusami*, laughing as the time of repast went on with various conversations rolling through the family. Father discussed the work that needed to be done over the crest with Mother. Meanwhile, Pele ate with relish whatever her mother placed onto her banana leaf.

Pele watched the banter between the brothers and joined in on the fun, allying forces with Sama, which added more reasons why Fano was left bristling as he conceded the teasing to Sama. Pele giggled, watching Fano turn from them, pouting as he finished his meal.

There was a brief respite after Pele cleared away the leafy as Mother tidied up the remaining staples into a small basket covered with banana leaves. She scraped the leftovers for Sole, who patiently waited for the leftovers. Sole sniffed the lot, pawing at the fish bones, and ate those morsels before gulping down the other starchy treats.

Fano filled a *tanoa* of water and handed it to their father first. After he dipped his hands to wash off the foodstuffs, Father threw the water a safe distance from them before motioning Fano over to retrieve the *tanoa*. Taking this from Father, Fano filled it again and handed the tanoa to Mother. Her hands were cleaned, and she returned the tanoa to Fano to dispose of its dirty water.

Father instructed the boys on chores left in the hours left in the afternoon. Mother reminded Pele that they, too, had to spend time weeding the watercress. The watercress will be ready for harvest in several more weeks.

Sama tied the basket on one of the cabin beams before setting off to the shade of the ancient breadfruit tree. He reached up to a branch and broke off several leaves. He handed two to his parents as they retired closer to the cabin as impromptu fans. The sun's rays gravitated toward the westward side of the house, offering shade for the weary. Pele went into the place and retrieved a mat for them.

As their parents lay down for the afternoon nap behind the privacy of the pupugi, Pele joined her brothers under the shade of the symbiotic golden pathos that had snaked its way from the hollow roots of the breadfruit tree to the tops of the uppermost branches. It anchored itself to the sturdiest part of the tree before its leaves congregated at the uppermost center. This cavernous root was a favorite hideaway on the most humid days. It offered shade and the earth's coolness to the somnolent. Pele slipped into her previous bed and settled to wait out the hottest part of the afternoon.

The boys had grabbed banana leaves and mile-a-minute weed as bedding before them, too, turned in for that much-needed nap. Sole dropped at Pele's feet and nuzzled his nose into the arch of one foot before he closed his eyes, content with the day's feed.

The women from before returned to their perches in her mind's eye, sneering and cackling like angry hens. If this was not real, why did they come back? She cried to herself lest they see her. Mother was at the center of this menacing crowd, fending off the mob as they closed in on her. Pele could not stand by and watch her mother disappear into this flurry of bodies.

"Stop it! Soia!" She is of diminutive stature, said authoritatively. "Go away! Leave my mother alone!" A looming figure closest to her reached over, wrapped her fist around Pele's ponytail, and slapped her into the hard road beneath her feet. The strange woman hauled her girth and laughed at the crumpled figure at her feet.

Leata looked over at the young slip of a daughter before she yelled, "Pele! Go home! Don't let them find you. Go now!" Bloodied at the mouth, Pele scurried from under the feet of this offensive monstrosity whose bloodshot eyes and gaping mouth snarled at her. The stranger yelled obscenities after her as Pele ran with her heart beating in her ears.

Minding her mother's urgent cries, she ran home to find her brothers. She looked around, and not a soul was home. Where were they? Oh, where? She paused for a cleansing breath before she realized that they were alone. The boys had left with Father for the town. How can she help her mother out? Quickly, she had to think. Going around the corner of the house, she saw it. Grabbing it, she hurled it over her shoulder as she ran out, grabbing two bullets out of the box. She hurriedly shoved these into the gun.

The women hecklers surrounded her mother as they furiously yelled and kicked at her. "Lou mea fiapalagi! Isa!" They chanted over her mother as she cowed in the middle.

Pele shot off a warning in the air. Startled, the mob turned toward her. Caterwauling, they made a short chase after her. Pele shot the second over the heads of the leaders. As though they were one vile spirit, they morphed into a plume of acrid smoke.

"Mother! Mother!" Pele cried, searching for her mother. She ran over to where she saw her last in the middle of the crowd. "Mother!" Mother! Where are you? Where have you gone? She cried.

She sobbed well into the quiet of the night. Her mother lost to her, and no one knew but her.

The kingfisher watched the commotion from above his perch amid the fan-like leaves. He cackled menacingly. He relished the fear that he struck in these earthbound souls. As a hen and her chicks scratched away at the soft dirt beneath the mango tree, the kingfisher flapped his wings and screeched his way down at his victims.

The frantic mother hen squawked angrily at the murderous beak as it swooped down at her and her chicks. She ran furiously to shelter her young with her wings as the six bright coats scattered wildly in a panic. Before the mother hen could right herself, the kingfisher picked one out and pecked at it with all its might.

The maniacal kingfisher, quite happy with the mayhem he caused for the afternoon, re-settled back on his perch partially hidden in the fan-like leaves. He watched as the mother hen clucked and hurried to assemble her chicks back to the safety of the mango tree.

One of the chicks lay motionless in the aftermath of the melee. The hen clucked over it, hoping that it would stand up. Part of its head was bloodied over its blonde fur as its eye socket bled out. Its mother, seeing that it was hopeless, moved on to gather its five siblings and settled them down under her wings. The afternoon's chaos was too much for her young. She could only let them cry and shiver under her protective wings.

The abandoned chick lay still for fear of a repeat attack. Yet, none came. Our Good Father also heard his mother's call before that but was lost in the deafening silence. He struggled to get up on his feet. Again, the mangled creature chirped out for his mother, but she didn't answer nor come to his side. He chirped a little more before he heard her clucking. Her comforting hum came from around another side of the mango tree. He shuffled toward her, hoping to find solace with his family.

Mother Hen saw the bloodied mess before her and stood up. Her cowering chicks fell out from under her, horrified to see the bloody pulp. Too much of a reminder of the horrors dealt with by the kingfisher, she squealed at the bloodied mess, hoping it would go away, rejecting it. She hoped that it would find a way to die out of sight. It was no longer one of hers.

December gave way to January that year. Time found the family busy as ever with the keeping of the plantation and its many crop harvests: bananas, manioc, watercress, cacao beans, a few coffee plants, taro, and immense yam roots. Most mornings broke with no cloud in the sky, offering yet another clear, happy day spent in the village's heart. After an incredibly humid morning, sudden downpours in the afternoon up here provided respite from the hordes of mosquitoes that tortured them throughout their legions of chores with their parents.

On Sunday, after the mid-afternoon toana'i, Father took to his books behind the pupugi. The boys played with their homemade carts fashioned out of old branches cut from the *milo* tree with wheels made from bottle caps they had found below in the village. They sequestered the farthest side of the cabin where the melee did not disrupt Father.

Pele helped Mother as she mended and hemmed the family's lavalavas and the lavalava sheets by holding the hems in place while Mother sewed from one end to the other. To keep Mother's stitching in place, Pele fetched the cast iron filled with hot coconut shell charcoals and handed this over to Mother. Mother ironed, folded, and stacked the lavalavas before handing them to Pele to stow away in the wooden chest.

Cotton pulled out kapok pods that had fallen to the ground and dried further in the blazing sun. The little black seedlings had to be manually picked out of these. Pele and the boys helped Mother throughout the weeks with the daily cotton picking and sorting, as the cotton had to be dried before it became stuffing for their linen.

Mother and daughter sat companionably to sort through the scrap fabric and sewed them into miniature pillows. For fun, some as pillowcases for her dolls' beds. Pele held up the small pillow for her mother's approval. Mother nodded as she inspected approvingly. "Your stitching is coming along, Pele. The more you practice, the better your little creations will get." The compliment was as warm as a ray of sunshine to her young back. Who knows? Dresses would follow soon, and the list was endless! They'd work on dresses for her dolls in the avapui hedge when Mother had time.

Sole winced a bit but seemed to be holding his own. Pele smiled to herself. The family hound found himself wedged between being the surrogate mother for an unlikely adoptee and the wish of the hound for personal space. Pele hurried over to a corner of the grand room and found the hole in the planks they used to peer below into the crawl space.

With his hindquarters spread-eagle on his belly, Sole looked about as rested as a mother hen. His head rested on his front paws. By his head, the fledging King-King was constantly chirping into Sole's ear between the young rooster settling down and nodding off into a nap. Sole promptly closed his eyes and settled into catnap, relieved at last for the respite from the racket. If anything was true of his new ward, he was noisier than Pele.

"What are they up to, Pele?" Sama had stopped playing to see what Pele was watching through the makeshift peephole.

"Shhh!" She pointed wordlessly to the crawlspace with her index finger to her pursed lips. "They're sleeping!" With a hand over her mouth, she giggled. She moved away to let Sama have a look. Their rescued chick bedded beside the exhausted mother hen, Sole.

"I dare say King-King is going to be okay, Pele." He pulled him up onto his knees and sat back on his haunches. "He's going to be one cranky bird. *E so'o nei ia oe.*" He grinned ear to ear at his indignant sister. Satisfied by his wince, she boxed him on the shoulder before she sat up and hurried back to Mother's side to pick up her sewing.

The afternoon was quiet enough and had cooled considerably. Pele leaned up against her mother's back as support and continued sewing. Mother sang to her in her melodious voice as she was often wont to do on these bucolic Sunday afternoons.

Lota Nuu ua ou fanau ai! Ua lelei oe i le vasa e. Ua e maua mai luga O le tofi aoga! Samoana! ala mai. Fai ai nei le fa'afetai I le pule ia maua ai O lou nuu i le Vasa e. E! Ua lalelei Samoa. Lona valevalenoa. Ia mo'omia ai ou fanua. Samoa, ala mai! Ua e sui lou tautai Lou mamalu ia mau ai? Tuputupu pea mai. Talu nuu ua feagai! Nu'u mamao ua e maua ai. Mea lelei e ati a'e. Lou mamalu, ia mautu. Mataupu tau Iesu! Ia fai oe ma nu'u tumau, Olaola lau fanau. Ia viia e fa'avavau. Le ua pule aoao!

"*Pele, fai mai le mau le Tusi Paia lena ou a'oa'oina atu ia te oe.*"

"*Esoto 20:12; Ia e ava i lou tama ma lou tina, ina ia fa'alevaleva ai ou aso i nu'u o le a foa'iina mai e le Ali'i lou atua ia te oe.*"

"*Lelei tele! Ia fa'amau pea le mau lena ia te oe 'aua le olaga e tumau pea nei mafutaga o matua ma fanau.*" Father continued so they could close the evening prayers.

As the afternoon slowly waned, the horizon over the island darkened considerably. Father rose from his reading, looking up from the well-thumbed pages. He eyed the skies from his side of the room.

For far as the eye can see eastward, clouds churned and whirled over the horizon. In time, there was a silence that had settled over without forewarning. The absence of birds chirping nearby; the bothersome kingfisher was strangely quiet. A growing sense of foreboding came over him. He closed his bible and put it somewhere safe beneath the linen and his ali. Swinging the pupugi to the side, he walked into the living area, where the children played near their mother.

He looked over to his wife and the children scattered over the planked flooring. "Leata." The wife looked up from her sewing and met her husband's eye. "A storm is brewing." She dropped her sewing on her lap. Pele stopped, too.

"Boys, come with me." He walked out of the cabin, disappearing to the back. Sama and Fano hurried after Father, both concerned over his abrupt, curt call. Mother and Pele hurriedly put away their sewing, pulled up the mats, and threw them over their meager belongings. With her heart in her mouth, Pele did as Mother asked of her without complaint. Father was bothered by something as he hurried out of the cabin.

Sama rushed over to Father. Fiso yelled at him and Fano, "Boys, we have winds coming. Help untie the blinds quickly!" Fano hopped onto a jutting corner of the flooring to pull down the sennit that held the blinds in that corner. The double blinds came down with a soft thud. Sama hauled several planks to Father and dropped them at Father's feet.

"That's enough. Find the hammer and some nails." Father dropped down the back blinds from behind the main living area. Sama hurriedly returned with the tools. He handed these to Father. Fano grabbed one end of a plank and held it up on the opposite corner of the lot, while Sama held up the center as Father nailed it against one of the main poles. They secured all the cabin's blinds to these structural poles. Once done, Father moved toward the roof.

"Check on Sole, Fano. I'm going to help Father with the roof." Fano went around the front steps and dropped to his knees to see if Sole was still under the house. Relief settled over him as he saw the dog bedded down in his bedding of ferns and an old mat Mother gave them for Sole.

"Stay down there, Sole. You hear me?" Fano re-emerged and walked up the steps to check on Mother and Pele. "Mother, do you need anything here?"

"Come help us move everything to the corner." Mother pointed out the sleeping mats rolled up for the children. "Move those toward the chest and bind them down!"

One raindrop hit the step before the downpour came down hard and fast! There was a steady stream within ten minutes of the first. Father and Sama were still on the roof.

"Fano, tell them to come down before the downpour hits harder. Hurry!" Mother pulled the sennit from the blinds to shield their belongings and linen to the side so the downpour wouldn't hit. Pele helped her by stacking everything that was not secured to the sheltered corner.

Gray and stark as everything was stripped of their places, and nothing but the tapa screen was still in place. Pele mused that something was so horrific about the grim scene before her. She held her mother's hand as they sat down, watching the thunderous clouds rise and pour onto them. Sheltered partly by the fruit trees around them, the winds haven't blown directly at the cabin. Not yet, at least.

Father and the boys entered the front, drenched to their bare skin. Mother hastened over with lavalavas to change into while Pele fetched more for them to use as towels.

"It's going to be hard," Fiso predicted gravely. A look of concern crossed over Leata's countenance. *It cannot be helped. It is in Our Father's hands, I say.* He glanced around the immediate clearing. "I hope we see the worst of the winds before nightfall." Father grimaced as he watched the rain pelt down harder every second. "Fano, make sure you get the lamps burning before nightfall. We're going to be in this for a while. Sama, get the barrels and leave them under the awning."

The brothers went about their assigned chores. Fano grabbed the work tools and shoved them under the crawl space lest they were swept down the slope. He handed the essentials to his father and brother.

Father looked heavenward. "We must dig around the back so we don't get flooded out. Sama, come with me!" The brook to the cabin's right had turned into a flash stream bearing down hard on the watercress beds, uprooting the bumper crop from roots.

Sama rushed forward, grabbed one of the shovels from Father, and started digging a trench from the far left rear side of the cabin while his father hurriedly dug from the right. Thunder rolled and clapped threateningly while the sheets of rain came down on them. The roof of the cabin thankfully held up. The copra trade with the town palagis had paid off as Father had bartered for tin roofing, which helped hold up the thatching. They dug the trench four feet deep to thwart the streams of water coming downward from the higher ground from flooding the crawlspace.

Sama peered below the crawlspace. Sole was cowering in a corner as the booming thunder roused him from his nap. "Father, I have to move Sole out from below!" He called the dog over the din to no avail. He ran back toward the front of the cabin and wrenched his way behind the steps. All he could see were the iridescent orbs on the dog. King-King's alarmed chirping became shriller as the din became unbearable for both. Sama called out to Sole and coaxed him out of his corner.

"Sole, *sau!* Come here!" The dog inched his way toward Sama on all fours with his tail tucked behind his hindquarters. "That's right! You're not afraid of all this mess. We've been through worse, old boy!" Sole wagged his tail hesitantly as Sama coaxed him more until he was in Sama's arms. Sama backed out of the crawlspace with Sole in his arms. He pushed the dog into the cabin as Mother stood, waiting for her husband and son to escape the storm.

"Mother, he has to come in!" He yelled over the loud din. "The water's coming down hard out back!" Fano came from behind Mother and took Sole by the scruff. Sama went back under and re-emerged with a very wet King-King. Sama handed the chick over to Pele. "Dry him, Pele, and try to give him some heat." Pele nodded; she was frightened by the looks of what could be a dying chicken.

"He's not dying, Pele." Sama laughed as he laughed at Pele's stricken look. "Dry him, and he'll be good as new. He's a survivor." Pele wondered about this as King-King looked anything but well with his fledging feathers so damp and limp. His missing eye made him this menacing talisman.

Father and sons kept at it until the channel fused in the middle. They turned and ran to the front side of the cabin, guiding the runoff into the gulley that flowed alongside the watercress lot. The booming cacophony of the rain with the accompanying thunder surrounded the family. The flora from Mother's garden bent under the weight of water on leaves and flowers. Rivulets ran down in eddies and dropped into the trench before streaming, cutting off the water from the crawlspace.

Pele scooted closer to Mother as the thunderous rumbles from the heavens rolled, roared, and boomed with phantasmal lightning. King-King was warm in one of her scraps. His working eye was closed as he shivered dramatically.

Sole hunkered down at the rear entrance with his head between his front paws, wishing the storm would go away or to ease up so he could return to being a dog doing what he needed—exploring the plantation for tasty treats. To be cooped up with King-King was not his idea of an ideal Sunday afternoon, as there was nothing restive about that venture. About that bird.

Father and Sama inspected the trench again before the night met the storm's darkness that blanketed most of the early afternoon. Father and Sama returned to the front, dragging the shovels with the machetes. They were weary and worn from the constant, chilly onslaught, ready to escape the rain. Both changed out of their lavalavas into dry ones.

Coconut oil lamps hung from beam to beam, swaying back and forth as the wind broke through slats in the blinds. Mother tied from the long branches they hammered into the beams. In the adjacent corner from the armoire was an inside fire pit that burned coal for Mother's iron and boiled tea in the evening. All other foodstuffs had to be cooked in the outside umu. The hole was now their source of warmth as the temperature outside plummeted. Father went into their makeshift room and returned with his spectacles and bible.

More severe than ever, they had seen him, "Children, come." Pele scooted up next to Mother, leaning into her side. Mother asked Fano to retrieve her hymnal from the chest. Sama sat in between their parents while Fano sat down in his place opposite Sama.

Father offered a benediction of thanksgiving of grace and asked that the Good Lord watch over his young family, their land, and the families in the village below and shelter their relatives elsewhere on the island. He prayed that they weathered the harsh hurricane as well as can be.

With a rousing amen, Mother started into her hymn out of the Congregationalist hymnal. *"Ua so'ona olioli nei lou loto…"*

Father accompanied her throughout the hymn. The boys, already versed in the Sunday services' hymns under their parents' tutelage, followed their parents' lead. Pele listened on and savored the simple melody. The howl of the wind outside the cabin got louder as the rain picked up its second wind. It would be a long night, but she hoped it would leave them unscathed.

She thought about their livestock, the few hens and roosters, who often slept in Mother's *sugi* trees in the storm. *Lord, be with them,* she mused between the Lord's Prayer and her mother. *Even the pollinators that help keep Mother's garden blooming. But you can have* all *the kingfishers in the world.*

"Pele!" Mother's voice pierced through her reverie. "Pele, please mind the prayer."

Father peered over from his side of the mat. *"O ala a po'o ua moe fo'i?"* Pele sat cross-legged, with her arms crossed and head slightly bowed. Her breathing was suspiciously rhythmic. Fano grinned, knowing that if Pele were sleeping, Father would have a scathing lecture for her.

"Lo matou Tama o ile Lagi—afai o lou finagalo lenei, Ia e alofa ia matou manu uma," Pele continued fervently. *Watch over the helpless and other families who haven't had a chance to run from the storm, dear Lord.*

Father chanted. "Oh, Lord, please hear my daughter's plea for Your leniency over the creatures she looks after so passionately." He glanced over to Mother meaningfully. She placed a hand over her Pele's. "Fano, please continue."

Not to be outdone by his sister, Fano broke into a sing-song litany of ills of the world and its possible fixes if the Good Lord investigated these matters. As he continued with his laundry list, Pele bowed her head again. And in the middle of one incredibly long stream of hail and brimstone, her mind prayed that Fano would stop. She rolled the cricks off her back, and gradually, the lull of the rain got the best of her. Sleep crept into her brain, its restorative powers thorough. In his perch closer to the heap of heated rocks, Sole also rolled on his back comfortably in his slumber. King-King snored as a fledging chick came next to him.

As the family prayers came to their natural end with Sama finishing the order of the children, Mother sang a hymn, and the men followed her lead. Pele was startled back to life and her surroundings. She hummed along and hoped she found them on the right note. By the look on Sama's face, she stopped before she wailed louder than the storm outside.

The storm lasted three days. As the dawn broke on the third day, the sun's rays penetrated the overcast gloom. Along with it came a rainbow, a promising sign to the children. They had prayed often enough as a family over these several days, but it was time to go into the world and survey the damage. It was no later than eight in the morning when their parents gave them leave to venture out as a family to look over the damages from the storm.

In front of them, the damages to their hillside were stark against the formerly lush growth. Mother's garden was in shambles. Chicken that had survived the last torturous days gathered at their usual rallying point, drying out their feathers in the rising sun's warmth. The umu lean-to had collapsed and was little than a heap of burned wood and scattered fronds from its roof. The torrential rivers had washed out the watercress plot save for a few tendrils. Dozens of banana trees snapped in half, with turned-over saplings up down the incline. The devastation was overwhelming.

Pele ran over the stepping stones to the *avapui* hedge to check on her dolls. She shimmied through the stalks on all fours, most broken in half from the winds. In the center of her haven, her playhouses were no more than rocks strewn about. Her dolls were now merely sopping messes of old papaya stems with no life or character.

She sat back on her haunches and sobbed. She bit her lip so no one could hear her. No one would understand what these dolls meant to her. *No one*! Mother had made them for her, something that had not been passed to her by her brothers. Now, even the parent-to-child moment when Mother made them was passing through her tiny body as she wept, inconsolable for her unbearable loss.

Father went up the path to the crest of the property with Sama. More of the older trees had fallen over the trek, making it strenuous to stroll up the usually short walk. Mud caked over their bare feet as they steadied themselves from sliding farther down the slope. More banana trees were turned over at the roots or bent down in the middle.

Sama felt his father stiffen at the sight before them. Fruit lay scattered up and down the hillside. The loss was a severe setback as what was marketable was either on the ground or washed down to the waterfalls below them. He could only imagine the time it would take them to clean up the storm's aftermath. It all was overwhelming, and the recovery weight was evident in Father's eyes.

"I can stay home from school a couple of terms, Father," Sama said more to himself than his father. "I'm sure that they'll understand." Father quietly assessed the loss some moments more. Sama shifted from one foot to the other before clambering over a fallen tree to move up from his tenuous foothold.

The winds plowed right through the windward side from his high-end perch. Little was spared as more devastation paralleled the winding road to their home below in the village. Banana trees snapped twigs in the path of the powerful winds. He grimaced as he thought about their relatives in the town and beyond.

"Son, it's pretty serious," Father said matter-of-factly. With a hand on his son's shoulder, he stood beside Sama, seeing what lay before them. "But no, I will not have you staying home from school. You must finish what you started, and Mother will not hear that you stay out of school."

"I know, but whom will you have to help you?" Sama and Fano had only four more weeks left on their school break. "Even if we start today, there isn't time to get through both sides of the hill, Father. If you do this alone without us, it would be futile."

"God has provided us with a living, Sama. Let Him be our reason for hope." Father smiled at his son's doubtful look.

Ua fai atu fo'i iā ia, na ou sau le mai le manava o lou tinā, o le ā ou fo'i atu iā ia lavalava na foa'i mai le Ali'i, ua ave'eseina fo'i e le Ali'i; ia fa'amanuiaina le suafa le Ali'i.

Naked, I came from my mother's womb, and naked, I will depart. The Lord gave, and the Lord has taken away; may the name of the Lord be praised.

We are not Job, Father. Sama thought mirthlessly, yet not daring to say this out loud.

"Never be too comfortable with your gifts, Sama. Do not get so comfortable that you stop praising the Good Father." He swept his hand over the landscape and the once-verdant hillside. "We're only temporary guardians of the land, Sama. Remember this when you, too, stand here as you inherit this."

Father walked off and, with his machete, cut down the fallen fruit trees. Sama rolled the cricks from his neck, squelched the rising sense of overwhelming desolation for his parents, for their family, and followed in the wake of his father's footsteps. He started on the adjacent lot and cut away at the debris. The day was still young, and they had a hillside to clear. Father and son worked companionably; the sound of machetes non-stop in their determined goal to set the plantation back into some palpable order.

Fano gathered the green bananas that had broken off their stalks and piled them into a spot. These will be as feed for animals. Salvaged crops were set aside for collection for umus. He hurriedly lifted fallen branches off the lime and citrus trees, cleared the brambles, and picked the fruits that covered the ground.

Leata and Pele had spent their day cleaning the brook, patching the irrigation flow, and replanting watercress back into the beds. Pele did not complain in the least. The avapui patch wasn't the same anymore. It wasn't the safe sanctuary that she once thought it was. She looked at the knoll and sighed. Her sadness was palpable.

Why do You put us through so much, Lord? We spent three days praying and singing hymns, hoping that You would spare us this grief! Our parents must work hard to provide us with a home and food. All that my mother gave me? Gone, too. Her garden is near ruins. Why us?

I hope I don't find yet another reason to have this conversation with You again, Father.

The sun beating down on them didn't bother her. Mother tied a section of her lavalava over Pele's head to help keep her calm. Mother rubbed dark mud over exposed limbs as the hordes of mosquitoes were horrendous in the aftermath.

The intricate cut-and-slash work lasted well into the mid-afternoon hours before Father reappeared with the boys behind him. Fano hauled in baskets of wasted fruits, from lemons to papayas to green bananas they could otherwise use as a meal staple or leave to ripen. Father and Sama dropped their loads by the overhanging awning of the cabin.

Father looked at Mother pointedly and shook his head. She understood the gravity of the moment. He headed to the brook where his eldest knelt to scoop water up in his cupped hands to wash his burned face, and the back of his nape reddened from the sun's burn. Father followed their sons.

Father glanced over at the collapsed hut that housed the umu. He advised against the rebuild as noon was giving way to evening. They will build again tomorrow. They can make an umu on its side without the shelter. He assessed his children's grim faces and knew they needed a reprieve from the loss and tremendous recovery work they had before them.

As they closed the umu an hour later, it was time to do something less time-consuming. The massive yam leaves were the covers this time around.

"Children, let's head down to the waterfalls." Cool baths and an unhurried approach would help them forget their aches and pains. Yet, even the thought of heading down the precipice was too much. "Mother and I will go with you." That helped brighten them up a little. "Pele, you want to piggyback down?" Sama asked with a tired smile. She looked her brother over and shook her head.

"No, thank you." She took his hand into hers. "It's too hot. I don't feel like being the little pig today." Fano came up the rear and walked without much conversation or meanness. Maybe that was God's short answer to her harangue earlier, she thought to herself. Perhaps it was too humid for them to care much for small talk. Whichever the case, she was grateful for the respite. And the *quiet*. Sole and King-King came with the children, their jostle in the undergrowth the only ruckus on the way down.

Their parents followed them. "Be careful heading down," Mother warned, knowing the children knew this. Minding her was another matter. "Just be careful." She fretted about this in better times as they hiked the trip several times a week. Now, with the steep descent bound to be even more dangerous, an accident up here was bound to be fatal. The children acknowledged her with synchronized "*Ioe*."

"I am sure they understand this, Leata." Fiso pushed banana leaves and debris out of the road. They followed a short distance behind their children.

"I'm just reminding them. There is nothing wrong with reminding the children that the path may be dangerous after these rains," Leata responded a little more sharply than she intended. Her shoulders dropped a little. "I'm sorry."

"No, you're right, Leata," Fiso conceded. He knew the pallor hanging over his family was immense, and the weather wasn't helping matters and starting *over*. They had to start over. Do as much as they can with the time they have with the boys before leaving for school. Even recovering a quarter of the plantation was a better start than none. The boys will be home for a term break in another two months.

"This land will break us, Fiso. It'll break our children," Leata said out loud. "The boys will work it as long as possible but must move on." She ran a hand through her dark hair, tired from the laborious morning in the sun. "They *must* move on," she whispered more to herself than her husband. He grabbed her by the elbow, holding her back from the trek.

He slapped a mosquito on his upper bicep. "This is their family, Leata. You know this when you came home with me." He sighed. Leata fixed him with a hard stare.

"I know what I was in for by marrying you, but we have children now. Their future, not ours, is something that we must consider." Leata wiped the sweat from her brow. "Their education is necessary, and I won't let them have less. They must be able to live beyond *this*."

Fiso knew that Leata was right. His sons were receiving the best education available on these islands. He knew his wife's family thought she married beneath her, but this was the least of his worries. Education comes at a cost. This luxury was paid for with the earth's resources and fruits now beneath their feet.

"I hear you, Leata," Fiso urged her on as the children were almost out of their direct line of sight. He rolled the cricks from his neck. "The children will be educated as you wish, but that education is not free."

"Don't try to appease me, Fiso. The boys' education is *our* future as well," Leata reminded him. "They do well? So will we. Was this not what you also wanted? Whatever the cost, the children must come first. We can't falter." She swept a hand over the effects of the storm over the hillside. "We cannot let *this* become the alpha omega of their lives."

"I know this, Leata. I *know* this." The conversation between husband and wife has come to its natural end. There was little that Fiso had not heard from Leata on this issue. Leata could not help but feel that they had hit a wall that could not go away between them. To each, the growing silence of their thoughts of their family's future had roosted between them. The concept of a separate *lumana'i* of their children is beginning to diverge in opposing directions.

"They'll return to the land, Leata. They will return after this worldly education and live on this land. It is good out there, but they must not forget that here is the land of their ancestors."

"There is not much left to their future if they wholly depended on the land to support them, Fiso. Life out there is changing, and they will, too."

The children were in the pool, happy for the cool respite. They were oblivious to their parents' burdens, worries, chores, and this brutal humidity.

Leata wished they would always look back on their childhood and hold these moments as threads of their youth. Their struggle together would be why they stay and prosper together as a family, even beyond the verdant acres of Olo'ie. They would venture beyond Samoa, beyond Tutuila's boundaries, and find something that defines them without their parents. This ambition is what Leata wished for her young children. Modernity was knocking on their door, so much so that even Fiso could not ignore the changes facing the children forward moving.

Father, with his sons by his side, worked on the land and rebuilt, recovering some of the immediate damages to the hillside. The plantation was the future of the children's stake out on the world. They had to understand that they were born on this land, and someday, they would know it was their salvation. These foreign wares and goods can only sustain them long before they return and appreciate all they worked for during these years before they stake their flags of independence. Even though their mother believed otherwise, Fiso was adamant that the estate would sustain the children.

The seasonal rains came once again one evening as the family sat and watched from the safety of the cabin. The children were languishing on the mats, looking out with some concern. They worked day and night to replant the plantation, and now time was running out for the boys as they looked forward to the eventual travel into town as they traveled back to the boarding school. To another civilization, it felt, another world that was not filled with the arduous work to upkeep a living that their father wished they would take on from him.

This world is not a life I want for myself! Fano didn't dare say this out loud, but he thought it. There was something more significant and better about life outside this rural world that their father confined them during these school breaks. *Maybe I will find a way not to come home next time. They wouldn't miss me here.* Father leaned on Sama to be the apparent heir, while Mother, whom he didn't doubt loved him, didn't have enough sway to further his position as the second son of the family. No, they wouldn't miss him here. He would find his living out in town.

Sama rolled onto his side and glanced at his mother's sunburnt hands. He wasn't opposed to coming home one day to stay permanently and take the plantation over from his parents. His heart was *here* on the plantation where their parents' wealth lay; eventually, as the eldest, it was his inheritance. There was something fundamental about being Samoans and owning the land they lived on and cultivated. They paid no taxes to the palagi landowners. These planters and farmers built and tried to enslave natives as the kavige, servant folk who ran around in their lavalavas and kowtowed to them.

He would never bow to a foreigner. No, he will learn the ways of this palagi ruling class by being in the lion's den, much like the prophet Daniel. Without that knowledge, he would not be able to do more about moving forward with his plans for his parents' efforts. This land was his destiny as the firstborn son.

The sheets of rain pounded the roof. Pele couldn't help but fear that God had sent her this exact answer to her impertinent demands not long ago. The rapid growth of the avapui patch was a godsend, as well as the whole greening of the hillside once again. Her sanctuary was thick enough to hide her from the world, her parents, and her brothers. To recapture her world once upon a time? It was not going to happen on this rainy day. *Okay, I get it, God.*

The children were not mesmerized by the torrential rain as the afternoon wore on into the evening. There was no joy among them about this rain. There was too much loss tied into the last storm that there wasn't any time for play. "Go out there and enjoy the rain," Father said firmly. "This is not a storm." There was a sun shining behind those clouds out there. The birds did not disappear, nor did they call out warnings. This healing rain fell over the land, a time of replenishment. Yet, an emptiness yawned across the estate.

"The rainbow, Father?" Pele asked. "Is this *His* rainbow? *His* promise that he'd never leave us hurting more than we need to?" Pele stuck a spindly leg out there, letting the rain pound down on her toes. "Why didn't He send it sooner?"

"Pele, God isn't on a short leash to tend to our every want and need." It was a strange concept to attribute to the omniscient Father, but he had to instill something into his ever-precocious, ever-curious daughter. She infuriated him and made him proud in equal parts. He was often astonished by her mindful ramblings, yet, if he had to admit it, Pele challenged him more so than her brothers. She was precocious, more intelligent than a wily octopus with questions that he wasn't always ready to answer.

Stung by Father's admonishment that brook no room for debate, Pele watched the rain splashes on her ankle and shin. Why then teach them the goodness of a deity that would drive them to ruin? That would endanger their family's chances to move forward if He took away how her brothers could thrive and take their family along.

She did not understand a god that could take away her little peace on this hillside; the tenuous hold that bonded her to her mother was left over from Mother's love for her sons. She didn't want to grow up and be the proper wife that her mother was. Her mother certainly had ideas of what she should be doing; leaving home was not one of those options that Pele wanted to ever think about.

However, her chances of leaving home? It is not impossible, yet not a swinging *yes*, either. She had to be aware of Father's moods. Within Father's moments of clarity are her fighting chances for a real future. Pele will have to live a more adventurous life away from this world that already belonged to her brothers. She had no chance of inheriting this land since it was deemed that it would be male heirs.

"Pele!" Sama broke through her reverie. "Come back to earth." He smiled at her worrisome brow. "We're going to be okay." He offered her his outstretched hand. "Shall we?" They walked out into the rain and relished the coolness that it provided them. Sole and King-King joined in the fun.

At the end of the week, they will rejoin the world beneath this haven. The children will take changes with the ebb and flow of the ocean. The Pacific before them was yet another facet of their world, unlike the earth beneath their feet. The sea gave and can take all away from them when incensed by the acts of man. There was a reverence and fear about the cerulean, clear ocean. Their ancestors were famed navigators who traveled the open seas, fearless in their adventures. One among them wished to be as daring and adventurous as those men and women who dared to go beyond Samoa. Who else but one of them?

With His good graces shining upon them, they will prevail. The good fortunes of the land will catapult them beyond the village and put their father's name much further than he has ever imagined. Sama knew their parents depended on him to accomplish something more than they had in their lifetimes.

As the rain poured on them, each child thought of the world above the village. They reveled and thrived in the quiet family life up here, away from prying eyes and far from the world's hustle and bustle below. Their laughter echoed throughout the hill as their parents watched them play. The plantation would recover soon enough, and winds of good fortune would indeed return,

Fiso believed. Something had to break even for them in this place, as this land could not be the death of their family, as Leata believes.

Fiso called the family closer so that they could say their evening prayers. It was merely four in the afternoon, but it might as well have been midnight. The rain eased into the evening's twilight. The faint buzz among the evening denizens was back. His children came closer into a circle. The sense of gratitude was palpable among the family.

Lord, we ask for your guidance as we get through our dailies. Please be merciful as You watch over us. Lead us through our trials with love. Show us kindness when there is none among our brethren. Remind us there is a tomorrow with the promise that even in our darkest hours, there is belief. Please be with our sons as they return to school in Samoa; guide them back to our family there so they may be graced with Your gifts. May they always know the importance of family in good harvests and how to reach out to others in times of woe. Father, I ask for Your hand on our daughter's road to her realization.

Could you help us be good parents to them? Help us through these moments when we must let them go.

We leave our fates in Your hands through all Your goodness, Our Good Father.

The children slept with the weariness of the day off throughout the night— no thought to the future or the past. Little now sustains, but they unto themselves. It is hard to see hope here when there isn't any sign.

They slept each with dreams of anything beyond their home shores. Someday, their father prayed the boys would see life here. They will see this land as worth returning home to with their own families. He will see his grandchildren gather in the future and appreciate the work they do now for them. In time, they would understand the perseverance of their ancestors. What great joy comes over him when he thinks of what herculean efforts to cultivate the land in his living can mean for his grandchildren and the generations of Spaffords. He hoped his sons would see beyond hard work and know this was not about a singular inheritance or heir.

Every day he added to the plantations, he thought of his sons and their return home to take over. While the world is changing and foreign wars are knocking on island shores, this remains home. No matter how far removed they travel in their search for meaningful lives, Olo'ie will always be theirs.

This has always been the way—their Fa'aSamoa was tied to the land, the *tautua, a'iga,* and filial piety. This was always the way between Spafford fathers and sons. His daughter will move on and hopefully bear some grandchildren who will help support their paternal cousins.

Lord, please bring them home when they've seen enough of the world and let them do what needs to be done here. Let them know that all he strives to do is for a future for them.

II. 1910

Le Lalolagi
The Land Beneath

The sultry warm day settled into an airless night. She had never seen people sitting with her parents and eating with them in the front room.

Who are these people? Why have they come? What has happened? These people—why, oh, why are they here?

What can they possibly have to do with their parents? And where are her brothers? The term break was today, and the boys were due home from town any day now. She was so happy awaiting their return now that months had turned into mere hours. Even seeing her annoying brother, Fano, would be nice.

But Father had not gone into town. Instead, folks had come to call. Her mother had instructed her to prepare the sleeping mats and remain in the kitchen. Father's maiden younger sister, Aunty Lesina, came in to help with the week's errands while her parents played host during this open house.

Unseen behind her parents in the hallway, she could not help but hear them talking heatedly over something or *someone*.

Father looked grim but resolved. "She needs to go, Leata. We cannot hold onto her. She is growing up and needs to be in school."

"I know this! You don't need to remind me!" Leata riled, "But does she need to leave this young?" She fretted with her husband, "She is so young, and her brothers will not be there to look after her."

Father batted her hand off. Leata grasped his upper hand again. "Please reconsider. She is our only daughter. How can you be so cold and let her go?"

Let me go. Where am I going? Why will Father not listen to Mother, to her pleas? Shouldn't I go away from them? Who would look after me?

"She must be formally schooled, Leata. Was this not always your wish for the children?" Father replied firmly. "She's just as capable as the boys, if not smarter. If she has a chance, she must leave now. Please get her ready to leave when the boys return to school."

These strangers laughed merrily, their boisterous voices carrying from the front. They entertained themselves now that tea was over. After all, what could they take so seriously when bountiful foods, a place to lay their tired selves from their *malaga*, were readily available?

Pele shrunk back into the darkness of the night, and with a fist in her mouth, she wept unceasingly. She should be happy, but this was not how she envisioned her adventure. Not so soon. How can she ever leave home? Leave the faitatala Sole, and then there is King-King, now a full-fledged pearl-colored silky rooster, holding his court with the hens. These were her best friends, and leaving was kin to lopping off her hands. They needed her as much as she did them.

She was not her brothers. Going away to boarding school was as natural as breathing air for the boys. They were experts at leaving home after breaks, hopping the ferry, and waving from the aft before becoming mere dots on the horizon. She wasn't old enough to traverse the village on her own. If anyone asked her, she didn't want to. Yet, Father didn't doubt that she was old enough to leave home on her own. She wept until she hiccupped herself into a troubled sleep.

This future all felt so familiar. *"Pele, no one's conspiring to take you away. It was all a dream. Just a foolish dream!"* Sama, my dear brother, it's not a dream anymore.

Father meant to take her away from home. She wouldn't see her mother, brothers, or home even longer. The abject sadness was overwhelming. Tossing and turning in her bed set above the bundle of sleep mats, she could not find a comfortable position. The tighter she squeezed her eyes, the more she saw black, blue dots. Sleep was not forthcoming, she sighed. Why even bother? She bolted up and dropped her bare feet onto the cool floor! Pele smoothed down her lavalava over her thin knees.

The loud voices and laughter of guests carried from the front of the house. It was late, and folks were still talking. She crept out the back door, knowing no one would miss her as the high tea was served about an hour before.

Lights from well-lit lanterns shone from their palagi home, a Queenslander in the middle of these verdant hills. The house was still so new; she was not happy there. There was something so cold about the solid walls, about a room on one far end of the house from her parents. This house was not their hillside cabin.

As she held up the wall for fear that someone might hear from the front, her heartbeat drummed a painful beat. She didn't know where she was going, but anywhere was better than tossing and turning all night. The linen she helped hang up earlier with Mother flapped in the slight breeze.

Then Sole was suddenly beside her, ever faithful in the moonlight. He sat down on her toes, much to her chagrin. "No, you're not going to stop me, Sole. *Halu!*" Sole refused to budge despite Pele's pleading. She shooed him some more. As that didn't convince Sole, she pulled her toes out from under his rump. He whimpered as she fixed him with a mean stare, her grimace plain in the glow of the moonlight.

"Come with me or not. You choose. Sole. But if you so much bark out again, I will *never* speak to you," Pele admonished. Sole solemnly followed the young miss, not at ease with whatever she was up to, but he must be with her whenever that disastrous deed comes to fruition.

Pele followed the grassy path toward the beach. She went traipsed by the pungent flowering pandanus trees, bending aside the waxy branches of the Panax hedges that lined the road. Over the knoll, she came to the robust ancient Chinese lantern tree, its trunk covered by lichen. Armed with knobby, twisted massive branches, it was a great source of many fun days after pulling weeds with her mother, a preoccupation they kept from day to night. Forbidden to be alone during the day, Pele can only imagine how much trouble she'd be in *now* if she were discovered. Sole camped his tired soul below her.

Hiking her way up to the forked branches, Pele sat down in the cradle that formed from the junction between these two branches. The stars glittered brightly against the navy-blue indigo skies as the moon canted slowly over the hillside. The tide was low, and the exposed, dry coral stink was especially pungent but not unpleasant.

Well, at the very least, Mother fought for her. *That was some consolation.* The dams rose in her eyes as her nose dripped down onto her upper lip. She looked as the horizon allowed; the stars twinkled as they wished, oblivious to her woes. Sole caught sight of several hermit crabs scurrying about and went to investigate. They hurried forward to the edges of the water as it lapped at the shore.

She scooted a bit in her perch to lie down on the branch. Skillfully, she rolled onto her side as she often did when she was here. Watching the stars shine brightly over the precipice of the earth, Pele closed her eyes.

Dear Universe, please hear my prayer tonight. I know I have often asked for favors, but today, it would mean something if you heard me. Who would care for Sole and King-King and help Mother with the chores? Do I need to go? Can't we hold the business of schooling off? Well, if you're up there, not so busy, can you please tell Father to keep me here? Fa'afetai, o Pele.

Sleep came easy to the faithful. Pele felt herself walk back home in her dream state with her steady companion, Sole, beside her. She felt a lump creep up her throat as she looked down at his inky brown eyes. He wagged his tail in response. How can he know her despair? Heartsick, she whispered her fears, hoping God would hear her between prayers.

Pele was startled and tried to grasp hold of the branch beneath her. It was seconds too late! The branch gave way, and she fell to the sandy ground below. Her head hit with a sick thud as she collided with the edge of one of the hollow roots.

Sole ran over to her prone body as he heard her groan and wailed aloud. He hurriedly licked the trickle of blood dripping from her forehead. The pain was excruciating. She couldn't catch her breath. It was painful even to try to breathe. Sole, sensing the moment's magnitude, ran up the knoll along with the home. Even if his barking alerted all to Pele and her shenanigans, it couldn't be helped! She was hurt!

Sole bounded up the wooden steps and started barking at the back door. The merriment continued unabated, so it was unlikely that anyone would hear him. Sole howled the best way he knew how. Hurried footsteps were bounding toward him. He bellowed a little louder than before and barked unceasingly at the door.

Stepping out onto the lanai, Sama came out to see Sole. He set down his green coconut on the railing. He wondered why the dog was putting up such a stir. He smiled at their faithful pet, "Sole, *ole a mea ete so'ona pisa iai?*"

Sole barked on, twisting his body, and took off running. Sama was not sure what had Sole so excited. Perhaps not seeing him for the last school period has made him miss the boys more than usual.

"What's wrong, Sama?" A resonant voice asked him behind him. "Is everything okay?" his guest came to stand next to Sama on the lanai.

"Oh, it's just our *sa'a*, Erich." Sama shook his head, laughing. "I think the devil's gotten into his belly that one!" He reassured his schoolmate. His brother was in the front, reveling in the attention of their aunts and uncles. Fano liked that stuff, whereas Sama was happy hiding in the kitchen.

Erich looked after the dog as it watched them from the bottom of the steps. "Sama, something's amiss. He's standing there as if waiting for you to follow him." Sama looked back down at Sole. "Oh, he's okay. You're such a worrywart, Eliki." Erich was not convinced. Something wasn't right. Before he could say something, Sama's aunt Lesina stepped out of the kitchen, grinning at the boys. She guffawed at Sama's wry smile.

"Alu e va'ai ou aiga, Sama. O oe lena o le autu na usu mai iai le malaga." She giggled, laughing even louder as Sama winced. Lesina was only three years older than him but still his aunt.

Yet, she told no lie—it was true. The guests were here to speak to his parents about his marriageability and a possible pairing with their daughter, who did not have to accompany the malaga. Marry someone sight unseen, Sama grimaced.

"Soia!" Sama grinned good-naturedly despite Lesina's constant teasing. "Let Fano marry her! He seems to crave that kind of attention."

They talked about the term and how he was doing at school. More importantly, whether he had thought about what to do during the break, they caught up with school's happenings, being away from home, and the prolonged arduous plantation harvest here. The storm was seemingly years ago when they were up at the cabin. In time, Father's hard work had paid off. The plantation had given them a boon harvest two years following the last hurricane.

While Lesina chatted with Sama, Erich walked down to greet Sole, anxious and standing with his tail between his legs. It must be odd to have so many strangers at home here, walking about in a massive yard that was all of Sole's territory. Erich smiled to himself.

Sole wasn't impressed by the new arrival, this sprite fellow. He got up on his fours and bounded toward the steps again to get Sama's attention. Sole whined and growled at Erich as the boy tried to reach out to him. *Something's wrong, all right*, Erich thought out loud. "Sama, something's going on with Sole. He's not going to stop unless you follow him." Nephew and Aunt looked at each other, smiling.

"Erich, are you a seer?" Lesina called out jokingly. Erich's intuition told him something was out of the ordinary here. He did not have to be clairvoyant to know. Sama noted his friend stiffening. Even Lesina noticed how serious Erich had become.

She sighed aloud. Sama sure had some friends, but they were primarily good boys. Her handsome nephew wouldn't pick otherwise.

She adjusted her lavalava tied over her mu'umu'u. "Go with Erich and see to Sole. *Masalo o iai se mea e talatala le loto o Sole. O na toe omai laia ae le'i uma le inuga ti!*" Lesina returned to the inside kitchen. She waited for the last calls for food or the wash pan, even at midnight.

The boys called Sole, who was waiting on them outside the span of the burning kerosene lamp. He ran, hoping the boys would forget their human rationale and follow him. Sole looked back to see them running after him. *Good, so good!* He barked some more, heralding the urgency of the moment. They waited for them to hurry up and catch up with him.

Sole wanted them to tend to something at hand. Sama suddenly understood. Erich stopped and looked at him curiously. "Sorry! Sole likes to chase crabs. That's what the mutt's been chasing! He wants us to go on a lama with him."

Erich stopped and then chuckled out loud, relieved. He joined in with Sama's contagious good humor. "That entire ruckus for a fling with an *uga*? Even your dog is maoback, Sama." Erich shook his head, amused. Sole was already over the knoll. "That's some determined dog. We ought to join his little game of *igave'a* with the crabs!"

They slowed at the crossing and walked over the rooter vine that vociferously covered the knoll. They surveyed this end of the beach, noting how the cleansing winds blew in from the vast Pacific. He now understands why his best friend was so fond of his parents' hold out.

It was quiet here in Taima, less populated than the town center, and his parents' homestead was in Apia. Sama was a country boy, showing his leanings at school. He was outstanding in their agricultural sciences classes, botany, and farming. Here, his best friend was in his element.

The moon was closer; even the ocean seemed vaster than he'd ever seen elsewhere. Or was he spending an hour in the sun on their ferry from school? He sent word to his parents about his adventures in the countryside. Once he received their permission, he was on the ferry with the brothers. They were out by the beach looking for hermit crabs with this wily, stout family dog.

Sole bounded across the stretch, already twenty ahead of them, barking up a storm. The boys saw his tail disappear in the distance. They hurried along to see what Sole was so darn excited about in the dark. The boys chuckled at his enthusiasm. They hurried along the sandy path with the lamp swinging. Sole barked again and bounded farther down the beach into the bend of the knoll.

In the moonlight, under the shadows of the *pu'a* tree, they could make out the shape of a mass. Sama's ebullient laughter seeped out; a creeping fear coursed through him. Has something washed up with the tide? What has Sole dragged in? He broke into a run. Erich followed his friend, wondering what had upset him.

There, by Sole, was the unmistakable crumbled figure just within the shadows of the massive tree!

Sama knelt next to the figure as Erich caught up with him. Sama's shoulders dropped as he realized who this small, inert body was. He moved around to Pele's head. "Pele! Can you hear me? *No! No!*" Sama's dread gave way to panic. Erich pulled his friend away as he leaned in closer to her.

"Don't move her, Sama! Go get your parents!" Erich urged. "She is breathing, but please hurry!" Sama sat back on his haunches, dazed. Erich grabbed his friend's trembling hands. "Please hurry, Sama. I'll stay with her here! Go now!" Sama leaped to his feet, trying to clear his mind of the dread and totality of the horror of discovering his sister here and hurt, tattered as one of her rag dolls.

"Watch her, Erich! Please!" Sama begged unnecessarily. *Lesina! She will know what to do.* "I'll hurry back with help." He sprinted up the sandy path, hurrying back to the house, bounding around the back, hoping Lesina wasn't in front of the guests. Several women were with her in Mother's kitchen as they were readying tea for the guests. He rapped at the window to get her attention.

Lesina peered up from her chore to see her frantic nephew waving her over. She handed the *laulau* over to another one of the other women to take out to the front. Waving off a concerned look, she excused herself from the busyness of the kitchen to walk to the back to find out what had Sama so excited.

Sama hurriedly explained what had happened to Pele, trying hard not to cry. Lesina listened intently, and as concerned as she was, like Sama, she did not want to throw the gathering into a panicked frenzy. She had Sama run around the back room to gather a mat and a few lavalavas.

Sama went, and Erich thoroughly checked Pele's vitals. Sole, faithful stead as ever, stayed with them. He circled and whimpered helplessly. "I know, Sole! I know!" A slight breeze came in from the ocean, cooling off the day's humidity. Erich took off his lavalava and covered the unresponsive Pele with it. He still had his parochial school shorts under that. Pele had to be kept warm.

"Sole, *sau!*" He urged the dog closer to lay on her flank while covering her from the easterly winds with his body. She was small enough for him to tower over. She pitifully moaned as he laid for what seemed like an eternity for Sama to come back with help. Moaning was good. She was coming around.

"Pele! Pele, can you hear me?" Erich whispered urgently. "Do you know where you are?" She was startled at the sound of a voice. Opening her eyes, Sole was staring at her intently. Then Sole was talking to her. Could this be His answer to her fervent prayer? Her dog was talking to her. She was thankful, but what could Sole say to Father that Mother hadn't already said? What was Sole doing on top of the tree?

"Sole." Talking to Sole strangely hurt more than she believed possible. She panted between breaths. Her head was throbbing. "Why are you up here? What if you fall?" Sole winced, burrowing his sandy nose into her chest. She winced in return.

"Don't move, Pele." Erich scooted closer to warm her. If something was broken, he didn't want to aggravate her state more than necessary.

"I won't, Sole. But I am so tired," Pele muttered, almost inaudibly between breaths. "Now that you can talk, please tell Father I don't need to go away?" *Please tell him that I am so important to you and King-King; tell him that boarding school can wait!* She was exhausted beyond belief. All this cool air can be so comforting, such a wonderful part about being home. Where she was going couldn't possibly rival the beauty of the home. *No way!*

Erich was startled by how well-spoken she was. The sister that Sama spoke of so lovingly. He chuckled. "You're right, Pele. Nothing as beautiful as your home on earth."

"*Our* spot…" Pele gasped sharply. She expelled each breath slowly, trying to focus on Sole. "Something's wrong, So-le." Alarmed, the pain in her temple threatened to send her over. She grimaced and gritted her teeth as she closed her eyes.

"Stay with me, Pele. Don't fall asleep," Erich exclaimed loudly into her right ear. "Stay with me!"

"Stop yelling at me, Sole," Pele replied petulantly. She opened an eye and glared at her friend. Every limb weighed so heavily. "Can you stop it? Pl-please, don't yell at me. I'm n-not deaf!" She closed her eyes. "I don't want to argue with you. Will you talk to Father?"

Erich couldn't help but grin at the pluck in the fallen. Even though he was mistaken for Sole, that wasn't as important as it was to keep her from falling into a deep sleep. Not right now. "Pele, I'll tell Father. I'll tell him you're not ready." No answer. "Pele!" He rose and hurried to the other side of her. "Pele! Pele!" She was unresponsive.

Sama dropped down. Next, his breathing labored as he ran up to them. "How is she? Did she say anything? Did you talk to her?" He searched for Erich's face in the canted moonlight.

"No, not I, but to Sole!" Sama was unsure how or what Erich meant by that remark. What mattered was that she did wake up, and she had talked to one of them. Be it Sole or Erich, it mattered not.

Lesina dropped down to her knees next to Pele. She grabbed her niece's hand and felt for a pulse. It was faint but firmly there, which was good. She hurriedly felt around Pele's ribcage. Gently, she prodded. Pele winced and cried out. Lesina pulled aside her niece's lavalava. She looked at the boys, "Sama, light that lamp now. I must see her before we move her. Hurry!"

Sama lifted the glass to the kerosene lamp and quickly lit the wick with a matchstick. Lesina checked her for broken bones or ribs, running her hands over Pele's midriff. She motioned to Sama to lift the lamp higher. The purplish bruising around the gash at her temple was prominent.

"She's tender around the ribs, but nothing broken there." Lesina took a clean lavalava from Sama and ripped it in half. She gently dabbed Pele's forehead. She sighed out loud. "I don't have to worry about splinting her." She shook her head. Lesina looked down at her niece's prone body. *Only Pele can find the lone rock underneath this tree,* Lesina thought tersely. "She isn't supposed to be here, I tell you. And we can only imagine what will happen when your mother finds out."

Strapping the other half of the lavalava around her midriff, Lesina motioned the boys to move her steadily onto the mat. "I want you to take her to my place and make sure no one sees you. Do you understand? I'll finish the cleaning at the house and make sure no one is looking for her."

Sama and Erich nodded in agreement. They hauled Pele over the knoll on a makeshift litter, Lesina following behind them, and the kerosene lamp extinguished lest anyone spot them on the beach. No one appeared from one side to the other. Sole bounded next to them, following the boys with Pele while Lesina disappeared into the beaten path.

At the fork of the road, they broke into different directions. Lesina's humble faleo'o was another few yards beyond the impressive palagi house. Lesina waited to see them walk onto the marked dirt path toward her place before squaring her shoulders back and hurrying toward her brother's house. Clambering onto the steps, she went around the back, hoping no one saw her.

"Where are you coming from?" Fano stood in the shadow of a beam. She snuck right by him in her haste. "Has something happened?" Lesina whirled around and looked at her nephew. Unlike Sama, she had to mind her way around this one.

"Nothing to concern yourself with!" Lesina replied to him a bit more sharply than she had intended. She calmed her breathing. "What are you doing out here?"

"Nothing to concern yourself with!" Fano retorted as he moved away from the beam and hastened back through the back of the fale just before she did. If she were not afraid of her Maker, she longed to reach out and touch that boy as she watched his retreat.

She wished her brother would discipline this one a little more often. He minded only their parents, leaving her wanting to strangle him sometimes. God forgive her for her thoughts, but Fano was trouble, and if his parents leave that impertinence unchecked, he will only get worse over time.

It was a godsend that he hadn't noticed that Sama and Erich were not around. It's best not to fight this battle, not right now, at least. She walked behind the blight on her taro leaves and did the night's chores.

Nearing Lesina's faleo'o, Sama and Erich adjusted themselves, approaching the front side of the faleo'o and facing forward with Pele between them. As he motioned to Erich to lower his end of the mat, Sama jumped onto the side of the flooring and hauled himself onto the flooring. He pulled up several sets of blinds. Sama jumped back down to the front of the faleo'o beside Erich.

They grabbed the litter on their respective ends and lifted her shoulder-high so they could ease there on the flooring. Once there, the boys jumped onto the flooring and hoisted Pele onto the plank floor, Sama dragging her forward, careful not to jostle his sister too hard. *You did it this time, Pele!* Sama thought. He shook his head as he looked down at her in her repose. Now, it was about keeping this incident from their parents. What could have possessed her to venture out there in the dark?

Erich collapsed beside Pele on the other side of the mat while Sama flanked her.

"Is she always this adventurous?" Erich smiled, staring up at the intricate rafters. Hanging atop the posts were herbs that Lesina had gathered and was drying. It was now apparent to him that Sama's aunt was a healer.

"Always," Sama sighed ruefully. "One of these days, Mother is bound to have a heart attack over Pele's antics." He rolled over onto his side, gazing down at Pele lovingly. He smoothed back a curl that had fallen over her temple. She will wake up with a massive headache. One thing was sure: he was not missing any stuffiness back at the main house.

Erich looked over at him. "We've all of two weeks here. This break should be fun."

Pele stirred in her troubled slumber but thought she heard Sole talk to her again. And Sama? Could her brother be home already? Has he come home? She had to get up and greet him! Her eyes felt so heavy and weighed down by a boulder. Where was she?

"Pele!" Sounded like Sama. How was this close to her? He was only in her dream, she thought. Her tongue was stuck to the roof of her mouth. Why can't she open her eyes? Why did she hurt all over?

"I don't think she can hear you," Erich answered. "Maybe she's hurt more than we know." *Sole!* He was still talking. That's a good sign. She reached out tentatively, feeling for him in her urgency. She swung a foot, and it fell over her ankles. Maybe God gave him legs to carry her home.

"*Sole*?" she whispered, husky from the effort it took to say his name. She tried again. "Sole? Is Sama home?"

"Yes, he's come home, Pele," Erich answered.

Sama stifled a laugh as he watched Pele struggle to feel 'Sole' in her semi-comatose state. At least she was talking. Erich glared at him wryly as Pele fell heavily against him in her effort to find the family dog. From her heavy breathing, she was asleep once again. She had curled closer to Erich with a foot and swung over him, and she insisted in her sleep to stay close to him.

They remained that way until Lesina came back from the main house. She watched the trio sleep as they were. Sama had fallen asleep on his left side, with his arm over Pele, while she was curled under Erich's armpit. He slept on his back with an arm slung over his young face. She laughed as even Sole had squeezed in between the kids.

Lesina pulled a large lavalava sheet out from the bundled linens and lovingly covered them. The mornings were cool these last days of October. She settled the children before sitting on the corner of one of the poles and pulling out a tobacco pouch. Swiftly, she rolled one together and smoked one as she contemplated keeping her niece with her without her parents finding out what had happened here. The girl has a way of getting into fixes that will get her in serious trouble.

She smiled as she thought of the many times Sama had to bail her out. More of a father figure, Lesina was grateful that she could always count on Sama regarding family. However, the children were hers as well. On most days, she had control of the situation. *Most days*, but not of tonight's fiasco.

Birds were cawing once again on this cool morning. Upon the glow of the morning's first light over her ten-year-old face, Pele stirred and immediately felt pain from her bruises. She opened her eyes in protest. Glancing up at the ceiling, the detailed sennit work on the beams looked familiar. *Aunty Lesina's!* What was she doing here? Did Aunty bring her over, and she couldn't remember? She yawned, rubbing the sleep out of her eyes. She turned her back before realizing her head was resting on someone's arm.

She turned to look and saw an unfamiliar face with curious, quiet eyes staring at her. Specks of sand they were, set against a fair-complected face, a curiously hawkish beak, with flaxen straight black hair.

She stared right back at them. "Who are you? Why are you sleeping here?" Could this be one of her cousins? Everyone who came home to them was an uncle, aunt, or cousin. But this person was no one she could remember from previous encounters with family visits.

"I am Sole," Erich reminded her from the night before when she addressed him as the family dog. "Pretty hard fall you took there, Pele. You're lucky that Sole came looking for your aunty and brother."

"Well, then I should thank Sole." All the love that buoyed her spirits she lavished on Sole had been a significant investment. Eyes narrowed at Erich, "Are you making fun of me?" This stranger took such liberties with her feelings. Then the audacity to even address her as Pele?

Erich heartily laughed as outrage crept over her face. She pulled her head off his arm as if in protest. Rushed, Pele gasped as a sickening wave of nausea rushed from the pit of her stomach to her head. She rolled away from him as she felt a wretched burn of her stomach contents coursing up her throat, and she needed to hurl. Erich sat up and pulled her into a half-sitting position, hastening her toward the flooring corner.

Erich gently urged Pele to the edge to get her to relieve herself onto the ground below the file's elevated flooring. He rubbed her back as she crouched over and vomited vociferously. Sama stirred, stretched, and rolled over onto his side. His face was away from the sun, and his sick sister was under the care of his best friend.

Erich held Pele's brown wispy hair from her face as she relieved herself of her stomach. The dry heaves worked through her, shaking her to her core. She braced herself against Erich's arm and rocked steadily forward until the last shudders were out of her system. Erich slipped a hand between her shoulder blades and steadied Pele.

"Do you think you can stand up, Pele?" Erich saw the road to the creek around the corner of the fale. It would do well to hydrate and dip her into the stream so she could clean herself of the foul smell of regurgitated food.

He kicked Sama in the foot to wake him. "Sama, you must get up and take Pele to the creek. She needs a drink and a little clean-up." Sama stirred a little but did not get up. Erich pressed on. "Sama, get up, Mate." Sama peeled an eye open but did not get up. He looked bemused and exhausted in one fell swoop.

"Where is my aunt?" Sama asked sleepily. He stared at Erich as though seeing him for the first time that morning. Sama glowered at the balled-up shape of his sister, laying an arm's reach away from him. Rubbing his eyes with the back of his arms, he rolled back to stare at his sister's sad, huddled form. Again, he was between wanting to strangle her little neck and loving her out of her injuries.

Erich could see the exhaustion in Sama, but this had to be done. "Get up, Sama. Let's take her." Sama pointed out Aunty Lesina's basket of soaps and botanical potions. Erich gathered the soap and the loofah and waited for Sama to get his sister, Miss Sleepyhead.

Sama reached down and gently picked her into his arms. She was lighter than a bundle of bananas. Gangly thin limbs on this girl, but she seemed in good spirits and health when she woke.

Feet onto the dirt path from the fale, Erich gently treaded over the worn path, trying to clear the brush before Sama, who was trying his best not to jostle his sleeping cargo. She turned toward his chest and wrapped her thin arms around his neck, a little tighter than his comfort, but he was sure she would fall out of his arms. The path wore thin in parts, so he stepped a bit into the grassy knoll that flanked the steadily flowing waters. Up ahead of them were the falling waters of the source of the creek bed.

Sama walked into the waters and slightly dipped Pele into the translucent depths. She yelped at the coolness of the water as it dripped over her face. Goose flesh immediately rose on the back of her arms and her legs. She sputtered and tossed about but knew he was right. She did smell something seriously foul.

Pele took the soap from Sama. "Please." He left her to sit off the bank's side with his back as she tended to her constitution. *A little nap*, Sama thought to himself.

The morning sun rose over the draft horizon without asking the sleepy hamlet's permission. Basking in the warmth of the rays, Pele revealed for a bit. She scanned her view briefly before she turned to her brother. He woke as she touched him timidly. "I am done." She shuffled her threadbare belongings in her hands and crawled back as he turned over. He smiled at her before he smacked a mosquito on his forearm. And another bloodsucker was hovering over for a turn.

He motioned her over to sit by them. She plopped down unceremoniously to be next to them. Erich rolled over on his back as Sama stifled a yawn. It was still early yet. Sama slumbered between them.

"Do you like it here?" She shrugged her thin shoulders. "Is that a yes or no?" he laughed at her grimace.

She pulled at a blade of grass between her crossed limbs. "This is home. What is there not to like?" Maybe he was trying to return to her brothers and tell them anything less than happy. If she said no, it would make it to her parents. If she said yes, he would leave it at that.

It wasn't. "Do you miss your brothers? When they are away, I mean?" He probed. He wasn't looking at her but rather at the morning sky above them.

"Yes." It was truthful, short, and without room for misunderstandings. She was happy either way. It was great to have them home so she wouldn't be on Mother's shortlist—to call for chores, to discipline if something wasn't right. The point was that there would be others to keep Mother company, and she, the unruly and the ungrateful, would be off the register of ill-mannered children when her brothers were away. There were no others to yell at when something went amiss at home. The list was very short, Pele groused.

"Do you miss having a sister?" He rolled over to gaze at her. He didn't look at her but rather through her. "Someone whom you can play with?" He had two sisters and three brothers a few years older than Pele. All of whom were younger than him. Their family was quite busy, and his parents often looked to him to help the children, even disciplining them when they were either away or preoccupied with other business. This task was a godsend.

Most days, he could play judge and jury. His siblings sorted out their arguments while he was their parliamentarian, the tiebreaker, who sorted out the infractions and who was right or wrong.

Pele shrugged her shoulders. She didn't miss what she had never known. "Is that a yes or a no?" Erich rose to his full height, which might as well have been a willowy reed to her.

"It's neither. I don't have sisters, so I don't know," she said out loud. It was as honest an answer as the day was long. Pele shifted her belongings under her arm as he helped her up.

Erich asked for her towel, went to the water's edge, and dipped its frayed corner into the calm waters. He motioned her closer. Erich dabbed at the angry abrasion in her hairline, wiping off the caked blood. She winced out loud but refused to look up at him. Erich chuckled at her stubbornness a few days more before the welts would calm down. Hopefully, by then, without notice by Aunty Leata.

"I suppose that's okay, Pele." Erich extended a hand to her. Sama rolled over and stood up. She placed her hand in his while Eric guided them through the tall grasses on the creek's bank back toward Auntie Lesina's fale Samoa.

"Thank you for seeing me to the waterfall and looking after me." Shyly, a regular crimson flush crept up her face. She walked ahead of Erich, not seeing his amused grin while Sama dragged his feet behind them. She walked on as she could not afford to answer her brother's questions about last night. Pele walked up the steps to her aunt's fale Samoa and dropped her wrapped belongings by a pole.

It was nearing seven in the morning, and it was time for her to return to the house. "Has Mother called for me, Sama?"

Sama was wide awake from his brief slumber. He sat with his legs hanging from his perch on the side of the fale Samoa. "No, she hasn't, but you mind telling me what you were doing up on the pu'a tree without anyone out there?" Unlike Erich, who was sitting on the other side of Sama, this was her brother asking. His annoyance was evident.

"I wanted to see the night fishermen." These men came out of the villages and fished exclusively at night. The fires from the coconut fronds burned so spectacularly against the indigo nights. She often watched them unobserved on the massive pu'a tree there as she often did without her parents' knowledge.

Now, that was a memory long erased from her mind. The bruises throbbed. Unfortunately for her, this was not so for her brother and Erich.

"I heard Father tell Mother I *must* go away." Her bottom lip quivered as Sama came home at the end of his term later that year. "Why must I when I can learn from all that you do from your fancy schooling, and you've always been so good to teach me? So has Father, but he tires of me lately."

Sama stopped slapping his bare arms. Then he laughed out loud as clear dams welled up in her eyes. "So that's what's bothering you? *Really*?" He chuckled, relieved that his wild child hadn't thought of something more sinister. Killing herself over something so petty was enough excitement. "Pele, you're going to love school. Like we do, right, Erich?" He nudged Erich, who hurriedly nodded in agreement. At fifteen, they were the big boys on campus. Or so they liked to think.

"There will be other little girls your age, and you'll have no time to miss home." Erich wondered if sending her to a world of hens and arrogant girls was worth it. He could relate to Pele's reluctance to leave home if this was home for him.

"I understand, Pele." Erich inhaled deeply, looking around at the greenery before them, the cry of the kingfisher piercing the morning quiet. "I do love it all." He spread his arms, expansive and vast. "Sama, I don't know if *you* know what you have here, pal." He chuckled at Sama's quirked eyebrow.

"Better than you think, Uso." Sama slid back and rose from his perch. He yawned as he ran a hand through back waves of hair. Pele was grateful for the resounding pep talk, but still, she was anxious about where she would fit into 'that' world so far from her.

She was fine here at home, where no one ever asked after her anyhow, where her classmates were a dog and a rooster, who were not so opposed to hearing her out as she repeated Father's lessons or a reading from the boys' anthologies. And if the mammals were, they either fell asleep or wandered off.

Life was uncomplicated here in the clearing: quiet, lovely, and predictable. She didn't have to fuss or fight with folk who didn't understand her. While Father was quite aware of her precocity, all Mother wished for was that she was proper in her mannerisms and etiquette—how she sat, how she addressed her elders, how Pele talked to her parents, and how she walked.

"Be polite, gentle, and stately, Pele!" Mother sat with salu nearby. *Aga malū, aga tausa'afia, ma aga fa'atamali'i.* This scrutiny as Pele bobbed up and down to her count: how to walk politely in front of guests. How to sit like a girl with legs crossed over and her lavalava tucked. She had to sit, serve tea, and turn slightly to the guest. On and on, these rounds with Mother went. Once upon a time, life was so simple. She could run up and down the hillside without being told to come in, to stop playing like a heathen. She had to wear her lavalava tied securely around her breasts, which were barely there.

"Modesty, Pele." *No one ever looked at me. Why so much change?* Her body was changing, and there was a significant difference between her and her brothers. It isn't as if she did not know this, Pele mused resentfully. Every day, Mother reminded her to be a proper daughter. Devote her life to the sound, righteous things those young women did, obedient and quiet in the presence of her relatives and elders.

"Am I that disagreeable in your eyes, Pele?" Erich nudged her out of her reverie. She looked up at him from her weaving, her eyes blank. "The weight of the world is on your shoulders." He laughed at her bewilderment.

Pele shifted to be sure that her legs were folded under her. To be sure that the weave of the woven blind was falling right, she busied herself with righting the frond without answering Erich. He was no guest here, she thought to herself. He fell in with Sama, another older male kin to mind, and kowtow to around here.

"If you flip it properly onto your lap," Erich motioned her closer so he could show how to position the front so the leaves would right onto the next section and not bow under the tucks. She took her blind back from him and fell into a more harmonized rhythm than before when she sat on the front and was closer to weaving a mat than a blind.

Erich brought his leaf over. "How is school, Pele?" *She has sprouted some,* he thought to himself. There was something that brought out the protective brother in him. It has been a couple of years since he has had a chance to return with Sama. Sama spent some of the following school holidays with their family to save the arduous travel back and forth.

"Painful." Glum and low, she replied. Based on how Sama saw things here at home, she was thriving at the local primary school.

Erich laughed at her displeased expression. "But you are here at home with all that you love. You know, your brothers and me? We *must* be away for the school year. That's ten months of never seeing you. Or our pets."

"You don't know what being with girls is like." The constant prattle about who knew the cutest boys went on forever. Who among friends was going over to someone else's home? No one asked. This exclusion was all right by her. She did not want to be, and then Mother would say no. Mother was strict but loving, and Pele could not bear it if word spread that her mother was old-fashioned.

Never mind the usual mean bullies who were loud, foul-mouthed, and obnoxious. They were the last bunch she wanted to know about home and her parents.

It was her turn to bring the bouquet to school that Monday, she excitedly exclaimed to Mother. Even though it was only Friday afternoon, she was so happy to think of her bouquet's bright-colored array, and Mother would help her pick from her massive garden. She could hardly wait for Monday morning when they would go through and find just the right blossoms. It was all she could dream of now!

"Always start from the center to the outer colors, Pele," Mother instructed, clipping some of her red *sugi*. "You can take this with white plumeria blooms and these greens, and you have a beautiful *teu* for this morning." She neatly tied the blooms with a string of sennit before handing it to Pele. Barely containing her happiness, she hugged her mother tight and hard. Leata held her child to her, wondering at her enthusiasm. She had not seen her run off alone without so much of a goodbye wave.

Her father watched her from the hill as Pele ran from their home toward the main road. She had a good grasp on her way now and did not need her parents to help her get there. Two miles were child's play for Pele. He settled back into the hillside for the morning's planting.

The hike to school wasn't as late that morning. The wind blew hard at Pele's face, but she was determined to make it to school without stopping along the uphill climb. Her gunny sack was across her back with her class bouquet.

The road to the school campus was another half-mile inland. Once on it, Pele saw other children coming in from all directions. The foot traffic was heavy and choked in places, but all this chaos was okay. She carried the day's bouquet for her class, which was all that mattered.

Suddenly, someone yanked her gunny sack hard from the back. Pele lunged backward before steadying herself, trying to hold onto the girl standing before her.

"Oh, what do we have here?" Pele sidestepped and moved out of her reach. The Wall, as she was known, moved with her. Outweighing Pele's lithe form by twenty pounds, taller and older, she sneered down at Pele. "I asked you what you had, pissant." She had an entourage, three more girls out of the eighth grade. In between these monsters was one of Pele's classmates. The Wall's younger sister, Filoi, Pele's class 'princess'.

The Wall shifted her weight from one side of Samoa to the other. "Is this that one, Filoi? The teacher's pet?" Thirty girls must have been heading into the school campus, but Pele was one pushed into the hedges. She stared defiantly at the massive older sister, ready to fight her. The other girls blocked her exit and held her gunny.

"Please tell your sister to give me my bag." Pele wanted nothing of this business. She looked around at these eighth graders, then slowly realized why Filoi had brought her older sister.

Filoi laughed sharply at Pele's concerned look. "Ask her yourself, smartass. You seem to be capable in class; why not here?" The other three girls circled and forced Pele back into the tall hibiscus hedges.

The Wall pushed her swarthy face into Pele's, with that bulwark of a nose inch from the younger girl's. "What's so important in the bag?" She turned the gunny sack upside down.

Pele's notebook fell out, as did the bouquet. Pele dropped to her knees to grab them when heavy feet stomped on both her hands. She wailed in pain and hollered at them to stop as they rubbed her notebook into the mud. The Wall ripped the bouquet from Pele's vice-grip. She beat it against the hedge until all the stems were bald.

Pele stopped fighting. She rose from the hard ground, and before anyone could stop her, she lunged forward and spat into the Wall's face. The bigger girl yanked Pele's plaits, slammed her back into the ground, clambered on top, and punched Pele's face unmercifully. The Wall shredded Pele's cherished white cowl-neck blouse as she bashed Pele against the rocky ground!

"Oka! Fusu! Loa fufusu!" Spectators jeered at the melee, jumped, and hollered at the combatants. There was a reverbing chant from the crowd who had stopped to watch the commotion to find the pugilists and, in horror, this frenetic biblical battle between David and Goliath. Others who were nearer to the campus ran back to see the melee. Show people among the crowds stirred the masses into a mad frenzy, calling out names as if the girls were racing *fautasis* on the water.

Pele blindly sank her nails and pinched her attacker so hard in those fleshy thighs to stop the pain of those fat fists. The Wall toppled off immediately, screaming in excruciating pain, grabbing at her thighs as she sobbed. Pele found a cleansing breath as she rolled to her side, gasping for air. *How many pigs did this one swallow during toana'i?*

Pele scurried from her, her face battered and bleeding profusely. Pele knew little reason as she swept up a sizable rock. The crowd parted as the creeks did during summer storms around the isle. Her budding breast bared to all who witnessed the beating—bared to the jeering audience whose brown faces became a melding sandstone.

A booming voice rose above the mad, insane cacophony! *"STOP! Stop it right now!"* The principal's voice was twenty miles away, but she was there. The teachers peeled the Wall off the ground and ran to stop the fight between Filoi and Pele. With the principal this close, Pele dropped the rock out of her hand.

"What happened here?" Pele did not bother to answer. She saw bits of her notebook scattered over the ground under the scores of feet of the *faikala,* the circle of nosy gossipmongers there for the show. The spectators parted as she limped over to get the pages. Blood dripped from the side of her brow harder as she hurried to grab pages between the feet of the masses. There, she saw a stem from her bouquet, rugged and bare of its former glorious bloom. She snapped it up.

Pele parted the crowd as the principal waited for her to stand beside the Wall. She rushed forward, and as the principal stared at the unrepentant mess before her, she pushed the plump woman out of her way. She swung her arm and hammered the stem with its thorns into the Wall's bulbous nose. The loudest scream for miles echoed throughout the village. Blackbirds took flight and squealed the news to others!

"Ai kae! Alu ai polo lou tamā!" Filoi screamed in Pele's direction. The daughter of the village pastor, this was fine form. She stopped in her trail, reared up, and came face to face with Filoi. Pele stood back and hurled a fist into Filoi's right eye. The thunderous contact with bone echoed throughout the *malae.*

Grace school did not convert the Wall over, nor did it keep the Princess's mouth clean. The teachers were afraid of them. Secondly, their parents were important school patrons besides being powerful clergy.

"Get her! Don't let her leave here!" The principal yelled at the teachers, who were dumbfounded and shocked. Yet, they could not help but feel that Pele was justified and that Filoi deserved that.

Pele grabbed the cover of her tattered notebook, tied up her torn blouse, shouldered her gunny sack, and left. While both women tended to the Wall and her injury, Pele ran from the crowd and hiked back up the steep hill. Homeward to her parents, she panted. She hurried across the footholds while she looked behind to see if she was being followed.

As the fight's anger and adrenaline left her battered body, dread began to set in with every step toward home. How will Mother react? What will Father think of her? She could hear the commotion at home a mile out. Pele felt the side of her head bloody and bruised from the beating; the closer she got to her house, the more her heart sank. Sole spotted her from the front steps, started to bark, and ran up to her. Her faithful steed and friend. Her *only* friend.

"Your daughter was out of order! She started this fight at school, beating up the pastor's daughter. Have you not taught her any manners? Why now, we must expel her!" The village mayor and his board entourage were there on their doorsteps. Her mother's worry and anxiety were all apparent. Pele's heart began to thump in her ears. The sound of rushing waves converged in her eardrums as she tried to muster some former bravery, a cacophony she could not hear from.

"Pele! Come here now!" Her mother had her *salu lima* in hand. "Come now!" Judge and jury. This little committee had delivered their testimonies, and she had not reached home. Leata must dispense her daughter's punishment in front of these disapproving, austere strangers.

Father came out from the back of the house upon hearing these raised voices. They hadn't reason for company or expected any loud commotions without their sons home on term breaks from school. He walked up to stand next to his wife, a presence so prominent among the uneasy gathering.

"What is this commotion about, Leata?" He addressed his wife rather than the crowd. Fiso glanced over the uninvited five, six people in front of them only briefly. "Why are these folks on our front door?" Leata explained the news from the school, which was now relayed to their village mayor.

Fiso listened intently, never losing sight of this advanced party who had descended to tell them of Pele's egregious sins. "What is it that you hope to accomplish here, Mayor? You've relayed the news. We've heard you out. Now, you must leave my property and my family." He reached over to his wife's side and pried the hand broom out of her hand.

Leata nervously looked over to the mayor and apologized. "Please, thank you for the time you took from your day to come over. We will see the issue and apologize to the pastor's family soon." She attempted to diplomatically explain her husband's autocratic order and keep their attention from Pele, who milled a fair distance from them, standing her ground in the middle of the road to home.

The mayor looked at the others, feeling there was little they would accomplish today. They bid the Spaffords a terse farewell and left. They strolled past Pele and grimaced at the sight of her injuries. Yet, there was a fair feeling of collective purring pleasure as they thought of the corrective actions that her parents would take shortly. Her father, brief and abrupt, appeared ready to take justice into his massive, callused hands.

Pele walked the last fifty feet to stand in front of her parents. Leata shook her head and adjusted her lavalava, "We send you to school to learn. And you have brought home this outrageous shame? Have we not taught you better? Do you know whom you have hurt?" She implored her daughter, looking for answers from this mulish girl. How will she, the mother, ever look at folks in town? Forsooth, the humiliation!

"Fiso, aumai le salu lima! Tafefe le fa'alogoka!" She reached out to her silent husband, looking for the hand broom. And for his support, she was about to discipline their obstinate child.

He straightened a little and looked at his wife, unamused. "You were going to beat her so village gossipmongers can relay the news back to the rest of the world?"

Leata bristled at the admonishment, at his condescending tone. "I resent your insinuation. Pele needs to be disciplined, whether in their presence or now." Discipline had to be imposed, even if these were not the pastor's daughters. Pele was too much sometimes, and the girl didn't even know it. Fiso felt she was too strict with Pele. She knew her husband—he refused to pull in the reins.

He tapped his slipper, shifting his weight to and from. "You were willing to take their accounting of the facts without hearing Pele's account of the unfortunate events? Did you think to ask Pele at all?" Fiso threw the hefty salu lima to the step, which fell with a thud.

Leata replied disbelievingly, "Have you seen her face? Look at that face and tell me that she is innocent. That she hasn't harmed those girls?" She grabbed Pele by the hand and roughly dragged her forward to stand before Fiso.

She raged on. "Look at her, Fiso, and tell me this is innocence!"

Fiso looked at Leata nonchalantly, almost uncaring. He knew his wife felt isolated and torn from home since their marriage when she discovered that home was a virgin jungle. Moreover, he knew she felt stuck in a rut since Pele was born. He knew of his wife's lingering sadness but not how to comfort her when she was in her head about her sadness.

What should have filled her life with joy and love with the birth of their only daughter did not. In her first year, Pele almost died as Leata left for town to recover from childbirth. The baby was left to his younger sister, Lesina, to nurse with coconut water as there wasn't a wet nurse within a mile of Ta'imā.

As a matter of this course, it is apparent that his daughter is closer to his sister than his wife. The break between mother and daughter was too great for all to try and mend. This, too, has remained contentious between the women.

Over the years since her return, he let Leata vent her anger for these reasons. She is a wonderful wife and mother to their children—most days when she was present.

He turned Pele toward him, her bruised, battered face, with those familiar almond brown eyes brimming with tears staring up at him. "So, tell me what happened, daughter." This was her father asking as he let go of her chin.

Little can better her circumstances than the truth. Or her chances of surviving her father's austerity. She started with her arrival. Then, there was the ambush by the Wall and Filoi. The bouquet that meant so much to her was ripped and thrashed by the sisters and their faithful tautua. "I had no choice but to defend myself."

"In defending yourself, you had to stoop to their level, Pele?" her father asked, unimpressed. "What have I taught you about retaliation?"

Pele thought about this, reluctant to echo his teaching. "To never give in to violence and to come to you beforehand." The thought of running from bullies to find her sire was an inconvenience. Scaling the craggy terrain was something she could only do twice a day for the four school days she had to attend.

"Did you come to me this morning?" Fiso asked of her, knowing fully that from the scale of the current scandal, he was asking the obvious. "What do we do when you do not listen, Pele?" The question was rhetorical, but he wanted to point out that she should stick with it for her lifetime. He wanted her to say this out loud so he could discern that she had listened, heard, and understood him the first time they had this talk years before.

Pele hung her head in shame. The disappointment on his face was more than she could bear. She went to her mother to get the switch from a hibiscus branch. It was weathered and well-used over the years on all three children.

She handed it over to him, her fear so palpable. Her heartbeat was in her ears, painful and irregular. Before Father asked her, Pele flattened out her palms. "I will not resort to pettiness." The first of her lashes. "Before I act out, I'll come to you and Mother for help."

"Do not upset my mother and mind her until the end of her days." If not *mine*, she sobbed to herself. "I'll not sass her back as though she were not my parent!"

Her voice trembled hard as the fifth lash fell. She stifled a cry out. "I'll be more aware of who I am, my family, and the importance of who we are here." She rubbed her bloodied hand against the dirty scraps of her school blouse. "I will be more respectful of elders, even those not family." The seventh ripped skin from her right palm as he dragged the switch. "I'll not be careless in my actions."

The ninth order of conduct fell on numb palms. "I mustn't follow others blindly." Her nose ran down her tattered, filthy shirt onto her bare chest as she blinked hard against the relentless pain.

The tenth fell on open wounds. Pele whispered in her cracked voice, "I cannot go on doing whatever I wish. Permission before forgiveness, Father." Her punishment complete, she glanced over his shoulder to see her mother immobile and expressionless, waiting. There was no comfort forthcoming from her. This was her due.

"*Aue! Aue!*" Lesina ran up from her house to see her brother ask Pele to wash and put away the hibiscus switch. Her mu'umu'u pillowed in the slight breeze. "*Oute ofo lou le alofa! Lenei lava mea o kamaiki! Fa'afefea na e so'ona faia le teinetiti?*"

Enraged by the horrid reasons for Pele's disciplining, Lesina stared at her brother and her stoic sister-in-law, who stood unmoved by Lesina's rage. "*Aumai le teine oute faia!*" She hugged Pele's thin, weeping body to her ample bosom, staring hard up at Fiso. "*Auoi! le lua le alolofa lenei alu'alu toto!*"

"*Ia ave mo oe pea fai ua e poto lou faitama.*" Take her, then, as you are the resident expert on child-rearing. This is to the unmarried maiden Lesina. At twenty-two, she was certified as the spinster aunt. The title was bestowed upon her by her family and village—much to *her* uncaring stance.

Lesina stared at Leata, stood up, and faced her squarely. She pushed Pele behind her. "Oh, this is rich. You came here with uppity sensibilities and talk of the town, complaining about all this, of your inconveniences since you came with my brother. This!" Lesina swept her hands expansively. "This *godforsaken* hole, as you've called it, and *us* as the rednecks. As if we can never measure up to your folk!" With four children over these past sixteen years, she has been the babysitter to Leata. They were not even friends.

Fiso listened emotionlessly to his sister's tirade. He returned to his chores, leaving the women to fight their differences. This was not his place. Let the women find a solution for Pele. His sons were settled and thriving in Apia; little else mattered.

Meanwhile, Pele will be groomed to be a wife to someone suitable for the family. The fight between his sister and wife? It was of little concern to him. Pele will grow up to make a good match and wedding.

"Pele, go get your stuff and come with me." Lesina was exhausted and refused to give voice to more of her repressed anger. Pele scurried forward and entered her parents' home to gather her meager belongings and ragged papaya dolls. She gathered her few clothes and tied all of them into a lavalava.

Her mother stood at the opening of the lanai. Pele stared at her blankly, opened her mouth, but closed it—her *mother*.

"Aunty, I have everything." She buried her tear-stained face into her bundle and avoided looking at her mother, her shoulders back. Lesina grabbed one of her niece's bloodied hands. This child, whom she has kept alive since birth, is now barely allowed to live as a child. They walked from the lanai to the little road to Lesina's Samoan fale.

Leata watched her child disappear into the hedgerows with Lesina. She called out to them to bring Pele back to her, but she had no voice. She fell to her knees as the years of great misery and grief torpedoed into every fiber of her being—the wailing of a motherless child. All that sorrow that no one could take from her. All she wished for was that she could be more to her daughter! Yet, she lost this war and her daughter to Lesina in one sitting this afternoon.

"It is for the best." She wept still, long and in earnest. These years she has tried to bring her child to her were lost. The opportunities when she could have loved her child are gone with Pele's every footstep to her aunt's fale. Oh, how she tried to bridge this gap with her last child. Any chance this could happen was gone in its finale with the easterly wind.

Around the bend, away from seeing her brother's grand house, Lesina paused. She closed her eyes in some regret.

"She loves you, Pele," Lesina gently pressed on as she pried open Pele's fists, the girl wincing with every stretch of her tendons in the flickering light of the coconut lamp. A mean poultice of ripe *gogu* fruit and *sugi* leaves was spread over each of the palms and buttered the ripped skin. "There are reasons why your mother cannot care for you right now." She tore part of her lavalava, wound the cloth, and tied each carefully over each medicated hand. This was the best she could do for her young niece.

"One day, I hope you can forgive your mother, Pele. These times are not the easiest for her," she whispered positively. She pulled Pele into her embrace before anything happened to either of them.

"I don't understand, Aunty." Pele's shoulders shook from the pain of the whole day. "I don't know why she can't just love me." She wept into Lesina's shoulder as her aunt kissed her forehead, hugging her harder into her generous bosom. Lesina swept Pele's hair from her eyes. Those rainy afternoons, cocoa-rice eyes wailed ten years of living pitiful and lonely.

This unfortunate child of her older brother lost to her mother since birth, a daughter born after sons she is. Lesina thought of a grander scheme to keep her niece from a fate cloistered as hers. The child needed so much more than Samoa could offer her. This intelligent, delightful being was born of another womb but her child in all manners of motherhood.

Lesina thought of her friends. Some in Apia, of those in Hawai'i, and hope began to sprout. It would take some time to hear back from anyone, but anything will help her cause. With her heart in her mouth, she sat at the step of her fale and looked for the constellations. These were God's paintings her father had told her about so long ago.

"Lord," she implored. "Please look after my kei. I come to you with little on my mind but for Pele. She is deserving of love. She is worthy of a fighting chance. Please give me the means to move mountains out of her way. These circumstances are not her own, but she is stuck in them. Lord, I pray for mercy. I pray for love and grace for this child. I ask of You to grant me the means to move her on to a better and safer living."

Lesina nervously searched for her tobacco leaves. She needed to smoke something, something more potent than usual.

The horizon darkened against the disappearing light. Lesina gently rolled Pele onto her left side, tucking her head onto the comfort of a pillow, her breath lingering and muted against the symphony of crickets out in the open grassy knoll. Glimmering moonlight peeked through the spaces between the *laupola* as the blind flapped back and forth in the gentle breeze as evening fell over the isle.

Now she will wait for God, Apia, and Hawaii, whoever should answer her first. She prayed for all of it to happen in one sitting. There cannot be any pause. The ships were delayed these months due to the inclement weather barring the harbor as it was the end of the year. If she did not move Pele now, her fate would be left to this village, which was not enough for this child. She agreed with Leata that they were isolated and sheltered from the world, but she did not want to give Leata another reason to resent them. Or Pele, for that matter.

There was also news of war brewing in Europe. The Germans spoke of the worsening conditions back home in Germany. Some were fretting about what would come of their plantations as the earlier war in Apia stopped commerce for several years. These were uncertain times in Apia, and it would be foolhardy to take Pele there even with Mother's family all over town. They had cousins who could care for Pele in her absence. It was an option as Fiso planned on sending Pele to board for school. However, it would be the last resort. Hawaii offered a more appealing haven, but they had no family near the cloister. She loved the sisters there, but what of Pele's care?

She rolled another cigarette, staring out into the horizon as Pele slept. Crickets worked up a symphony as the darkness rolled in from the west end of her house. The smoke from her rolled tobacco wafted across the light of the lamp.

Later that month, an answer to her prayers came through. Lesina packed Pele and her paltry belongings with her brother agreeing to her plans. They traveled toward town to catch the steamer. This was about new beginnings and a fighting chance to be more than a wife and mother. Lesina knew she might be pushing off her ambitions to her niece, but she was unapologetic. This was an indigo child, and her parents were oblivious to her. The travel north was uneventful. Lesina prayed every morning for miracles to gather on behalf of this child.

Sister Ingrid was waiting for them at the convent in Hilo. She was as no-nonsense as ever and as intimidating. However, Lesina trusted her with all her being. Not long before, Ingrid had been her counsel and confidante. Even as she was expelled from the convent in Honolulu, Ingrid stood by Lesina. They relocated the priest to England but afforded little time for Ingrid to fight for her charge.

Sister Ingrid was at the Basilica for a reason. She was no longer in contention to be Mother Superior. The idea of starting life at forty alone in an increasingly dangerous world beyond the convent was too much to bear. Even when she is now a ghost, she didn't mind—a life of prayer and devotion to the Good Father was beyond man and their avarice.

After a tight, warm hug, Lesina moved Pele from her back. "Sister Ingrid, this is Pele. I know she will be safe here with you. Please look after her in my absence." Sister Ingrid bent down to look at Pele directly.

"Do you know who I am, young lady?" she asked, friendly and open. "I will be your guardian while your aunty is in Pago Pago. You think we can be friends?" Pele nodded, hesitant and shy all at once. Her aunt was leaving her here with strangers. Lesina straightened abruptly from kissing her forehead, and Pele started to cry. The winds died down with Lesina's fluid withdrawal.

Sister Ingrid folded the weeping child into her embrace as Lesina left without a glance backward.

Lord, tell me that I am doing the right thing! This is a cross so heavy on me. If she looked back now, Pele would be back on the ship. This will defeat all she has done and fought for to move Pele from home.

"Lesina! Lesina!" Pele cried out to her aunt. Lesina was farther down the path. "Please don't leave me!"

Sister Ingrid let her cry her little heart. Once upon a time, she, too, knew what it felt like to be left behind. She was much younger than Pele when she was dropped off in front of a Midwestern convent.

Keep walking. Do not look back. The end will justify leaving Pele now. Lord, please give me a sign that what I am doing is right!

As the ship sailed out of Honolulu Harbor the following day, Lesina looked back and saw a rainbow over Hawaii's hills. The Lord promised that all would be righteous after calamity and strife. She hoped this, too, would be Pele's fate. One day, Hawaii will be a footnote in her history, and Pele will be more robust and happier, better equipped to cope with anything that her parents could dream up.

Hear my prayer, for I do not know what will come in my absence. Please keep my Pele in Your good graces. She is just a child, and I am trying my best. Please do not cause her harm, but let her know that every moment she is here on Earth is for her greater good, Our Good Father.

Book Two

I. July 1917

Le Folau
The Sail Home

The sun rose slowly over the distant horizon. The captain, taciturn, thirty-four, as tall as his nose was long, stood at the entrance looking over his crew and the stores as they came aboard. As a crew member in previous positions, Mister— now Captain Michael Parsons—has sailed these waters several runs to the southernmost parts of the Pacific. Commerce was booming in these times in and around the islands. Due to the demands of the Pacific route, he was at the *Williamson's* helm, leaving little to chance. Not the *Forester*, but certainly, it has proven its seaworthiness.

He inspected the mixed crew of eight *haoles* and seasoned local sailors. They were fit for the seas before them, but how they will get along while it is underway will be something to be seen. His first mate, Buchanan, had the unenviable job of assuring that the ship would not fall to a mutiny. The quartermaster reviewed the inventories of supplies and the cargo they carried. This count did not include the eight passengers among them. Seagulls squawked and followed the steamer—a prayer for the Good Father's blessings before they set sail.

And one for *Tagaloa*, father of the vast ocean before them. This ocean belongs to Him, the Supreme Creator of life for Polynesia, long before the English and their Lord landed here. It bodes well for sailors to give Tagaloa tribute before setting out into the Pacific. Having sailed this route often as a first mate, Michael Parsons firmly believed in petitioning all the gods for their graces whenever underway.

The crew stood at both port and starboard sides with Captain Parsons at the bow as they sailed out of Honolulu Harbor, the waterways busy with ships of all classes, with constructions alongside the port. In these summer months, there was not much to be worried about on this sail due south.

This was their ninth morning at sea since they departed from Hawaii's port in Honolulu. Eventually, rumors that they were close to arriving in Pago Pago pass through crew members to the women. They were in an adjoining room to Captain Parsons' stateroom and secluded from the others quartered beyond the narrow hallway.

Lesina surveyed her three sleeping wards, her niece Pele, for whom she sailed into Honolulu to return home. She loathed to do this, but with her brother's permission, she did get Pele away from Eastern Samoa and the provincial life that was the fate of most girls. Grow up, fill in, and get married to another family with their dowries in tow. Some never returned to their families. New home lives left little time for local girls for family visits.

To thwart this norm, she bought eight years for Pele. They would have lost Pele two years ago. No—Lesina corrected herself—*she* would have lost Pele. Why now, at nearly eighteen, she is almost a spinster. *Like me*, Lesina grimaced at this, a painful reminder to herself. In the past year, her brother has received word that a suitable suitor is asking for her girl's hand. With her nephews settled into their own lives, Fiso felt it was time for Pele to return to sit down with the potential groom and his family.

Her brother is getting sentimental in his old age, Lesina reflected, not unkindly. Moreover, Leata acquiesced to his decision to bring Pele home so she could plan the wedding's leulumoega after the dowry was decided and the costs of food and fine mats were apportioned to the tautua.

"What is keeping you up at this hour, Aunty?" Pele had come up from the cabin to stand beside Lesina, slipping her lithesome arm into her aunt's as she stared out into the horizon. Lesina flicked her tobacco roll into the churning ocean beneath them to look at her niece.

Her niece has blossomed into this stately, graceful, long-limbed young woman standing beside her. She wasn't as petite as her mother or as filled in as her aunt. Taller than the average Samoan girl, Pele has grown up built for love. Solid, steady on her feet, with a voluminous cascade of her mother's earthy brown wavy hair braided to the middle of her back. Her lips were wafer-thin yet pouty at rest. Pele's face was her mother's, graced with her father's ancestral secrets. Lesina owned some of those genes, but she was not her brother's daughter, the perfect blend of both parents. *There*, but not acknowledged. Old, 18th century old.

The suns of Hilo have summered her over, with her alabaster skin bronzed from her prominent forehead to her ankles. Those bright, raw almond eyes were clear as rain on a summer's afternoon home in their Olo'ie.

The demand that newlywed wives have children within the year of marriage is a deep-seated expectation. This antiquated belief was part of the agreement between families. No one ever asked what the womenfolk wanted or wished for their daughters.

Lesina's disquiet grew as she thought of this pedestrian fate that Pele was now party to by association. If she had the means, she would find another answer to Pele's future even further away than Hawaii. So be it if she spent her life plotting a better life for her niece!

Lesina sighed, taking her niece's face into her callused hands, and placed her forehead against the younger's. "I love you, Pele." She searched this face of her blood. She loved her niece with all her being. This feeling was parenthood. "You know why you're coming home, right?"

Placing her hands over her aunt's cheeks, she said, "I have an idea." Pele was not oblivious to the happenings back home. She was aware of local news of her parents and siblings via letters from Lesina. More than this, she admitted to herself, maybe that of Erich. She wasn't ten; perhaps she would merit more than Sama's little sister in *his* mind.

She knew that her parents had agreed to a suitor. To whom she worried. Why was this wedding her fate? Eight years at the Basilica have blessed her with an unfettered Catholic education, a home, and two sisters—two of whom she is taking home. No one ever claimed two unrelated orphans at the end of the winter's break from school. She might as well have been one, too. They had weathered the holidays with her as her parents never sailed from Samoa to see her. Her aunt came to see her every other summer in Hilo and did her best to fill her in with news of home when she did not make the trip by letters. Now, she is to return to Tutuila, the main island of Eastern Samoa, marry someone she did not know from Adam, and give up her personal Eden. Again.

Even her aunt did not have an adequate answer about her betrothed's identity. She did not know who he was or what hole he hailed from at this juncture.

Lesina wrapped Pele in her embrace. "We're going to get through this together, Pele." Even if it killed her, she mused to herself. Her kei was born to be more than some village wife—mother to a tribe. So much more, Lesina insisted to herself, even if she was here as Fiso's emissary.

"How are they, Lesina?" Her father occasionally wrote about home and what their hillside looked like. She longed to see them—they were her parents, after all. She missed home so much that they couldn't possibly understand if they'd let her stay for a while before shipping her off again.

"Growing older, Pele. They need you three to come home, but I'd like to see your brothers there before you," Lesina answered truthfully. She inhaled her smoke, "This takes the burden off of you."

Pele scoffed. "How do we do that? When I get home, I'll leave without unpacking my bags."

Lesina was undeterred. Something will happen to benefit all. Maybe not Fiso and Leata, but whatever happens will.

Kiele Chen was up, fully awake, and was folding down their bedding—a few sheets, with a few pillows, which she rolled into their sleeping mats. A couple of months younger than Pele, she barely stood shoulder-high to Pele. Her hair was as dark as midnight on a rainy night. Whereas Pele was taller and straighter, Kiele had enough curves and bends for both.

Fast friends from their early introduction by the nuns at Basilica, they remained inseparable since they arrived at the convent at ten with barely a stitch on their backs, hands, or the safety of family names. Her parents lived at Kalaupapa. Upon learning that her parents had Kiele in their care, the Church preemptively removed Kiele with other young, healthy children and relocated them to Basilica's grounds.

There was no judgment upon revelation. The girls held each onto one another about rudderless as lost ships after a summer storm. Pele could not think of a good reason to grow a nose over her friend. They agreed that they would be sisters through their joys and sorrows.

Oh, how Kiele missed her parents, too, but knew she could not be reunited with them, perhaps for the rest of their lives. Here with Pele and Iolana, she had sisters and, hopefully, a family awaiting them. Lesina welcomed her as if she were her biological aunt as well.

Kiele woke the younger Iolana so she could wash with them before they started their day. The girls walked from the port to bow daily, ensuring they stayed out of the crew's way. It helped break the monotony of daybreaks, squawking seabirds, and nightfall.

Fresh water was a rarity; the women welcomed the few chances to bathe. Pele insisted that they have showers this far out from land. Every second day, the four women were given quiet time at the back of the steamer to wash and do their laundry with some water from the stores. The men and the crew took to the bow. It was the best way to manage personal cleanliness in the cramped quarters.

To better accommodate their bathing, the women secured their impromptu shower with their lavalava out of sight from the men. The little soap they had today had to wash four bodies. Pele drained their two gallons of rainwater with a gourd and poured just enough over each to wash their hair and bodies. The sparse soap was shared among them as they stood next to the cabin window; the sheet hung on a line hid them from the men at the stern.

Pele scrubbed Lesina's back, who washed Kiele's, who in turn did the same for Iolana. This was a more prudent way to shower, given their lack. The girls thought of the comfort of their waterfall at Basilica with its ease of access and endless water supply. They must make do with these few gallons as Captain Parsons gives them here.

A kind man, if perfunctory. He was a bit pleasing if one looked at him from the side, but otherwise, he was a nondescript palagi.

Today was humid, and the sun was bearing hard down on the deck, on the women and the crew. They languished inside over three hammocks and padded mats on the rough-hewed floor until Pele was done holing up inside. It was easy to lose her mind waiting for sunsets to give way to another day—little changes in their routine over time.

"Miss Spafford?" A knock at the door, a rapid rap. Which one? Lesina rolled out of the hammock and looked at the door's peephole. It was the cabin boy standing on the balls of his feet. Pele flew over to the other side of the cabin, stifling a giggle at Lesina's look of outrage at her impertinence.

Lesina opened the door, a little peeved. Sweat flowed down between her breasts when the breeze caught her unawares. The young man noticed the discomfort among them. "Ma'am, Captain Parsons would like to know if you and your wards would dine with him tonight. The menu is paltry but better shared. He told me to tell you that."

Lesina looked at her ragtag crew. Pele signaled a no; the other girls looked gamed. "Let the good captain know we will be there tonight for dinner. Thank him for the invite."

Something was better than dry soda crackers, melted butter reconstituted, and salt beef. There was tea, but more was needed to have every day. There was coffee but without milk to help make it bearable. Dinner with the captain is bound to awaken their palates.

So now—what to wear? They looked over their belongings and found that the closest to a reasonable dress code on a superbly hot steamer was to share their bed lavalava sheet. They cut the sheets and fashioned simple dresses. If there was anything that the nuns insisted on teaching them, it was the skills to keep a husband once parents secured grooms. Going to dinner on the steamer was not exactly how they thought they would have their first formal dinner and probably not how the nuns believed their skills would be best used.

Neither here nor there, Pele thought out loud. After spending their morning on this project, she needed a break. She got up from the floor, stretched out her legs, and rubbed the small of her back. Her fingertips were sore from sewing with her needles, but this could not be helped.

"Tita, I don't think we will have enough to cover all three of us. I'll find something in our chest." Pele was not about to sit through the rest of the balmy afternoon worrying about what she would wear to this outlandish affair that Lesina promised they would attend this evening—Captain's table or not.

Kiele looked up at her peeved sister and laughed. "It's okay, Pele. Little *pilikia*! I sew for all of us." Pele looked at Iolana, who was sitting with Lesina.

She loved that girl since she found her tucked into the root cellar of the rectory. There was such an instant kinship with her that Pele could not explain. Perhaps if she had a younger sister, Iolana would have been it. The young girl had arrived that afternoon and had slipped out of Sister Ingrid's hands, only to be found in the root cellar, deathly scared and wailing.

Pele gasped when she held her hand out to bring her into the light. Iolana had a partially healed scar on the right side of her face. It was black, purplish, and angry. At first, she pulled back and sought the darkness. Pele had other ideas not covered in any script among abandoned children. She pulled Iolana gently into her arms. At fifteen, she was nearly a child smaller than Kiele.

"You are going to be all right, Iolana." It was a sight to behold a child carrying another. Sister Ingrid looked on, caught between the need to intervene and let the girls find themselves.

Pele opened the chest they dragged from Hilo across the harbor to the *Williamson.* Captain Parsons looked down at them, unamused by the amount of baggage the women had stashed by the starboard end of the steamer. He sent two of his crew to bring up the valises and the war chest. No one noted that the majority belonged to their guardian. Over the years, the girls had barely added to their wardrobe at the Convent of the Benedictine Sisters.

"I'm sure I've something in here that is bound to be right for dinner," Pele announced to the others. She hurriedly rifled through their collective belongings. However, little appealed to her. "What I *need* is a shower." She slammed the cover of the chest down, flustered.

Iolana found a couple of hand fans and handed one to Pele and the other to Aunty Lesina. The heat was unbearable at two o'clock. Kiele looked up from her cutting and agreed it was time to walk out to the upper end of the steamer.

They headed toward the bow, where there was a slight breeze. Pele broke off and looked at the ocean from the starboard side. She could see for miles with an unbroken view of the Pacific.

Would he be good to her? Did he come from a good family? Would he take her sisters when they married? Can they not allow her to get acquainted with him? Will her parents give her a break and let her stay home during the engagement?

She bristled, swearing at the thought that this man was waiting for her to come off the boat. They didn't even know *her* anymore, and *they* were her parents.

Pele kicked the twine debris at her feet from the miles of rope above her head. Even the sails were not flapping. "Iolana, come and help me, please." She could feel a rash spread over her skin the more she thought of the fate she had selected for her.

They strung the makeshift screen across their customary post at the stern. Iolana let Pele have some blissful quiet and solitude away from prying eyes. She kept watching as Pele swung up her sarong behind their threadbare screen.

They hadn't seen other passengers and were six days from Pago Pago. The crew was under strict orders to stay away from the women. Let these days pass uneventfully, Iolana thought for all their sakes.

Each girl was lost in her thoughts when a sailor on the crow's nest called out to Captain Parsons. "Storm ahead, Captain!" Captain Parsons turned to see where the seaman pointed, and with all that was certain in him, they could not outrun the coming storm. "Get down!" He called his first mate to plan their escape as they had, at best, an hour to move the steamer around. The crew scattered as the frenzy touched down on the deck as their skipper barked orders. He looked back at the horizon. He called for the anchor to be dropped ahead of the bow. They were going to have to ride this one out.

At the stern of the ship, Pele was oblivious to the noise of building commotion around the bow, with the crew running to secure the sails. Lesina and Kiele were rushed into their quarters. She had lathered her soap and seeded it through her hair. The heat was enough to call for a haircut! The sweltering mornings woke her to wish she was as bald as Buchanan, the first mate.

"Iolana? Can you pour some water over me?" A gourd of water poured over her head. She hurriedly scrubbed her scalp, trying to use her rations better. "Can I get another and pour it slower this time?" That would be her allotment for the day. Maybe a week if they didn't run into a storm soon. The water poured slower than before while Pele washed the rest of the soap suds from her tresses. Then it stopped. The ship pitched to and from as waves pounded against the lumber of its hull.

Pele laughed heartily. "Oh, Iolana, can I borrow some of yours?" Her face was covered with suds. Sweeping her wet hair, she called out to her sister. No answer. She felt for the lavalava screen so she could wipe her eyes. She peered out and saw no one. Something was awry as she could hear the men yell over the roar of the suddenly choppy seas. Iolana must have run to cover earlier as the rain began to fall in earnest.

The storm was over the ship, and it crashed hard that afternoon. Pele adjusted her sarong around her legs when she felt the floor give way under her bare feet. The wind was knocked out of her lungs so fast as she landed on her bottom. As she lay there in shock, the pouring rain pelted her. *Great, there comes my shower. Drown me, Our Father?*

She let the hard rain clean her off before she tried to roll onto her stomach, which proved to be more complicated than she thought. Pawing at the floorboards, she tried to steady her way up to sitting on her haunches. Onto her knees, she tried to steady her ascent against the window of the cabins. Her right side was so battered that she could feel the throbbing pain shoot right to her brain.

As she clambered up, the ship pitched again. This time, she landed even harder on her left side. She waited for the boat to stop rising before attempting to stand up and tiptoe to the cabins. Holding open palms to thwart the rain, she couldn't see anything but the black clouds forcing the afternoon into darkness.

Two hands reached down and grasped her waist to pull her up on her feet. As she tried to hold onto these decidedly male hands, she blindly tried to feel for Lachlan's arms as anchors.

The ship tossed once again, forcing her forward into his arms. She landed in thin air, slammed against his length, and slid down his waist. She felt something in her grip.

The floor and she were becoming fast best friends. Pele blinked against the sheets of rain, trying to find her way around her savior and the sea. She felt his feet planted solidly on the planks of the floorboards. She shuffled onto her knees and tried to stand up using those as guides.

Blinking against the rain, she sat back on her haunches before this man. She shielded her eyes from the downpour. Two bare feet led to their bare knees, to his bare thighs. Oh, no! She could not continue further. Blood flooded her face as she dared not imagine. In her hands was a lavalava—the color of tapa *elei. If this was his lavalava, then that made him Samoan.* On this boat?

"Can I have my lavalava?" He asked sardonically, staring down at her as she held it so tight that he'd have to pry it out of her vice-grip. As she wouldn't look up at him, he took it out of her hands and wrapped it back around his waist, letting it fall mid-thigh. Her curiosity would kill her, but first, she needed to know.

The rain calmed as the black clouds passed as quickly as they had appeared on the *Williamson's* trek. The part in the dark skies broke open and gave way to a rainbow as a ray of the sun gave way. *Not so long ago,* Pele thought to herself.

He looked her over, from her feet to her face, lazily as if to challenge her to ask. His full tattoo stood against his fair skin as it was raised and coarse to the touch.

She did not. Tawny eyes stared back at her from the depths of a face that wouldn't be so hard if it were not for the scraggly beard. Darker than the hair wound atop his head, he stood with his arms folded and feet planted on the planks beneath them. Older, maybe about Sama's age. He was tall as he looked down at her. *Down.*

Pele felt the hair on the back of her neck rise. Her eyes roamed the length of a leg and spotted a reddish crescent-like birthmark on the back of his knee where his left thigh started. She struggled up again as the view was anything but welcoming. He reached down again and helped her stand up. The contempt was unmistakable.

She pulled her hand from him. *"Fa'afetai lava."* She turned her back on him and walked to the entrance to the cabins. *What a buffoon!* She was irrational and petty, but something about that arrogance got her goat. He needs a haircut, the idiot!

Considering the circumstances, Lesina and the girls were almost dressed in their finery. Pele was still looking over their collective wear. She found a cambric shirt, maybe Kiele's for Mass, and Iolana's skirt, which was inches shorter. Time was of the essence, and it would have to do with this dinner that would happen as scheduled. As if they had not passed under a storm hours ago. The food was committed, and the cook was instructed to serve.

They walked into the galley and headed to the long dinner table. Folk sat next to Lesina, who sat beside the captain. Kiele followed, with Iolana between her and Pele. The décor was not as bright or as welcoming. It was a room for men and little else. As they sat waiting on Captain Parsons and his crew, four men followed them shortly and made their way to the other side of the table.

They were dressed in crisp Sunday shirts and their formal lavalavas. Even on bare feet, they were not small men by any figment of one's imagination. The two younger boys were about Pele and Kiele's ages and looked less authoritative than the others as their youth was telling. They all had long hair and tied their tresses up in orderly buns.

If God sent a giant to sit at the table with them, to watch over the mere mortals, this third man was that embodiment of Angel Gabriel. Yet, such kindness emanated from him as he looked at Lesina, apologizing for their delay. The last of them, Pele, had already made *his* acquaintance. Her offended backside bristled at his lazy scrutiny of her. She looked up from her lap and met his stare head-on, refusing to back down from his quizzical gaze. A bit of it was dismissive and insolent, rolled in one fell swoop.

A little amused at her choice of dress, given that he had seen her nearly naked a few hours earlier. There was a hint of rebellion in that upright, pert nose and almond brown eyes. She was younger than his usual fare. Someday, she will make some man a great wife as she was built for childbearing from the sight of all of her attributes this afternoon. The idea amused him. That hair bound up like a schoolmarm made him chuckle to himself.

Meanwhile, he was sitting with her, waiting for dinner, she thought crossly.

"*Ia o a'u o Maifea.*" The bigger man spoke to Lesina; his voice was gravelly and gentle. "*O lo'u tausoga lea o Lachlan.*" This introduction points to Pele's stranger. "*Ma ole fanau tama lea o lo'u tuafāfine.*" He pointed out two teenagers next to them.

He had traveled with the cousin six months ago to pick up his nephews who were in school in Honolulu and decided to wait until the northern summer before traveling home with their charges. The boys were in apprenticeships and slated to work back in Apia for an accounting firm owned by the Germans. Tala'i was older than his brother at stalwart eighteen, while Mataio, at sixteen, stared at Pele, instantly smitten. He met her gaze and blushed as she held his attention steadily with a gentle smile. Over his head was his uncle, Lachlan McAllister. She saw him looking at her inscrutably.

"*Oi! Ia manuia le malaga! Na ou sau e a'ami la'u kei lea…*" pointing out Pele toward the end of the table. "*Sa luga le a'oga o taupousa. Ia ma nai ona uo ia, o teine Havai'i.*" Lesina introduced Pele, informing them that the girls were at the Basilica and they were now traveling home.

Michael Parsons walked in with his first mate and two others. He greeted all amiably as much as a captain does after an afternoon storm would. Before he sat down, he noted the split between the men and women before him.

With a conciliatory look to both sides, he asked, "Can I have you mix a bit?" Lesina remained at his side while the Samoans and the girls exchanged seating. Maifea moved to sit next to Lesina. Lachlan moved next to Captain Parsons on his right side. Pele left Iolana where she was while she went to sit with the enemy. Tala'i is next to her, while Kiele is at the end with Mataio and the first mate. The other palagis sat to Iolana's left.

"I am not much on world affairs, but my faith asks that I am reasonable in all my actions." He grinned at his guests and encouraged them to talk while waiting for Wilhelm to serve dinner. The lanterns along the walls were luminescent and lit warmly over the room.

Lachlan looked at his side and said to the schoolmarm, "I hear you and your aunt are from Pago Pago. Are you returning home?"

"Yes," Pele replied without explanation. "And you?" She, too, can play poker. There was that arrogance from this afternoon. She knew what she looked like. She didn't need him to stare at her like she was overdressed. She was—in ill-fitting clothes.

"The same. We are heading to Apia, however. Are you familiar with German Samoa?" he asked conversationally. "Have you ever been over to Upolu?" He was pleased that she was articulate and direct.

"No. I've relatives inland, but I've not been there. My brothers spent their years in boarding schools and are probably more familiar with the locals than I have ever been." *More so than I will ever be.*

Pele didn't want to think about what awaited her once home. Nor did she want this man to know how lackluster her destiny was. She felt for her rosary under her starched shirt. The fabric fit snugly around her chest, but this could not be helped. Kiele was much smaller than she was. As she sat straighter, she inadvertently made this an apparent fact between the two girls.

A keen sadness draped over her, and while he could sense her quiet resolve, he wanted to ask why. Not that he thought she would reveal the reason, but he liked her company. Now, she was beside him, not glowering at him from across the table, wishing he was a roast pig over the Sunday umu.

He was revered by women, or repulsed his feminine company, equally for the same reason. Most days, it is the former. Pele Spafford fell out of both categories, and this intrigued him. His companion now wished he would fall into the singular hole in the ocean's floor or was resistant to his charms. He'd like to think it was the former. Feeling for her rosary was a new one for him. She smelled much better than his burly cousin on the positive end of the seating arrangement. He won't tell Maifea that, but the soft smells of the sun, ocean spray, and *moso'oi* were better than any man aboard.

Wilhelm, the cook, plowed through the door with much fanfare that they all stopped talking. "We have some of the best *huli-huli* chicken with potato salad and haupia!" He announced, proud of himself. He called out to the seamen who carried in the platters. There was also some fruit from the stores atop the plates.

Captain Parsons took it upon himself to say grace before their first shared meal over the past week. He prayed that his guests would be kind to one another and that they would get through another week safely and get to Eastern Samoa before the storm season. The *Williamson* will stop in Apia for stores, but they must depart for Fiji before the middle of September.

The revelers sank into their meals. Then someone exclaimed, "The chicken is not cooked!" Others followed suit by checking theirs. It was unanimous. The chicken was in varying states of alive and crowing out the five o'clock alarm.

First mate, Buchanan, felt so wretched and vomited to his side. His mates followed suit. Captain Parsons asked that they leave the stateroom. This was not before Iolana projectile vomited onto Mataio's plate with such accuracy that it was clear that no one would eat in peace.

Wilhelm was beside himself with remorse. This wasn't how he imagined the meal to pass. The German chef had good days, but the storm left him shaken and in the store's liquor shelf. He apologized profusely, hoping to restore his reputation in the morning when he could offer a better breakfast. People who were not sick picked up their port and haupia and filed out of the galley onto the deck. Kiele volunteered to take Iolana to the cabin so she could lie down. Lesina replied that was well with her. She stood with Captain Parsons at the railing, relieved to see the stars again.

Pele stood a little closer to the starboard side, dreading the idea that every nautical mile brought them closer to Pago Pago. She braced herself a bit. A breeze would do her soul well before she clambered downstairs to watch over her sisters.

"Some shillings." He pressed the coins into her hand. She was puzzled by the offer but took his coins. He laughed at her bewildered stare. "To buy away your woes."

"Is that how the Scots do it?" she asked curiously and without malice. She wasn't aware of any such ritual, but she would take his money.

"The Scots of Churchur."

She tried to see his face in the dark, whether he was pulling her already bruised ham hocks, stealing her pride already in tatters as he had witnessed in broad daylight.

"I don't remember hearing of such a place," Pele replied. She knew then he was a yokel. "Is that a village back in your highlands?" She stood with her hands crossed over her chest.

He laughed at her sassing! "It's Christchurch. In a manner of speaking, a village in the South Island."

"Oh, ye of the New Zealots?" Pele didn't figure he was, but then his Queen's English was quite pronounced. "Are you and Maifea true cousins?" Even that sounded backhanded of her to ask.

He looked at her merrily and laughed at her first real question since they met. *"Ioe, e ma tausoga i ma tinā. E ā?"*

"Leai se mea o iai. Na'o la'u fesili a. Fa'apea o oe se a'oa'o po'o se faifeau tala'i." Even in the hills, there was news of varying religions settling in Honolulu. Sister Ingrid often read the news to her girls between morning Mass and devotions. Some were so new that it was hard to distinguish who was in the islands in their earnestness to act as agents of God or as agents of the infamous thieving Americans.

She dropped her hands from her fold, then extended a hand to Lachlan. "It was nice to meet you, Mr. McAllister. *A o'o se taimi e ta toe feiloa'i le lagi mamā."* Wherever those blue skies should appear. *Just please, not too soon,* Pele threw out into the universe.

Lachlan watched her walk across the deck and disappear down to the cabins. No glance back at him. There was no defeated hang on her shoulders or feminine hysterics. No, Ms. Spafford did not care for him. He honestly didn't know if this bothered him or if he should feel relieved. *Stay away from Samoan women,* he said to himself. Besides, she was too young to be courted.

The idea of wooing her when, if the circumstances were right, was not unappealing. Pleasant, a little daring, and met with a superb match. Granted, she'd lose that burly attitude in time. Who knows? These affairs were tricky and downright stuff of Shakespearean plays. He will tread with care. In any case, if he did not carry out his intentions properly, someone was bound to get hurt, and he wasn't ready for an angry family to remind him of his lack of attentiveness to their potential bride!

A stiff, loud pound came at the door, waking the women from a deep sleep. Lesina sat up, confused about what day it was. Could they have arrived earlier than scheduled? If so, she had to get the girls packed and moving! She was weary of ship life, and no matter how excellent the company was with the Captain and the McAllister group, she was ready to get off the ocean and onto land. No matter how often she has traveled this ocean to visit Pele, land and home were much too precious in her regard. Her heart plummeted as she saw Pele's form tightly wound under her sheet.

"Ms. Spafford?" It was the first mate, Buchanan. "Ma'am, I need to speak to you! It's urgent!" The pounding went on—if she were drinking the night before with the men, she'd be so angry. It was loud enough to wake the ghosts of Samoa. And a wicked hangover.

Lesina threw her mu'umu'u over her head as she called out, "I'm coming!" What could be so urgent? She opened the door to a frantic Buchanan.

"Ma'am, our third mate is sick! He has not recovered since dinner." The disastrous dinner of a week ago. "It looks more serious than food poisoning. Captain Parsons said that you would know what to do!" Mason was Canadian but had a wife in Apia waiting for him, and she was also expecting their first child.

Lesina listened to this litany and went back inside to grab her satchel. Buchanan led her to the back quarters for the crew. Men lined the wall as they watched her come through the narrow walkway.

Mason was in his bed, tossing back and forth in writhing pain. He was hot to her hand. Febrile, Mason was incoherent, calling out names that no one knew. Mother, wife, daughter? Be it as it may, she wasn't leaving much to chance. She took the skirt of her Sunday best mu'umu'u, halved it up to her hip, and tied a knot. She could not have her skirts encumber her movements to move about the bunk area. She stood up and looked out into the alley as variegated faces stared back at her.

"Clear the area! I need you all to move to the top deck! Take your beddings and air them out!" she yelled out. "If possible, wash yourselves and get into clean garments." She turned to Buchanan, belaying her anxiety. "Please go get the captain!"

Buchanan ran out through the flurry of men, trying to collect their clothing and bedding as Lesina ordered them. She threw the bedding from the bunks nearest Mason so the men who owned them could haul them up to the top deck.

As Captain Parsons fell below into the sleeping quarters, he knew something was awry. Lesina stood with her hands on her hips, waiting for him. She went closer to the entryway to meet him to avoid bringing him closer to his sick third mate.

"Please instruct your men to follow my directions! Mason has a fever and is delirious. There is no telling what is going on with him now, but I can tell you, we can't have the men bunk down here." Lesina mopped off the sweat from her brow. She brainstormed ideas of how to manage Mason's condition with Captain Parsons.

There were little ventilation ports in the crew's quarters as bunking was a simple dog pile of sleeping men. Captain Parsons knew they could not leave much to chance as they were due in Samoa by the twenty-sixth of the month if he was to move from there to Fiji on time in September. There was the business of rehiring sailors as four men would disembark in Samoa for their families.

First, he had to deliver Lesina and her wards to Pago Pago as he had promised Sister Ingrid he would.

Lesina went to their quarters to rouse the girls. She instructed them to dress and cut the remaining lavalava to pieces as calmly as possible. They were needed to help with Mason's care. The girls followed Lesina's orders and rushed to and from to prepare for the day.

A canvas was secured to pitch as a tent at the port side of the stern. This was to keep the sun out of the deck and cool the area. The girls scrubbed the floor while the McAllister men pitched in by building a cot for Mason. Lesina instructed them to get a few lavalavas and fashion when all was done. As the McAllister group was not bunked with the crew, Captain Parsons asked four crew members to go below deck, move Mason out of his bunk, and bring him to the quarantine area. However, he could not afford to get the others sick despite the conditions.

The American Navy stewards were brutal, exacting keepers of the Pago Pago harbor, and the *Williamson* would be turned away if he sailed with sick crew and passengers. He did not want to get on the wrong side of the harbormaster. He needed to follow along with Lesina to keep the ship's manifest healthy.

The rest of the afternoon was spent cleaning the decks and the quarters with all-hands on deck. The girls cleared their room of clutter, straightening out their mats and the floors. Clothes were pulled off the makeshift clothesline and stowed away. When the mopping was done, they drifted above to see Lesina and her ministrations to Mason. Kiele stayed with her to do the immediate chores with Iolana on hand to move washcloths. Pele was sent to ask Wilhelm for lemons or limes from the stores.

He was in hysterics and planned on dying on the spot if she asked him to go down below deck. *"Nein, fraulein!"*

Given that the world was at war with Germany, being German on an American steamer was hardly popular. He had found his way from Dutch Pennsylvania to San Francisco, a great hub of commerce on the western Pacific shores. Moreover, he was a second-generation German before becoming the mortal enemy. Besides, no one aboard had any qualms about his nationality as much as they did about his cooking. Captain Parsons was magnanimous about life and was like his aunt, Sister Ingrid, when running a tight ship without inducing chaos among its passengers, these special guests, and crew.

Pele left him to seek comfort on his deathbed. Lesina was waiting for the citrus and could not wait for this man to recover. Upon opening the storeroom, the conditions were sorry at best. Her shoulders sank in defeat, looking around the area and the goods haphazardly stowed, still in boxes without labels. There were live chickens and a pig in cages. Her stomach plummeted as she tried to sort out the chaos.

"Looks like you need some help," Lachlan noted as he stood at the door. She had not heard him come but wasn't expecting anyone else to come.

"I think that is the understatement of the times, Mr. McAllister." She grunted as she tried to get around the wooden boxes, some cargo while others were stores for the steamer. She could not reach the citrus unless she moved some packages out first.

Defeated, she came around the stacked load to look at him. "Can you please, though?" She wasn't strong enough to move a mountain to reach the citrus stows. Added to her misery, she felt claustrophobic and dirty from that day.

"I can if you call me Lachlan, Pele." He smiled wryly. "This is already a long day. We needn't be enemies. Besides, I think we are a little past that business, *Miss* Spafford." He was right. She could use his help more than she would if she started this independently. Lachlan called Maifea and their nephews down to help sort out this madness.

As the men moved the boxes out or to a side, Pele swept, scrubbed, and rearranged.

Lachlan moved the animals out of the way toward the porthole. Finding the citrus, Pele gave Mataio six to take to her aunt. This work was going to keep them busy well through the afternoon.

They worked quietly as shipmates, sorting out the food from cargo and salvaging some of the fruit bin and the salt beef kegs from the living. Lachlan and Maifea reconstructed a more considerable pen to house the remaining chicken and the egg layers. Pele hoped they would arrive in Pago before looking down for a meal. She hoped against hope but was aware that a delay or hungry men would end the lives of these animals.

An idea came to her. Hope and enthusiasm were a heady mix, but she wasn't above working the advantage to her benefit.

"Why don't *we* cook for the remainder of our travel?" She turned to Maifea and Lachlan. "There are enough of us on board; maybe we can help feed us better than Wilhelm. He doesn't mean any harm, but we must get home alive." The men, dirty and sweaty from the chore of doing the heavy lifting, were not above saying no to such an idea.

"Oi ae a le Siamagi lae luga?" Maifea asked, doubting that they could avail the man of his galley. Yet, Pele had a point. No one wanted to be next to be laid upstairs in Mason's cot. *"Ia o ai la faia ma tatou fono fetalai?"* Pele looked at them pointedly.

Maifea saw her smirk. "Oh, I'm not the man for the task, Pele." He laughed nervously as he rubbed his beard. "No! Oh no!" throwing up his hands.

"That leaves you, Lachlan." They both laughed at his outraged incredulity. Lachlan blanched at her audacity to ask this of him. Both she and Maifea crossed their arms over their chests.

Pele nominated him outright as he was charming enough to deliver the effect they sought, and Maifea gave her his blessings. As far as the two-thirds majority was concerned, Lachlan was prettier than both combined. Wilhelm would be charmed right out of the galley.

"We can arrive alive and well to our destinations or blame you for everyone being sick. So those are your choices," Pele said matter-of-factly. There is a war going on in Europe. Here, they were all trying to get home alive.

As she had Tala'i and Mataio scrub the galley with vinegar and lemons, she went into the sunlight to see how everyone was faring. The sailors picked up their bedding after sunning while others were fishing alongside Maifea and the embattled Lachlan near the stern's starboard side. They were onto her idea that they needed some other protein than that down below.

Pele shielded her eyes from the glare of the afternoon sun, scanning the deck for her aunt and the girls. They were hidden from view as they had draped another sheet over Mason's cot.

"Ua mai oe, Aunty?" she asked as she approached the tent. "If you want to rest, I'll take over the watch." Lesina smiled up at her gratefully. She rubbed her shoulder tiredly as she stood up. Pele sat beside Kiele and Iolana, pushing them into the afternoon sunshine. Never in her life has she felt as dirty as she was after the storeroom, but that cannot be helped.

There is no fathomable reason they should all be walking around like Frankenstein's minions. She can add the younger boys to the Watch; hopefully, Mason will make it through the night.

At twenty-five, Mason was weathered and beaten out of his body. Lesina asked that she help him breathe. This was to be done by holding the bag over his mouth when he started to wheeze. His breaths were labored and shallow. She wrapped her lavalava around her head before she leaned into him. Mason's eyes rolled as he tried to fight her.

"No! Please don't leave me here! Don't leave me ever!" He edged toward the opposite side of the cot, vomited the contents of his stomach, flopped back down, gasping hard, and fought against something in his fevered sleep.

Pele fell back and away from the cot as he rolled to his side and stared at her with dilated pupils, lifeless and clear. "We are all going to die if we go home, Miss. Tell Captain if I don't make it. Tell my wife I tried to warn everyone. Can you do that? For thine is the kingdom and the glory… Oh, Lord, please spare the children! Spare my wife, Filoi!"

He thrashed out at her, hitting her squarely on the left side of her face, sending her sprawled over the one end of the flooring. Pele, dazed, quickly clambered on him to keep him on the cot. The man outweighed her by two stones and so much so when prone. She fell back and promptly ran out of the tent.

"Lachlan! Maifea!" Between them, they subdued Mason before he passed out. His eyeballs rolled to the back of his head. "Please hold him while I get my aunt!" Pele ran over to the cabins. Her heart thumped hard against her ribs and was in her mouth as she ran down to Lesina.

The evening settled over the ship while they were palsied in groups; the foreboding stillness settled over it. The constellations were out and brightly shining over the indigo dark of the earth in repose, but there was little pleasure in their sparkling light. The ocean was so calm that one could walk on its ripples.

The sailors and the passengers gathered toward the bow to pray and pay homage to their fellow. The clamor of the day, the exhaustion settling in them, kept them edgy. Lesina had the men help her lift and dress Mason appropriately. She laid his personal effects on his body. The men took over to wrap his ravaged body into a canvas and secured him by ropes at his neck, waist, and ankles.

The usually calm Captain Parsons was beside himself with grief and anguish. This was not how he envisioned his maiden voyage as captain to begin. It was an awful way to think, Michael admitted to himself. He was not without sorrow about losing his third mate. However, one's first run at captaincy determines one's reputation through the fleet.

Lesina began the prayers. Her voice trembled through the preamble. *"In the name of the Father, the Son, and the Holy Spirit."* The Lord's Prayer gathered strength as the others chanted in harmony with her.

"Our Father in Heaven: hallowed be thy name, thy kingdom come, thy will be done on earth as it is in Heaven. Forgive our trespasses as we forgive others who trespass against us. Give us this day our daily bread.

Lead us not into temptation and deliver us from evil. Amen.

May you find peace and salvation in your next life, Mason Cahill. May the waters wash over your body and deliver you to your new sail. God's will has come. May He grant peace to your survivors in Samoa."

The men lowered Mason's body into the calm seas. They waited; some cried as they heard the body hit the waters. The deck slowly cleared as there was little left to do now in the aftermath of the tumultuous day and evening. Lesina and her wards walked toward the cabins to retire for the night.

Out of the dark, Lachlan approached and pulled Pele from the entourage. She was too tired to protest or put up a fight.

"I wanted to see how you're faring." He pointed at her swollen face. "That doesn't look good." He traced her face with his fingertips.

"I'll have my aunt look at it in the morning." Exhaustion blanked her mind; all she wanted to do now was lay her head down with her sisters.

"Perhaps we should have *toana'i* tomorrow with everyone, Pele." He seemed sincere in his query. A shared meal would serve as a farewell in earnest among them.

"Whatever you think is proper. We'll help." She was too depleted to think, plan, or even think of food, too tired to be responsible for yet another event on this ship. The urge to get off it was egging her to the cabin. The lack of space was getting the best of her manners.

"Goodnight, Lachlan."

She was so sad for Mason, for whomever he had left in this world. May someone among them find cause to tell his wife in Samoa. Yet, she was even too tired to cry. No, it was too much for her to do so in front of Lachlan. Stooping low at the entrance, she walked into the room.

Lesina was fast asleep while Kiele and Iolana were waiting for her quietly in the hammocks. She pulled off her dress and lay down in her chemise, pulling what lavalava was left to cover her legs. Kiele dropped out of the hammock and lay beside her on their mat. Iolana did as well. The girls lay with arms and legs over one another as they did as children at the Basilica. Twenty-three days and Hilo seemed like a post-script, a chapter once upon a time fairytale. If truth were told, she missed the cloister's assured tranquility. Now, she felt this overwhelming doom that came with this arranged marriage waiting for her.

Too much, as she rolled over. *Everyone will die!* Why wait? Her shoulders shook in the dark as she wanted to scream and yell at someone. Anyone! She was sad, angry at the world, at her parents. Maybe even at Lesina. There was so much she could do better than be a wife. Be a *mere* wife, she angrily cried.

In the dark, she wept pitifully into her arm. Kiele heard her misery and rolled closer. She held her sister as Pele gave voice to her anger and sadness. Iolana scrambled over to the other side of Pele and held on to her sisters. As the hour passed, they slept, all too tired to process their future in the coming days.

Pele woke up hard in the early morning hour. The girls were still wrapped around her in their slumber. Their breathing was rhythmic as the waters beneath rocked them gently in that familiar lullaby of the night. She extricated herself and popped the door ajar to let the cool morning breezes enter the room.

Lord, please send me a sign that this is my righteous future. Why, Lord, is all this so hard for me to believe? Can I not go home to my own family? To all that is familiar and mine.

Always so much to bear, my Good Father. I will understand that if you do not answer me in the next few days, then I know Your will and not my own will come to pass. Thank you for always standing by me even though you have forsaken me. Lord, hear my prayer!

The familiar sounds of sleep rolled on as the night did. The miles to home shores are getting shorter, she knew. Despair rose as she tried not to think about what awaited her. She stepped into her dress in the dark before slipping on her robe from Sister Ingrid. "To keep you warm in your travels, my child." There is so much regret and love in that departure from the convent. She passed through the gaping entrance as quietly as possible without raising the alarm about her leaving.

Standing on the steamer's stern, she watched the stars turn and sparkle throughout these night skies. Somewhere up there, they say. Yet, she could not feel anyone or His presence.

She looked out as the stream flowed behind as the boiler churned its energies over the doldrums of the Pacific.

Here, rather than have futile conversations with a god she cannot see, she can have them with Him in person. Little keeps her here—family, few friends who can go on without her. She was an extra player in those new motion pictures. It was time to go. Pele clambered over the bottom railing and swung a leg over. Better here at sea without ties to the land.

Two hands out of the dark reached out and caught the back of her burlap hood. She slammed unceremoniously on the stern deck, falling on her already bruised posterior. She gasped, trying to catch her breath before staring at the stars and the angry face above hers. Pele stared back, enraged, if not more.

"I'm not going to ask what this is about." He looked at her, angry and in disbelief about what he had witnessed. Little could be so wrong to merit this severe of a turn.

"You've no right." As she struggled to right herself. He made no move forward to help her sit up. She did anyway before leaning forward and standing up. "No right to ask!"

"Even so! Are things so terrible that you think this is the only way?" He looked bewildered and unamused by her insolent attitude.

"You know nothing about any of this. Nothing." She righted her hooded smock before standing before him, challenging him. Before he could answer, she turned on her heel and walked away from him. He went after her and pulled her back.

"Then make *me* understand, Pele. What are you thinking? Do you not think that your aunt and friends would not miss you? Don't you have parents waiting for you?" She gazed at him, over and down those long legs, before leaving him without explanation.

That bloody disdain! Thank God he doesn't have to worry! Damn Samoan women. Yet, something about Pele's open defiance set him on edge.

She pulled her smock off her slip and took a lavalava off their makeshift clothesline. The girls were still fast asleep. She wrapped the ends and swung them around her neck. She tidied the corners of her sarong before lying down.

Thank you, Lord, for keeping watch over them. Her shoulders shook as she cried in a tired ball of confusion, anger, and angst. Her eyes popped open, wiping her eyes from the exhaustion and adrenaline. Sleep came unawares to her wearied mind.

The McAllister group was on the deck. They found their way through the galley kitchen to cook their Sunday toana'i. Maifea led the parade of dishes to the table. The younger men followed him with the rest of the boards of food and aromatic morsels set on top of plates. Wilhelm stood aside nonplussed but relieved that he had not toiled over all this gloriousness. The food on the table was out on the deck; it was time to sit and partake of the bounty the men had gathered and prepared.

For the Samoans, the Sunday repast was superbly substantial. It was time to gather to celebrate their imminent arrival, to recover some composure from Mason's death, and even to say goodbye as they were over this sail.

Captain Parsons called for Lesina and her wards. He hoped they would arrive on time in Pago Pago. Lesina, Kiele, and Iolana came to the table. As they approached, Maifea glanced up kindly.

The men waited until the women sat down, as did the embattled crew. Pele's absence was apparent as plates were passed and laden with food. The men were curious, but Lachlan did not ask. The meal was quiet as thoughts of Mason's passing were still on many of their minds. Conversations were solemn with one's neighbor.

When done, they returned to their posts without complaint or want for company. Lesina retired with the girls to their quarters once they finished cleaning up with the McAllister men. The earlier chatter between them was subdued, polite as though this was among strangers.

Lesina's sadness and anxiety were eating at her. Life was about to change so much for all of them and, most of all, for Pele.

The setting sun burned as it sank one sliver over the horizon. The evening blaze was golden all over them, washing them into their journey's purple and crimson end. They were ready to go ashore. Any shore will do. There was sadness here on the ocean, and there was no good to be had if they remained aimlessly floating without a home. She has sailed more than enough ships between Eastern Samoa and Hawaii to see Pele at the Basilica, but none of those previous ships bore a death.

On the side of the bow, men stood smoking, with the waves breaking and lapping against the steamer. The smoke wafted between them. Maifea and Lachlan were lost in their thoughts of their homecoming. News of more rigid lines from the New Zealand administration would take some time to adjust to once they were on land. The wanton depravity of their respite in Hawai'i may have dulled their senses, but they were aware of the hardline expectations back home.

They could not afford any conduct unbecoming in their fathers' companies. They were the sons returning home to take up their positions among their families, and these were not roles to be passed on to the younger boys or the next generation.

Maifea skipped past the issues of being the firstborn. Still, his father didn't see any stoppers by leaning heavily on him to serve the more prominent causes for the village, church, and other more significant Fa'aSamoa responsibilities. He was his father's orator. He was groomed from ten and has become an outstanding steward of language. His English was flawless, leaning slightly toward the Americans than the local Kiwi patois.

Lachlan will follow his father into the import business. Travel was becoming more routine and would pick up now that New Zealand was the new sheriff in Apia. He will have to find a network of Kiwi businesses to move forward from his father's network. Times were changing, and if he moved this business forward, he would be in the country to state some of his ideas with or without his father's blessings.

As for love, his parents were clear about his future wife. His mother, of course, had already found a girl that she swore would make him a good wife.

He was not about to live like a monk while she sought that soul out.

II. Summer 1917

O Fanua O Ou Matou Tamā
Land of Our Fathers

The commerce on Apia shores was pulsating with humans. Businessmen were three-deep, followed by servants who followed in their wake. Auctioneers were calling out costs on fish from that morning's catch. Others were weighing the mountains of copra stockpiled near the pier before Chinese laborers hauled them off in a flurry between ship captains and plantation owners threading their way through the undulating crowd.

Captain Parsons sailed another twelve hours over to Apia's port. The US Navy refused to let the *Williamson* into the island after discovering Mason's death on the ship's log. Kept at the mouth of the Fagatogo harbor during the inspection, he was immediately told to pull anchor and sail to Samoa or Fiji.

"Why are you turning us away? I must let some passengers off and pick up the copra here."

The mustachioed senior class petty officer scoffed. "Sir, move on with your crew and passengers. Immediately!"

With that brusque dismissal, Navy officers from the port authority pulled their anchor up and pushed their fruit ship to shore. The Navy sentries waved the *Williamson* to sail onward to its next destination. Where? They did not care, but this steamer was not landing on their shores on their watch.

Captain Parsons turned way, flushed and angry from the encounter, and told his crew to be ready and set the *Williamson* to sail onto German Samoa. The Navy detachment here at Pago Pago was not hosting them, and the women were now his responsibility to put to shore in Apia. It was the best he could do.

Lesina ran up to him, hoping to intervene after coming on deck and seeing the heated exchange. The officers were still within hearing distance. She and the girls needed to disembark here at home and face whatever awaited them sooner rather than later. Their only way home was getting farther away by the minute.

"*Oi*, you!" She angrily waved at the first officer who came aboard with his entourage of two military police. "We need to get home! The ship isn't coming in with us!" The sarcasm was not lost on the officers.

"If you aren't this vessel's surgeon, I advise you to be quiet, Ma'am," he ordered, dismissive and pompous all at once. With the flip of a backhand, that was all he needed to say to this offensive woman.

The officer curled his waxed mustache and jeered at her as she ran along. *Damn natives! So pertinent!* They wanted to be coddled when they needed a good tossing. Over the knee or bed, it didn't matter. "Go to Apia! Arrange your quarantine over there, then telegram us in two months." With its unfortunate captain, he waved the *Williamson* summarily onward and with this mad woman staring *down* at them. They sailed back to the shores without as much as a glance back at them.

"Why were we turned away, Captain?" Lesina spun to face Captain Parsons, who was as frustrated as she was. She began to sink to her knees and cry. More than getting home, her livelihood was here in Pago Pago. If she had to house and feed the girls, those means were here, a few short miles inland.

"Because of Mason's death on our sail."

"But he died of pneumonia! What could we have done? And what does that have to do with us getting off in Pago Pago?" Weariness tore at her nerves, her mind thinking about her brother waiting for them at the shore. She and the girls would swim home as they were this close to home. However, Iolana was too small for that swim. The evening tides were only suitable for a dinghy to approach the mouth of the harbor.

The day was getting worse by the hour as they sailed to Apia. The McAllister party came onto the deck with their belongings and luggage, dressed in traditional tapas. Maifea came to Lesina to thank her for assisting them during their journey home.

"You're welcome, Maifea." She briefly touched his shoulders and pressed her cheek to his. He reddened as he felt her soft skin against his beard. Lesina laughed as he blushed.

"*Oi, o lea outou malaga i Apia ma matou?*" They had missed the Navy denial while packing and bringing their luggage on deck to prepare for their disembarkment in Apia.

"The Navy said no to the Williamson." Lesina pointed to the last of the green hills of Pago Pago. "The girls and I couldn't disembark at home—so now we are going on with you all to Apia."

"Oh? Please come with us if you need somewhere to stay until they allow you into Pago Pago. Our village has a lot of open houses, any one of them open to you and the girls to use."

Lesina mused out loud. "Oh, thank you, Maifea. Should we ever need your assistance, we will find you."

"You have a need right *now*, Lesina." Lachlan walked up to them, hearing bits and pieces of her conversation with Maifea. *"Omai ma keigeki. E tele matou fale e fai ma outou faletalimalo."* He assured her they wouldn't be a burden on their families or village.

Lesina considered this for a spell, then thought better. The girls were on her mind. Without the company of her nephews, it wasn't proper for them to be there in this unknown village under the auspices of these unmarried men.

"Fa'afetai lava mo le agalelei ma le aga'alofa. Both of you, but I must decline. *Ona o lou fanau teine, te'i fa'apea outou aiga ose ulumoega lea ua solo atu."*

The cousins looked at one another. They laughed at the idea of the rise that such an idea would incite in the village. Their mothers would be up in arms if they brought the younger women as brides and dowries with unknown worth and lineage. Lachlan didn't want to go through that hassle yet again.

However, this wasn't an ordinary woman. Lesina was a *taulasea* and would be more than welcome in the village. With her skills as a native healer, Lesina would be given a home and place with her *keis*. Her proposed home can serve as a haven for those who sought medical care; the palagi physicians in town were not keen on coming into the villages to see patients.

"There is more than enough room among us, Lesina." Maifea shifted his weight, further noting that he was an anomaly at six feet four inches tall. Lachlan was slightly built at six-two and was less intimidating than his cousin, but that did not make him any more approachable in comparison. Besides, he has grown fond of these young women who have gotten through the arduous journey with them. "Please consider our offer, Lesina."

Later, an idea occurred to her as she stood at the rail. She sought out the men to ask before Apia came into view. "Do you know where there is a Catholic church?"

"There is one in Apia right in town. The *Immaculata* is open to guests if you need us to drop you there," Maifea offered, looking at Lachlan for confirmation.

Lachlan nodded his agreement. He had no hurry to get home just yet. *"E leai se mea o iai, Lesina. Afai o le tonu lena mo outou, ia ua lelei."* He, as Maifea, would instead like to take the women home. They'd work out the details later with their womenfolk and families.

Maybe this was a better delay, Lesina thought. "I'd like that, indeed! *E sili ona matou nonofo le taulaga e iloa ai taimi o malaga o va'a na matou toe fo'i laea i Pago Pago."*

The men were from farther out in the country along the Beach Road but could come if they were sent to help them move. Lesina was assured of this and felt comforted that they had made friends with these men. Toting the three girls, she needed as much help as possible.

The blur of spoken German and Chinese, dogs barking, and laughter in Samoan showed signs of life here in Apia town. Pele, Kiele, and Iolana stared at the crowds in wonder. This is about as diverse a place as they've ever seen before. They were excited to be off the ship. Before following Lesina and the men, they bid their captain farewell.

"Thank you so much, Captain Parsons. Hopefully, all goes well with your business in town." Pele held out her hand to shake it graciously, and he did so with a rueful smile.

"I am not sure your aunt likes me right now, but I, too, bid you good tidings, young ladies, and the safe harbor with the Immaculata! It should be but a month before you can travel home from here. It is closer than Hawaii, that is certain!" His crew had disembarked as well for a short liberty. With his parting wave, the girls watched his retreat. His sandy hair became blurred as he bobbed and wove through the busy-minded mid-morning crowd.

The McAllister party found horses and a cart for hire, which they brought back to the edge of the market, where Lesina and the girls were told to wait. Lesina fretted that they were imposed upon when they could find their way if they made their way through the market and onto the main road. Most of everything was on the main city street, she thought. She regarded their fellow passengers cum friends and protectors kindly, but she was not keen on being an imposition when it was easier to do something alone.

The horses neighed, and their gait slowed as they neared the women. Tala'i drove a team of two geldings, pulling a cart behind his uncles. Mataio sat in the back, happily whistling. His joy was evident as he breathed in the air of Samoa. He did not want to make the trip to Hawaii anymore. He would have to tell his parents. No, maybe his uncles would be kinder and gentler. Then, *they* can fight his cause against his parents' disapproval. He missed them. He missed his old friends. Tala'i was used to all this travel, but Mataio could live without its arduous sails.

He laid back on the wagon's bed, staring at the blue skies above Samoa, and reveled in its welcome: not a single rain cloud or temperamental summer squall. Even if he had to work the plantations for the rest of his life, he could not be persuaded to return to Hawaii. His father wasn't one to take to rebellions. Sometimes, Mataio wished that Maifea was his sire. He was unattached, so easy to talk to, and didn't care much about the seriousness of the future. He wanted to grow up to be him, not his autocratic father. *Please, Uncles, please help me!*

The girls sat on Lesina's cedar chest while their guardian stood off. Kiele and Iolana were awed by Saturday's market's hustle and bustle. The Basilica of Hilo was remote and peopled by only caretakers of its grounds. Here, all these different faces were such a change for the girls. While they looked out to the main corridors, Pele gazed at the undulating crowd east of the market. She happened upon an elderly lady who stared back at her.

Wispy gray hair framed her face with the hint of her formerly reddish-gold hair, swept up in a bun away from bright, twinkling candlenut eyes. There was such great love in that gaze that Pele wanted to bask in all of it. She raised her head slightly as if to acknowledge Pele. The younger could not help but smile back at her.

Pele laughed out her merriment as this kindly soul winked back at her. Pele stood up to go to her to greet her properly. She hurried off the chest and jumped onto the ground beneath her slippered feet.

"Pele, come on!" Lesina called out to her.

"Just a minute, Aunty!" She felt relieved to be off the boat, and her prayers answered, stumbling across this lovely woman. The universe was talking to her.

She had to meet this kind soul before her. She had to! Several mortals passed between them before she looked over to where the old lady was and saw that, sadly, she was no longer there. Pele felt so let down, looking over the heads of the crowd moving in and out of the easement. Disappointment settled into her. She could not shake the sadness that came on full-force. *Lord, let me meet her again.*

Joining her party again, she looked up at the men sitting on horseback. The boys loaded all the luggage, the crates of dry goods from Hawaii, and the beaten valises. Iolana and Lesina were in the back of the wagon, sitting against the back of the boys. Kiele settled in the back of Maifea, riding with her legs to the side while holding on to him, as natural as a child born to Hawai'i's *paniolo* of Hilo's ranches.

The men had changed into their daily lavalavas when they had gotten the conveyance and horses. Maifea's bare flanks highlight his *pe'a* as a *tulāfale* against *koko* Samoa smooth skin. It was to be expected, but he was more than Lachlan's cousin. That meant he served as translator and speaker for their village, more paramount than most young men his age.

Lachlan was his *soa,* and as Maifea's partner in their tattooing session five years earlier, he did not display his malofie. Maifea has either given up his position as an orator or, by death, has vacated the title and role his father and village elders have bestowed him, and only in these instances would Lachlan show his own.

Pele considered her options and thought climbing the wagon with her aunt, and Iolana was best. She walked back to ask Mataio to pull her up so she could sit on one of the crates without acknowledging Lachlan, who was staring down at her impatiently. Daylight passed them as the sun canted on the horizon, and they had to get on the road home, another twenty miles east of Apia.

"You can't get on the wagon. It's already loaded to capacity." This was the first salvo fired if there was ever an insult so blatant. Lachlan did not spare her feelings as she intently avoided and passed him by for the wagon.

She stopped in her tracks and stared up at him.

He glowered down at her. "You must get up with me. Hurry up!"

"I can walk," she said, staring back at him. A deep red flush crept up her neck and cheeks, then her face at his backhanded admonishment. He shook his head and jumped off his stead. He came around and grabbed her by the waist. He lifted her roughly onto the back of the horse, much like a sack of rice.

As she rose in the air, the left side of her dress ripped to her mid-thigh. Lachlan didn't apologize as he openly stared at her bare leg, torn clothing, and chemise as she struggled to pull herself upright. She grabbed the horse's side, which seemed as onery as its rider. Lachlan threw her other leg on the other side so she could sit astride. Once she was upright, he mounted and took the reins from Maifea. Lachlan did not meet his cousin's curious, burning gaze.

Something was wrong between these two. Whatever it was, Maifea hoped his cousin would get it right before they left the women at the convent. It's good that Lesina did not witness this sour encounter between his cousin and her niece. She wasn't a woman who minced her words.

Maifea turned his horse and Kiele toward the open town path. The boys had turned onto the main road and drove the wagon ahead.

"Put your hands around me, Pele." Curt and abrupt. He wasn't putting up with any of her defiance. Pele obeyed willingly and locked her fingers around his waist. She leaned onto his back, pressing her breasts against his unyielding spine, and swallowed the rising bile from her stomach. She was tired, hungry, and could live without this boorish man. The sooner they get to the convent, the sooner she will see the last of him. *Hopefully, she mused ungratefully for the rest of the time they were here.*

She thought this was a fate worse than that awaited her at home. This detour was comparable already. Swallowing her rising palpable fear, she leaned into him, with her cheek to his back as she braced for the ride. She closed her eyes and hoped they only had to go around the corner.

It was the longest, roughest ride of her life. Those five miles were among the worst so far in her years. The bile of her last meal was in the back of her throat. They approached the busy roundabout of the cathedral before them; Lesina hopped off to knock on the door to find Mother Superior.

Pele, with her head throbbing, was ready for them to stop. Her mouth was dry from the air passing them by as Lachlan pushed for time through town. She peeled her cheek from his back when he stopped and tried to rub blood back into her jaw. Before she knew what was happening, he lifted her off. So unprepared that the winds were pushed out of her lungs. She wailed as she slid down his length, with her ripped dress and chemise riding up her posterior. She grabbed him around his neck to stop her unceremonious descent.

He unhooked her vice-grip, her long legs locked around his waist, and dropped her foot from the ground. Pele stared at him as she tried valiantly to regain her balance. She opened her mouth and abruptly closed it again before she reached out to push him out of the way. He angrily batted her hand from his chest. She lunged forward and vomited all over him. The contents of her last meal on the ship were splattered all over his shirtfront and feet. She bent to her wobbly knees and cried out in shame and anger.

She pushed off him and stood straight, wiping the corners of her mouth. Not giving him the time to yell at her, she grabbed the two parts of her dress and chemise together and walked off to rejoin her aunt and sisters. He was quite finished with this woman.

Lesina secured approval from the French *pere* of the parish that they could stay with them until the next ship to Pago Pago moored in port. It would be a month as commerce between the isles took precedence over passengers. She thanked the McAllister group and waved to the girls through the side gate of the cathedral. Kiele looked over and waved her farewell before helping Pele into the cloister.

As the boys unloaded the chest and valises, the younger girls followed Lesina's lead. Mother Superior appeared after being beckoned by a Tahitian novice in residence at their *pere's* behest.

"You didn't have to be so rough with Pele," Maifea said as they continued their road home. "*E lili'a le keige.* She doesn't do well with heights." He looked over his cousin's ruined shirtfront. He deserved all of it and wished Pele had eaten more at breakfast that morning. What a churlish cur Lachlan has been since they came off the *Williamson*!

"Is that what she told you? You could have told me beforehand, Maifea." Lachlan brushed off some nasty bits of bread and eggs on his shirt. "Whose side are you on anyways?" taking water from Maifea to wash the crud from the shirt. It was a pristine white an hour ago.

He was a little antagonized by his cousin's lack of sympathy. Pele seemed to have made a lovely impression on him, and now Maifea was smitten by her charms. *Stupid choice, Cousin.*

"Stop being an ass, Lachlan. Pele hadn't said anything to me. Lesina told me before we started to find a way to get her over without all this. Middle of the wagon would have been fine; even blindfolded, she would have been better off than riding with you." Maifea turned on his heel to get to his horse. "Not sure what went on with you and that girl, but you need to stop it. *O lou fa'akamakama e ta'uvalea ai uma tatou.*" He called the boys to continue as it was time to move on toward home. *Ua lava fo'i le vaega ole malaga.*

Six months away had been too much for him. The winter in Hawaii was colder than here at home. Even the extreme humidity was better than the more frigid trade winds through the hills of Manoa. They were not saints. A little too much of the palagi's whiskey and rabid debauchery was the way of the palagis on Waikiki's beachfront at O'Malley's. After productive days, they were down the hills with sailors and Honolulu's underbelly drinking their fill, sowing their oats with local *wahine ho'okamakama* for the money they could skim off transient men. Love had nothing to do with any of it.

He looked over his cousin and nephews and was glad they were home. He was happy that they brought the boys home safely and that the cargo made the sail intact. Moreover, they were alive. He needed to return to his roots. Hell, *they* both did. He turned toward home, not waiting for the damn *afatasi*. Everything got old over the six months they were away.

"Ai kae! Kakou o loa!" Maifea was weary of the road and needed to feel the mats of his parents' home.

Lachlan chuckled, *"Ai ma oe!"* He rode ahead to the boys, leaving the brooding Maifea to bring up the rear. Let him think about what he will do. That girl deserved it.

The boys were happy enough that the sight of home came up ahead. They could hear the merriment of villagers who had sighted them atop the plantation.

"Loa ua taunu'u mai le malaga! Fonō lōlō loa taunu'u mai tama!" The excited calls gave way to songs from all over the hill—pounding tins resonated throughout the village's boundaries.

They were so not worth all this commotion, Maifea could not help but think. These folks spent most of their lives serving the ranking chieftain, including his father. And he was so grateful to see everyone, but he was exhausted. He was tired of the ocean and the road this far from home and only wanted to lie on a mat behind his parents' house for several weeks.

The *popese* lasted well into the evening until midnight, when all the significant speeches were made. Orators, old—while the young listened—spoke of the olden heydays and their yearning for those times between cups of 'ava. He wanted a break to return to his old self without all these excessive celebrations. His mother insisted otherwise. She regaled him with news of young village women and those who have come in from afar on wonderful *malagas*.

Lachlan looked exhausted. The younger boys were nodding off while sitting behind elders more on the *paepae* of the *faletalimalo*. The guesthouse sat on the raised foundation of the river and the cobalt stones of the ocean.

Manumā, Maifea's father, finally called to end the *popese*. This night of song and dance was their way of welcoming family, especially those who have traveled afar. His son and grandsons were home at long last!

It may be the time that they all stayed home for a while. The long months were taking a tow on Maifea's mother, and his parents were not getting any younger. There was also the matter of his nuptials now that he was suitable to marry at twenty-seven. If not here out of the *au'alumā,* of the high chief, then some fortunate girl of these *malagas.*

These sister communities helped mothers and their life's aim to find suitable brides. Maifea could choose one of these women, Manumā thought happily, and with a wife, reason for Maifea to settle into his own homestead. His older son had other issues to cope with and couldn't be depended on if his parents' lives were at risk.

Lachlan found his cousin sitting on a fallen beach hibiscus tree, smoking a cheroot in the dark. He wasn't invited to sit down, but he did. He had to squash this growing rift between them. Moreover, he wanted them back to their even-keeled selves. They were always brothers without tension or a crossed word since their grandmother raised them together.

Maifea handed the cheroot over to him. "Something is amiss, Lachlan. I could feel it in town. All those foreigners on our shores, and we haven't much control over our futures." He stared out at the ocean beneath the starlit skies. *Their* families, *their* homes. He missed all these things when the night sky seemed closer than ever on the voyage home.

"Hey, why so glum? Things will ride themselves out." Lachlan handed the cheroot back. "I'll see my father in the morning and find out if he needs us to work immediately. If not, maybe we need to take time off and travel for your parents."

Maifea stood up, tired and sad all at once. "Samoa has changed since we left, Lachlan. *Masalo o iai ni tulaga ua tatau na ta fa'alogologo iai.*" He stared at his cousin, hoping he would understand what this undertow was about. Maifea knew that Lachlan would not join any rebellion against palagis.

Ronan McAllister was not a man to cross in business or life. Least of all is Lachlan's participation in any improper rebellion with natives. Even his aunt was dressed as some proper palagi woman here in the village, and little anyone wanted to discuss that part. His mother wasn't on speaking terms with her older sister. However, neither sister intervened between their sons. They were their mother's sons.

"See about your parents, Lachlan." Maifea made up his mind. Eventually, he will find the others, with or without his cousin. Everyone must pick a side. He knew his cousin wasn't cut out for conflict, especially in these early days of the battle for self-governing from the superpowers pulling strings to their American puppets in town.

"You wouldn't do anything, right, Maifea?" Lachlan wasn't as daft as Maifea believed him to be. He knew that his cousin was sending back letters to leaders at home from Hawaii.

The question was moot. "It shouldn't matter."

"*Matou. Outou. Latou. Tatou.*" Lachlan looked at him, aware that his cousin needed to be reminded that joining the agitation would jeopardize him, their families, and their village, Punae'e.

Maifea lit his cheroot and exhaled noiselessly into the night's stillness. This wasn't a fight he fought with Lachlan. This was *his*. He will find the others who were gathering in the hinterland. German Samoa was fast losing its face over the three years since the New Zealand administration took over as the Queen's agents in the Pacific.

Lachlan wasn't without his reservations. Manumā could lose his reputation and ranking in the village if Maifea were named among the rebels *if* he was. Many allied with the present New Zealand administration. Negotiations were still being bandied about town between governments. Even the United States had her hands in the local pot. The more foreigners came to their shores, the less willing they were to listen to Samoa's ranking chieftain.

Maifea prayed, without fail, for peace among all. He wasn't opposed to the presence of the palagis. Yet, they didn't come without issues or demands of the native populace. He, his parents, brother, sister, and in-laws were all part of this nation, and he wasn't about to play the second citizen to these foreigners. German, Kiwis, Americans—he was not some second-class citizen to any of them.

He wasn't oblivious to the news of unrest stirring in the eastern and southern counties. If he had to serve as his father's matai, then he would. This is so important to him that even as the favored son, he wasn't so far from the leadership. His father's school peers were among these men. *What could go wrong?*

Lachlan returned to his mother's home here in Punae'e as his father had a residence in town and didn't bother to come to the village. The travel was too hard on his aging senses, he said. His mother was always welcome to stay in town all year, but she chose to come home for weeks with him in tow. She left his sisters in town as it was a better option than to sit here and watch their cousins toil, as though this were the norm for all of them. Her children did not have to stoop to such levels. They were Ronan McAllister's daughters and need not be part of the commoners' strife.

In Fele's opinion, Sala missed her opportunity for *this* good life. She rebuffed Ronan's courtship, and now she must deal with the *fa'alavelaves* and all the usual drama with the rounds of inaugurations, funerals, weddings, and the *malagas* with her Samoan husband. Sala didn't blink an eye.

Fele knew that her sister did not envy her. If Dickens was missing a cast member from *David Copperfield*, Ronan McAllister was the missing Uriah Heep. There was little to like about him from his appearance, but even his shrewdness and single-mindedness put off others who must do business with him. He might have hit every ugly tree branch on the way down, but his children were spared. Their mother's Samoanesque genes helped save them from the relentless rounds of bullying. They were not the talk of the town as the reigning princesses, but they were not remotely ugly.

This was an exception about the McAllisters, about whom Sala often laughed at her sister. Little convinces her to think she is in the wrong for saying no to the palagi. Sala went to her marriage, knowing it was for her family's sake rather than love.

"How is your sister? Does she need any help with the wedding?" Manumā asked as he heard his wife enter through the back door. *"Tuli iai Maifea e fai mea ma lona tausoga."*

"Oh, the usual. Please talk to the extended family about the contributions to Lachlan's dowry." She sighed.

Sala thought about the number of fine mats they would gather in the following months for the *a'iga faitele* when the domestic exchanges happen. While she did not begrudge her nephew for his nuptials, she wished Maifea would be as likeminded and find a woman soon.

She would like some grandchildren from Maifea soon as she and his father were not getting any younger. *"Maifea, ua ea?"* Sala called out to her son as he stood staring out in the dark as if waiting for something or someone.

"Ua le ā?" Maifea said without turning around.

"Le fa'atali atu ia oe! Ua uma na e iloa ua tatou a fai sou avā!"

Maifea thought of blurting out his emphatic disagreement but then said nothing. She was already so preoccupied with his aunt's long to-do list that he didn't need to add more stress to her plate. If the qualification of a wife to his mother were that he had to find a local girl, he would get to it when he got there.

Sala looked at her son over and down before she let the matter slip back into oblivion before she lost her son. He wasn't so patient today. Something was bothering him.

"Something going on with you, Son?"

"No, why do you ask?" Maifea stopped himself from snapping. This was his mother and will always be his mother. Yet, she had to understand that he was a grown man, almost thirty. So, twenty-seven wasn't the milestone, but he was old enough to consciously make such choices without her help or that of his aunts.

"Well, you're distracted for one. And two, you don't seem to want to be here. Your father and I miss you dearly when you are away."

"Mother, I'm fine. *E tele o isi mataupu o lea oute pisi iai.*" His exasperation was getting the best of him. "I'll be home for church. I'm coming back to spend the weekend." He could sense his mother's disenchantment. He could feel her impatience. However, he'd like to choose his wife when he gets around to it. Right *now,* it was not that time.

Her son didn't think she knew. Other mothers have also noted the disappearances of their sons on certain days. There was a foreboding to what was happening. What he and others were up to, she prayed that all would work out. She prayed that his father did not find out. Add air, food, and water, and these kids think they can no longer talk to their mother.

Oh, Son, I only pray that you find peace in this living. So much about the world is changing, and I hope you find your way around safely and with love. With these things in mind, Lord, hear my prayers. My son is so young and needs love and guidance whenever possible. Do not let him go into this world without hearing me out.

Later that following Sunday church, she came across a twenty-year-old girl. She was fair, seemed to speak well, and was unmarried. Her parents were of the Old Samoa—landed, titled, and connected. She told her husband to consider a *talatālaga* with the girl's family so they could have a discussion that might yield a wedding between families.

Manumā winced at the suggestion as he was sure that Maifea had his ideas of a wife. "We should let our boy find his way around this, Sala. He has a good mind on those big shoulders."

"We need to nudge him in the right direction."

"Sala, a le'o le mea ea lea e ga'alo so'o ai le tama? Faitalia ia Maifea ma lona filifiliga!" Manumā protested, standing for their son. Let Maifea make his own choice of a wife when he is ready and not because Sala thinks she is a matchmaker.

III. April 1918

Le Vavalo
The Vision

Their market day was the busiest as they gathered their wares to barter and sell in Apia. There was much to look forward to today as they celebrated Iolana's birthday. The girls rolled off their mats and folded their sheets, stowing both near Lesina's cedar chest.

The trip to Apia was a once a month's adventure, so they were up early and ready in their best dresses. Lesina was just as happy as it allowed her to meet with her fellow healers and compare notes on their findings with new native medicines. The joy and merriment were contagious as they got horses from the catechist to make this trip. Lesina traded her services as a healer for the two horses.

Pele walked around their fale and dropped the coconut blinds while Kiele let the cats and dog into their small yard of over three acres. Iolana carried their baskets to put them close to the horses. She was stronger than her older sisters, took less time to gather the lemons, and worked the plantation without complaint. Kiele was more adept at gathering Lesina's herbs and leaves than the others. Nursing came naturally to her, so she followed Lesina around most days, cataloging and writing notes as Lesina dictated when exploring the ravine, hillside, and plantation as they gathered native medicinal plants and noted their whereabouts.

Iolana happily passed her by as Pele put on her wide-brim hat, burning around her gills as she was not going into town. Her sister was about to turn eighteen in May, and they were all so excited. There was much to look forward to as Lesina had promised they would venture to town to watch moving pictures at the Tivoli. It has been nearly a year since they arrived in Apia.

After a month at the *Immaculata* rectory and no answer to her telegram to Fiso, Lesina found a small estate near Apia in the hills. It was time that she moved the girls out, even if into the virgin jungle. She negotiated a lease with the Apia See to be caretakers of the parcel and paid something to their charities over time. Henceforth, their home was now called Teuila Hill.

Steadily, her reputation as a healer grew among the faithful of the parish. She made a humble but reliable living that could support them. She had become the midwife to the palagis, the Chinese, and the Samoans for miles around Apia and the nearby communities. Lesina offered her services to all without prejudice. The palagis and other foreigners paid enough to sustain her work with her fellow Samoan women who could not pay during their *failele.* They had enough to eat because of many grateful husbands. Kiele traveled with her, so she had a helping hand with the newborns, and the girl had a natural affinity for nursing, more so than the others. In exchange for her services as a midwife, Lesina received live chickens, the catch of the day, and the plants she needed. From other patients, lavalava bundles and fine mats, some of which she gave to the parish and convent.

In time, they have settled into a home they are proud of. While her Pele wasn't of the healing arts, she could grow things out of the earth that no one could imagine. The terrain around their fale was Pele's masterpiece. There was little the girl didn't think of, especially when Lesina needed native plants and herbs. Most grow in their garden due to Pele's efforts.

While their home rested on Sunday, Pele went to the village and sat with the elderly women after morning Mass. She was happiest there as she returned with cuttings and grafted plants. In exchange, she helped serve the Sunday meals for her foster aunts and grandmothers.

Bougainvillea of deep reds, fuchsias, and oranges were trained over their fale and small kitchen. The smells of jasmine regaled their senses in the early evenings when its creeping vines bloomed profusely. Trees and plants that were already on the land, Pele spent most of her days pruning, retraining, and fertilizing. She was on her knees, digging and planting away while babies were born and as Iolana tended their little plantation.

The four cats and the lame dog were Pele's idea of adding to their menagerie. She may not tend to women, but Pele had an affinity for collecting homeless strays. Lesina let her do so as she knew that if Pele missed anything over the years, it was her pets left behind in Olo'ie.

These excursions into town were a good break for the girls. They have all done so well in helping create their spacious home, one that will have to do until Fiso gets on the ferry to get them. Lesina knew her brother wasn't happy with her, but he would have to bear up and say no to courter for a daughter who hadn't come home in nearly a decade. In the meantime, all three girls were thriving. She was reluctant to think of the day he would come charging for Pele. That would not end well.

That was neither here nor there. When Fiso comes, he will see that Pele is more than just a bargaining chip for his alliances with potential in-laws. Hopefully, he'll know they have come to a living of their own merits.

Kiele was on her steadfast stead, O'o, who was more theirs than the villager who loans them out to Lesina and her girls for trips into town every month since his son was born. They were often called the unknown *au'alumā*.

With a bit of finesse, Lesina hopped on and sat behind Kiele. Iolana had the reins of the second horse, Mulu. He was affectionately called this as he was constantly chewing on something. *Aigutumulu* was named for his voracious appetite, but the girls found he answered better with his nickname.

Pele came around with a crate to help her up on Mulu's back. She lunged forward and grabbed the horse's left flank. Mulu sidestepped. Pele stared at the blue, cloudless skies above them. The laughter from the others was almost deafening.

Kiele snorted the hardest. "Pele, you need to give this up and come out and learn." She got a sour stare from below O'o. Lesina laughed until she couldn't stand it anymore. She joined Kiele in their merriment at Pele's predicament. This was not one of her best moments.

Iolana stared straight ahead. "You can do this, Sister." At sixteen today, Iolana was soft-spoken, as the other sisters were not. Seeing Pele wasn't trying again, she leaned forward and whispered commands in Mulu's ear. The persnickety horse looked mortified.

"The only reason I'm near this confounded animal is that it's our way to town." Pele dusted off the back of her lavalava dress. The dirt was not coming off. "I'll stay behind." The trip to town was a treat, but she could live without the horseback ride. She has not improved her equine skills.

While a relatively straightforward way out to the main road, the path was of hairpin corners and through the church's terraced taro patches, where Iolana worked with some of Tava'esina's Catholic congregants to care for the food stock that the See considered necessary to keep in store at the Immaculata. The root harvests were plentiful, so they distributed what was not sold for commerce back to the Parish.

Kiele got off O'o, "You're going with us. We've been cooped up in these hills long enough." They had skipped Market in April. Now, they needed to go.

While not as tall as Pele or sturdy as Iolana, Kiele made up for it with grit and determination. She held the crate while she gave Pele a boost over Mulu's backside. She thumped against his spine but held on as Iolana scooted back to support her. Once settled, they slowly descended so the horses were not hurt.

Apia, as usual, was busy with commerce. Folks were hawking the harvests, especially breadfruit, bananas of all kinds, and other exotic fruits grown by natives and the Chinese who've married local women. Most of the older German settlers' homes lined the beach at the west end of town, with the Americans nearby. They, too, were here for the markets. Some sent their housemaids and men to make their purchases for the Sunday meal. Some vendors hawked trinkets, necklaces, and souvenirs at the harbor appeal to foreign tourists as they come from the mainlands.

The women dismounted the horses in front of the market. People were milling around, bartering, selling, and loud guffawing among sellers. Iolana took the horses' reins and walked them across the street to wait for the traffic while Mother and her sisters tended to the house shopping. The myriad of colors blended well and floral lavalavas were pinned to twines strung from poles to trees. To help combat the humidity, fans were selling off the tables faster than most green produce.

Lesina and Kiele threaded through the crowds to find other market healers, looking for moringa saplings and other plants that would grow well on their side of the hill. Pele threaded among the produce sellers, bending over to inspect root crops like taro and its leaves, Cavendish bananas—the *fa'i palagi*—and smaller breadfruits for their toana'i on Sunday.

Bartering with sellers was great fun, as they went back and forth for a good sale. In the end, Pele paid each of her sellers a fair price. She knew the value of hard work and how much it took for some to bring their produce to market.

Spying Iolana over the bobbing heads of the crowds between them, she waved to her to bring over the horses from her side of the road. The baskets of a few crops, taro, taro leaves, coconuts, essentials such as *moso'oi* oil, and two lavalavas for her sisters were the cost of the market today. She can wait for her lavalava until their next market day. Besides, she did not venture beyond home for much except for visiting her elderly women gardeners. Even then, they did not ask that she dress up. They were such a godsend, Pele thought. More than this, it was time that Iolana got something pretty, even if it was for Mass.

Iolana sidled up, turning O'o to his side so she could load the baskets from Pele. While she steadied these on his sturdy back, Pele went around to O'o's head and calmed him as the commotion of the market's crowds was getting him a little anxious. Mulu was unbothered, but he was busy with a tasty treat from a Chinese vendor who passed them and remarked in Samoan to Iolana that he looked like a good racing horse if he and his family could look him over.

Iolana wasn't fluent in Samoan yet, but she understood his question. *Oh, Pele, please hurry.* And there she was, waving at her like a lunatic with her red scarf over their heads.

Pele came to O'o's flank to see about her little sister, who seemed upset. Grabbing a couple of mangoes, she handed the ripe one over to Iolana while she bit into her *mago oka*. "Hey, what's going on, Sissy?"

"Oh, you know, strange people," Iolana replied nervously. She was ready to return to Teuila Hill.

"There are a lot of them around." Pele gently reached for Iolana's hand, placing it into her own. Surveying the crowd for the idiots who bothered Iolana, "Which ones? So, I can get Mulu to sit on them!"

"I think we ought to get on the road already, Pele."

"All right, stay here. Let me find Lesina and Kiele." Iolana was adamant and turned the horses to ready them for their ride home.

Pele surveyed the internal section of the market and saw Lesina's head bobbing as if she was striking a barter with her plant dealer. Kiele was turning from a Chinese vendor speaking to her as if she understood his rapid-fire Cantonese.

She did not. Her father was part-Chinese, yes, but she was never taught to speak her father's Cantonese in their home in Hilo. Petite and sun-kissed golden, Kiele knew that local Asians thought she was one of them. This didn't sit well, as enough of the local Chinese accused her of being a Samoan impostor. The days when she was Kiele, the girl from Kona, were long past her. Her life was here in Samoa now, as she could never return to Hawaii or Kalaupapa, where her parents were in exile. *Lord, forgive me!*

As Lesina looked up and saw Pele approaching them, she mimed her back and waved at her niece frantically, hoping that Pele would look toward her right. She did not.

The collision with the young palagi lady hit her like a cannonball as she walked straight into the path of the crossing crowd of women in their white summer dresses and parasols. Pele fell back when the hard part of a parasol hit her on the right side of her face. She was stunned by the blunt force, unsure what and why it happened. The impact of wood to cheekbone reverberated over the stifling air. The market fell silent without preamble!

The middle-aged matron looked about her entourage of seven, asking after their wellness. She looked down as Pele bent her waist, nursing her bloodied cheek.

"You must remind them that they are not to cross or speak to us as though we are lowly," she said to her younger charges. "This is what you do to keep them in line." She flicked her wrist as though she had touched untouchable filth. "Come, daughters. We must get home."

This godforsaken place. If they didn't become mothers to litters, they were whores on the dock. Bare their nakedness in full view of men. This one was bound to be one of these fates—the former was more likely.

A Samoan lady in the same finery motioned toward her daughters after the palagi and her three daughters.

"Mrs. Hansell, are you all right?" someone called from the gathered crowd, looking on.

"Nothing that soap can't wash off," she answered airily. She turned to the Samoan lady who followed. "Fele, please! Tell the filth to stay out of my way. You once came from this stock. Without Ronan, you'd still be living in all that squalor!"

Fele looked embarrassed and angry, but she did not answer. She pushed her daughters forward. The girls looked more like their palagi father. *Thank heavens,* she thought to herself. She had to find her son and get out of the market. Where was that boy?

Pele, breathless and in shock, all in one fell swoop. Lesina fought against the crowd as she sprinted toward her niece.

"Go ahead and wait for your brother, girls, while I look over something." The matron bobbed through the gathering crowd, parting the menacing crowd with her open parasol. *"Move out of my way, you dogs!"* The filth of it all. The parasol moved through the crowds, pale against the sea of brown faces and bodies.

Pele's eye bruised into its purplish shade as she stood with her aunt. Lesina angrily swore back at the crowd, panting from the effort to get across the market square.

"Aunty, I don't know why!" she cried, her tears stung as her eye swelled, and Lesina folded her into her arms. "I didn't do anything wrong!"

Lesina leaned into her niece. "Pele, listen to me! Go with Kiele and walk back to the horses. Wait there for me." Kiele carried their basket filled with plants. She let Pele lean against her shoulder as they walked through people staring at them. Faces mired with anger, pity, and, among them, obsequious apologists.

"Ana e vaai le mea lae ete savali iai, fenū le sasa a oe le fafine!" You wouldn't have been hit if you had looked where you were walking.

"O loa le fale ae le'i omai ni leoleo!" Go before the police come!

"Fea oulua matua? Le mea tuli mai oulua aunoa ma ni matua—oka oka e!" Where are your parents? This is what happens: you are unsupervised, running about like heathens! And on cried the clarion advisement board among the throes.

The girls paid no heed to the heckling and the jeers. They had to get to Iolana, who was waiting, unaware of what had happened until she saw Pele's face.

Lesina turned on her heel, ran the distance to the retreating women, and caught up with the Samoan acting lady-in-waiting. Or whatever she was to these overbearing idiots. *The Queen of England*, she could care less. To strike a child—her Pele? No, these monsters needed to pay for their sins!

Whirling on her heels, Lesina coughed up enough saliva and spat in Fele's face. *"Isa! Lo mea tu sameme! Fai lou masiofo e vaai iai! O malaia uma ia e outou toe seleseleina i se aso o loma mai nei!"* she cursed angrily. *"Fai mai ua loa lotu ae na'o amio leaga mea e maua!"*

Fele was taken aback by the vitriol. Stunned by Lesina's curse, she whimpered. *"Tinā, o le'o o a'u na fasia lou tama! E fai lata ia fanau fa'amolemole!"* I didn't hit your child! I, too, have children!

"Ana o oe se tinā lelei, na tatau nae taofia le palagi pua'aelo le la ae leai! Ua tutusa uma outou ma fiatagata!" Lesina sneered angrily. "You mark my words—you will know great sorrows! And they will hit so close to your homes—you and that monster!"

Lesina dropped back into the crowds, returning to the girls. This woman dared claim she was a good mother and had her children but failed utterly to protect another's.

It was time to go home to their hills. It may be time to book that passage home. The idea wearied Lesina. Those presented problems. She wasn't ready to subject the girls to the separation that would come with Pele's nuptials.

She ran to join the girls. "Get on the horses! We're going home! Whatever we can't carry, leave it behind." Lesina lifted Pele's face to see the black and purple shiner. Vowing under her breath, "Oh, my love, I'll see this to its end, don't you worry." She hurried the girls forward, with Kiele and Iolana holding their reins, leading them away from the market. The last she wanted to see were manservants from the palagi.

Anders' was at the corner of Market Street, at the opposite end of the corridor. A Danish immigrant and his family ran the hub for the powered elite of Apia. Men assembled in corners in leather chairs as they talked of the war in Europe, the local politics, the changing of the guard to the Kiwis, and their profitable business ventures.

"Man, come here!" Commander Campbell bellowed from one side of the tables. "Come here and tell these folks that they are fools."

A boisterous Midwestern American, Anthony Campbell, was a man who was used to being obeyed on demand. His attaché was this young Samoan who would go far if he stuck with the Americans. Or so *he* has been told.

That bellicose coarseness belied a man passed over for captaincy, cut off permanently for vice-admiralty. Twice. At this point in his career, he would rather be in Southeast Asia with its exotic women, but no! He mused unapologetically about the downturn in his career. He is out here in this tiny backwater holdout for zealots and whores.

It's a pity we Americans didn't land before all these hypocritical English missionaries or their predecessors. What beauty these isles would have been! Coconut trade and the prime opium passage.

The Admiralty's executive officer, CAPT Adam Willis, sent them over on official business a week ago. An adventure to which he promptly added the frequent detours to the infamous gentlemen's club, Anders'. Several times over, he admitted to his men unremorsefully. These negotiations on the waterways and marine rights with the newly assigned New Zealand agents of the English monarchs haven't been fruitful, but he could not return without a formal agreement. *Assholes.*

The commander lit a cigar while the others looked on with barely veiled disdain over his coarse American manners or his overt lack of them. The committee included the local Consul, the former German select officer on demotion, the incoming New Zealand consulate general, and several businesspeople, including Ronan McAllister. Commander Campbell personally chose his *tulāfale* for the Americans, with three other young, robust men of the *Fitafita* as bodyguards and crew aboard the American *SS Wilson*. He didn't need more than an attaché to take on these pretentious Kiwis. Four years after they were appointed as agents of the Queen, they were cycling out their current officers.

"This is Mr. Taisamasama Spafford, the Navy's best weapon, son of Tutuila. Spafford, meet Massey's men from Wellington." Campbell pulled on his Cuban cigar and blew out smoke rings into the faces of his fellow negotiators. "And some of these local businessmen." Campbell had no patience—bringing commerce persons to a political meeting was not how Americans conducted their state business and policies, especially these social climbers.

Tall, distinguished, and in his double-breasted suit, the debonair Sama reached over the table to shake hands with the English agents. Not one stood up or shook his hand. Sent to Stanford by the Americans, and this is what he gets? In *his* backyard?

The former German governor and his consulate general shuffled slowly to their feet and reached over, conciliatory and resigned. Sama shook their hands with respect but briefly. If there was anything time among the palagis has taught him, it is about the value of language and nuanced speech.

Sama dropped the books with their maps heavily on the tabletop. The Americans drew out zones with the proposed demarcation line between the Samoas. He pointed and marked the map with the exact points by their coordinates. The German gentleman looked over the boundaries and appeared unbothered by what the Americans proposed. They pointed this out to New Zealand's representatives. Sama continued his presentation on the American position in Tutuila and its seven islands under their side of the Protectorate.

As Sama closed the meeting with the agreement, he handed the pen to Campbell to seal the Navy's communiqué on behalf of the Executive Officers, including Willis, waiting back in the Governor's Mansion. He stood to the side as this happened.

Once the meeting ended, Commander Campbell stood up and thanked the New Zealand party and their company men. He offered them drinks to conclude their deal. The party decided they had family matters to tend to this Saturday afternoon. They got up promptly, shook Campbell's hand, and left. They did not acknowledge Sama, who stood off to the side of Campbell, as the former being his senior officer; this was the way of the protocol of the Navy Admiralty.

The Germans chose to stay and drink with their American peer. They were on the tail end of their time in Samoa, so why not enjoy it? At best, they were not leaving as deportees four years after Brit's handmaidens moved in lock, stock, and sheep.

"The enemies of my enemies are my friends," Campbell called the barman, Anders' son, Pierre. "Sama, sit down. You've earned some refreshments, young man. You did exceptionally well in rebel English. I'm sure that was a burr in their wannabe-English claw." Campbell guffawed.

Despite his conduct flaws and flagrantly surly attitude toward the Admiralty and Navy, Sama liked Campbell and his brusque, burly manner. Beneath all this was a tried-and-true Navy man. He had had enough and was ready to retire to a farm in Nebraska. Sama knew that Campbell's days were numbered once they were back in Pago Pago.

He took the absinthe, hurriedly swallowed, and let it burn its way down his throat. Sama choked and gasped as the liquid fire hit his stomach liner. Campbell clapped on his back as a mother would a colicky baby. The younger man apologized for his novice experience with spirits.

Campbell heartily proclaimed, "You have a lifetime ahead of you, Spafford. Good liquor should be something that you invest in once you have some earnings to speak of." Campbell knew that Sama was receiving a mere pittance against his palagi colleagues. It couldn't be helped as he was about to be fired; however, politely, the Navy liked to call it retirement when openly asked. Nonconformists have no place among the rank and file. In time, the boy will make a name for himself. Campbell was sure of this, with or without the Navy's endorsements.

They drank another round, and with their Germans counters, they toasted to the absent Kiwis, who made their excuses of home and hearth and departed. Hysterical laughter ensued as they re-enacted the Kiwis' indignation at the idea that they were told of staunch American policies by a local boy. A local Samoan *boy*.

Sama looked over toward the bar area and saw a very familiar face. He laughed at the sight before him and politely excused himself. Campbell waved him off while he got his local gossip with the Germans. He strolled over before reaching the two men who were having their beer sitting atop bar highs. He laughed merrily.

"Well, if it isn't Erich Hansell!" Sama announced himself as he pulled Erich into a half hug. Erich was so surprised by his friend's appearance that he broke out of Sama's hold. They had not seen each other since the end of their long years at Marist St. Joseph's.

Seeing that it was Sama, he tossed his head back and laughed merrily. Sama seemed much taller than he, self-assured and the handsome American man about town with his formal suit.

The years disappeared as they laughed and hugged one another. Erich hurriedly introduced his friend, Jackson Lachlan McAllister.

"Lachlan is fine." As he extended his hand warmly. Sama grasped it and shook it enthusiastically. "You're with the Navy entourage?" Lachlan had seen his father sit in the corner with the other distinguished gentlemen but had not seen Sama with them when he and Erich walked in earlier.

"I take it that was your father, Mr. McAllister?" Sama asked airily, stifling a cough.

Erich choked back a laugh. Indeed, Old Man McAllister was many men in one sitting.

"For better or worse, that is my sire, Mr. Ronan McAllister." Lachlan laughed without rancor. "Unfortunately, I am not the golden son by any stretch of the imagination." He, too, sat back as Sama listened merrily in on Erich's update on the family.

"How did you end up with a very American name like Jackson, Lachlan?" Sama asked, curious about the correlation.

"My mother's attending was a very American Navy doctor." Lachlan laughed. "When they were stationed here, Mum decided to go into labor. Dad didn't have much of a choice at that moment."

Erich looked at the far corner where the older men were still arms-deep in politics. Time passed over these older sentries, and they didn't even know it. The Americans were better aligned with the Germans than they will ever be with the incoming Kiwis. That much he knew—he wished Geneva understood the difference between Europe and Samoa. He prayed they would recognize that the same children as immigrants are not their parents of the Old Country.

"How's your mother these days?" Sama asked Erich soberly. Mrs. Isla Hansell wasn't often seen when he visited when he and Erich were at school at Marist. For his part, Mr. Gerhardt Hansell was busy downtown being the consulate general's press secretary. The younger kids were left to their own devices, supervised, and cared for by local nannies. Erich was both parents in lieu of when he was home.

"Oh, you know she fancies herself as one of Queen Victoria's long-lost granddaughters and that we are her subjects rather than children," Erich shared, a little sadly. "She has lucid moments now and then but no significant improvement. Father thought maybe we needed to take her home to Munich, that she needed home, but they lasted about a year. Father can't tolerate those harsh German winters anymore." He called over to the waiter.

He would never call Germany his home as he, with his siblings, were Samoan-born and raised here in these balmy climes. He'll have to find a Samoan wife if forced to go home by the Kiwis.

"Se'i toe sau le matou mea inu ia, fa'amolemole lava!" Erich said to the barman. *"E totogi le kamaloa lea sau mai Tutuila matou pili."*

Sama looked outraged at his friend's gumption before laughing and handing over his emptied glass. "The Admiralty doesn't pay me enough to marry, but I will foot this round," he agreed as the barman looked at him for confirmation. The men removed their jackets and settled into the settees as the drinks were served.

At the door, a shadow fell over its opening. Lachlan saw his cousin Maifea standing there in his Sunday best. He wore a clean white shirt and a formal men's *lavalava* with pockets. Lachlan waved him over as Maifea tried to bring him to the entrance.

All stood up to greet Maifea as he walked over. He looked concerned but cordial as he glanced curiously over the other men. *"Sau! masalo ke masagi le au Malisi ia."* Introductions were made before they all sat back down.

"Oi! se fa'amolemole a! Toe sau ma seisi mea inu mo si tamaloa lea mai le tua!" Sama called out. *"Lea ua taunu'u mai le tamā matua o Tuamasaga!"* Uproarious hilarity broke out among the fast friends.

"Matuā tele ana tala. For someone from America's footstool!" Maifea teased. He took his glass of whiskey and held it up. The others had a few or maybe more before he came upon them. *"Ia manuia!* Let's toast to friendships, old and new! Ourselves, our fathers, our countries, and the palagis trying to rule us!"

Conversations wove in and out effortlessly among the young men as the afternoon wore on and the sun canted.

"I came to tell you, Lachlan, that I heard about some trouble at the market this morning."

"Oh? Of what?" Lachlan moved his glass out of the way and dropped his feet off the ottoman.

Maifea looked around at the others. "The girls were involved." Lachlan looked at him blankly.

Erich said, his brow furrowed. *"Ga tupu se fa'alavelave?"*

"Fai mai na pa le misa anataeao le makeki." Maifea looked a little uncomfortable. "Among women."

Sama and Erich looked nonplussed. Why would this fuss among women be relevant to them?

"Your mother was spat on." Maifea looked at Lachlan, who became flushed with anger.

"Why? And by whom?" He angrily asked Maifea. How and why did this happen? Of course, his father was here kowtowing to the delegate when he should have been with his mother.

"They said Lesina." Maifea was uncomfortable.

"As in the woman with her three wards on the ship?" Lachlan was incredulous. Why did the one who appeared so reasonable and calm during their voyage home do that to his mother? Of course, she didn't know it was his mother. But why be so spiteful?

"Wait—whom are you talking about?" Sama interjected. "You guys were coming from where?"

Maifea tossed his whiskey back. "We were in Honolulu and came in last June on the *Williamson.* We had other passengers with us."

"And you said you know of this Lesina and three girls?" Sama questioned further. "Was one of them named Pele?" Sama was confident that this was the ship the Navy had turned away, among others, since last year. This was his aunt and sister with two others he did not know.

"Why, yes, Pele was one of the girls. We dropped them off at the Immaculata before we went home. Lesina is a healer and midwife to the villagers and parish," Maifea offered, wondering why this mattered to Sama. At least, that is the rumor he heard this morning. They hadn't heard anything about them since leaving them at the convent with the *Pere* and Mother Superior.

"Oh my God! My father told me they were here, but I didn't come to see myself as I've just gotten home from California."

"Who are they to you, Sama?" Maifea asked, almost afraid to know. "Do you know them?"

"Lesina is my aunt, and Pele, my sister," Sama said, now really concerned. He looked over at the flushed Lachlan. "Look, before you judge my aunt harshly, we must find out what happened out there."

Erich was now caught in the middle of Sama, his oldest friend, and Lachlan, his family. One thing was clear—they all needed to keep cool heads until they found out what happened among the women for Lesina to have spat at Fele.

Commander Campbell bellowed, "Boy! Come here!" It was already six o'clock in the evening. "It's time we leave." Sama got up and shook the other's hands. He held his hand out to Lachlan, who wasn't as interested as before. Sama dropped his hand to his side curtly. He grabbed his jacket from the back of the settee.

Maifea was mortified and apologetic, "Let's get together tomorrow and find Lesina and the girls." He, too, wanted to know how and why this transpired in the middle of the day at the market.

Sama agreed that he'd meet them at the Immaculata's doorsteps the following morning before he took his leave of the others. He thanked Maifea for the news of his aunt and sister, even if it was not all good.

The following day was overcast and humid. Maifea and Lachlan spoke with the parish *pere* when Erich rode up with Sama. The other men, too, were on horseback. To combat the heat, they were all in lavalavas this morning and cambric shirts.

"They live in the hills now, according to *Pere*," Maifea said as he mounted his horse. Lachlan came around to his ride as sullen as he was yesterday.

"E fai e Isla le fasiga le teinetiti ae fa'asaga mai le ika lena fafine ia a'u," Fele cried. *"Ua leiloga ni kala ua lafo mai!"* Lachlan loathed hearing this. It was not his mother's duty to carry the sin of another, he heatedly thought to himself.

Sama hurried the men on to find the women this morning. He was anxious to see his aunt and sister and move them from here. They didn't belong here. Besides, his parents were expecting them back home. Even if his sister must marry this village idiot back home, surely it would be a kinder fate than living on this godforsaken hill on the graces of the Apia Diocese.

As Maifea rode ahead, he was told that the women were caretakers upon the hill of a small parcel that the See let them tend on a freehold lease on the condition that they would cultivate and care for the land as judiciously as possible. This meant they had to source an income from its bounty and use the farm's profits to promote charitable causes.

Iolana heard the horses before they appeared down below at the head step. She stuck her head out of the banana trees that she was clearing. These were men and were strangers. She ran up to the fale to warn the others of the approaching riders.

"Lesina! Lesina!" She gasped breathlessly. "Men are coming up!"

Lesina hurried around the back of the fale and grabbed one of their machetes. "Kiele, stay behind me with Pele." Lesina came out of the hedges leading to their fale to see who dared come up without permission. Oh, these folks did not know who she was. This was not a thoroughfare.

"Lesina!" Sama called out. Lesina heard him but could not fathom why Sama would be there. *Oh, no! He has come at Fiso's behest!* The riders came up to the last landing before the entrance to their fale.

"Lesina!" Sama closed the distance between them and wrapped his aunt in a bear hug. He kissed her cheeks, forehead, and side of her head. Lesina laughed and cried as if she had not seen him for years! She hugged him back fervently. This child, this remarkable man, too, was hers.

She glanced over his shoulder to the other men waiting on horseback. Maifea, she knew. She closely scrutinized the others.

"This is Erich, my friend from Marist, who came home with me, as you may remember. I gather that Lachlan McAllister and his cousin, Maifea Atafua, were both on the *Williamson* with you." They all dismounted and waited for her to invite them to sit in the fale.

Lesina took note of the men behind Sama. Recognition crept in as she saw who they were. Lachlan, as did Maifea, had shorn his long locks and was now wearing his hair close-cropped to the scalp in line with local men. Maifea's *soga'imiti pe'a* was visible as he sat astride on his horse. As his father's orator, he did not have the choice of grooming here on land with his new cropped cut.

"Ia malo lava outou usu mai," Lesina started. *"Omai!"* She led them toward their fale. Iolana came around and took the machete from Lesina. Whomever they were, they were going to live a while until Mother said otherwise.

The women's home here at Teuila Hill duly impressed the men. The grounds were immaculately kept, with a garden of plants on one side and flowers on the other. Vines were trained onto roughly hewn trellises while the near back of the fale exploded with colors of all sorts.

Pele is here. This was their hill once upon a time with their parents back home. She has re-invented their Olo'ie here.

They followed Lesina through and sat as she motioned.

"Lesina, there is the matter about what happened at the market. That woman was Lachlan's mother." Sama started as they were motioned to sit in the lanai.

"Is this all that you rode up here to see us about? That some feelings were hurt?" Lesina called the girls out. "Do you see that face? Do you think it's right that your sister was beaten, Sama? By your best friends' mothers?" She turned to the others, "Who proclaims themselves mothers and watches the child of another get assaulted? How do you defend the indefensible?"

Sama saw his sister come out from the back of the fale and close the distance between them. He had not seen her in the last eight years. Even as Sama tried to visit her at the Basilica in Hilo, they told him the family could not see novices. He had not asked Lesina why Pele was a novice when their parents were not informed.

Seeing it was Sama, Pele hugged him hard, her whole childhood in his arms. So much time she had passed them that she had to look back up and search for this familiar face, now aged years since she last saw him.

"Where have you been all this time, Sama?" she laughed and affectionately tapped him on his shoulder. "You didn't write or even come for a visit!" She surveyed him up and down and laughed!

He chuckled. "Don't you worry your mind about all that business, Pele! We're here now." He hugged her to him again before scrutinizing her face and bruises. Grimacing, he traced her battered side, "I'm so sorry this happened to you."

Pele looked at the other men. "I am, too." She moved out of Sama's long shadow and arms to look over the other men. She walked toward Erich. "It has been a while, Erich. I hope you've been well." She offered her hand before he took it and hugged her warmly.

This was not the precocious child of those visits to their parents' home. She has grown into a beautiful, unaffected woman. Even at nearly eighteen, she had filled out in all ways, making it hard for him to remember that she was his friend's younger sister. This was not the child he had met years ago.

"We seem to meet at hard times, Pele," he began hesitantly. The apologies he has had to make to staff and acquaintances on his mother's behalf were enormous. "I must apologize to you about my mother. She's not in her right mind these days."

"Please, don't." Pele looked at him solemnly. "Not to me, but to my aunt." She pushed him forward to Lesina. "Aunty wasn't too pleased."

Lesina looked at Erich and sighed. "You are not your parents, Erich. However, I will take your apology for your mother's actions." She looked over at Maifea and Lachlan. "Girls, say *talofa* to our old company."

Kiele came forward and shook hands with the men warmly, as this was Pele's brother and his friend, then with Maifea and Lachlan. She chuckled at the sight of the men's close-cropped haircuts. They were far from their seafaring days months ago on the *Williamson*, with scary beards and longer manes of fearsome warriors.

Maifea laughed at Kiele's curious looks. "We are civilized as well," he offered as he swept a hand in Sama and Erich's direction. "We *can* be." Kiele smiled warmly as she turned from Maifea to his cousin. "Hello again, Lachlan."

Standing offside, Lachlan greeted Kiele politely, cheek to cheek. He didn't have a quarrel with Kiele; she was easy to get along with as their month on the *Williamson*. Kiele bent with the breeze—that gentle, that lovely, and so welcomed.

Pele squeezed Maifea with joy and easiness. He was as happy with her calm friendship. Moreover, Pele has never meant any meanness to him. She asked after his nephews and was genuinely pleased that the boys were thriving.

She moved to stand in front of Lachlan. "Imagine seeing you again under these circumstances." Her arrogance and open disapproval instantly aggravated him as she stared at him from her bruised face. How gorgeous she was, in any case!

She expressed coolness when she meant to roast him over an umu. Here, it was possible, unlike their voyage home. It's about as subtle as getting hit by a sledgehammer or a rock to the forehead thrown by this woman. Pele would hit her mark if she did the deed in a black hole.

Before he could reply, she pressed her lips softly to his cheek, to the other, before she dropped his hand and walked over to stand by Lesina and Sama.

Why even bother? He stared testily at her nerve, then with a hasty retreat before he could react. Maifea did not look at his cousin.

"Now that we are reacquainted," Lesina started, "I apologize to you, Lachlan, for I didn't know it was your mother."

Lachlan thought about it and sighed. "It was rude, Lesina, but I'll accept your apology on her behalf."

Lesina looked him over and let it go. It was the best she would get, given these awkward circumstances. Anger was not going to resolve the matter. Not today, at least. However, a meal would help ease the mood.

Iolana was excited about seeing Lesina signal to bring forth some food. Pele cut down some banana leaves to lay the mats with some food. She went around the landing of the fale and dropped to her knees to lay them out properly between the men on the one side while they were outside smoking cheroots and drinking spirits they came up with and them, her aunt, and sisters. As Iolana handed her food, she placed it across the leaves evenly. Kiele came with the broad leaf of the breadfruit tree to fan over the food and keep the flying bugs from landing.

While Pele was busy with placements, Lachlan couldn't help but watch her. She was fluid with her actions, moving deftly throughout her preparations. She was older now and seemed more resolved than when they arrived in Apia nearly a year ago. They had not crossed paths, as he and Maifea were busy with life back home. There hasn't been a respite as they had to adjust to life with the Kiwis in charge in Apia. Commerce has flowed slower due to the transition between their outgoing German consulate and the incoming second round of the conservative Kiwis. This impacted how his father's import-export business happened in town, directly affecting how he and Maifea spent their time.

He was glad to be home here in Samoa. There was little that Hawaii could offer them in entertainment or liquor they didn't already have here. Instead of cold beds and Hawaii's women of the night, he is here and is close to family. Of course, the occasional run to Apia for the nightlife and some company of women was the offset. Women he didn't have to see in church or sit with when his mother had tea. It was bad enough when he had to sit with their prospecting mothers.

Emily Schumacher offered him a solution to his marriage issue, but something didn't sit right with him about her. His mother was certainly happy about the prospect, as she was proper and the daughter of one of Father's business acquaintances. She liked him well enough with her pleasing personality and pleasant face. Yet, he could look at Emily all day and not feel anything.

Perhaps his marriage was to be that calm. That uneventful. He was confident he would have to find a mistress if forced to live with a creature as ethereal as Emily. Ethereal without emotions. He would be surprised if she were not frigid.

Not as much as he did in the presence of this battered woman before him. Admittedly, he could go from rage to lust in one fell swoop in Pele's company. She didn't know it, and thankfully, neither did her brother.

Pele looked up and caught him staring. She deliberately stared back before she stood up from her hunches and went to the back of their open kitchen. They sat down to partake of the repast as the men were dressed in shirts and lavalavas, which made it easier for them to sit. Lesina and the girls sat from the other side of the leaves and asked Maifea to say grace.

Conversations were easy as the day was long. Iolana and Pele sat on Lesina's left side while Kiele sat on her right to face off Sama and Erich, with Maifea at the center and Lachlan across from Pele on his right. She ate quietly, passing the food over to Iolana. They raised a few livestock, but she was not eating them. They once had names. Lesina knew and told them that this exception was for the company. *Some* people were not worth the sacrifice.

In exchange, Pele took Iolana's fish. La'auli ordered his tautua to bring up some of the day's catch and part of their stables to help barter for services and medicines that Lesina had rendered for the village families and children.

"They, too, had names." Lachlan jeered like a storm cloud out of nowhere that broke into a flood by the fale.

"Do you play tulāfale for them?" Pele queried. "Do you hear them protest for their rights?"

"I may," he said under his breath. The others were busy talking about the new government. Lachlan thought little now than to turn this woman in front of him on his lap.

"And do you feel relieved now that you have done good and honest work for the citizens of the oceans?"

"I do." He casually dragged his taro across the banana leaf, placed a piece of the tender chicken atop, and ate it without shame as Pele looked at him.

She reached over, took the same amount of his octopus, and ate it as though she were famished. Loudly and with bits of food in her mouth. "Goodbye, fe'e," she hesitated as though she was a five-year-old child with her shiner. She pursed her lips, unrepentant and uncaring, at his blank stare.

She continued her conversation with Iolana and Erich without missing a beat with the occasional side glance at Lachlan, who sat with a bit of unwanted mirth upon his sensuous lips. She ignored him throughout the rest of their toana'i.

The young women were relieved to be out of sight as they cleaned up the meal. Tea was served to their guests as they sat against the poles. Leaving Lesina to entertain the men, the girls washed and bathed in the nearby pool. It was good to escape the fale before she took that fight up a notch.

"Or two," Kiele said as she scrubbed Pele's back. Iolana was busy being a fish swimming to and from in front of them.

Pele needn't explain what her difficulty was or why. "Do you find me petty, Kiele?" she asked plaintively. "I'm not sure if I am angry at him or can say yes to whatever he tells me to do at the snap of his fingers." Kiele pulled her sister to her and hugged her through her laughter. She gathered Pele's hair and put it all atop her head.

"Well, is any of this worth the fight?" Kiele laughed at Pele's hurt feeling. Singular and sassy it was.

"I don't know. However, I feel I must correct what Lachlan thinks of me. It's as if he is determined to walk all over me when he comes close enough."

"Does he have a reason?" Kiele was ever the reasonable soul among them. The fair, logical devil's advocate. "Don't play with that man, Pele."

Pele thought about it, and maybe he did, but why does he make it about her? She wasn't anyone to him. She turned around and faced Kiele.

"I don't know. Maybe I annoy him on the spot or something." She snapped her fingers. "This fast, Kiele."

"And is it so unfortunate that he thinks little of you?"

"Maybe it is. A little bit." She squeezed her pointer to her thumb. Kiele dropped under the water, laughing her merriment in noiseless bubbles. She popped to the surface, and her laughter echoed through the little valley. She was dunked under again before Pele left to think about her issues with this man, passing the family fish, Iolana.

Their baths were attended to before the girls quickly slipped into their sarongs and knotted them. They walked on the path, talking about the day's encounters. There were villagers in the Tava'esina valley, whom Lesina and Kiele will look in on tomorrow.

"Think Sama will take you home to your parents?" Kiele was sure that this eventuality would break them from one another.

That, too, has crossed Pele's mind. She wasn't sure what to do anymore as she did not want to leave her home with Lesina and her sisters. She had a bargain for her father, but how could she make him see reason? She owed her parents obedience and love, but too much time had passed. She didn't want to marry someone she didn't know or *love*. How can she not do their bidding without seeming to be a bad daughter? Permanently moving away is too much for her to take on once again if this marriage came true.

The prospect was closing in, and as much as she loved Sama, he represented her parents and everything about their home. She could join the Immaculata as a novice, but that was too great of a choice to combat the return home. She was sure something else was out there for her, but it was not coming to her fast enough.

"Universe, and all that is great and small between us, please show me a way to help without making it the answer to my parents' wishes. Please let me be of use so that I may pay back the kindness of others to us."

Sama decided to stay with his aunt and sister and the girls. He wanted to discuss this issue as his father is pressing the matter. He needed Lesina's reason and mentally searched for an answer good enough to stand up to his father's scrutiny.

The other men took to their horses. They gratefully expressed their appreciation for the meal and the hospitality. The girls walked them down the narrow and winding hill before the turn into the main road on the coastal Tava'esina as it was nearly evening, and the road down was steep. Iolana walked with the lead horse's reins, holding a coconut lamp. Maifea thanked her as they walked the horses down, careful not to spook or hurry them, thus possibly breaking their forelegs.

Kiele took to Erich's horse as he rode in the middle of the pack. Pele watched him from behind and thought of her childhood fixation on him. He was so handsome then, and while he aged into these good looks, she yearned for something that was best left buried. She liked him well enough; perhaps she should let this infatuation be for her sake. Yet, if he wasn't her brother's friend?

"Shall we declare a truce, Pele?" She was closer to Lachlan, who brought up the rear of the pack. He was undoubtedly feeling generous.

Pele hung back, glad for the darkening skies above them. "I didn't know we were playing war." She pressed her hand against his horse's left leg and steadied him down the terraced stone steps. "You are Germany," she added as generously as she could.

"As you wish, useless Allies. Am sure you imagine yourself as some useless resistance fighter."

"Vive la France! Ils ne passeront pas!" She mockingly crowed. She was glad he did not see the crimson flush that crept up her face. As the horse whinnied loudly, she stopped to calm him. They could not afford to scare him into a downhill gallop. At the hairpin corner, she brought him to a standstill before the turn into the side of the hill.

He snickered but knew better and let the moment pass them. There will never be any end to this animosity between them. However, they needn't kill these priceless animals and others. Besides, Pele was helping get him off the hill. Or was she? He didn't know whether she would have if her aunt and others didn't ensure a safe trek.

Lachlan felt a little remorse for this part of their disagreement. "I hope we can start over once again, Pele."

She turned the horse into a slower gait to continue the ride down. As numb as she was, Pele nodded. *All this anger was useless.* She knew he was angry about what happened on the ship, but he never let her forget. He looks at her, and she instantly remembers his disdain and anger that night.

"Someday, when we aren't mortal enemies in combat, Pele Spafford, I will take you to eat in Apia." He meant this.

"You are not my enemy, Mr. McAllister," she replied. "One day, you will understand. Until then, please don't assume you know me well enough."

"I agree," he conceded. Lachlan didn't have any wish to harm her. Or think less of her. Or leave her feeling that he would! He couldn't help but smell the faint but familiar *moso'oi* flowers from her skin.

Pele came around his horse's flank and walked companionably with him. As they went down to the final turn in the road, she offered her hand up to him. "I am sorry for my part in this. May we meet in another lifetime under better circumstances." Before he could respond, she went to bring up her sisters, who were already down by the road.

"Goodbye, Pele," he said more to himself as he watched her back disappear. He didn't merely see her retreat from him. He *felt* it.

Regret, maybe even grief, the further she walked away from him. Yet, he could not close the enormous gap between them now. She was not taking any apologies or a genuine truce between them. That ship had sailed with her on it, and he was standing on the shore wondering what he could have done better. No, he knew he could have done better. She was lost to him. The finality of that realization hit him as the storm out at sea did.

If he were born to his aunt, he would have taken this other road.

With his Navy officer and entourage ready to sail back to Pago Pago a week later, Sama sat down with his aunt and sister. Kiele and Iolana busied themselves so the family could be afforded their privacy. The girls hid nothing from one another. However, Kiele knew this talk and felt the Spaffords needed space to discuss these family matters.

"I must leave in the morning, Lesina. We need to come to an understanding about what to tell my parents."

"Let them know that Pele is well and happy here. I'm her guardian, and she lacks for nothing while we have been here at Teuila Hill," Lesina said resolutely. "I haven't raised her to be merely a wife."

"I don't think that is going to fly with Father," Sama mused pensively. "You can return with me and reason with him together."

"Then tell him to give me a year. What is the difference between Pele's eighteenth birthday and her next? She'd be more mature and ready to take on in-laws, versed with the Fa'aSamoa, and even pop a dozen children," Lesina reasoned with footnotes. "I'll see to it that she has a doctorate in married to the in-law arts."

Sama was between disbelief and laughter. "It isn't that extreme." He looked to Pele for help to counter their aunt's rally. Pele shrugged and laughed.

Lesina scoffed. "Do you ever worry about being a woman in that household, Sama? I think not!"

"That's unfair of you, Lesina. I'm merely the messenger." Sama threw his hands up in the air.

Lesina felt no pity for either of these sons. "You can be a good owl and take that back to your parents."

"You don't want to come home with us?" Sama cajoled with a grin. "The Navy schooner is comfortable, and you don't have to wait for the ferry at the end of the month."

Part of her wanted to take up her nephew's offer, for she yearned for their own space and home without depending on the Apia See's offer. However, the consequences were far more significant than she wanted to bargain for. "No, Sama." With that, the discussion ended. Lesina wouldn't let go of Pele without giving her a fighting chance to be what she could be. Then, after that, she can be a housewife. She needed to hone life skills such as the in-law arts and her kitchen wares, which required time and effort.

Sama pulled a couple out of his shirt pockets and smoked a cheroot, handing one to his aunt. She smoked hers without hesitation. Good tobacco was hard to find during the governmental transition, and tariffs were harsh. The Chinese dealers were not as giving without currency, so she didn't have luxurious gifts such as tobacco come by these days.

That aside, she made a comfortable living that provided everything for her and the girls. Some were humble offerings of food and lavalava, while others were monies predominantly from the west end German quarter that were substantial enough to pay into their rents with the See.

"You know, Erich has grown into quite a handsome young man. I don't know how he came from such polar parents. Do you?" she blew at the ashes at the end of her cheroot.

"Oh, he is that, indeed, Lesina." Sama laughed at how adeptly she changed subjects.

"If this transition weren't so chaotic, I'd talk with the father. Who else but Erich could be good enough for our girl?"

"He isn't the man, Lesina," Sama deadpanned. He was uncomfortable with the idea. Erich was an old friend but not one he would consider for his sister. "Erich has his people, and Pele is not equipped to be part of that circle." The Apia parties were the stuff of rumor mills.

Lesina thought as much but wanted to hear this said out loud for the present company.

Taking Pele to the local half-caste cotillion wasn't something she aspired to do. *"Lelei a nofo Samoa ile Samoa."* It rang hollow, but it was still a good idea. It was best that, as a Samoan, one married a Samoan.

"Aunty, that is not what I said," Sama protested. Yet, he knew she was right. Everything had a place and time here in Samoa, and Apia's social elitist circles were just that. Those folks were not going to change for Pele. Or better her chances to crash those parties. *"A lelei a le nofo Samoa ile Samoa, ia tatou o loa i Pago Pago."*

"No, not right now. If Pele is going to marry, she will go for the right reasons, under the right circumstances."

"She will be eighteen this month, Lesina. Most girls would have gotten their dowry and gone to their marriage homes by now. *Ua leva na tatau na sauni lona leulumoega!*"

Pele was tired of this conversation. She agreed with their aunt that she was hardly marriage-minded or ready, but what disappointment would this be to their parents? Unsure of what anyone could bring to their home, she was not about to build any good alliance with her father by stalling here in Apia. Yet, she would merely disappear into a marriage tethered by obligation and the tautua to in-laws.

Sama sighed, undone by the rationale for Lesina's fight. "I hope you both have a more amenable answer for Father by next April." He would take his diplomatic skills home once they disembarked in Pago Pago. He grimaced at the idea of discussing the same reason with his parents.

"Sama, have you considered marriage? Perhaps the answer to your father's will is your own." The firstborn son here was the fervent advocate for his sister's marriage, groom unseen, but he has yet to volunteer. Even if Eli left the monastery and went home to their parents, Sama would still be the eldest.

He had no answer to this. Moreover, he had no desire to do so when he had career opportunities in the diplomatic corps. He might be back in the States to work for the Admiralty.

"No. My ambitions do not lie at home, Lesina." Sama blanched at the idea of giving up his post. He liked the Admiralty, unlike Campbell, his senior officer. Besides, even if he aspired to run, their parents would find out in a moment as the unofficial telegraph machinery was faster than the electric one in town.

"I'm not speaking to your ambitions, Sama. I'm talking about this idea about a marriage in the family." Lesina flicked the ashes off her cheroot. "Or maybe Fano can take this on for all of you." The idea was dead in the water before she said it, but desperation makes one consider all avenues.

Sama kicked a few rocks around. "No, I don't think Fano wants to return home." Now teaching, Fano was nowhere near home. He was on the polar west end of Tutuila and will probably stay as a transient teacher through his time with the fledging bilingual teaching corps.

Lesina resigned herself to the fact that her keis would probably not return regardless of what their parents had in store for them. Her father would turn in his grave if the land deed passed to her or Pele. Yet, a year could present an answer that they all need.

They all got up from the mats. "Go well with the Navy, Sama." He was so handsome and had grown into his long legs. Pele came around and walked into his embrace.

"Stay hopeful, *tama'i monti*." He tipped her face upward. "Stay close to Aunty, Pele." Sama kissed her forehead. He let her go reluctantly before pulling his aunt into their embrace. He let them out of his arms with regret before he grabbed his hat and walked resolutely down the hill, where a man and horse were waiting for him. Campbell was not leaving him to conspire an absent without leave run in these hills. These hills were denser than those in Tutuila, a mere thirty-one miles from west to east along the coast. In comparison, it was much easier to lose someone here, and most natives did not talk to palagi authorities.

Pele and Lesina watched Sama's downward progress to the main road. It wasn't pretty, but he was getting there, and they laughed and cried as they saw the last of his body.

Lesina mused about the changes in her keis. They've come far for the betterment of the family. With each accomplishment, they are further away from their parents' ambitions. The sons were not going to return home any time soon. Meanwhile, she was hanging onto Pele by the ends of the girl's braid.

The resolution to Fiso's dreams about the estate was precariously in jeopardy. Whether he was aware that his son's ambitions were anything but near home, Lesina was sure he wasn't aware as neither son appeared to have had that talk with him. Now she has a year to move him on Pele's freedom. The idea felt like a boulder just rolled off her shoulders. Imagine what the same for Pele.

As Sama rode back to town and eventually sailed home, Pele felt acutely aware that they were no longer children. She took her aunt's hand and pressed her cheek into it.

"Maybe we should just go home, Lesina," Pele said to her, to no one. "The more we stay out of Father's sight, the harder this becomes on all of us." Kiele and Iolana as well.

Lesina had not heard this from her niece before. "No, don't cave in, Pele. There's so much that you can do, and it can *be* before we go home. Don't let this discourage you."

"Father will disown us once Sama tells him we are staying here." Pele sat down next to Lesina on the landing of their fale.

Lesina sipped her lemonade as she thought about this before shrugging. "Let him." Her brother was a hard man but not unreasonable. Her sister-in-law would protest and probably call her bluff. The battle of the Pacific again, but if these delays saved Pele from the loveless business of marriage to some unknown man, she would fight it without hesitation or doubt.

"We are going to be okay, Pele." She pulled Pele into her arms. "Your brother will survive his run home."

"I worry about what could happen with Kiele and Iolana." If she was packed up and moved, it was unlikely that the in-laws would take her adopted sisters.

"They will stay with me if it comes to the worst-case scenario," Lesina called the girls from behind. She wanted all the girls to hear her out. "I'll not let either of you go anywhere but stay with me even if Pele had to leave us. That is a major IF."

Lesina had no idea what could change in a year. Hold the girls and pray. Pray long and hard that the Good Father will be on their side. In the meantime, putting the girls back in school could solve the issue.

"Lesina, how about if I went to the convent?" Pele asked. She wasn't opposed to the idea. There were obvious benefits to all if she did. Life's quiet was also appealing if she had to be honest with her family. Not that she minded home chaos, but if she chose any life over marriage, the convent was a viable option, her understanding of the pressing issues above and beyond.

Little during their time at Immaculata told her that life would be anything but academic, quiet, and with the children. She loved her lessons from Mother Superior at Immaculata, a kindly older French woman who delighted in her penchant for learning. The girls' help around the rectory and convent was welcomed to help with Sunday Masses and cleaning the humble chapel and the grounds that always needed care.

Pele grew plumerias and white gingers along the fences. Maybe one day, children will flock here to harvest their blooms. The idea warmed her. Children's giggles as they prepared for their *po pese* for their parents would be so wonderful to witness. Moreover, Mother Superior was thankful for the hedges created by the plants.

She missed them. She truly missed them, but she wasn't sure she would give up her life and freedom to base her critical life choices on their ambitions. Maybe becoming a nun would offer a solution. Her parents would let her stay home by letting her come over for holidays or lodge with family on the west coast during Masses between parishes.

Kiele brought her mat over while Iolana carried their sheets and pillows. The girls sandwiched Pele between them, feet and hands locking Pele in this impossible embrace until they rolled in hysterical fits of giggles.

"You are not going anywhere, Pele Spafford. You are grounded to the corner! That's as far as you're going, you heathen," Kiele intoned seriously. The girls rolled in merry convulsions at that nasal voice, so fresh in their minds nearly a year since departure.

"Oh, no! Not Sister Siobhan!" Pele groaned. "She had it in for me." She rolled over and wagged a finger in Kiele's face. "You were her favorite child, Missy."

Kiele wiggled, "Yes, I was! I hadn't a reason to rebel. Someone had to be good, for the woman was key to the kitchen."

Iolana giggled so hard. "Yes, those buns, Kiele."

Pele stared up at the intricate pattern of their roof. "You know, all this bother, for little me." She turned to her side and stared at Kiele, pulling Iolana's hand over her hip so the younger, too, was on her side. "It would free my aunt to move on with her ambitions."

"I'm sure she doesn't even think that way, Pele," Kiele answered with a knot in her throat. "Lesina would never let you go without reason. I mean, all these years, to give in now?" Iolana snuggled closer to Pele, adding her agreement.

The girls hugged and slept fitfully, limbs and legs over one another. It was always their way out of crises. Life has to offer them a reprieve from all this.

"Father, I can make this choice myself. Why does any of this have to be so complicated?"

"You cannot sit at home without a husband or not have children. You should go back to your aunt if that's your goal. At least you'd be serving the Lord, unlike your aunt, whose fortunes will always be contingent on people and their whims."

"She does honest work, Father. She helps people, many of whom palagi doctors would not even see in their clinics and the hospital. She has delivered a generation of babies!"

"One day, these doctors will take over, and your aunt will be out of work. I want you to have a home and children. Olo'ie is for your brothers, and you know this."

Pele rolled her in her sleep from one side to the other, warm to the touch and troubled. She awoke, startled and a little angry. In the inky dark, her sisters were still here next to her. She heard Lesina read aloud in the flickering kerosene lamp. Pele scooted to the edge of the lanai with little chance of falling asleep. She gazed up to the starry heavens. *Please, Lord!*

The blooms were teeming over Teuila's hillside the following week. Pele spent her waking hours pondering on her late-night talks with her brother while digging holes up and down the fences. Bees and other residents of the hill gravitated toward the blooms, which she allowed as there were enough to go around. Enough to be food, ornamental for home grounds, and used in oils that she experiments with, some for Lesina, while many were tested on her sisters. The more she felt bonded to plans that other people planned for her, the more she dug and planted, grafted, shifted, pruned, slashed, and burned her way through the hillside. Iolana watched her sister and knew it was best to leave her alone and work on her green harvests.

As the sun's glow canted, the digging slowly halted. With a shrug, Pele reknotted her bun on top of her hair. A gentle breeze blew through the hill. Facing it held on, she could see miles of the ocean beyond the outskirts of Tava'esina below them. Denizens of the village flittered to and from their business and errands of the day. All the while, she reeked of earth and sweat, sweet and lovely.

Pele lay beneath her red gingers and watched the clouds pass her between sleeves of leaves. On her side, she stared at home between the spaces of the long green stalks. All the things she wanted to accomplish on her Olo'ie fluttered in her eyes in a dream-like state.

"You cannot sit at home without a husband or not have children." No one has died of being a spinster, Father. Lesina not only remained unmarried but was of more help to the community than some of these upstanding folks among the chieftain.

IV. September 1918

O Fisaga o Suiga
The Winds of Change

The usual cacophonous hawking at the market came early as Lesina and the girls walked through, bartering and haggling for produce that balmy September morning. Iolana came in as they found a friendly boy happy to watch their horses. She was glad to hang back and see the other stable persons from the German quarter but delighted to go into the market with her sisters.

Kiele and Lesina walked ahead, looking for medicinal plants, primarily for analgesics, to help with their midwifery work. Pele wandered behind Iolana, looking for hot food vendors. They found them at the far corner of the market and were cheered by the choices of fresh, hot cross buns and bread. Lesina gave them a shilling to pay for the family treats. It was so rare that they would find the bakers in time, but the girls were so contented to have something for their Sunday morning tea when they did.

The baker was an older German gentleman who was quite happy waiting for the girls to look over his loaves of bread. Married to his Samoan wife for the past twenty years, he was spared deportation as the Kiwis transitioned into power at Mulinu'u four years earlier. Friendly locals were few and far apart as much of German Samoa was systematically dismantled and intentionally erased from the face of Apia. Twenty-five families have been deported since the takeover four years ago.

"How can I help, girls?" he asked as he readied a paper bag. The girls giggled; their eyes widened happily at the selection this morning. Herr Johann loved these girls as they came in with such joy.

"There is so much to choose from, Herr Johann." Pele finally chose a sourdough loaf, two brots, and four hot cross buns. It was enough to keep them dunking in their Sunday teas. She turned and handed Iolana her hot cross bun. Her younger sister was appreciative and ate it with relish! Pele laughed at the cheerfulness emanating from Iolana, who so deserved the treat.

"Girls, wait." Herr Johann went through his wares as the girls began to walk away to find Lesina and Kiele. He handed Pele a quarter block of butter and a jar of papaya jam. "Please, go ahead. Let your aunt know that we send our regards." Lesina had delivered their first grandchild almost a year before, and they remain thankful even now.

They thanked him sincerely, with so much gratitude for his kindness. The appearance of butter was rarer these days, and reserves were rationed for others more fortunate than them.

As they passed through the market, a group of other young ladies came through to Herr Johann, Emily Schumacher among them. She and her entourage of three young ladies were followed by men, who walked by leisurely between parasols. As Iolana passed them, one bumped against her shoulder on purpose. The offender flinched out loud and stared at Iolana as if a dirty foreigner had accosted her.

"Oh, look, a darkie." The group looked over at the offender. Iolana surveyed her way out as Pele was already ahead of the throes of bodies. The bullies were in their white dresses and fancy slippers. She did not want to get into a fight with these young women.

"What, cat caught your tongue?" Milicent Riley continued to prod at Iolana. "Do you understand English?" The American teased meanly. The others snickered spitefully as they lowered their parasols.

Iolana felt trapped, and the familiar claustrophobia crept up her throat. *Never pick a fight in the town streets,* Lesina reminded them of their rules of engagement while at the market as they departed Teuila Hill.

"She can more than understand you." Pele demurred. "You're not worth her time." When she couldn't see Iolana behind her, Pele retraced her steps through the crowd.

She stretched nonchalantly to her full height next to her sister, towering even the repugnant crowd before her, among them the American consulate's daughter. She broke through the semi-circle and took Iolana's hand to move out of the area with her.

"And you are?" Emily came to the fore from behind her entourage to see who this was. Who dared speak to them as though they were commoners?

"Never mind who *I* am—who *we* are. Please do not address my sister unless you have something to say to both of us." Pele moved Iolana to her side and smiled apologetically at Herr Johann for the unnecessary spectacle unfolding in front of his kiosk. Pele sneered at them. "Here in Samoa, and act like you are our betters! Go back to your black holes!"

"Pele." A man strode out from the back of the gathering crowd. "It's good to see you both." He looked on to see if the others were with Pele and Iolana.

Pele breathed a little easier hearing that friendly, familiar voice. *Talofa, Maifea! O ou palagi toi ia?*"

Maifea threw his head back and laughed in merriment at Pele's utter disgust. "*Leai, tuafafine! O tagata a Lachlan.*" Maifea broke up the simmering hostility between the entourage and introduced the girls to the others. "This is Emily Schumacher, Lachlan's betrothed," he said as he pointed out the young lady at the group's center.

Pele surveyed her up and down at the tart who spoke to her. She had nothing more to say to her or her bloody friends but turned to Maifea. "Wish him my best. *Manuia outou!*" Pele tucked Iolana's hand tightly into the crook of her arm and walked away from the group after acknowledging only Maifea's presence.

"My regards to Lesina and Kiele, Pele!" He got a backhanded wave back. That girl wasn't giving an inch.

Lachlan came out of a neighboring stall, seeing his group milling around Herr Johann's. He saw Maifea waving back at someone but didn't know to whom that was. Emily seemed flushed while Milicent simpered angrily.

"What's going on, Maifea?" he asked casually, unsure if anything was.

Maifea guffawed. "Pele was here getting Iolana." From the looks of Emily and the girls, it appeared that it wasn't a convivial meeting. Not that he was surprised one bit. Emily did not take to being spoken to by locals. She could barely tolerate Maifea, but he didn't care, and Lachlan didn't make his cousin a choice.

"Oh, where are they?" Lachlan was curious as it had been months since they were on the hillside to see them. That last meeting did not give them room for an invite back.

"About there." Maifea pointed out the girls who were hurrying away from them. Her hair was tied up, browner in the sunlight these days. That girl could wear burlap and still be all woman with her curves as she moved expertly through the crowd mid-morning.

"Who is she, Lachlan? I see you're both familiar with her," Emily unhappily asked if the pertinent monster even knew Lachlan.

"No one you need to worry about." Lachlan grabbed a cheroot from Maifea. Pele wasn't a discussion he wanted to speak of to Emily, especially when they were due to marry in November. The men left Emily and her friends to haggle over bread. They headed off to Anders for some drinks.

"How was she?" He swirled his whiskey after they settled in a corner away from others waiting on their womenfolk as they went through the weekend market day.

Maifea looked over at Lachlan. "You better stop." He knew what his cousin was asking.

"I could be asking about the younger sister." He sipped his whiskey. He looked over at Maifea. "I take it that it was not a happy collision."

"No, and you are not asking about Iolana, either." Maifea deadpanned. "You better get your mind on this wedding with three months to go, Lachlan."

Lachlan took a soda cracker from Maifea, who was not drinking. He chose to call for tea and the soda crackers over as they had not had enough time to stop for breakfast earlier. Whatever he felt about the Kiwis, tea traditions continued unabated in the isle.

Maifea handed Lachlan a plate of franks and eggs, who declined it. She was in the market, and he had to find a way to see her, even if only to say hello.

Maifea looked at him, unconvinced of his cousin's intentions. "Leave her alone. She didn't seem surprised that you are betrothed to Emily."

"How did that subject come about?" Lachlan came off the heels of his chair.

"How was I supposed to introduce Emily to Pele? Your 'friend'?" Maifea asked incredulously. "Look, Lachlan, we have your wedding; that is all. My aunt will not hear that I helped you do something foolish."

"No." Lachlan felt as though a noose was tightening around his neck. He got up from the table and threw a couple of bills.

He ran out of Anders before Maifea could react. He had to find her, apologize, and maybe even start over. He couldn't go on with the wedding without making peace with this woman. She angered him and drove him insane with emotions that he was ready to tuck into a dark place, but she made him *feel* these things.

He has spent months thinking about their last meeting and how he could have done better, but the time to make amends was lost. Lesina didn't extend the invitation. Maifea has been busy with so many *fa'alavelaves*, the cyclic rotations of births, baptisms, birthdays, chieftain inaugurations, church dedications—and so on.

Until today.

He ran back to the backside of the market. The girls were not here by themselves. Lesina had to have been out looking for homeopathic plants. Those dealers were closer to the Chinese side of the market. He went through the market uncaring about who saw him or what they thought of him. If he did not see Pele today, he would never do so again.

Pele felt the hair rise on her forearms. Her heartbeat pounded harder in her ears. She handed her satchel to Iolana to carry for a minute. They were standing up against a corner near Lesina and Kiele, both busy as they haggled for the prices of these valued medicinal plants.

She went through the back side of the stalls, hurriedly looking for space and distance from people as she felt so wretched. As she half-ran to a suitable spot, she turned and slammed against a man. She reeled from the impact and stepped back on her heels to see who, what, who she collided with! Arms reached out to steady her from him.

Pele looked up and stared unbelievingly. "Lachlan." She pushed herself back to her feet, her eyes teary. "The next meeting with you will kill me for sure."

Lachlan held the torpedo out from him and stared at her as she rubbed her bruised nose. He stared at her as if seeing her before him was too much.

"Pele," he breathed. He grabbed and hugged her as she felt the bridge of her offended nose. This woman. He pulled her out of his arms. Lachlan stared at her as if meeting her for the first time. Not that their first meeting was the stuff of envy. His show of affection took her aback.

Pele stared back at him as if she had known him all her life. At times, it certainly felt that way. "Is something going on?" she smoothed down her smock over her lavalava. "You look lost."

"Pele, I wanted to apologize. For all of it. The ship. Here. Whenever we met, there was never an opportunity to really talk to you. Now, so much time has passed, and I wanted you to know I'm sorry."

"Yes. It's been rough, but I agree. I, too, am sorry that we haven't gotten along." Pele held out her hand to him. She chuckled as she noted his dry look. She fiddled with her lavalava, refolding its long lines along her left side as her arm fell back to her side. "So, I heard that you're getting married." She mustered all the cheer she could find in her soul, but even this felicitation sounded empty.

Deflated, he affirmed her statement. "Yes, and I heard from Maifea that you have met."

Months of teas and talks between families, the discussion about homes. His father wasn't vocal but wasn't openly set against the nuptials. After all, the possibility of a family merger was advantageous and even prosperous if the tides were right with the Kiwi administration in town.

"Sort of. It wasn't the best meeting with such folk, you know." She shrugged. "I'm not sure what you could have in common, but neither here nor there." Her stomach wailed out its protest. "It was nice seeing you again without the horrors." She meant it and laughed.

He knew she meant it but wasn't happy that she did. "If I could have redone this, I would, Pele." Suppose luck was on their side—if better circumstances existed. Suppose he could get out of this. There were so many ifs that his head spun from the number of things that had gone so wrong.

"Please don't worry too much. It seems so ironic that we are here in the hills to get out of my betrothed to someone I don't even know, yet here you are marrying your own," she said matter-of-factly. "Who knows, we can all be best friends and meet for bridge?" Her eyes widened innocently as she batted her eyes.

"We're quite the pair." He cupped her face. "I'm sorry that a better life isn't on our side, Pele." He kissed her forehead, her eyes, and her nose. Then he tipped her chin before kissing her lips softly, persuasive and arduous. Inquisitive, she kissed him back, offering him comfort and assistance. He tasted like sweet tea left out in the sun. She giggled into his kiss before he broke it, curiously staring at her.

"Sorry, sorry!" She started laughter burbling up from the well-spring of something warm and good. There was something so good about being here now. Admittedly, there was this burgeoning sense of sadness, but that could not be helped. In all these months, she wanted to make amends and move forward. Maybe as friends to start.

He stared at her openly, smiled, and threw his head back at her cheek. Giggles wasn't precisely what he inspired when he kissed women.

She stepped back and smiled. "I do regret that we don't have the luxury of being friends, Lachlan. Yet, know I wish you so much happiness and love. Perhaps, between us, we will find something worth writing to one another about."

Lachlan appreciated her optimism. Yet, as a married man, he could not see her, write her, nor have this conversation in passing with so many eyes and lips around them. The noose was closing around his neck, and he didn't know how to escape this predicament. His parents were set on settling this alliance with Emily's father. What could be more advantageous than their two families uniting over the children's union? In a year or so, they could be graced with grandchildren who would be their foothold legacy in Samoa.

"Don't look so grim, Lachlan," Pele averred. This is the way things happen around here in Samoa. There could be no other way when families were determined to merge. She thought of her inevitable union waiting for her once she was home.

"It doesn't have to be, but we are both stuck with these familial responsibilities," Lachlan reluctantly agreed. Pele wasn't as grim or pessimistic about their fates. *Don't be so daft, old boy! Say your goodbyes and let her go.*

He felt his heart in his ears as this was probably the last time he would see her.

"Maybe in another living, we'll meet up again. We're friends now and shall remain so." Pele thought of their children or grandchildren finding one another in years to come. Perhaps they will have a kinder fate, and those children with gentler parents who would allow for better, who'd allow them the chance to marry for love.

Lachlan lamented, "I'd like to think that was possible, too, Pele. I wish I had come to you sooner."

"Why? Our chances made us arrogant and unbending." Pele turned to him with regret. "I wish this weren't us." She touched his cheek with the back of her hand. "You should get going before they miss you."

Lachlan pulled her to him. She put a hand against his mouth, almost jokingly. "Please, we are friends. Not lovers." She pulled out of his arms and walked away from him. Lachlan sighed and knew this moment of freedom was over.

The farther she walked from him, the more regret ate at her conscience. Her family was looking at her expectantly, motioning her to join them over the far corner of the market. Pele felt her feet anchored to the earth and was unable to move. Her heart was in her ears, coarse and raspy, threading painfully.

She ran back to him, passing people, feeling the immense loss of her life unravel! Now! Or she would lose this chance to fate, too. *Please, let him be there. Why do I feel this is his funeral?*

He was still standing where she had left him with his back to her. She grabbed him by the arm and kissed him chastely on his lips with all the burgeoning ardor in her. What she had so little experience in practice, she made up for with enthusiasm! He kissed her back fiercely, and her thin lips felt bruised when he finally let her go.

She stepped back to look up at him, a little hoarse. "Goodbye, Mr. McAllister." Her melancholy leaked out of the corners of her eyes. She shifted her smock and left.

Pele felt like her world was caving in, but she need not burden him with her sadness. A minute ago, she was so ready to let him go. All was well with her soul, even with Lachlan's wedding in the coming months. Now, her every step away from him felt keenly like death and the funeral march of a loved one.

"Tita, are you okay? You look like you've lost the world and all of us as a whole."

"Turning over leaves, I suppose, Kiele." Pele blinked. She didn't know what to feel other than this abysmal sadness, and for once, she felt so very alone.

They walked about town with airs of superiority and little to offer other than to be a blight on the local communities. They landed with their ostentatious lifestyles and sensibilities to impose on locals. That monster, Emily, was—no, *is*—Lachlan's betrothed. They stuck to their circles, and unfortunately, Lachlan was part of them.

The afternoon wore on unabated. Lachlan lamented the loss of every step he took toward his future without Pele. He walked to Anders with little but misery dragging on his feet.

Maifea was finishing his tea when he glanced up and saw his cousin walk back into Anders. "Found her?" he asked, even though he knew the answer.

"Yes." Lachlan sat down in his seat unhappily. He swirled his whiskey, sipping it like a drowning man.

"You went from disliking her immensely to wanting to see her like some desperado. What has changed, man?" Maifea raised a brow as he looked his cousin over.

"I wish I had been more honest about Pele than I've been," Lachlan admitted. "I let opportunities fall off to the wayside, and here we are." He had no idea how he would have sold the prospect of courting Pele to his mother. However, he was sure he would have done it well in time.

Maifea wasn't sure about that. "You know that Pele's family is from Tutuila, and I don't think your parents are sold on the idea that they are tied to the Americans or that her aunt is the *taulasea*." And that they are here temporarily, Maifea mused to himself. As a bonus to Lachlan's dance card, her brother was not impressed with him after their last encounter.

With the advent of Western medicine, the call for the local healer was exclusively a native calling. It wasn't that she was a healer. No, it was a problem for the McAllisters and their circle of friends to associate with the *help*.

"Does any of that matter, Maifea?" Lachlan called for a round. Maifea motioned for a glass and the whole bottle.

"Not to you, but it matters a lot to *them*," Maifea droned, much the devil himself. "You know your mother is keen on Emily, man. Voila! You're marrying in a few short months."

"I know this." Lachlan felt it. Knowing this and accepting it as a fact were two different ideals.

"Right now isn't the time to get cold feet. Besides, I'm your best man. The first line of my duties? Get you to your wedding day. *Sa le avaga li'i, sole!*"

He liked Pele, but his aunt would blame him for any issues if Lachlan rescinded his agreement for the wedding, *as if* her son did not have free will or a mind, nor was he old enough to have both. However, the shame that an elopement would bring to the family if her son didn't show up for the nuptials would be met with fury, lifelong damnation, and wagging tongues among the village gossipmongers. He loved his cousin but didn't want to be in his slippers. This marriage was not one of Maifea's grander ideas of what they should get into regarding their shared future.

Maifea felt a headache come on as the idea continued to plague him. The prospect of being beheaded and his testicles in a vice-grip, execution ordered by his aunt, was not one of his ambitions. As much as he loved Lachlan, Maifea would rather avoid his aunt for the rest of his life.

How do you marry one woman but love another? How does one go through life in a fixed marriage that is barely tolerable?

"Easy," Maifea answered out loud. "Let family dictate what and who you are. Think about the meaning of your existence as you grow old, grumpy, and unfulfilled *after* your wedding." Further, children needn't be born of love. They merely need to be delivered. Every landed family required heirs and workers. Their own was not without the want of progenies to carry forward legacies and prestigious surnames.

As the men near thirty, the cousins sat with minds in whiskeys in their grips, neither wanting to rewind the present problem. The more they did, the tighter the noose knotted around the groom's neck.

With Lachlan's fate fixed as it was, Maifea wasn't without his mother asking about *his* prospects. Mother may speak her peace, but he stayed away when she was especially keen and persistent. The parade of pastors' daughters was not beyond her ambitions.

Misery is relative and knotted like sails in a storm, churned waves of regret, grief, and unhappiness, equal gale-force winds blowing at them.

Fele busied herself with gathering massive fine mats and setting them aside for the VIPs from Emily's families due into Apia toward the end of October. News had arrived that her husband's New Zealand relatives were expected in the last week of October.

"O a ea ou mea o fai?" Her older sister, Sala, walked in through the opened front door without announcing herself. *Or ask permission to come in,* Fele thought to herself. However, her older sister was here either to advise or criticize her preparations.

"Fai i keige e aumai se ki, Suga." For someone who was always hurrying to get to town to shop, it sounded like she would sit a while—much to Fele's chagrin.

Fele sat with her at the cedar table she was so proud of, a gift from New Zealand when she and Ronan married nearly thirty years before. The clatter of her fine China was another point she knew wasn't lost on Sala. House girls who served that tea?

"I thought Maifea was here with Lachlan." Sala dunked her buttered cracker into the black-sweetened tea. Fele was also proud of the fact that she could afford such luxuries. Fifteen miles by horseback was long, and the men were not due back in another three hours.

"No, they went into town on business for Ronan." She asked the serving girls to fetch the fine mats for review.

"*Oi!* Then maybe my grandsons did not see things." Sala dragged her cracker out before the butter dripped into her tea. "They told me they thought they saw their uncle kiss a Samoan girl." At the market, of all places, those arched brows said plainly.

"What girl?" Fele felt deceived, and her anger began to simmer. How does news of Lachlan's impropriety travel nearly twenty miles this fast? "How can they be certain?" Her son was virile man, and she wasn't naïve.

Sala finished her crackers, dusted crumbs off onto Fele's floor, and stood up. "How many Lachlans do we have in Samoa?"

She continued sarcastically. "I'll see you in several hours."

Fele felt betrayed. If Tala'i and Mataio happened to see them, who has not? And why now? Has her son lost his mind? Did he want to sow his oats? Fine! But he needs to wed Emily Schumacher and not some local strumpet! No!

"You came over and now leave? After telling me this of my son?" Fele was miffed at how low-browed her sister could be.

"That's all you need to know," Sala said dismissively. *"O oe ā ma lou tama! O mea e toe selesele lava le tagata ia, a ea?"* Oh, the sow and reap scripture! Which is so rich coming from this woman.

"Oute ofo lou le alofa, Sala! Ia fa'afefea ma ou iloaina ni tala ia Maifea fa'apea outou alu atu ta'u atu ia 'oe? Ua matutua uma tamaiti ae lea fai lenei taua!"

Sala looked at her sister and could not remember when they last had a moment to speak honestly between them. It was a pity that their parents bargained for better things by looking for alliances with the palagis in town. Sala declined the first suitor, who raped her, and then brought her back to her parents on the back of a conveyance used to move pigs, with a complaint that she was frigid and would not be suitable to bear children. The enormity of the shame of this rejection by the palagi to their parents was immense. There was no talk about the rape. They didn't want that funny business to become fodder for the village.

Then Ronan came in a year later, groveled around town, and ingratiated himself with the farmers' import-export business. A course man, she was not about to accept his proposal when he plowed his way through the village. He wanted a cut into their parents' estate. The land was prosperous and fertile. She warned her parents that this was the cost of any marriage to Ronan.

Fele accepted instead. She didn't care about Sala's advice not to cave into this union. Many years later, with their parents gone, Sala did not let Fele forget what was lost from the village because of this marriage. "Stop blaming Ronan and me for what was agreed upon by our father, Sala."

"The land was not ours to give away, but all that money romanced so many elders," Sala lectured. *"Ia fai le mea sa'o ma mea tatau ma fa'afo'i le lauele'ele o tuaā i le alālafaga. E le nonofo mau ni palagi a'o ole sa'o lea mo tatou fanau ma latou fanau."* Do what is right and return the bargained land parcel to the village. Foreigners will come and go, but they will never settle. They will keep taking from us.

Fele refused to rehash this conversation with her sister whenever they were together, today being the least of them. She wanted her here as it was important for all to see them bond over Lachlan's wedding. Furthermore, she wanted Manuma to be their master of ceremonies as he was a unifier. No one bothered to acknowledge her husband; she has long given up trying to sell him to Punae'e. It was enough that children were loved. It was one thing they both agreed on—that they would never bring their differences to the kids.

"Lelei o la koso ou gafa i o ma o, Fele," Sala said diplomatically. She loved her nephew as much as she did Maifea but felt that if only his mother stopped forcing the issue, Lachlan would find him a proper, practical local girl, not some Kiwi strumpet. *But who am I to talk on this issue?*

V. November 1918

O 'Oli O Ti'otala
The Cries of the Kingfisher

The persistent wailing first came on a humid November dawn. The village below them was alight with burning torches as mourners gathered at La'auli's guest house. Rumors ran fast through the town and their neighbors in Tava'esina of their pastor and wife's deaths. No one knew how they came to their tragic deaths so suddenly, save for the travel they were on that late October week through Apia town as they headed west for a wedding the Pastor had officiated. Even more horrifying, they were told there would be no burial here in the village.

"Oh, what is becoming of us? Our Lord has forsaken us and taken our dear pastor and wife from us?"

"Why has this terrible malaise come to us?"

"Where are those palagis and their powers? Why couldn't they have warned us properly?"

"What god would let this happen to us?" The village mayor could not be found. They heard that he was on a mission to ferret news of this gruesome illness from the German and Kiwi doctors in town.

Women hurried to and from as they found mats and lavalavas as they were told that the road would leave the bodies of their pastor and his wife for the dreadful 'collection'.

"Aue! Le leaga ma le matuiā o nei tulaga ua fa'afesaga'i ma tatou tagata!"
Oh, the indignity that our loved ones are subjected to!

"Go and get Lesina!" La'auli said to a young *taulele'a*. *"Sili le a'ami le taulasea auā le kaikai na omai ni foma'i palagi ia tatou ma tatou aiga."* As he said this, the looks of horror on the faces before him turned from disbelief to anger to more weeping among the prostrate women.

The untitled man left as soon as he was told. He moved through the village to the dirt road up the hill. Yells and screams came from the east of the town. Two husbands were found dead by their wives. Young men ran to those houses to collect these men as lesser matai instructed them.

As the day passed its midpoint, they would find another villager who died after complaining of a headache. She bled from her nose heedlessly and could not stop shivering. When she did, an hour later, she died in her mother's arms without seeing her newly wedded husband, who was away with the village mayor on this truth-seeking mission.

Lesina heard of the troubles of town and the unexplained, rising death tows that began a week before. She was sure that the Spanish Flu was here now, and its news via the papers was not disseminated to villages.

The pandemonium of this morning in the town was telling. Pago Pago had closed all shipping lanes and inbound traffic. That was a sign that the government had erred on the wrong side. Now, the choice to go home was not even an option.

"Kiele, get the bag ready. We will have to tend to the sick!" Lesina looked up toward the blue skies; no cloud could be seen for miles. And yet, the wailing from the village did not stop. Kiele did as she was bidden, adding some sterile gauze pads Lesina acquired from the hospital. She also prepared the oils and the roots.

The arrival of a kingfisher did not help. It landed on the branch of the *fekau* and looked down at the mortals with a piercing blue stare. Pele saw it and keenly remembered the unkindness of its forbearer. She leaped from the lanai of their fale and ran, grabbing a small rock to throw at it as she did. It wasn't her intent to kill but to send it away. It wouldn't be moved even as the rock struck between its feet. She stopped at the bottom of the stalwart tree and knew then that something horrible had come to stay.

In the blazing sun, Iolana harvested the *lega* and *fiu* from Pele's garden and laid the turmeric and ginger roots on the mat. These were to serve reserves to their supply already in their powder forms. The ginger was pared in half as some were to be dried, while the turmeric would be pressed into its powder form. She also harvested lemongrass and red *ti* leaves. Placing those with the turmeric and ginger roots, Iolana followed their rock fence to the citrus trees, where she plucked orange leaves, oranges, and limes. Mentally tracking her supplies, Iolana knew they were dangerously low on coconut oil.

A shadow stood over her as she cupped her hands to capture a drink of water. Pele dropped the water to turn swiftly to the uninvited. A young man stood by her only to step back from Pele's defensive stance.

"Fa'amolemole a—na ou sau e a'ami le taulasea," he mumbled, his speech rushed and breathless. He stepped back to let Pele stand up to her full height. She stared at him and knew why he had come up for her aunt. He was disheveled and stood there picking at a leaf in his hand. He reminded Pele of young Mataio.

"O Lesina lae lugā le fale. Muamua atu." She motioned him forward as he was this far, and now it was only fair that he had permission to go up to their house. The kingfisher continued to sit on its perch, watching the exchange beneath. It did not move.

Lesina, with the young *taulele'a*, walked through the village, silent and observant. Women wailed as they gathered through the guest houses. Some were familiar to her in her care rounds through these last months. They were young, middle-aged, and older, and they were coming toward her, openly grieving.

Mats were gathered earlier and were ready for use. The flexible sleeping mats were set aside. The weeping continued without a break.

Kiele followed on Lesina's right side while Iolana and Pele brought up the rear of this entourage, taking their time. The young man introduced them to his mother and three sisters who were with the gathering of women. They exchanged greetings of the day before they walked through the crowd.

Lesina stopped. She looked for one of the senior wives and asked her to come forward. *"Fa'amolemole a, Tinā! Fai i uso ia e fa'avalavala!"* *Stand apart if they are to gather as such.* The crowd parted as she asked of them.

Lesina turned back to the road to the paramount chief's guest house. The villagers had laid out the middle-aged pastor and his wife here, respectfully minding their former spiritual leaders among them. Among the crowd was their *tulāfale,* La'auli.

Seeing no one around, she stepped to the front and carefully checked the bodies' rigidity. Dry blood stained the formerly young face of the wife.

Otherwise, they looked well and could have been just living hours before. *They were*, she told herself.

"Where were they when they came in?" Lesina sat beside La'auli, pouring and handing him his *moegalo* tea, which he drank more often than the imported teas from Fiji. Drinking steeped lemongrass in his family went way back before the missionaries arrived.

"From a wedding out west. They went for a week and came home yesterday. One of the church ladies found them this morning," the older matai told her. "We were told that we cannot have funerals for them. How can this be? Why do we roll them in mats and throw them onto the road like trash? How can we not mourn our own, Lesina?"

"A lea fai mai le tala ole fa'ama'i e faigofie lava na pipisi mai le gasegase i tagata o lo'o tausia o latou." Lesina reached over to grasp his veiny hand. His skin was transparent, as were his eyes, which were cast with a translucent sheen that came with his age at sixty-eight. "They broke the news worldwide, and here, the government has not come to the villages to tell you."

The talking chief held his silver fox handsome face in his callused hands. "Oh, what have we done, my daughter? Why have we been naïve and stupid enough to believe these foreigners were our friends? They came with their god, proclaiming theirs was more merciful than ours. And yet, they hide their deceit and hate by treating us like ignorant children!"

Old La'auli was an ally and always keen on looking after Lesina and the girls, sending foodstuffs and *umu* on Sunday from his hearth at Tava'esina. He believed in Lesina and her ministrations for his aches and pains over the year, and he had known she was a true healer among them. He did not force them to live in the village or mandate that they come for events. That non-inclusion was Lesina's actual cost for her care of him.

She sent the girls down to Tava'esina for various reasons. Kiele to gather medicinal herbs Pele had not grown or found impossible to keep alive in the hills. On her own accord, Pele went out to seek the master gardeners and sit through her *A'oga Samoa* with La'auli while Iolana went along in case there was a need to bring up stores. Needed, she made friends with some of the younger girls. They did not lack company, but being among those who cared for them gave them the familiarity with the village as they should.

He sadly shook his head as the wailing started over from another guest house. "You know, two men from the middle of the village also died this morning." Lesina nodded.

"If you don't mind, La'auli, I'll visit the families. I need you to secure these four guest houses. Please do not let anyone leave," he acquiesced and called for his young group of men who would serve as sentries for as long as needed.

From the early morning to the following week, Lesina, with Kiele, Pele, and Iolana, went through about thirty-eight of the fifty fales of the village populace, hurriedly calling out family members from their oldest to their youngest. All four of them wrapped lavalavas around their faces.

Quickly, Kiele triaged each in Lesina's shadow. Pele followed by taking the census of households. Throughout, Iolana held crying children as Kiele screened their parents.

The triages were moving along as Kiele moved as efficiently as she could before nightfall. They were learning more than some were willing to impart, while others were staunchly noncommunicative about their whereabouts, resentful and angry. Others were suspicious of Lesina and her skills. She was a healer but was not one of the foreign doctors trained at fancy schools and, frankly, knew more than Lesina. Before now, they didn't need her to look after them.

"Why aren't they here to tend to you and your families?" Kiele asked about the doubting Thomases. "Do you think you are *that* important to them?"

"How do you know? You aren't one of us!" One rotund wife spat at the girls. She was aiming for Kiele. "Maybe the delay is because of you, *Saiga elo!*" The 'stinky Chinese' slur hit and rolled right off her back.

"I am more you than you are of the palagis." Kiele turned to the woman who shouted this insult at her. *"Fa'apea outou o a'u le Hawaii na outou le fa'alogo mai laia?"* The crowd's venom because she was a foreigner was understandable but misplaced. She was not the enemy.

"Well done, Kiele!" Pele laughed out loud. She was so proud of her sister! Over time and during her extensive rounds with Lesina, Kiele has learned a lot, and Pele is grateful. "Well done, love!" With this rapidly boiling crowd, one had to be firm and clear in their intentions. Kiele was much kinder than Pele would ever be, even though *she* is Samoan.

Assured the girls would be all right, Pele moved through the fales, noting her census in her notebook. Looking through the corners of her present fale, she came face-to-face with the soul she had searched for at the market when they arrived in town.

Grandmotherly, she sat next to a pillar of the house with her fly-away gray hair tied up in a tiny bun. Her former golden-brown tresses were now threaded with silver, but she was proud of her crown. Her high, regal cheekbones with smooth skin untouched by disease or circumstances. Bent at the waist, her posture had dangerously curved over her eighty years. She looked at Pele and smiled a beatific, kind-hearted welcome.

"Ae tū mai la ae ua le sau totonu!" she chortled. "Come! Come inside, my child. No one is here to bring you tea, but sit with me."

"Ua fia fai sou kī?" she asked, ready to help. *"O fea lou aiga ua le omai e fesosoani?"* Pele looked beyond her toward the earth kitchen to see if anyone else was out and about. Only a couple of dogs, as sad as their dowager owner, sat faithfully in the back on watch.

"Ia lo'u tama lenā na tupu ai le fa'alavelave le Aso Gafua. Ua alu atu ai ia ma si ona to'alua ua toe fo'i i gagafō i lona aiga. Ua na'o a'u lava matou fale," she lamented. Her daughter-in-law has left since her son's death, one of the two men the wives found the week before. Her eyes watered over, and her sadness leaked out at the corners of her eyes.

Pele readjusted her lavalava as she ventured to the dirt and ash kitchen. A pot was on the makeshift table. She found water and lit the kerosene oven. She went to the back of the kitchen shack and quickly found the lemongrass bunch.

"Aua! Masalo koekiki sau seisi e fai se ka kī!" the dowager aunt cried.

Pele would not hear of any such talk. She was not one to state the obvious to this sweet soul, but her daughter-in-law was not coming back. There were no signs of any clothing in the old cupboard in the corner. Much of anything of any use to family was gone. She was surprised that the kerosene oven was still there.

Pele brought in the tea on a tin platter that had seen better days. To better its conditions, she had placed a cut banana leaf on it, which helped improve the appearance of the ionized tin cups that had also lost their luster and paint.

They sat convivially and talked stories. As her stories were told, Pele was more drawn to her than ever. Something about this old soul mattered so much to her.

"How remiss of me! I never asked you about your name," Pele said ruefully. *"Ua malie ka fagogo ae nei lava oute leiloa lou suafa."*

Her eyes twinkled with laughter. *"O lo'u suafa o Epenesa."* Pele sat back and was comforted by the knowledge that even her name presented. Now, it would be easier to find her should Pele lose her in the shuffles of people.

Presently, Pele had to find a way to care for her. Without family in the village, she needed to move up the hill with them. The loss of the pastor's wife was also a loss to the village's women's care organization. Some have left as Epenesa's daughter-in-law did with her children, while others did not come out of their homes. Pele could not in good conscience leave her behind even if her home was intact. Others have been ransacked or left behind, with animals milling about looking for their humans.

Kiele and Iolana were two fales on from Pele. They were busy with the triage of the last remaining families. She was told that an access road up in the hills would connect with their fale on its twenty-five-mile dirt road, which joined the north to the south and would probably be safest. However, it will take longer to get to the fork and several hours from the village's plantation to their home.

Finding young men to help was beginning to be a task that the girls found more arduous. Many have fled to families in the south to distance themselves from Apia.

Pele finally found La'auli, who was still home. A year ago, he was also the most coveted senior builder, the *tufuga,* and was often consulted in all matters of buildings all over Samoa. To keep Lesina and her wards safe and housed, he built their home open to the elements but practical and fitting for the hillside.

Now, he rallied some of the young men in his family to go with Pele to help move Epenesa. Many of his contemporaries have been left behind by fleeing families. If the girls were willing to help, he would offer them as many men as possible to move some of the elders to higher grounds.

Three showed up, two older than La'auli, while the other was barely out of his teens. They looked worse for wear but hopeful in their willingness to help. Pele sighed, a little disappointed, but their present company will have to do. They, too, were prepared to move south.

"La'auli, please come with us," Pele asked of the orator as they settled Epenesa and readied her for the move. "No one is here to care for you." She pointed out the obvious to her dear teacher.

He laughed as he sat on the corner of the *paepae* of his family's guest house. Unlike other homes, this was on a higher foundation of layered coral and river rocks.

"Pele, please do not be discouraged! I cannot leave our village when there are still families here. Some cannot move with young children while others have both elderly parents with them, less mobile than Epe."

The paramount chief has not returned for the fortnight since his departure. The circumstances of his delay were unknown, but it was not hard to infer what had happened. As the highest-ranking orator, he was the leader now.

A knot crept into her throat. They will find a way, but first, they must get those already gathered at the wagon to safety. Most, if not all, of them, and this move must include La'auli. Instead, he showed her the plantation horses with several mares and foals in the village.

"Please take the strongest of these animals to help you move these folks," he said firmly. "They have families waiting for them as well. I am no less important than they."

Pele called for the men to hitch the wagon as it was already noon. If they left now, they would retain light before the five-mile mark where they needed to stop for their own home. Iolana and Kiele came up to Epenesa's fale to help prepare her for the trip. They gathered as many mats as possible to serve as cushions as the wagon baseboards were not made to carry humans but copra to Apia.

As they loaded Epenesa on board, a crowd started to move closer. Epe was some eighty years into this village's history, and she was leaving for the first time since she and her husband retired from their pastorship twenty years before. She bore her late husband a son, who, at fifty-two, died on Monday. Their daughter died on the morning of her wedding day some twenty years earlier. Her husband lived without a soul. His death followed years later, but his dear soul died with their beloved daughter.

One woman hurriedly ran up to Kiele. This was the same one who called Kiele out the week before. Her former bravado has turned into desperate contrition. She carried a toddler and a baby.

"Please take my children. My husband is ill, and they cannot remain here," she cried as she pushed forth four children, from ten to infant—three young girls with their infant brother. The eldest held onto her brother as their mother handed him over, wrapped in the best lavalava that her mother could find.

Kiele reached out to the eldest girl and took the baby from her. *"Leai se mea o iai."* She had the girl load her younger sisters and had them sit around Epe before she handed the baby over.

"I worked for the Hansells in town and thought they would come out for us," she admitted, mortified. "Tell them that these are Elisapeta Lesoso's children," she said, shamed and humbled all at once.

Kiele took pity on her and waved her on, assuring as one woman to another that the children would be cared for as best as they could find once they were in the south. Younger at eighteen, Kiele wasn't without compassion for this former maid who was barely older than she and Pele.

Lesina refused to let them work in town for a good reason. Kiele now understood Lesina's counsel.

Pele walked out of the corral that La'auli had shown her. He hurried her along as the sun moved faster than they could have hoped.

She implored him once more to leave with them. This trip began with one move, but as she spied the wagon, Kiele and Iolana had problems saying no to those who had rushed out of their fales.

Iolana added the widow of the second man who died with Epenesa's son. She was the second wife, as his older children were the same age as she, barely thirty, with a five-year-old daughter and an infant son. Her stepchildren were not coming for their half-siblings even as news of their father's death had already reached them, three villages over. She clambered toward the other side of Epenesa with her children and helped keep the others together.

Pele looked back at La'auli, trying to convince him that little was left to chance. The flu was here in Tava'esina, and it was unlikely they would get the palagi doctors to come out to care for the sick.

"You know very well, Pele, I cannot." The paramount chief left three weeks ago to greet family arriving from New Zealand. "I'm sure he has met his fate in Apia. That leaves me in charge here at home, Pele. *A'o ou alu la, o ai o lea fai ma tamā matua?"* If he left, who would be the senior father here?

He held Pele in his embrace for a moment longer. *"Alu ma ia fai mea tatau mo nai tagata ia. Ave nai fafine ma latou fanau! Loto tele, ua e loa?"*

With her heart plummeting, she went over everything Lesina had told her to relay to the villagers. She hugged him once more before she let him go.

"Wait for us! I will come back with help!" She reminded him as she started to run toward the departing party.

Please, Lord, keep them in Your care! I know I ask for many favors, but please let this be one that You hear.

The clearance of the village had begun in earnest. Watching the flurry among the villagers, Pele felt the heaviness of responsibility on her shoulders. The wagon was filled with the young and the elderly while persons not sick walked behind, carrying whatever they could to help them in their temporary homes. The sadness among the worried faces was palpable. Without delay, they had to leave to make the best of the daylight. Dogs and cats followed their humans at the end of the trek.

As the infant began to cry, Pele asked his mother if she could carry him, for she was walking behind them. The wagon would be too rough of a ride. If he cried all the way, no one would have any peace, for two bawling babies would be hard on already frayed nerves. She grabbed one lavalava from Iolana and had her help tie the baby to her back.

"How long will this be, Pele?" asked someone walking from behind. "Are we going to take rest stops?" Some were hanging back. The climb along the hairpin corner was challenging for every footfall on the ascension. It was not suitable for the wagon, the elders, the young, or the ailing, who were among the group women and children with these few older men.

Pele adjusted the baby so that his head was covered from the sun. "Please be patient. Either we walk this through, keep going, or go back together." Both options scared her, but of the two, there was no way they could turn the wagon back down to the village.

Kiele dropped down to walk through the twenty-five folk who chose to come with them. Some children carried mats; others had baskets with food and produce across a pole. Mothers held onto several younger children. She went through the crowd and cheered them up from the rear.

Pele walked forward in front so that when she spotted the clearing, they could see the village below and the miles beyond to the ocean from their perch on the mountain. From below, on the *paepae* of the guest house, La'auli waved them on as he saw the wagon turn onto the access road.

La'auli was this tiny little figure out there on the malae. She cupped her hands and called out as loud as she could. *"Fatali atu!"* They had to find men and get back here. In her estimation, there was no way she was about to abandon this man.

"Ia taunu'u manuia outou malaga," La'auli whispered to himself as he hoped and prayed that the girls would safely get through the road trials. They would be on the south coast in three days if they pushed hard during daylight hours. *"Tofa soifua outou!"* He turned to Tava'esina with his arms clasped behind his back.

They ascended further into the mountain, slowly trekking around these sharp corners. Pele led in front of the wagon while Iolana pushed it forward from the left. The road was well-used until about a year before when all copra shipments went through Apia.

Two hours later, they were about five miles past the village. At the rate they were walking—*crawling,* Pele was not so sure they would make it south in less than four days. As Teuila Hill came into view, she called all to rest.

She encouraged those who needed water and food to take what they could out of their supplies. Lesina will probably return to kill her, but this trip requires sustenance as the children always want something to eat. She wasn't sure what the road held in the way of crop foods and fruit they could pick, but absolute assurance of food would do them right.

With help from some of the men, they unloaded Epenesa. Once off the wagon, Kiele helped Epenesa relieve herself before moving toward their watering hole. The road was rough and dirty, and there was no way that Pele could leave her here at home without seeing her through a bath and a meal.

It soon became evident that it was best that they stayed here for the night and started anew in the morning at dawn. The horses were let out of their reins and brushed down by Iolana and one of the men. Once done, they were corralled into the top side of the garden, where they hurriedly feasted on mangoes and guavas hanging off the trees.

Kiele went through the crowd as they sat in little groups, families of three or four or unrelated men who sat toward the upper end of the property talking among themselves. There were about eleven in addition to Epenesa here with them. She asked most how they felt, checking their temperatures and reassuring them as she triaged the children. As she did, she spoke in hush tones to their mothers about their options before the morning pullout to continue southward.

The budding nurse encouraged the mothers to bathe or wipe their children down when she was done with the group. She pointed out the pool with the creek for baths to them. To help others, Iolana went into their cedar chest to find lavalavas for most of them. Some could be cut at least in quarters of three yards each.

As it was cooler up here at night, Pele called the men in closer. These were the same souls that came to La'auli when she asked him for help. They were so thankful for the break that they were happy to help. She asked for a bonfire in the umu pit and the kerosene lamps to be lit. Kiele was pleased to share some of the new lavalavas and soap with them so they could have their baths in the quiet of the darkening evening.

"What's tea for this many people, right, Iolana?" Pele laughed. She was exhausted, but they had to make evening tea, and hopefully, this would help keep the children full until tomorrow. She reached over and hugged her younger sister tight and long. Iolana rarely asked about decisions they made now that Lesina was not present among them. Pele rarely let her go without knowing how much she was loved.

Iolana got their fire going while Pele measured out flour, the little Fijian sugar, baking powder, and oil, all of which she did not know how to replace before Lesina came home from the rectory. These were luxuries gifted to her and were not to be used until they had special occasions like their first set of actual holidays. However, she had mouths to feed, and that would have to be a worry she thought of after they were done with the road in, hopefully before the following Sunday.

Following Pele's lead, Iolana harvested the lemongrass from behind their homestead and wrapped them in manageable bundles. Once the water boiled, she dropped the bundles into it and watched it become the tea of choice. It took both over an hour to present tea. One of the younger children said grace before all were given tea and pancakes, which were devoured with delight.

All gathered between spaces of the *pous,* the supporting beams of the faletalimalo. A young teen girl and her mother volunteered to lay out mats. Epenesa was already on Lesina's side of the fale, on the sleeping mat with Lesina's ali. The wooden neck rest was preferred over western pillows by the elders. There, she slept peacefully as low voices of merriment and comforting gratitude were paid to the girls.

Gathering the few able-bodied persons, she went over the map from La'auli, which was fifteen years old from the heydays of copra farming. She honestly disclosed her lack of experience with the task at hand, but if they were comfortable with the idea, Pele and the girls would continue the road and learn with them. Because time was of the essence, the children had to stay and wait until they returned with help from the south out of Musumusu. The mothers agreed that they would remain behind with their children and help look after Epenesa.

With the flickering coconut lamp, Pele spread the map shared by La'auli. While it was patinaed by time, she asked the men if this road was still accessible with the resources they had at hand. One former copra farmer noted it would be a long and hard slog, but they would make it without the entire party.

The road formerly belonged to the German plantation owners, inherited by the New Zealand government in 1914, since the beginning of the Great War. It had withstood the pounding of wagons when the farmers went south to catch the American buyers and their steamers. Without maintenance in the past four years, they were uncertain of its viability or if it was still clear of undergrowth. No one had heard anything from the government about rallying points, so Pele felt this was enough of a sign to push forward. None of the families have heard from relatives, leaving them in a vacuum.

"We can leave everyone here, and Iolana will supervise the food rations. There is enough for about a week, giving all a good chance of surviving. Kiele and I will go on this reconnaissance mission with some women who are not mothers." That gave them a week to make something happen. They would get the party and move everyone if all was well in the south end. Pele didn't want to think of any other possible case scenario, but in the dark, she had to come to a viable alternative if the south failed to be the avenue out to safety and medical help.

The men thought about this before they agreed and declared this was the best plan they had at hand. Making this arduous journey without news or knowledge of what was happening in the south would be foolhardy, especially with children here.

As the plan was finalized and the women informed, they agreed. The three who were not mothers would go with them. Instead of taking the wagon, they would take the horses and alternately ride them. The party will take turns and rotate the horses out.

Pele moved through the sleeping souls, soft breaths from the children while she stifled laughter at the rhythmic snores of a couple of five-year-olds. The baby she carried earlier on the ascent was tucked under his mother's arms while she slept with her head in her hand. It was cool enough that some needed their sheets re-tucked under them. The slumber of innocents. She prayed for better situations for them. One day, they'd see more of the world beyond homes and shores when they grew up. Moreover, she asked for space for them to grow up without fear of a pandemic hitting them again.

She moved around them to find the reason for the movement. Lifting the sheet that covered Lesina's space, she found Epenesa facing away from her, sitting up with her head bowed, quietly praying. Pele sat down behind her in the same manner and closed her eyes.

Lord, I don't know what I am doing, but I will lean on You and the others to help steer these folks in the right direction. Please look after all of us and grant me the strength to make the right decisions. You are most merciful and will deliver us from this tragedy. Please help us help ourselves, Good Father.

I humbly ask these things of You, Father. PS. Please do not bring Lesina home just yet. I can have the house back in order soon, but not too soon. Thank you!

Lesina was adamant that they kept their spaces and home clean and orderly. Pele sighed as to what she would say had her aunt come home this evening. She looked around at the sleeping party; she wanted to cry and laugh at her aunt's expression. They have never had so many left shoes at the lanai.

Soft, barely discernible weeping broke the quiet of the night. Before her, Epenesa's frail shoulders shook as she cried over her bible cradled in her lap. Pele scooted closer and sat behind the gentle soul. Reaching out, she touched Epenesa on the shoulder, offering her strength, companionship, and solace.

Epenesa turned to Pele, softly whispering her love and gratitude. In the flickering light from the coconut lamp, her smile was gentle as she took Pele's hand into her own.

"You know I am old and useless to you and your cause, Pele. You should have left me behind." Her voice quivered as she whispered this to her. "You should have left me with La'auli. We are old and have lived rich lives already. You have these young people to worry about. Save them and go!"

"How can you say this to me, Tinā? You are welcome here, which is why these folks followed. They didn't come because they trusted *me*. They came because you are with us." Pele grabbed one of Lesina's lavalavas and wrapped it around the ali to soften the wooden headrest for the grand dame. "Please do not worry yourself. I'll go back down and get La'auli to come up with us when we get back."

Willfully tying him to a horse if he protested, Pele added more to herself than to Epenesa. *"Aua le popole fua oe! Lea ua e taunu'u mai ma le manuia."*

"Tatalo tatou Ali'i ia mou atu lenei fa'ama'i matuiā!" Epenesa answered fervently. "I prayed earlier that He stands and watches over you, my child."

Pele tearily held her friend's veined, freckled hands that had nursed a daughter born unto her and died as she was to marry in her arms—and raised a son who was faithful in his care for her in the absence of his father. This woman has journeyed all over Samoa with her traveling preacher husband and helped raise a nation-state of children who have moved on to be people who mattered. In her winter, she doesn't have a soul to look after her.

As they sat together companionably, Pele felt her soul knew Epenesa upon first sight. Finding this gentle soul again, she could only imagine God sent her to help her through this crisis.

Whatever comes, they will be watched after and cared for, Pele promised Epenesa and the Good Lord.

A whisper came through the blinds. Kiele woke, confused and exhausted from the day. Pele was on the other side of Iolana as they had always slept.

"Can you please wake Pele?" the man asked urgently.

"Is something wrong, sir?" Kiele asked through the coconut blinds. It was still early. "Can it wait until later?" It was not yet four as their rooster hadn't crowed.

There was some shuffling of feet outside. "No, please get Pele now." He was not going away any time soon.

Kiele turned from the blind. She loathed doing this, but she reached over and tapped Pele, who woke with a start and got up right away as she popped upright.

"We have to go, Kiele." She pulled on her muslin smock in her wakeful sleep. She threw her portion of their sheets over Iolana, who was still fast asleep. A throbbing headache popped behind her left eye. It couldn't be helped.

"Pele! Wake up, Tita!" Kiele knew her sister wasn't fully awake in her rush to dress. "There is someone out there who wants to talk to you!"

"I am! Please get ready! We must go, I know." Pele rolled over onto her knees, looking for her slippers in the dark. Find her shoes, and all will be well with the world. Kiele got dressed as well as she needed to steady Pele.

As they hurried to the side of the fale, a man from their party was waiting for them.

"Ua li'i, So'o?" Pele asked, yawning. This unabated exhaustion was going to get the best of her. She was still dreaming, seeing the Big Dipper behind her eyelids. They had to leave for the South this morning.

"Pele, there are boys out yonder that I need to bring you to. Please wrap your heads." So'o was one of La'auli's lesser matai, but here, in the senior's absence, he has taken the lead for others.

Kiele and Pele quickly pulled their lavalavas over their heads before the older man out from their home toward the road down the steppe. There, one of the younger men stood with dried coconut fronds as he stood as sentry to the fale.

Pele saw the flickering smokey light in the otherwise dark morning and hurried forward. "What is going on here?" The sentry turned toward her and stood aside to show her. "They are looking for Lesina, Pele." One of the two was in severe distress.

She ripped her lavalava scarf from her mouth. *"O Lesina lae o le taulaga."* With the light of the crackling coconut fronds, she looked closer. Upon seeing the faces before her, she gasped and cried out. "Tala'i! Mataio!"

"Pele! Oh, I'm so glad to see you! We came to get Lesina!" Tala'i, usually the reticent and quieter of the two brothers, blurted. His voice cracked before he could continue. "Oh, Pele, we need to find Lesina! No doctors will come out to us!"

Mataio rushed forward and fell to Pele's feet, sobbing uncontrollably. "Our parents are gone! Our grandmother, aunts, our cousins! All gone, Pele!" The sinking realization of what Mataio was telling her took a minute to register. Then it hit her as though the blunt force of a hurricane had slammed into her all over again. Mataio grabbed Pele around her hips and wailed into the muslin of her smock.

"What are you telling me, Mataio? *Tala'i, ua? E sa'o le tala lea a le tama?"* Pele cried out. "What do you mean that your parents are *dead*?"

"They got sick a week ago, and we didn't know why! We thought they ate something bad, but it wasn't!"

Mataio found them behind their partition, staring blankly at the ceiling. Near them in the lanai, their grandmother, Sala, who was lying next to Lachlan's mother, and their grand aunt, who was also found dead. They had all just been served a meal when they laid down that evening. Fele came from town feeling under the weather but had been over to see their grandmother plan Lachlan's wedding and to see the fine mats.

Kiele stepped forward. "Where are Maifea and Lachlan?" she asked, her voice thick with tears.

Tala'i cried out, "They're down by the main road. Maifea is sick!" Kiele ran to the house to get the medicine satchel they stored while Lesina had taken another for the Immaculata when she answered a call from Pere and Mother Superior. The rectory and its caretakers had all become ill a week ago. She had not sent word about her return home.

Pele gently unhooked Mataio's arms from her hips. "Tala'i, watch your brother." Tala'i knelt to take his weeping brother from Pele. She turned to the sentry and So'o, "Please come with us!"

Even as the early dawn's golden light spread across the horizon, Pele knew every step and cornerstone down to the main road. With her heart in her ears and throat, she had to reach Maifea and Lachlan.

At the bottom of the hill, Pele found Maifea leaning against the rock that marked the road up. While he was gasping for air, he acknowledged her briefly before he asked for water, his breath labored through hard wheezes. He was hot to the touch.

Kiele and the men arrived soon after Pele. Kiele triaged Maifea and knew that he was gravely ill. They had to get him up to the house quickly. She flew a flurry of commands to the men and wrapped a wet towel to his head. As the commotion came to a crescendo, Pele did not see Lachlan. Maifea was now in Kiele's hands, but she had to find Lachlan.

She looked around the horses, and there wasn't a sign of him. Then she ran down the trail and found Lachlan had toppled over the steep corner. He was hanging on to a tree root that jutted out of the earth.

"Lachlan!" she cried out. "Lachlan!" She swiftly took her lavalava, knotted it at the end, and threw that end to him. This left her with little more than a yard to use as leverage. She dragged it back up and thought for a minute.

"Pele," he breathed. "It's so good to see you." He attempted feebly to make light of the situation. "What are you doing here? Mother would not like you here, you know."

"Your mother would want me to help you, Lachlan," Pele yelled.

"You're not my bride, you know. But I told her that you *could* be." He laughed, cried even. His unbridled misery was very evident.

"I bet you did, Lachlan McAllister," she said aloud. Now, she found the revelation particularly hilarious. Pele could only imagine what Fele's face looked like when her son admitted his affection for her. She is of native stock and little else if one didn't count the Americans. *May she rest in peace now,* Pele thought. At hand, though, she had to save her son.

She looked toward the hillside to see if there was a branch she could use instead. Finding none, she quickly resolved to opt for the otherwise unthinkable with this man. It wasn't as if he had not seen her in a state of nakedness. She pulled off her smock and knotted it with her lavalava. This time, he caught it.

He fell next to her as she panted and tried to catch her breath after hauling him up. He wasn't bothered by her state of undress, with her breasts bound and undergarments. Those parts of Pele were very Catholic and brook little room for nonsense. Grateful for her tenacity, he untied her smock from her lavalava and handed both over to her. His clothing was torn at the seams as he struggled up the ravine and the ride to find Lesina.

Pele stood up to dress back into her smock. "Can you walk, Lachlan?" Knowing from the boys the immensity of their collective losses, she did not want him to sit too long. He was floating in and out of lucid moments.

He struggled to stay focused on the road back to the others. A slight wind blew through the trees and caught him unawares. He was swinging out of his mother's home and here on a forsaken hill. Pele walked ahead, but he couldn't understand why she was there. In front of him right now. Or why he was tied to her.

Pele saw that the men from the party were waiting for them. One ran down toward them before she held up her hand. "Please steady him." She asked for the other horse so they could move him onto it. The men complied and helped lift Lachlan onto his horse after she untied him from her.

As they sat down for their afternoon meal, Maifea and Lachlan were set up closer to the garden, a fair distance from the main fale. So'o and the other four men who came up with Pele helped build two lean-tos in the avapui patch. The ground was smooth and well-covered by its debris. The leaves helped keep all shaded.

Both men had been bathed, dressed in *lavalavas*, and seen by Kiele.

"Exhaustion and grief, Pele." Kiele leaned forward and picked up some fish with her breadfruit. "Maifea is sick, but Lachlan is as well as can be, given their circumstances." Hope floated for once amid this chaos. The sisters ate companionably with little to no conversation.

Pele looked at their fellows, the children, and thought of Epenesa. "Kiele, we must expand the house. Our landlord will have to understand. The more folk come here, the more it is impossible to move them south."

"We can move everyone back to Tava'esina," Kiele said, uncertain that was even an option since their departure a fortnight ago. She wasn't sure this was viable now that they were here and in the heart of the contagion. Moving Epenesa was not feasible, so she would have to remain here in Teuila Hill. Considering their current circumstances, Pele had to think about their choices, if any, now that they had added the former McAllister party.

Pele walked around and found the younger boys. Tala'i was sitting not too far from his uncles, his banana leaf with food in his lap, uneaten. His brother was curled up outside of Maifea's lean-to. He was keeping watch over them, unable to eat as well.

"You might as well eat while they are asleep, Tala'i," Pele quietly encouraged him. She sat next to him, too tired to stand up. However, she was too exhausted to sleep. This insomnia was going to kill her one day.

He closed his eyes as if warding himself against massive pain. "I can't believe they are all gone, Pele. I just can't." His voice broke, and he started to cry openly, his shoulders shaking uncontrollably. "They were fine and alive until this past week." In one fell swoop, the epidemic wiped out a quarter of his family. "It is everywhere, Pele. We had to roll our parents up and leave them by the road. That was all they asked us to do. Like garbage with no graves to mark their lives."

Pele let him weep. There was little that she could tell him that would ease his sorrow. Her helplessness was not helping her resolve anything. She took the food from him and covered it for later. Perhaps if Mataio woke up, he would eat. She turned to find that Tala'i had laid down, staring blankly at the blue, cloudless skies above them.

"Why does God put us through all these tragedies, Pele? As if we don't struggle enough!"

"I don't know, Tala'i. I don't have an answer for you." *God hasn't answered me yet. Why indeed, Father?*

"Why did they let this happen to us? They knew folks on that ship were sick, but still, they let them come ashore." The anger was palpable!

"Yes, they did," Pele sadly agreed. "Now we must contend with the consequences of their gross carelessness." Her heart fell to the bottom of her stomach out of fury and disbelief.

"I didn't ask you earlier, but who are all these people?" he asked curiously as he wiped his tear-streaked face. "I've been so busy feeling sorry for myself, my brother, my uncles even, but you have all these people here."

"We are preparing to take them south over this mountain road," Pele answered. "It is about the safest place we assume is clear of the flu."

Tala'i sat up, concerned. "Please don't—Maifea said that the villages leading up to the south are littered with dead people."

Pele was immediately alarmed. "What was your uncle doing out there?"

"We've family meetings as we were trying to negotiate with Uncle Lachlan's bride's Samoan aiga in Leafā, and he was visiting them before to help Lachlan as our family's *tulāfale*." This was about two villages from their proposed safe landing.

This sorrowful turn of events had to be relayed back to others. If they had to stay here, Pele would send word to Lesina. The three acres on loan to them wasn't enough space, but it will have to do until something better presents itself to them. To garner permission from the Apia Diocese was now something that she would have to talk to Lesina about.

She missed her aunt very much, but now the responsibility of these lives was in her hands. They matter as much as those who were cared for in town.

Pele sat with Tala'i until he fell asleep, unable to keep his eyes open. So much tragedy has hit them that she couldn't help them grieve for their unfathomable losses. Yet, she could care for them, keep them safe here, where life is calmer and safer. That much she and the girls can offer.

The sound of another fale going up reverberated through the hillside this morning. This extension was for the men and to help bring others closer to the central part of the house. The boys were well enough to help and joined in with the floor's weaving and construction. Coconut leaves fell from trees, lined the property, and were dragged back to the clearing. The day was clear, and it made it possible for folks to move fast, knowing that they had to complete this today.

Iolana returned from her harvest, dropped her baskets, and hurriedly found Pele among the men going over the build. She leaned over and said something into Pele's ear. Alarmed, she looked up at the sky and acknowledged what Iolana had shared.

"We must reinforce the fale and secure anything we need. A storm is coming," Pele urged, running around to inform the men and women who were by the extension. "Iolana, please help get the animals in place."

She hastened the women to help clear the debris around the new fale, with the young children helping them. The men came after them and tied down the new pous. They dragged the coconut leaves into the new fale, tying the bundles together.

She knew what the sudden stillness meant. Not a bird cried out or flew over. Time was not on their side as she knew the storm would hit sometime in the evening, if not sooner. The busyness of the day got even more flurried. Maifea and Lachlan were still recovering and remained in the avapui hedge. Meanwhile, Kiele gathered the women to move all the mats and bedding. The women cleaned the kitchen together, using coconut leaves to guard against coming winds and rain.

Tala'i took Mataio with him to get their uncles to shelter with the rest of the group. Maifea was out of danger but still weary, while Lachlan was kept in quarantine with his cousin as a precaution. This endeavor to find help for Punae'e was not doable now, as the last three weeks had been anything but ordinary.

The evening came as expected. Rain began to fall hard on the thatched roof, rat-a-tat-tat that gave way to the booming downpour. With the children tucked in next to their parents or caretakers, some cried out as the wind howled outside. Epenesa was also moved closer to the far end of the dwelling, covered with sheets. Planks tied that side of the roof as it served as the sleeping quarters for the girls and Lesina. It was the safest place to be should the fale collapse.

The grown-ups, including the sisters, sat outside in the more ample living space—quiet conversations and cautious laughter in places, even amid the riotous downpour outside. The boys settled with a few others from Pele's party and seemed to forget their worries for some time as they talked of school and compared places they had been. Maifea was going over something with Kiele as if teaching her some touchstone Fa'aSamoa language.

Pele took one of the fidgety children from Iolana, who was watching over the young as they settled for the night. Grace wanted her mother, Elisapeta, who stayed behind in Tava'esina. She shifted next to the little girl, sang to Grace despite the howling wind, and hummed with the wind so she wasn't fighting against the fury of Mother Nature for Grace's lullaby. She hoped that her singing was more soothing than that cacophonous mess outside.

Sitting at her back, Lachlan tiredly said, "Reminds me of meeting you." He gestured expansively to the pounding downpour. A gust of wind blew hard at the blinds, straining their ties.

"Crazy same, right? Here we are again," Pele answered him quietly, smiling. There was no anger or resentment. More softly, "I wish all pans out well for you, you know." Continuing this conversation would only lead to the untold tragedies he had already encountered: their dead families, Maifea, and the boys.

He smiled back pensively. As he looked at her, Pele half-turned to him, his face older but more unhappy than ever before. In the glow of the kerosene lamps, the shadows were more forgiving. She could imagine what a mess her bun was now, but given their situation, she didn't care about what she looked like to him.

Her knee touched his side as she adjusted her crossed legs with her ward now sleeping on her lap.

"Do you want me to take her?" he asked, reaching toward her to take Grace. Pele motioned him closer to her so she could move her sleeping child over to him. He gently lifted Grace from Pele's arms and placed her across his lap.

Pele turned from others to sit facing out from them. She uncrossed her legs and stretched her back a little until she heard her lower spine pop. Relieved, she sat up straighter and faced Lachlan as she leaned back on one arm, tucking the other on her shoulder as she tried to squeeze out a kink.

"You'd make a great father one day, Lachlan," she said honestly. He was a natural as Grace turned in his arms sleepily.

"But you're way softer, Pele." He laughed. "And probably smell better than I do."

Pele leaned into him and sniffed. Oh, he smelled like a man sleeping his day away. A little sun, a little of the red gingers that had surrounded him, and strangely, of earth.

"Yes, you do smell a little ripe. You can always stand in the storm outside for a minute or two," she answered, tongue in cheek. He was apologetic as he openly smelled his shirt and armpits. The gesture was so silly.

Lachlan laid Grace in the space between them and pulled off his soiled shirt. He threw it at her. Parting the blinds, some to the side, he slipped outside and was gone for about fifteen minutes. She heard him yelp and cry in shock as he was out in the cold rain. Pele laughed so hard that she keeled over her side to lie down next to Grace, oblivious to all this silliness and the storm's chaos.

Oh, the slumber of children, she thought achingly. All were safe and tucked in for now. They were not in immediate danger, even with the storm pounding outside. The children were sleeping with Epenesa near them.

Thank you, Our Good Father. Her prayer started and ended there.

Lachlan found her fast asleep with Grace pulled in closer to her. He sat down with his hair still wet from his impromptu shower, with a lavalava wrapped and tucked around his waist. She didn't stir as he sidled beside her. Most were nodding off, if not already snoring around the lanai.

Hours later, Pele stretched in her sleep and fell from her left to try and find comfort on her back. The five-year-old took up much of the area, so Pele rolled into Lachlan. He could hear more of the sounds of sleep around the fale; as suddenly it had appeared, the downpour had stopped. None that way or this, she rolled back to her left and faced away from him.

Lying awake in the dark, Lachlan grinned as he heard her snore. Not loud or clamorous, but she was holding her own, sawing a young tree or two. She turned into her sleep and tucked herself under his arm, curled up in the tight space between him and Grace. Finding his arm an unnecessary bump, she lifted it and draped it across her to get a better position on the mat. An hour later, she was tucked back under his left arm with her back to him. He would not get any sleep if she moved anymore. He threw a leg between hers, her bottom up to him to stop her from wiggling to and from.

Her snoring got louder before it stopped so suddenly. She ceased to breathe. Concerned, Lachlan leaned into her, trying to make out the rise and fall of her chest. Assured that nothing had gone awry, he closed his eyes, with his face in her soft tresses. She sighed contentedly. He was happy to be her pillow.

A leg was thrown over him, with arms around his neck. As he felt cloistered into cricks, Lachlan unwound Pele from him. He turned to his opposite side. Promptly, he found Maifea's massive back, and his snores were louder. He sighed.

He turned back to Pele and placed her leg back on his hip. He was sure she was laughing in her sleep. She cuddled closer and continued to snore, this time sawing down more Fijian sandalwood trees in her slumber.

Pele woke at the break of dawn and took a moment to recollect where she was and what she was doing. Staring up at the roof of the fale, their yesterday fell as puzzle pieces. The realization of the storm of the night before came flooding back to her. Snores were louder than before she fell asleep. *Thank you, La'auli. Thank you!* She turned before she realized that Lachlan had locked her in her arms. Pele sighed but stifled a laugh as he looked harried in his sleep.

Drip. Drip. Drip. There was no howling wind. Blinds rat-a-tat-tatted, but little else moved. The downpour had stopped, and, in the process, this stillness fell over the land as dawn broke. Their chickens were probably below the flooring as they sought safety from the storm last night. She so hoped but could not see or hear the horses tied to the back of the fale.

She regretfully left the warmth of Lachlan's arms to investigate what had become of their home. As he did the night before, she slipped out under the blinds to slip outside.

The humidity hit her hard. The sun was barely on the horizon, but its burning wet impact was oppressive. Her pores screamed for relief as sweat dripped from her before she could even say good morning to one of their cats. Pele looked for something to use as shade from the blazing sun.

Pulling down the brim of her hat, she went around to see the extension and found that the roof the men had put on was well across the clearing. All that stood the day before were broken matchsticks. Banana trees snapped in half; their fruits scattered throughout. The avapui patch was mowed to the bottom of its stalks. The yard was littered with fruits, the top of the breadfruit tree hanging by its skin.

Meanwhile, the horses neighed knowingly upon seeing her. Three were behind the fale, under the coconut trees, and the fourth sought shade and food. There were enough guavas and mangoes to keep the starving horse happy. Mulu's girth didn't indicate that La'auli's caretakers starved him. This was Mulu's best effort to bring attention to his culinary needs. Poor O'o and the others had not thought of leaving their post. Pele untied the horses so they could also share in the bounty. There was plenty for all four of them.

"Do you know where my mommy is, Aunty?" A tiny voice asked from behind her. "I miss her." Grace slipped her hand into Pele's fingers. Her hair was matted in places, and her feet were bare.

"She's below at home, Grace," she said, kneeling so they'd be eye-to-eye. "Perhaps I'll ask if she wants to come up."

"Can I come with you?" she asked, reaching for Pele. "I miss her so much, Pele."

"The road is a little too rough for you, but I'll use my long legs to look for your mommy since I am bigger." On the verge of crying, Pele lifted Grace and held her in the curve of her hip.

"Everything is broken, Aunty." Grace pointed to all around them. "All broken." She waved at everything around them. She was right.

"Not everything. *We* aren't broken, Keleise!" Pele said firmly, more for herself than Grace. "We'll just rebuild and make most of this okay for us again." She felt a knot in her throat. Her determination pared down to a shaky whisper. The plantation, the garden, and regrowing their crops? She didn't know where to start. Maybe moving down to Tava'esina was something they needed to consider when Lesina came home.

"Yes, we will rebuild everything back to what it once was," Lachlan said plainly. "We will help you. We are here, so why not help?"

Pele turned to find him standing behind her. Folks had woken up and were outside milling around, taking stock of the storm's damage. The men began to pick up the entire roof of the extension and stacked its parts against its foundation. Women went further down to pick pieces of the home blown out and lying against broken crops and banana trees.

"It's going to be okay, Pele. *Faifai lemu a tatou mea.*" So'o offered, was supportive, and committed to rebuilding the extension they had worked hard to put up the day before. "Not like we have anywhere to go from here."

Pele shifted Grace on her hip and looked at the men. "I'm sorry we are here, everybody, but thank you!" Her gratitude was boundless. She could not rebuild with only her sisters to help.

"You didn't plan the storm." Maifea came up to them from the extension. "I'm with these usos. We'll find a way to rebuild most of your home, if not better."

It took them a month to assemble everything back together and rebuild the extension to its last blind. It was hard work, but now done, the men had room to lay their heads down without fighting for space. The evening prayers that afternoon were about gratitude and hope. They unofficially named the extension after Tava'esina as a reminder that they still had family below in the village.

"As we are here, thank you to all of you for getting this extension completed. I know it is not much, but it will help us to have a place to live and sleep properly," Pele began. "Heading south using the road above us was the original plan, but as we've heard, the pandemic has also reached those villages. So now you can choose to see this out with us here, or a few of us go back down and see what has become of Tava'esina."

"I'd like to know what has become of my family, Pele," one of the women admitted.

"Not a day goes by when I don't think about my husband."

"If we leave here, there is no haven for us below. What if Tava'esina has completely fallen to the pandemic? We risk death ourselves!" A younger *taule'ale'a* voiced. Others murmured in agreement.

"There is so much we don't know by hiding here," one woman said sagely. "Your aunt has not returned, and we don't know her fate since she left for town."

"If we are going to die, Pele, it is best we do so at home." Another voiced, resigned and fearful.

Pele knew most would rather have Lesina here. Understandably, folks were doubting her leadership abilities because she was this young. "Lesina isn't here, but I stand in for her as the eldest of my sisters." Dissension rose from the crowd. "Those who want to go back tomorrow, come with us, and we will walk down together," Pele calmed them. "We will see about your homes, and if you remain behind, then that is a viable choice you choose knowing the risks. I only ask that those of you with children to please reconsider!"

Their tea was served and shared in the peaceful calm as they settled in for the night. Pele was glad for the consensus here. Later, Lachlan sat next to her with feet dangling over the wood flooring edge, handing her a tin cup of piping lemongrass tea.

It would be good for them to be in their homes. No matter how much Pele can push them to stay here at Teuila Hill, they would be uncomfortable doing so. No one wants to be in a strange place when their home is a mere walk around the bend and down into the malae. The homesickness was growing each day as they watched the village at the clearing in the road above.

"Thank you so much for keeping us here and helping us, Pele, but we must face our fates. If we hide here and are out of our element, no one knows what those may be."

Others murmured their agreement. It was time to see how the village was faring. Let their sorrow be with them and their families.

She will deliver them back to Tava'esina. With Maifea and the men here, it would be easier to do so with their assistance. While it was not entirely safe to see them home, the residents wanted to be around their homesteads and sleep in their spaces. All this was understandable because if she and her family were ever displaced, going home at the earliest possible moment would be right.

"Maifea, would you be opposed to helping us?"

"You don't have to ask, Pele. Of course, we will see to your missions." He laughed at her mock outrage. He tapped Lachlan on the shoulder. "Right, Lachlan?"

"Not sure why she didn't ask me when I was standing next to her," he teased. *"E na'o o Maifea e taulia?"*

Pele ignored him with sham indifference. "They feel comfortable with him." Lachlan laughed at the outrageous response.

"Oi, ete le kea ile palagi?"

"Ioe, matuā fiu e fa'atali pe aliali mai ou aiga ae leai ma ni isi na omai!" Pele replied with just enough mirth to keep the conversation light. She needn't remind him about the lackluster response from the New Zealand government's lackey in Apia.

"Hey, I understand, you know. I'm with you and all these souls." Lachlan splayed out his hands in a peace offering.

The sweltering humidity of February settled in the valley. They went through the village to check on those who returned home from Teuila; five caught the flu and died this week. So'o greeted the girls, his regret overt and palpable. He pointed out three bodies already wrapped in tapa. The stench of death was overwhelming and permeated the village throughout, from corner to corner. Familiar faces were among the dead.

"When will it ever end?" He cried out. "Leaving them out there goes against everything we believe in as Samoans. They were men of God, too." So'o turned toward the road already peppered with covered bodies. "They deserve better than this, Pele." She was aware of this, so much more than So'o thought she could.

The three girls followed through the maze of fales with So'o, noting the family changes. Some children sat alone, clearly orphaned. Other children were barely grade-schoolers caring for infants. Pele divided the chores among them as they moved the children out of these homes and into a makeshift gathering place. She called Mataio and Tala'i to help carry the little ones toward the church on the other side of the malae. There was so much to do here.

On the east end of the village, she gathered friends from before to help stand in as caretakers. With others and Iolana, they found food from some vacated homes. Pele waded through the milling crowd and enlisted So'o's help to move residents into groups.

Older grandparents found alone were helped out of their fales and placed near the mammoth churchyard so Kiele could triage them for signs of the flu. Most were still very healthy, while several had temperatures that were a telltale sign that they were sick and were pulled from the churchyard and into the deceased pastor's home, now the quarantine ward, as more sick people walked from other parts of the village with Kiele at the helm.

La'auli came to see the girls and was sincerely thankful for their vigilance for Tava'esina. Lachlan, Maifea, and a few others rode out at daybreak to find help in town. One of those highfaluting, fancy-schooled doctors had to be willing to come out to the villages and check the villagers.

Every door they knocked on did not bear one ready or a willing soul. Workgroups went from one family to the next until most of Tava'esina was covered. Others went to the churchyard to be with their families or to look for them. Men started two *umus* near the church to help use the felled fruits and crops and, secondly, to feed those who were now housed there.

The rebuilding of lives will take much longer, but whatever they can do in the meantime, the girls will help ease the pain and grief over their tragic losses together.

VI. 1919

Fa'atosina ma Samoa Ua 'Oi
Deception and Death

Lesina roamed through the ward as she had the graveyard shift. She checked through the more critically ill among those coming to the Immaculata in the quiet of the morning hour. The rectory and part of the main cathedral were now a clinic and hospital since November's deadly outbreak. It was at Mother Superior's behest that she came down to the Immaculata.

That was three, maybe four, months ago. Oh, how Lesina missed her girls. However, she didn't want to bring them here. So much has happened since the *Talune*, with so many deaths that walked in from afar, with folks collapsing and dying at the church's front doors. Some were put here purposefully to pass on the church's consecrated grounds. To compound the growing issues at the Immaculata, Pere sadly died two weeks ago at seventy-six. They could not keep his passing a secret from the local mayor as he was a devoted Catholic, and news burned through the parish.

Without word to the Kiwis, the old priest was buried in the churchyard as he had begged to lie in peace and to be interred on hallowed grounds. Another body was sent with the Wagon instead. He wasn't the first to be hidden from the authorities.

The Diocese sent word that Lesina and the supervising physician, a holdover German doctor, would continue to offer care and keep the clinic if needed. Mother Superior was to submit the reports as usual. As such, Doctor Mueller cared for Apia's elite, while the indigent, the natives, and the unknown came down through Lesina and Mueller's Kiwi resident doctor, Mr. Smith. Most days, it was a dodgy game of avoiding both in the same room or at rounds as the animosity rivaled the Somme.

She liked to think she had not gotten callous and unfeeling, but counting the number of the dead was now a matter of recordkeeping. No funerals were allowed, as bodies were not repatriated to villages once the New Zealand authorities found out.

Lesina went from bed to bed, taking vitals and checking on these critically ill patients. Others were here for palliative care, as some didn't have family members left. She sighed, knowing that these crucial decisions were not quickly arrived at by families who had to think of the greater good for the whole. The sick were left on steps or anonymously dropped off by the rectory in the early morning hours.

This check of the grounds was also part of her nightly duties. Few of the sick were a day in the bay since they became ill and could be cared for, but most were closer to death than not. She stopped crying after they sent two hundred dead to their communal burial over these past three months.

As a courtesy, Lesina wrote letters to villages with news of the dead to their families. She was sternly ordered not to do this when she was found out. She refused and continued to do so. No parent or spouse deserves to go without news of their loved ones.

She walked down the ward, covered some, and comforted those who were so ill that it was a matter of time. She held the hands of the young men who cried out for their mothers. Besides beds, she heard many more confessions, even as she begged them to wait for the catechist or the young priest who had taken over for Pere.

At the end of the twenty-bed lane, she happened upon a young lady who was out of place. She dressed nicely and made up as if she had just come from a party. Or she was going to one. Whichever is the case, she was in the wrong place.

"Are you the voodoo witch doctor I heard about?" she asked of Lesina. "I came here to see you." No pleasantries, nor did she try.

"No, I'm not, but I'm the closest to a female caretaker you have in these parts of Samoa," Lesina said without taking offense. "What are you doing here? You can't just walk in here if you aren't sick."

"You're right, but no one will see me right now." There was no desperation in her voice. "I was told that you are also a midwife by trade."

Lesina was immediately concerned. "If you're pregnant, you cannot be here. I can see you at your home if you need care."

The young lady looked unconcerned. She looked around the ward and exasperated, "No, I'm fine."

"Then you must go to the rectory." Doctor Mueller cared for the local palagis and half-castes housed next door.

"No, I don't want those folks to know I'm here." She swiped her finger over one of the bed rails.

"Well, then, you can't be on my floor." Lesina turned on her heel to get Mother Superior to explain this to the strange young woman. "There are sick patients here, and if you're pregnant, you can't be around these sick people."

"No, please, I need your help," she said flatly, catching Lesina's hand. "I need to get on one of these ships soon."

"Why can't you do that?" Lesina stood and looked. This was as she sat on the side of the bed with her hood covering her face. She didn't need to be involved in some family drama.

"What is your name?"

"Emily Schumacher. And I need you to help me with an abortion." In her mid-twenties, she was privileged, and she wasn't showing just yet.

Lesina looked her over. There was a visible roundness about her midriff, which she hid from sight under the skirts of her dress. "How far along are you?"

"Four months."

"Have you consulted with the doctors?" The last thing she needed to hear was Mueller's rants about protocols and her lack of professional boundaries. She was never to address her betters. This girl was not about to bring Mueller down her ward.

"I can't—they'll tell my father." Emily shook her head. "I thought, as a woman, you'd be more sensible—that you wouldn't ask me these stupid questions. Look, I'll pay. I have money." She clutched at her purse.

This wasn't the first time Lesina was asked to aid with an abortion, but this was the first time she had been offered payment for her services as if this were a negotiation between a man and a prostitute downtown.

Lesina feigned it as if she was seriously considering the money matter. Then she turned back to Emily. "No. Please go to Dr. Mueller."

"Then please help me get out of this godforsaken place," Emily pined. "Look, if you don't help me, I'll tell my father how incompetent you are. He is a patron of Immaculata, and that will be your end."

"Please go ahead and inform him of my name and place here at Immaculata," Lesina answered calmly. She rubbed her shoulder and turned to walk down to see other patients. "I suggest you also tell him that you seek a physician to help you with an abortion."

"You have to help me," Emily begged, running after Lesina. She was not taking no for an answer. "Look, I do have my own money. Isn't that something you *meaulis* lack?"

Lesina led her back by her arm to the end of the open bay, stopped briefly to pick up her bag, and then out of the cathedral. She handed the bag to the owner. "This is a sick bay, and I'll not have you living out your drama here. Go to Mr. Mueller, who can better assist you."

Lesina didn't want any part of her madness. Not that she has not performed abortions on those who sought them, but Miss Schumacher has the nerve to walk in the middle of people who are dying and ask? Perhaps Herr Mueller would be more receptive to her.

"I'll make you regret this!" Emily yelled at her from the yard of the church. "You will not know peace when I am done with you."

Lesina leaned heavily up against the door. Emily was still yelling at her. *Do not deal with fools*, they say. She repeated this to herself.

"Fucken meaulis, who think you're above all of us! You're nothing! Do you hear me? You will never be anything!" she screamed, knowing Lesina would not chase after her.

Lesina swung the door open and went toward the steps. "You are a vulgar person, Miss Schumacher! Go before I show you just how black I am."

Emily spat at the bottom step. "You'll regret this." She stared at Lesina malevolently.

She would have flown down the steps a year ago and pummeled this girl into the ground to teach her a lesson. This sad, humid morning? She felt little but this overwhelming pity for this unstable, unfortunate soul. "You don't deserve that child. I hope for your sake that you find a resolution. Go to your parents and get them to buy you respectability."

"Even my boyfriend, Erich, will come after you!"

"Who did you say?" Lesina looked down at her, dismayed. Erich didn't even seem ready to be a father.

"This is Erich Hansell's baby."

"So, what is your problem? Why are you getting rid of Erich's baby? Does he even know what you're trying to do?"

Emily went silent and walked off, refusing to answer any more questions and out of sight into the morning before dawn. This meauli knew Erich! She covered her head lest she was recognized before the morning curfew was lifted.

Lesina walked back in and shut the massive door. It's a pity she couldn't slam it to full effect. Without knowing why, she felt true evil trampled over her soul—*Erich's* child.

The Good Father, please find her help, for I cannot be that person. Not that she has not participated in these procedures, but because amid the pandemic, pregnancies do not go unnoticed.

A fortnight later, she sat at the ward nurse's desk and started a letter to her girls. So much has happened in the three months she has been back in Apia. Death was the moment's business, and little else went on in between. Not that she worried terribly about them, but she hoped the girls were looking after one another. If all goes well here, and they import Kiwi nurses, she will be on her way back to them. She has had enough of the town and its insidious politics.

"Lesina!" one young man called out. "Please come!" In the quiet of the morning, he startled the others. "Today, I'm going to heaven." John Lesoso.

"John, how are you?" Lesina came to his bedside, bringing a chair. He has been here for a month. Barred from family before the pandemic, he had been in and out of his good and bad days. At twenty-eight, he was a former town worker who caught the flu from one of his clients. This morning, he came out of one of his fevers, proclaiming that he had a conference with Angel Azrael.

She sat with her mask on next to him. Azrael or not, she was determined to have their usual round of stories and books.

"Lesina, I'm going home to Our Lord. There's little that keeps me here," John said matter-of-factly. "I don't have any family anymore. This old, and I'm an orphan." He sighed sadly. "It's good that no one is left behind, Lesina." He tried to smile through cracked, chapped lips.

Unable to keep his solids down, he was emaciated, a far cry from his former healthy self.

Lesina shifted in her chair and moved the lamp closer. She smiled, trying to be happy for him, with a lump in her throat. "I'll miss you, John. Please remember our friendship if you remember anything of this dreadful life in heaven."

"I was dead already before this, you know. Mueller had already given me about six months. How convenient that I get influenza now." He stared at her with his clear brown eyes. Deftly changing the subject, "You're the prettiest face I've seen this close. Pity, I don't have time."

Lesina laughed out loud when she sorely wanted to bawl her eyes out. "Oh, Sweetie, wherever you go, you'll have someone missing you here on earth."

"As it will be in heaven, Lesina."

"His will be done there, as it will be for us here on earth, John." In her sing-song chant.

"Yes, my love, and I applaud you for knowing your way around Our Father's house." He beamed at her.

"You were an accountant, right?"

"Yes, to pay a living, but I always leaned toward the church, you know. I'd have gone to seminary had I been of my own man. My younger siblings needed schooling, and my parents needed money to stay established."

"Are they still with us?" Lesina has never heard him speak of his family.

"Unfortunately, they died during the first wave of deaths. As did my sisters. I don't know what has happened to my brother." His voice cracked. Tears leaked out the sides of his eyes. "Just like *that*, Lesina. And here we are, about to do my last curtain call. Can you be my mother-sister-cousin? I find this dying business so lonely without my best girls."

"Of course! I so wished *my* girls were here to keep you company. You'd love them dearly!" The girls would have chatted with him in and out of his nine lives if he were a cat.

"I bet I would have. Anyone who survives an aunt like you? They are tough little birds. And that's all I need to know. But tell me about them now! Names, wishes, boyfriends!" his laughter bright Christmas tinsel in this morbid place.

He turned to his side to listen to Lesina regale him with stories of the girls he wished he had gained as sisters in his living. Life had other avenues, and while he was not regretful, he missed out on many good people. Dreams, attitudes, and outlooks.

Lesina also read books he hadn't bothered to enlighten his life with. He closed his eyes for a short while to take in the warmth of his lovely nurse. No matter what Mueller and other doctors said about not addressing her as a nurse, for she was the hired help, she has done so much for those who came here.

"Lesina, please hold me," he said suddenly, sitting up in bed. "I love you so much. I'm leaving, my darling!" John left on his terms six hours later this sweltering February day while holding onto her hand. Lesina wept from a place she felt she could not anymore.

When they moved his body with the others, Lesina saw his departure as far as she could, walking behind the cart in the afternoon rain. There were no exceptions for wakes, either. One day, she will drink a beer in memory of her friend.

Lord, I don't know how much longer I can do this.

She took her tattered Wordsworth and went to the tiny cubicle she used as sleeping quarters next to Mother Superior. A folded letter fell out from her book.

Dear Love,

I know it is shabby of me to leave you with so little happiness, but one day, enjoy that sunshine when you see the other side of the morning. Bask in it and move on with life. You have given me so much love, as you of others in your care, but you gave me love. I know I was your favorite man-child. I know it! Thank you for your consideration and all my readings throughout my stay. I should have spent more time in a library than the bars! Please take care of your darlings and let them be those organic beings! Let them fail, love, scream, be disappointed, angry, and sad about their bad choices—let them grow wildly! Let them come to their deathbeds with you to love and guide them through the walk to the Pearly Gates as you have me.

I will look in on you from time to time and let you go when I know you have mastered this business of living. Do not grieve for me. Go to the living where there is much to be done. Finish what you have started with the girls.

You are loved, Lesina. Always, and now forever, John.

The following months were a blur through the public holidays. There was no time for grieving, as people were moved from beds to burials without delay, and others moved out without respite. Men who carried bodies out soon were the bodies carried out of these tired walls.

In March, the promised Kiwi nurses came in from Auckland and were primarily assigned to the hospital, while two were sent to the Immaculata for its clinic and wards.

"We of the administration hope you understand where you are with this clinic, Ms. Spafford." Dr. Mueller sat with the self-appointed head nurse. She did the talking.

"Yes, I do." It was still early as the sun had not come through the church's stained-glass windows.

"While your work with your people has been flawless, and there haven't been any complaints, your position with traditional healing runs counter to our profession. This is a problem with some of our patrons."

"And whom may those be?" Lesina was woken early before Mass to go to this conference. There wasn't any forewarning here, even by Mother Superior. "In all my time here, I've never harmed any patients, nor have I overstepped my professional boundaries."

Herr Mueller, gray all over these days, leaned forward over the table. *"Frau Spafford, Wir sagen nicht, daß hier das problem liegt. Wir haben eher das Gefühl das Ihr Hintergrund und die mission dieser medizinischen institution hier, nicht zusammen passen. Unserer professionellen Meinung nach ist hier kein Platz für homöopathische Medizin in diesem Rahmen. Dies ist kein Ort für jemanden mit ihren begrenzten Fähigkeiten. Sie sollten sich vielleicht um ein Stipendium in einem Pflegeprogramm einer unserer Schulen in Auckland bemühen, sobald diese furchtbare Pandemie vorbei ist. Wir würden uns sehr freuen Ihnen dann eine position als Mitarbeiterin hier in Apia anzubieten. Oder auch nahe Ihrer amerikanischen Ureinwohner."*

He turned to Nurse Bowie-Legges and motioned her to translate with his usual superiority complex.

"Ms. Spafford, that is not what we are saying is the problem here. We feel that your background and this institution's medical missions are not compatible. Our professional opinion is that there is no place for homeopathic medicine in this setting," Nurse Bowie-Legges reiterated as if speaking to a petulant child. "This is not a place for someone of your limited skills. Perhaps you might want to check into a scholarship to the nursing program with any of our schools in Auckland when this awful pandemic is over; we would be more than happy to offer you a position on our staff here in Apia. Or perhaps, in your native American side."

Facing the firing squad, Mother Superior sat on her left side. She wouldn't meet Lesina's confused gaze.

Oh, how she missed her girls, indeed. "We are not at liberty to say who filed the complaint, but I'll note that you must part ways with the Immaculata. Effective immediately. I recommend you go back to the villages and care for the native population—your people—that way. Any help you can offer to stave off the number of the sick and the dying would be appreciated here in Apia."

Lesina stood up and walked out without shaking their proffered hands. Her anger simmered as she refused to acknowledge Mother Superior.

She fetched her valise and walked to the outer memorial yard of the cathedral, Lesina noted how Pele's green thumbs had become eternal here. *Maimau le galue siou kei.*

Mother Superior stood on the steps and watched Lesina walk out of the wrought iron gate. "Lesina, times have changed. You should have minded Mueller, *mon cher!*"

I should have left when you had no help, but I am not a monster, Mother Superior.

She should have known that without Pere, she had no ally among these snakes in the grass. She pondered her plans with the girls as she walked home to her beloved Teuila Hill. Her firing squad would be in the ear of the Monsignor, and it wouldn't be long before they were asked to leave the estate.

It may be time to go home. Still, Pago Pago was not allowing any ships or vessels to travel into its harbor, and it was unlikely that the Navy would open the waterways anytime soon. The irony of their fate wasn't lost on her. Moreover, her brother will skin her for the foolhardiness of this time in Apia.

She arrived home an hour later and realized how much she had missed the girls. Six months felt like a century. Perhaps it would not hurt as bad if she didn't feel the sting of betrayal.

Her loyalty to the wrong people will kill her one day.

"Good morning, Aunty." Pele set down the tea tray, putting crackers and butter to the side. It has been so good to have her aunt home. Home has gotten so quiet without people bustling up and down their hills. Those who wanted to go home did over these past three months since January.

Lesina turned over and said little. Pele moved closer to lean on Lesina's hip, lovingly nudging her.

"Tea is getting colder by the minute, Lesina," Pele whispered. *"Sau e fai tatou ki."*

"Please go ahead. I'm not hungry right now." Lesina was not feeling gracious this morning. "Go see to Epe's tea and then your keis." She pulled the sheet over her head. It was the third day since her return home.

Pele put aside the plate and tin teacup to the side and rolled into Lesina's back as if she were a natural appendage. The younger hugged her aunt fiercely. Lesina opened her eyes, a bit annoyed.

"Don't *we* mean anything to you, Aunty?" Pele whined laughingly. "*We* love you more than those idiots." She hugged Lesina tighter, pressing her cheek against her aunt's shoulder.

"Those idiots also own this land that we're living on," Lesina groused. "Can you go and see the others now?" She pushed Pele off her without turning around.

Pele hugged her even tighter than before. "I know this, Aunty." She fell flat on the mat behind Lesina. She grabbed Lesina's hand, making her aunt feel her face. "You matter so much; you don't know how much. I hope you hear me."

Kiele snuck in and lay beside Lesina on the opposite side to stare at her. Iolana took the top end—the ambush of her three babies. Lesina felt hapless but could not help but laugh out loud. Whatever awaited them, she had her girls by her side. She cried her exhaustion out. The girls curled in and let her.

What now? Where can she earn enough to feed her family? The ships were grounded, but some semblance of food was still available in limited amounts. Flour, brisket, sugar, and oil were their essentials.

All these goods required services or hard cash. There were enough charged accounts with vendors, but without anyone needing her services, it was hard to assess value and receive goods in exchange. The girls could not work instead of her. There was little left in town for them to do, with folks sick and the indeterminable nature of the contagion.

She could find that young woman and help her do as she asked, as awful as that sounded. That could buy them some foodstuffs. Then again, she loathed the idea of supporting such an entitled soul. It would be one thing to help because her life was in danger, or she had many children that she could not keep with paltry means. None of these were her case. Lesina erased the idea from the viable options she had at hand.

No, she had to find another way to support her family.

"We will make do, Aunty," Pele said in the dark. "We can make us work." So many food crops were probably lying about without use to those who lived in Tava'esina. The plantations weren't harvested, fell to the ground around them, and went to birds and wildlife.

"I wish I could believe this, Pele, but there has to be more to help keep you all eating well."

"We survived so much since Hawaii, Aunty, that we can live without half of the stuff we get because you bartered away your time and skills." Pele sat up and made a mental calculation of their needs. "We can do it. We'll survive this as long we remain healthy and mobile."

None of them fell ill and had taken precautions, as Lesina had told them. Now, with Epenesa, they were incredibly wary about their health around her.

"Pele, I worry if we can't stay any longer," Lesina explained. "They let me go out of the Immaculata, and there isn't any domestic work at the moment."

"We can ask La'auli for help if he can," Kiele offered. "Why don't we carry on and look after the Tava'esina folk? Hopefully, others will hear the news that we can still help." The palagi doctors had still not come up the coast. All the efforts by Maifea and Lachlan to move at least one physician here had been in vain.

"That sounds doable!" Pele sat up, excited. "While you two tend to the sick, Iolana and I can help with caretaking and any domestic help that mothers and children need in the village. We won't get paid, yes, but it will help make people believe they can trust us even if we are not their first choices."

"Oh, girls, thank you for your love and belief," Lesina said quietly. "If all else fails, we go home to Pago Pago."

"Yes, it's time to face my parents, Lesina," Pele said, crestfallen. "We can always keep that as an option." There were certain things worse than an arranged marriage.

"We'll cross that bridge when we have to, Pele." Lesina pointed out things that were more emergent than the trip home. One of them was about feeding their family. She had to come up with an idea; however, it may be time to leave for home. The struggle to stay above water has gotten severe as the pandemic has changed people's perception of Western medicine. As families are cautioned and told by imperialists to stay away from one another, it has not been well-received. There were talks of unrest against the current palagis, and it was getting louder.

VII. Spring 1919

Le Taga'imamao
Purposefully Fashioning Futures

In late April, Lesina got word from Monsignor. *Please stay, but you must have plans to move with your family. I can't keep you there indefinitely. As you know, you haven't an ally on the Board. I can only give you until the end of the year via* Eli, his secretary.

While her nephew and Sama's twin, she was reluctant to ask for anything more. This gave her time to plan an exit from Teuila with the girls.

It's hard to believe that they have survived the worst of the pandemic. Lesina mulled over this as she and the girls washed their linen. There is life since Immaculata, although she wondered about folks who came after. She felt for their survivors, if any, who never received word about their prognoses and end disposition. *Probably not*, she said to herself. I cannot save the world, but I can set an example for others.

Lesina was so proud of Kiele. She has mastered the art of identifying local medicinal plants of the local botany and has followed Lesina as an apprentice in training. Her recordkeeping skills have been outstanding, and she has learned so much since they were working with Tava'esina as folks returned home.

In a pre-influenza Tava'esina, the local census of four hundred and sixty-three was the count. Since November, the village has lost one-hundred-seventy-seven; many of their casualties were men. So many young widows now found themselves parenting children, head of families without hustan their parents or in-laws to help.

When they first came down to Tava'esina at the beginning of the pandemic, the number of residents varied weekly. Two months after the first deaths,

Grace's mother was found dead on a Sunday morning. She insisted that she return to work for the Hansells so the children had something to count on to support their home and schooling. Their mother died here alone and would not be a place to bring the children home. This hit Pele hard as the responsibility of keeping the kids meant that they kept their house in Teuila. They *must* keep Teuila Hill for as long as possible.

Lesina was especially taken by the little boy, Noah. They haven't had a boy in the family for so long, so gaining Noah was a godsend. He brought balance among the women and his sisters. Pele asked permission to change their names to Serenity, Grace, and Love, first with Lesina and her sisters and then with the church in Tava'esina by having the changes recorded for posterity in their church registry.

Honoring the children, she asked La'auli in confidence if they could bury Elisapeta on the edge of Tava'esina's plantations. They could not keep their mother's body for burial in Tava'esina, but when the kids were old enough, they would have a grave to return to. Pele promised them they would always come down and visit their mother with flowers.

Village children often ran up looking for treats from Pele and Iolana while the girls played with their familiar cousins. With so much laughter, Pele often left that to Iolana to sort out the children. Iolana firmly institutes order before she apportioned treats, tea, pancakes, or Fijian crackers with rare butter. Whatever Lesina gained as a family with the girls, part of those parcels also came down to the Children of the Chapel. They started with ten children last December. Now, that number has increased to thirty-two.

"If I were younger, Pele, I'd have a choice of women," La'auli said as he sat down for the afternoon repast. Pele sat with him and waved a breadfruit leaf to ward off flies who smelled the delicious fish and its soup. *"Ia manaia le nofo le Samoa le Samoa, a ea?"*

Pele choked, laughing so hard at the outrageousness of his cheek. She held her chest, trying hard to stop howling at the idea. He has been a widower for so long that no one can imagine him remarrying. Ever. La'auli could not be remarried, for he would lose his ancient, magical, beautiful soul.

"E te ata fa'apenā pei a le ata outou fale." he scoffed, then gently squeezed her hand. "Please come eat with me."

"No, no. *A'o tausami i'inei fa'apea matou aiga po'o lea mea ua ou peti iai!"* Eating two meals a day is most likely noticed by her family, which would cause much laughter and endless jokes.

"What goes on in the Big House, Pele? Are all well and safe?" he asked after them every other day as she came to run errands, see about his wellness, and take him around the village.

"Lesina is about to come to Tava'esina and do her wellness checks on the children." Kiele followed as she was wont to do for Lesina's clinics. They were in town to talk to the folks at Immaculata.

No family here had survived the pandemic unscathed. In one, the father and his children died while the wife and mother-in-law remained immune. In other severe cases, it left so many children orphaned. Families chose to adopt some orphans, while others waited for families traveling from afar to pick them up from their foster homes if they had survived the pandemic.

"Ua le tonu outou nofo'aga, Pele? Afai e fia fai se mea outou nonofo mau iai, omai tatou nonofo! E fa'apisa iai si ata fale iinei," he asked, hopeful for a different answer.

She sighed and covered her legs with her lavalava as she crossed them. "I don't think that's proper, Uncle. People will say we are taking advantage of your hospitality since we have no blood relations with you or Tava'esina. We cannot, and I even speak for Lesina."

La'auli looked at his freckled veined hands, wringing them in frustration. "I can make you my *tamafai,* Pele. You and the whole family. Then they can talk all they want."

Pele looked at La'auli with so much love and resolve. She wanted to cry, even laugh at his righteous indignation. "You know, I love you as my uncle. *E leiloa a pe ka aiga mai aso anamua, La'auli!"*—a bold declaration through her joyous laughter. She felt such an endearing kinship to the older man.

Quietly, she sighed, *"Ae la ka ika mea e leai ni ola."* To be angry over situations void of life neither of them can control was a lesson in futility. La'auli taught her this adage earlier in her A'oga Samoa studies.

The beloved teacher and builder pushed aside his bowl of fish stock soup aside. "So many things bar us from being happy people, Pele. We have families, but we don't have companionship. Now I am alone in this house and can't bring you all here to live with me."

She pushed his soup back to him. There was still a lot of fish in there. *"Se ae ika la ma e le taumafa lou mea tausami. E ave oe lugā e nonofo ma matou?"* She joked, but it was the next option on her list of to-dos. Of course, La'auli would not agree to such tomfoolery of moving into Teuila Hill.

"No, I wanted only the soup. Take the fish and eat it. *Manaia ga'otala ma malau mai faiva o nai tama ia ga lama anapo."* He hurried as a man with a purpose does. He was at the end of the fale's flooring before Pele could push the soup back to him. "When you're done, let's go for a walk. The day doesn't get any younger, young woman!" Pele gave the leftovers to her *keis* as they could afford to put on weight. They laughed at her expression as she blew her cheeks and rubbed her flat belly.

They slowly made their way through the malae, starting from the middle to the end of Tava'esina. Most families lived around the main field of the village, making it easier for them to approach. House calls were called from the yards, headcounts were tallied, and Pele took notes of their needs. Tala'i and Mataio followed behind them.

"Maua!" La'auli called out. *"O a mai lou aiga ma le fanau?"* Maua and his wife, two of five surviving children, appeared behind the blinds.

"Le manuia lava fa'afetai!" Maua failed to convince anyone.

La'auli took out some tobacco from his pocket fashioned into his lavalava. *"Le fai le tusigā igoa! E mo'omia se mea tausami po'o se fesosoani?"*

"Fa'amolemole lava lou susuga! Ua le mafai ona ou galue lenei vaitaimi!" Maua answered as a man who desperately needed a hand up.

"Pele, Maua needs provisions for his family. Make sure you bring the boys back with food for the family." La'auli emphasized.

"Absolutely!"

"Today, before you leave, please bring the *aumaga* around and disperse the foodstuffs we have at the malae thus far."

La'auli, Pele, and the boys finished their rounds as far west as families settled. Pele took the young men and cut the provisions to families as she was asked. These care packs were self-generated from plantations and shared resources as Lesina went to Apia and begged for help from the church and its board.

As the day settled, the sunlight long off the west side of the plantations. Pele walked through the malae to get the girls from the chapel. Iolana held on to the younger siblings running from them, all ahead of Pele. Lagging with a laugh, Pele thanked the mothers, the fosters of the day, for looking after their girls.

The day was winding down. Pele turned to La'auli, leaning in to touch cheek to cheek.

"Ia manuia lou po! Tatou feiloa'i ile taeao le Aso Lulu!" He walked up the *paepae*, visibly tired.

On the steps of the faletalimalo, she gave the boys some clean laundry and directions for the night as they would set tea for the house. Mataio leaned forward for his customary kiss on the forehead while Tala'i settled for the hug.

"Sleep well, and I'll see you all on Wednesday." With the last few hugs for the boys.

She called out her last evening call, *"Fa, La'auli! Fa, tamā!"* She chuckled as she heard him growl from inside the fale.

"O loa! La pogisa mai le afiafi!" he loudly admonished; his gray hair grayer the longer Pele dawdled outside. He worried about their walk home to Teuila Hill and the time it took them to get there, which was close to half an hour in daylight. The sun was already sinking on the horizon. Undeterred, Pele waved a backhanded farewell.

The sun was rapidly setting, but Pele couldn't see the girls as they gave chase after Iolana, who was halfway up the road. She undoubtedly heard the pursuit between Serenity and Grace, in any case, by the squeals and cries about the unfairness of shorter legs. To which Serenity hooted and hollered in their merry game of tuligasi'a. Oh, to hear their merriment! Her heart was bursting at the seams as the sounds of fussing children echoed during their walk up to their hill.

Closed mouths do not get fed, Lesina muttered, even if she had to pass the folks who took the job that she loved from her.

Lesina greeted the panel with forced diplomacy. Again, there was no way she could get help if she didn't ask the Church. Eli greeted her happily, motioning her to sit in the anteroom until the Monsignor was ready to see her.

"How are you, Lesina?" Eli was the near opposite of Sama in features, a perennial tan with Leata's fairness. She hadn't thought of her sister-in-law for a long time. It was almost strange to even greet this son with his mother's eyes staring back at her.

"I'm fine, Eli!" She leaned cheek to cheek and hugged him. Even though he had spent his lifetime with Lesina's parents, he was still her nephew. "How is the old man?" The Monsignor.

"Well, you can be happy that he is a *generous* man. This meeting was not something the others were keen about, given your history with them. You might as well have been excommunicated after you walked out of here."

"It couldn't have been helped. There are things called principles." *And loyalty and compassion,* she added to herself. Besides, she had long left the church mentally years ago. So, any other official removal would be an alignment.

"Please, go in now." Eli cleared the way with the swoosh of his cleric robes. *Go, Aunty, go!* He cheered her on with some familial pride.

Pele heard a wagon coming through the dirt road and thought it was odd this early the following day. Aside from the frightful undertakers, no one drove through here. The truck came closer and closer until it stopped by La'auli's faletalimalo. She was helping foster the children today so that other mothers could tend to their families and errands.

It parked, and the young man dropped out of the vehicle's passenger side. In the balmy coastal village, his cleric robes were a sauna. He slipped out of them and came around in his seminarian uniform. He walked up the steps to find La'auli.

Pele told the others she was going to see what was happening. She walked over to see that La'auli was shaking the stranger's hand. As she walked up to the men, she was jolted by her startling resemblance to this man, as was he of her. As were La'auli and the boys! He saw her as he came up closer to him and laughed out loud. He quickly warmed up and recalled that Pele hadn't known he was close by in Apia until now.

"Hello, little sister." Eli laughed as she did. "I see our aunt didn't speak of my existence since before Christ." Pele walked into his arms, as natural as rain nourishes the earth. He felt, smelled, and hugged like Sama. This was all she needed to know to affirm her family relations.

The holidays of 1919 were imminent. There were little but sure signs of this around town, for a valiant effort was made. The men gathered at Anders again, where the often-boisterous mood was somber and quiet. There were so many missing now. The pandemic dragged on, although fewer people died a year later.

Lachlan returned from Christchurch, where he repatriated his father's ashes in August. Maifea accompanied him as he was the representative of Lachlan's maternal family to pay the customary respects to Ronan's family. Fele's death a year earlier did not deter Ronan and his businesses. There was no sentimentality in his father's stance. If the truth ever came to light, Ronan mourned Sala privately. Privately all until it became public when he said so to an audience here at Anders' in a drunken rage. Ronan hadn't even blinked an eye when his wife was also lost to the pandemic.

Ronan was his father, but it didn't mean he had to like or respect him.

"I'm going out to see the boys. Pele has had them long enough," Maifea announced ruefully. "I miss them."

"As do I," Lachlan echoed, swallowing his whiskey. "I miss all of them."

"Yes, I can agree and drink to that." Maifea was especially keen on seeing the girls and how all at Tava'esina have managed since they were gone.

This trip abroad was too much for him, and frigid New Zealand was his last for a long time. Besides, home to the young women would be a more welcome sight than his cousin, whom he has lived with for these past three months on this evolution. Unlike Hawaii, there was little to do in the cold for an islander who wasn't used to life indoors.

A young man came in, stood on Anders' doorstep, and scanned the tables. When asked to come in from outside, he politely declined. He looked around once again and then made eye contact with Maifea.

"Lachlan, get to the hotel, and I'll see you there." Maifea got up and paid for their table. He walked out purposefully and left with the young man.

Lachlan was confused by his cousin's abrupt departure but knew Maifea had other business that he did not speak about. Maifea wasn't keen on sharing with him, which was all right for now.

He stumbled into the early evening, over to the hotel row of Apia's oceanfront properties. Lachlan cut through the lobby, intent on finding their room. He found the steps only to be accosted by a young woman who called out to him.

"Hello, Lachlan," she said flatly. "Imagine finding you here." No, he could not, as he didn't know her.

"Who are you?" He stared at the woman before him, addressing him as though he was an intimate friend.

"Why we could have been married a year now."

The realization sank hard, and he was instantly apologetic. This was Emily. He did not remember her with so much makeup.

"You look like you've just seen a ghost."

"So much has happened since I last saw you, so forgive me for being remiss." Rather than stand on steps where people passed them staring, he led her to a seat toward the lanai of the hotel.

"I guess you got away now that we are not engaged anymore."

"I think there was a lot more going on, Emily. I lost my mother and sisters last year, so I didn't beg off for shits and giggles." Lachlan motioned for a waiter. "Who are you here with?" He looked beyond her shoulder. The last thing he needed was to have some persnickety father give him the evil eye. Or a beating.

"My father is meeting with the administration. Oh, boring stuff." She rolled her eyes. "What are you doing these days?" She pursed her lips seductively, trying to take his attention away from her face, as she could only imagine what she looked like to him.

Lachlan thought about an answer. What *was* he doing now? He can sort out his father's affairs and accounts and move into the Apia house. "This and that." He was about as imaginative as he could be.

"I thought I'd find you sooner rather than later before anyone tells you," She admitted.

"Tell me what, Emily?" He pushed out his chair to lean forward to hear her over the gathering chaos below their veranda.

"You could have been a father by now, Lachlan."

He leaned closer. "I could have been a *what*, Emily?"

"You know, a father. To a baby," Emily hurriedly rushed. "We can always start over."

"So, you're telling me that there was a baby." He vaguely remembered sleeping with her a night after partying with his old alum friends. Beyond that, he could not remember a thing about Emily. Yet, there was a child.

She stared at him. "Why, yes. You weren't around, and I was so scared to be pregnant and alone. I went to that Samoan woman. She is so good at what she does." She rubbed the rim of her glass as she looked at him.

"What Samoan woman, Emily? You didn't even bother to find me or see if I wanted the child?" Lachlan was on the edge of his chair, trying to process what she was telling him.

"Lesina, right? She worked at the Immaculata until they fired her for doing what she did for me." She fingered her napkin. "Aren't you glad that you know now? We can start over and try again. She said I was well and could have other children if I wanted to."

"Emily, I'm sorry you had to go through that alone. If I had known, I'd been with you." He stood up and said his farewells. He had to process all this by himself. There was a child, and no one was informed about it except Emily and Lesina.

"Lachlan?"

"Yes?"

"Thank you for not bringing that darkie of yours. I know he's your cousin, but I don't like it when they're all over the business," she commiserated.

Lachlan closed his eyes before he turned on his heel and walked back to her. "Don't speak of my family in this manner or at all. I'll do the right thing by you, but don't you dare ever speak of or about my cousin."

She watched him climb up those steps and fingered the hem of her napkin when he was out of sight. Emily swirled the ice in her glass and tilted the liquor. She stared out at the harbor and sighed as she placed the linen napkin across her lap.

A smile slowly crossed her lips. She sipped her lemonade and waited for her father to finish up with the administration's representatives. She ought to remind her daddy to stop consorting with the inconsequential minions.

Maifea could feel Lachlan's preoccupation as he said something to him on the ride into Tava'esina, and his cousin looked right through him.

"Hey, what's with you? Cat got you all riled or something?" Maifea teased.

"Sorry, I was just a little distracted, is all," Lachlan answered. "How did things go with your meetings?"

"Well, in fact," Maifea replied shortly. He didn't volunteer any information, and Lachlan didn't ask. "This trip up the coast will be good for both of us."

The ride to Tava'esina, a short ten miles, was quiet and introspective for both men.

Lesina heard from the boys that their uncles would visit and possibly fetch them. Neither seemed so happy about the idea, as they settled well with La'auli and their routine walk up Teuila Hill. This was their family now. They asked her to talk to them, especially with Maifea. She agreed to do so when they arrived in Tava'esina. Life would be incomplete without the two boys. They were such good company to the girls who had folded them in as their brothers.

Add the four children, Grandmother Epenesa and Puni, Noah's nursemaid, and the house was bursting with energy. The house has certainly increased in size as it has love and harmony. No one could have thought they could come out of Hawaii and inherit a diverse family.

"Lesina, there is a full moon tonight. We should go down and take everyone out for the palolo run!" Pele suggested as they had their morning tea. "It'll be good for everyone to get out, and we can stay with La'auli."

"That we can do. I'll ask Puni if she is good with keeping the littles here at home. Get Iolana and Kiele to help prepare the mats, and we'll head down. I'm sure your brothers would love the overnight visit."

The younger girls could barely contain their happiness. This was their first round at the annual festive run of the island's caviar. The spawning of the coral worm was long anticipated by those who waited for the first moon of October. It had been a year of unspeakable tragedies, and Lesina knew it would be good to see her family relax and be part of something happy. They've all had and seen enough sadness to last them a lifetime.

There were scattered men along the shores when they came down the embankment. They waved at them, welcoming them to the plentiful bounty the sea was about to offer. A slight breeze blew through as the equatorial summer started.

Pele and the girls clambered through the undergrowth from the pandanus trees to get to the beach line, careful to avoid the thorny parts of the leaves. It was only about three o'clock in the afternoon, but this would give them time to get their spot before others came out at nightfall. As soon as they were on the sand, Iolana dropped the mats and a couple of baskets.

She hurriedly straightened them out under the shade of a leaning beach hibiscus tree, spread out the hand-stitched quilt blankets, and then told Pele before she ran down the length of the beach. Serenity looked at Pele for permission, which Pele granted her readily with laughter.

Serenity broke from Pele's slower stroll after she got the okay and chased after Iolana with sheer joy, leaving her slippers behind her in the sand. Pele watched them both and laughed at the freedom they felt as they hooted and hollered at the skies and winds. The sound of successive splashes was loud and a clear enough sign of what those two were up to! Kiele giggled as she looked at Pele.

"They can do their own laundry, Pele." Kiele rolled her eyes at how much laundry they go through as a family.

"Yes—and haul their stuff uphill tomorrow morning!"

"It's so nice to rest for a bit and not have anything to do, Kiele," Pele mused. "We haven't seen you or Lesina for a spell before sundown." She spent more of her time growing crops. Even as their tenancy ended in December, leaving the land in good standing and food crops others could use would be ideal. Her efforts showed in her callused hands and the corners of her feet.

"I know—there has been so much else to tend to. Life didn't stop because of the flu." She pulled out the banana bread she had baked this morning, leaving three for the boys and La'auli for their teas. "People are in need and haven't access to any medical care because we've been stuck back here."

A thought crossed Pele's mind just then. "If we have to leave Upolu, do you still want to come home with me, Kiele?"

There was a pause. "I'm not sure, Pele. Honestly, I'd like to stay here. I've found my home here," Kiele said hesitantly. "I'll go with you if you want me to, but I'd like to stay here."

Pele laughed, reaching over for Kiele's hand. "You can stay here, go with us, whatever you feel like doing—you do." As she said this, she felt a shadow of sadness creep over her. Her sister not coming with her would be hard to swallow, but it was bound to happen.

Kiele took to nursing so naturally that it would be wrong to take her away from her work here. She is established and speaks enough Samoan now to communicate well with locals. Most have become accustomed to Kiele asking these questions and going through their homes, even if she *is* Hawaiian. Lesina sang Kiele's praises without a slight bias. Her aunt was not an easy taskmaster, so gaining her respect was enough of a character reference.

"Do you want to go home, Pele?"

"Honestly, I think I am ready—or near it. This living on someone else's good graces is not sitting too well," Pele bemoaned. "I think my parents can write off any grand marriage plans at this point. Besides, being stuck here amid the pandemic will not sit right with any interested groom."

"Pele, do you mind if I tell you something in confidence?"

"Sure, what?" Pele replied, looking curiously at Kiele, crossing her eyes. She screamed in mock outrage at her *tita's* fist in the air.

The boys came stumbling down the dune, kicking at the sand beneath their feet. They dragged over a basket of coconut husks, staples in green baskets, and some fresh green coconuts. Behind them, Maifea and Lachlan followed with mosquito nets and more baskets.

"*Talofa,* ladies!" Maifea greeted Pele and Kiele happily. He wrapped his lavalava up to his waist and wore it as *malo.* He was cheek to cheek with Pele, picking her up in an exuberant hug, then the same merriment with Kiele. With his jaunty walk, he walked down to the water's edge. The green of his *malofie* stood out today.

"Wow, *ua pe masa le kai!* You can smell the ocean today, ladies," he said observantly, wriggling his massive nose. The sun beamed off the sea as the afternoon turned slowly to evening. "Good time to go looking for sea urchins!"

Kiele laughed and looked at Pele, who ruefully shook her head. "Go ahead, Kiele. I'm going to watch our teens." As much as she would have loved to walk across, the sight of the reef line turned her stomach.

Lachlan came from behind her. "You can go if you want."

"No, it's okay. I should watch the girls." She turned to see him come around, in his lavalava draped to his ankles. "I see that Maifea is having a good time airing out." She laughed merrily.

Lachlan smiled but didn't say much to her. He sat down on the mat next to her. "So, what has been going on with you?"

"Grow everything and anything to help support our family. It's been quiet, you know. I'm glad for this respite," she answered. "So much sadness, so many families only shadows of their former *aigas,* Lachlan."

Lachlan looked at her and said nothing. She queried, "Are you okay, or do you just need a minute?" He stared off into the horizon, preoccupied.

He suddenly got up and went down to the beach where the kids were playing. Pele was baffled by his unfriendliness and distemper. She would have gone after him, but Iolana and Serenity had returned to her and asked for food. Pele sighed, sadly wondering about his sudden dark mood, but it seemed redundant and prying even to try. He'd probably speak of whatever burr in his paw when he was ready.

Before the moon peeked over the corner hill, voices carried over the breeze as folks passed through the shallow ends of the shore with their kerosene lanterns and burning coconut fronds. There was laughter as people met with families they hadn't seen over the past year. Women with billowing *mu'umu'u* shirts cried out for barrels and baskets.

All her keis were out there enjoying the hunt for the coveted *palolo,* the caviar of the Pacific. She waited on the knoll as she watched after their lavalavas, some leftover food, and mats. The night was still dark, but they had to get to La'auli's soon. When the moon moves over the sky, this will end the festivities as the worms will be swept out with the tide.

It was so good to hear people talk loudly, make fun of others, and carry on boisterously. It was so *healthy*, according to everyone but her belly.

"We have so much, Pele!" Serenity pointed out their bounty. "Now what?"

"It will be so great to share with everyone!" Iolana felt so accomplished as she rushed up toward her with the bucket. "But how do you eat this, Pele?"

"Your guess is as good as mine, girls. I've never eaten it myself." Pele wriggled her nose. "We're going to have to watch the pros do so." She laughed at Iolana's expressive gaze. Lord, please make sure that no one gets stomach issues. Coming up to the girls, Maifea and Kiele also dropped a bucket, with the boys dragging barrels of the most fantastic loot yet.

Lachlan hung back as he watched the ocean tide come in, people trekking up the knoll with their barrels and baskets in the distance. He took out a cheroot and lit it, pulling a drag.

As he stood there, he heard a voice from behind him. "Open your hand," Pele told him, smiling at his pensive grimace in the moonlight. He held out an open palm. Pele pressed the shillings into his hand and gently closed his fingers around it.

"When you're ready, Friend." She turned to leave him there for some privacy.

The others have long disappeared above the knoll and are at La'auli's faletalimalo. Pele found her way up to the footpath, following indents in the sand, and followed those through the low branches of the pandanus grove and the *lautagitagi* row. As she turned the corner, her lavalava caught the bougainvillea, tearing it off. Mortified, the more she pulled, the more the lavalava ripped.

"Hold on—I'll help you!" Lachlan turned to the task of untangling her from the bougainvillea. When he did pull her lavalava, it was in tatters. Pele gratefully took it from him. She motioned for him to turn around. Even if her sensibilities were in tatters, she wasn't as bared to him as she was on the ship. A lot of her had filled in, and she wasn't into showing her assets to anyone, let alone, Lachlan.

What she wanted out of the bits of fabric and what became of them were two different realities. She *felt* his eyes on her back. She heard his shameless laughter as she hurried forward to La'auli's faletalimalo. Even in the pitch dark, she knew those eyes.

"Wait up! Pele, I'll help!" he called out. She didn't wait for him. "I swear!" He was overcome with laughter at her indignation and the haste she made to get away from him.

"You're the village idiot, Lachlan McCallister!" His laughter was riotous and unrepentant. Pele flushed profusely in the dark, hurrying ahead without looking back.

The boys were in the umu, as was everyone else, gathering the food crops and preparing the meal for the afternoon meal. Because their harvest was on Thursday, they could not wait until Sunday's toana'i to prepare their bounty. Lesina and Kiele were weaving baskets from coconut fronds. Iolana fetched water for the boys as they scraped breadfruit and taro. Lachlan and Maifea were further up in the plantation to bring the umu coverings.

"It is so good to have people around." La'auli smiled through tears as he prepared the palusami. Pele sat with him as he was teaching her how to scoop the coconut milk into the taro leaves that they had harvested and washed earlier. In her infinite reasoning, Grace was on her back after being left behind last night, which was enough to make the tyke cling to Pele.

"It is quite lovely to see everyone out and about," she agreed. Looking at her borrowed uncle, she was sincerely happy to be here with everyone.

The village was ablaze, with umus being made in most households. Most folks were visiting La'auli and were happy to see many people with him during the post-palolo harvest. Some stayed to talk stories, and others picked crops they could add to their umu. Lesina packed *ti* leaves of palolo and dropped them into the baskets so that she could take them around to older villagers who had lost able family members. The girls went with her. The feeling of community this morning made the day feel like Sunday.

Pele started tea for her hodge-podge family as soon as Serenity had a good grip on the portions. Lachlan had fetched the green coconuts as she was thinking more *vaisalo,* as all other options were too time-consuming. She scraped the coconut meal out of shells into a pot for twenty coconuts. Pouring the coconut water in with the young coconut flesh, she also shifted.

Lachlan dropped the massive bundle of banana leaves and sought Pele out. Maifea laughed as he saw his cousin hurriedly walk off. He dropped his load of bananas and mangoes for the family. Meanwhile, Lachlan was well done with Maifea's orders to climb the trees, just about every tree along their path. Lachlan had mounted them with his lavalava and shimmied to their tops to harvest fruit while Maifea shouted orders from the ground and laughed his tyrannical life away.

Maifea howled in merriment as Lachlan gave him a baleful look in his haste to find a kinder taskmaster. He threw an overripe mango at his cousin's retreating back while the boys looked on and guffawed at Lachlan's disgust as the freckled fruit hit Maifea bullseye between his shoulder blades. The man did not even flinch but laughed louder at Lachlan's attempts at a payback.

Grace was asleep on Pele's back, which was a sight to behold, as the younger held on even as Pele worked. The work of scraping coconuts was fascinating, and she laughed between balancing Grace and scraping her coconuts.

Pele felt the load of some thirty pounds doubled on her back lifted off. She was startled but relaxed as Lachlan took the sleeping child into his arms. He put his index finger up against his lips as Pele glanced up. He carried Grace to the fale and gently laid her down before rolling out a mat and getting a sheet to cover her.

Grabbing the coconut frond, Pele cut the tip of the leaf stem to fashion into a whisk. She took it to the pot of coconut and its meal. Lachlan took her cue and moved the pot to the earthen upright oven as he took over the whisk from her.

Pele moved around him to get some kindling for the fire and to prepare the tapioca. She squeezed by Lachlan, who was happy to be her assistant to avoid Maifea.

"So, he made the palagi climb?" she merrily asked, knowing it was most likely the case. It was much easier for Lachlan to do so as Maifea up a tree was fanciful.

"That he did. Without mercy." Lachlan hurried around to the side so that Pele could take over. She laughed at his look of exaggerated weariness and shame. "Even my feet have calluses in places I didn't know I had!"

"Oh no!" Pele bent at her waist, guffawing at the sight of his feet. They were rough. That she had sent him to find coconuts earlier made her feel a smidgeon of guilt for his discomfort. As the vaisalo came to a slow boil, she had him taste the piping hot porridge. When he nodded in sheer pleasure, she handed him the whisk.

"Keep the tapioca from sticking, please." This was while she prepared the bowls and crackers.

As a family, they ate their meal in companionable gaiety as La'auli led the prayers while Pele and the girls served the dishes.

"*A, Lesina—matuā aualelei ka au'alumā.*" La'auli chortled. He was very grateful to have an extended family amid the massive losses around the village. "*Manaia mea uma!*" Lesina sat next to him, enjoying the respite, fanning herself as she glanced out at the kitchen as her girls served. Before tona'i was served, Pele packed up fresh baskets of food for Maua and his family, which she sent with Mataio and Tala'i to deliver. If she could send out all the palolo, she would find random families to send them to.

Maifea sat on the opposite side, with Lachlan and the boys following. Pele and the girls sat close by as they waited out the calls for replenishment and handwash tanoa.

When the first of the toana'i was over, Pele and Kiele sat with the younger girls in a semi-circle, regaled with a lot of giggles. They enjoyed their food on banana leaves under the shade of a nearby *talie* tree. Grace sat near her knee while the others faced them, while Love sat in Pele's arms, eating her fish happily as fast as Pele could sort it for her.

"Want to try the *palolo*, Keleise?" Her kei looked at the speckled blue swimming worms and sat back, refusing to go next to the bowl. They laughed at her look of utter disgust.

"You should try some, Pele," Kiele said as she took more of her breadfruit, relishing every bite with *palolo* on top of its meal. "It's so good if you don't look at it." So'o's wife hummed her agreement, laughing out bits of her taro. Iolana was penitent and shy but so agreed with the majority.

Pele looked at a lump of worms intently with one eye. The others fell back, laughing. Here, a demarcation line was drawn between the righteous and the palolo eaters.

"Grace said it for both of us. Right, Keleise?" She begged off and chose her usual octopus. As Kiele ate her mouthful with relish, Pele heard several crunches between happy, loud grunts. Like crisps snapping. She glared at her sister, who only openly snorted at Pele's disgust.

Between bites, Pele declared happily, "It's been so nice today, girls. Thank you for helping, my loves."

"Why couldn't today be Sunday?" Iolana opined as she dug into the palolo. "Be so nice to rest when we're done."

"Who says we can't, honey?" Pele answered as she moved Grace to sit in front of her so she could properly sit while she ate, facing Love. "Go get us mats, Iolana, so that we can nap this out." It was a lovely day as the winds blew through the village.

As they cleaned up, Maifea came out to help clean. "Please, don't." Pele laughed as he took the laulau and leftovers from them.

"No, you ladies served us, so now I wait on you all. You are indeed the best *au'alumā* ever!" He winked at Serenity, who giggled. Here, Iolana stood up to help him before he told her to sit and enjoy the day with the others.

Lachlan followed him from the fale, leaving the younger boys to listen to La'auli's *fa'agogo*. He offered a cheroot to his cousin, who took it. The men smoked theirs while Pele and her loves enjoyed the excellent weather in the shade of the massive *talie* tree.

For once, they were not running from rain or hiding from sweltering humidity. With the mats laid out, giggles, belly laughter, and snorts rang out as Pele told the young stories of old Samoa, of an ungrateful mouse who hitched a ride on an octopus. Serenity called out that the mouse sounded much like Grace, who cried her disagreement. Pele sighed as she pulled Grace closer, winking at Serenity, assuring the older girl that it was okay, for it was too wonderful of an afternoon to be cross.

Once upon a time, she was wailing in protest when Fano called her the mouse. The mouse did turn into the fruit bat who found their redemption in cleansing crops. Redemption that she, as the older mouse, now was in the kitchen serving up tea and biscuits with Lachlan as her waiter for the main house.

A couple of hours later, after the girls had ample naps, Pele started to pack baskets as Iolana and Serenity packed their bedding. Grace tried to help but was sent to Lesina to help get the young ones ready for the walk home. Kiele pulled their sparse overnight bags, grabbed some food baskets, and walked them to the corner of the fale. Maifea grabbed a long stick and threaded the baskets through. He would see them to Teuila. As the girls said goodbye to the boys, Lesina came down to the *paepae*. She hugged and kissed the younger boys as well before turning to the road home.

"Tofā, La'auli. O lea matou o ma teneiti!" Lesina called out as she headed toward the main road where the others had already started home to Teuila. The girls began the merry chase while Pele laughed with Grace's hand in hers, watching the craziness behind them. Seeing the fun ahead, Grace let go and shuffled after the bigger girls. Kiele kept Maifea company behind them as he brought up the baskets.

Lachlan joined the girls to come up the rear and took Love from Pele. She appreciated his help as she rolled a crick out of her neck. They padded side by side, as Pele walked with her elbows akimbo.

"Don't you ever get tired of the hike?"

"I can't imagine life elsewhere, Lachlan." She replied with a smile. "It's funny that when we spend all day with La'auli, we don't want to go home. But once home, we don't want to come down."

"I wish I could help, Pele. I really wish I could." Lachlan said more to himself. He began to hurt in a place that he kept hidden from this girl. As Love weighed heavier on one shoulder, Pele asked him to let her take her before the steps up to the house, grateful for the break this far.

"No, the least I can do is get you both home."

La'auli stood with his left arm behind his back and waved at the women and Maifea as they departed. This was the problem with visits. He was always saddened to say goodbye to his Teuila Hill family. He watched from the paepae yet another departure. *One day, they will stay.*

All set aside and put in their proper places, Pele and Kiele set aside a meal for Puni. There was so much ado over the *palolo* and pickled sea cucumber from So'o's wife as Epenesa ate with more gusto than she had most days. Her clouded eyes smiled their pleasure over the treats. Pele called Serenity over with a fan to ward off any evening bugs from Epenesa and Puni.

Pele took Noah out of Puni's arms so she could eat peaceably without little arms on her face. Even though it was only an overnight trip, it always felt like she was leaving the world behind. Noah went in his bassinet fashioned by the men out of sennit and decided that he was going to sleep through dinner. As everyone settled down for the night, Lesina went to lie down as well, but first, her prayers, lest she not get up again with the Good Lord's graces.

Maifea settled down next door in the extension after putting away the staples from the day's meal. He watched the breathtaking sunset from the corner. Kiele happily sidled up next to him, sitting by a pou over. She handed over a green coconut to him. "How did Pele take the idea of you staying behind?"

She replied shyly. "We are going to be okay."

Maifea looked at her with love and care. "Yes, we are, Kiele." He put his hand over hers. They sat watching the sun settle over the western end of the horizon. She leaned over on his shoulder.

VIII. December 1919

Ti'otala Ma Pepe Lele
Kingfishers and Butterflies

The children were up and cavorting outside of the fale at the break of dawn. The rising sun's rays caught Serenity's blondish hair and set it afire. She held onto her dark horse, Grace, chasing down the incline, screaming after butterflies. Or she tried to! Love sat next to her sister, sucking her thumb.

"Seren! Love – a lea!" Grace giggled as she snuck up onto one sitting on a milkweed plant. "Come look!" It was a monarch butterfly, fluttering to and from leaves. Grace stood and laughed, her hands on her knees as she tried to see if the butterfly would stay long enough for her to hug.

Pele stirred from her sleep, scooted onto her right side, and stared at the rising sun at the bottom of the blinds. Missing from her arms were Grace and Love. When she heard that familiar squeal, she rubbed the sleep from her eyes and sat up. Pele saw that Serenity was missing from her spot and knew the poor girl was outside with her sisters. *Grace,* she said tiredly. Where did she get all that energy?

"Ua, Serenity?" she called out to the girl. She would have to tie bells to Grace so all would be set on alarm and wake up in time. Serenity was no match for that child. Pele laughed to herself, as tired as she was. It was time to get up and greet the day. And Grace.

"O lea sola Keleise lalo le pā, Pele!"

"Alu e koso mai!" she hollered back. *That child will kill her before her twentieth spring,* she thought helplessly. If not mindful of the steps, Grace could tumble down the hill. She and Iolana fashioned and hammered a gate in place so it wouldn't happen to the children as they traversed way up and down the hill.

Kiele bounced up from her sound sleep, startled. "Something happened?"

Pele was already on the go looking for her slippers. Kiele watched and thought she had to get up and help with whatever emergency. Pele motioned for her to go back to sleep.

The offender was still by the milkweed plants and staring intently at the butterflies. Pele came up next to her and stuck her face between butterflies and her budding entomologist. She got a toothy grin minus three.

Pele straightened and put her hand out to Grace. As they walked toward the fale, Grace had about ten reasons why it was barely dawn on a Friday, and she was this far from Serenity.

"I wanted to see the *pepes*, Pele. They disappear quickly during the day, and I wasn't out to make you worry about me," Grace reasoned, rushing to get all points in at once. Pele looked down, and she laughed at that toothy-minus-three smile warmed up.

"When Serenity is watching you, you mind her, Grace. I'm not going to tell you this again." Pele tried to be stern. One day, she will regret it, but the child is just five today. "Don't you sass her, either!" At a safe distance, knowing Grace wouldn't fall, she let her walk on ahead to apologize to Serenity.

Tea followed after world peace was restored. Iolana took the girls to bathe while Pele and Kiele stayed behind to clean up after the morning's repast. Pele went in to check on Epenesa and picked up after her. The dowager aunt motioned her young friend closer.

"Pele, I'm tired. I'm going to take a nap. Look after your keis. *Fai fa'alelei teneiti. Ou manuia na.*"

"Don't worry, Epe! They will be okay. A little scolding now and then doesn't hurt." She laughed as she unfolded the blanket to spread it over Epenesa, covering her from feet to head.

She motioned Pele closer, who sat back on her haunches and securely tucked the sheet under Epenesa. "Pele, I love you. Thank you for being family when I haven't any left." She kissed Pele's hand. *"Se'i fai si ata moe laititi na fai laia ka kala, a ea."* Pele smoothed Epe's thinning gray hair that was tucked into a loose bun. Oh, the days when hair was dyed with lemon, Epenesa once told her. "This would be good for yours as you have such thick hair." Pele laughed at the idea.

Lesina was drinking her cacao roast at the back end of the fale. Pele sidled up next to her aunt. "Good morning, Aunty."

"Morning, my banana souffle!" Lesina put down her cup. "Soon, we'll have to leave all this behind."

"Well, La'auli would welcome us with open arms."

"I know, but we must get into our place." Lesina didn't say it out loud, but Pele understood that her aunt thought of all the issues with living with La'auli as landed and connected as he was. It was akin to being minions to a lord in the same house. The villagers wouldn't take it too kindly, especially now that influenza has reached its most tragic point. The last they would expect is non-related family camping with their orator. Lesina served a purpose as the taulasea, but unless she married La'auli, they did not have the right to live with him.

Her aunt was not the most ardent marriage advocate, let alone that to La'auli. She wasn't opposed to the man. She was opposed to a forced marriage regardless of their circumstances.

"Well, there is always the option of going home," Pele said quietly. Lesina visibly flinched, and the side of her lip twitched. "I know it isn't something we want to consider, but we'll always be outsiders here." Regardless of their relations here in Samoa, they will always be foreign cousins who align with the Americans.

"I know, Pele. However, the work and need here is plentiful and is so immense that it'd be wrong to turn my back on these folks." There was never an end to births and women who needed help birthing a generation. To leave them with little access to care would be inconceivable for her and her girls!

They sat together and took in the blessed sights in relative silence. Kiele found them with Pele lying with her head on Lesina's lap as she softly sang a lullaby. Kiele walked up and sat behind Lesina. She crossed her legs, leaned close, and placed her hand on Lesina's back. As Lesina sang on, Kiele started to cry. At the same time, Pele wept in her aunt's lap. Her lullaby spoke of the importance of staying close to home and caring for their folk as is customary.

Where will home be now?

It was Chapel Day for the young girls, and it was time to get them out with their cousins and aunts. As Pele crossed the churchyard, one of the women standing with the chapel's children reached out to her.

"Are you caring for Elisapeta's kids?"

"Yes, myself and my family. Why?" Pele asked, concerned. The woman didn't look like anyone she had seen before in the village.

"I am, *was* her best friend."

"Oh, I'm sorry. I should have found you sooner." Pele looked over at Serenity with her sisters. "Did you need something?"

"Oh, no. I wanted to know if you knew that the kids have a father."

"Yes, the husband. He also passed away." Pele replied matter-of-factly.

"No, that was her husband. Have you looked at the kids?" she asked in disbelief. "You *know* those were not his."

"I'm sorry, but who were you to Elisapeta?"

"I was her best friend," she said smugly.

"Well, please don't speak ill of the dead, as neither of us were there." Pele made off to walk over to La'auli's fale. She stopped and turned back to Peta's best friend. She fought the worry she felt creep up into her heart but could not let her go without knowing. She had to ask. "Were you interested in taking the kids?"

"Why no! I have four of my own!"

"And you don't know of any siblings or parents?"

"Her sister will not take the kids," she scoffed. "*O ulu elaela le kamaloa palagi lena faigaluega ai Peka.*" These were bastard children of the master of the house. She revealed it as if she was imparting a national secret. She did but to the wrong person.

Pele knew something was amiss when she first took the kids from their mother. However, it wasn't something she was about to investigate then or now. This did confirm the rumors that she was afraid to acknowledge. The children were innocent of their parentage, but this could mean she had to find their father. That the children were Gerhardt Hansell's? Pele wasn't informed of this tidbit; she has been worried. She had her selfish reasons not to look further.

As she walked up La'auli's fale, a strange cart was in front of it. La'auli sat there watching the palagi on it, who looked perplexed, hot, and bothered in his penguin suit. He was overdressed, and given how humid it was today, he was overtly out of place.

Pele looked at La'auli and wrinkled her nose before approaching the stranger.

"Sir, are you looking for someone?"

"Yes, I am, Miss. This gentleman doesn't seem to understand anything I'm telling him."

"He is deaf, mute, and numb, so please excuse him." La'auli cast his eyes elsewhere in sham affront. Pele stifled a giggle, "How can I help you?"

"I was told that I can find Ms. Lesina Spafford here."

"Yes, she's my aunt, but she isn't home now."

"Do you have an idea when she'll be here?" he asked with barely veiled annoyance.

"I do. It will help us if you tell me why you need to speak to my aunt."

The man waiting for the palagi called out to Pele, "*Fai iai koekiki koe fo'i i Apia.*" Pele turned back to this gentleman and informed him what the driver had said. The driver was understandably in a hurry—the sun was canting, and town folk did not believe in being in back villages beyond sunset.

He shifted his spectacles. Ichabod Crane came to Pele's mind. *Oh, Sister Ingrid!* "Please let Ms. Spafford know that I'm a solicitor from town. I need her to come and see me. I'm here on behalf of the estate of John Lesoso."

Pele took his pen and wrote the name down in her notebook. "Please let her know I have urgent business that I've been trying to find her for the past four months." Pele could not even remember the day before, let alone what they were doing four months ago.

Once out of earshot, she looked at La'auli, "You, Sir, are a stinker. *Makuā leva na i le kamaloa ae ete le fesosoani iai?*"

La'auli paused, then guiltily, "I'm sorry, Pele. *Fa'apea seisi ole lotu ua sau.*" He was right to worry. Agents of the Congregationalist Church were bound to be here someday soon, as were the independent aides of the Apia Catholic Diocese. Most of the village was Congregationalist, and their marriages, births, and deaths of the past sixty years were all duly recorded in their registries. Both churches were bound to come in and record the dead. *Or are they?*

She hoped that Eli would come as the noted agent of record on official business. It would be an excellent way to say goodbye to him. No one was able to visit the Monsignor's secretary for ordinary calls. This saddened her immensely.

"Pele, why did Mommy have to die?" Grace asked out of the blue. She looked up at Pele with that upturn face and nose. Those amber eyes were bound to be the object of a husband's love.

"I don't know, Grace." Pele wasn't aware of the Good Father's planning committee's decisions, but she didn't want to pass on anything less than the truth to the girls.

"Do you think she's looking after us from heaven?"

"Yes, I'm sure that she looks down and sees you all. Especially after you, Grace." Pele laughed at Grace's wide-eyed grin.

Serenity came up next to them. "Grace, stop asking stupid questions." Grace stared at her sister, horrified by Serenity's anger.

Pele stopped Serenity and sent Grace up ahead. Once Grace was up beyond with Iolana, who had Love, she turned to Serenity. "You don't have to be harsh with your sister."

"Yeah, well, our mother? She was never around for us. Our father *was,* and look at what happened to him." Pele stopped to stand next to Serenity. Although she was ten, she was the ghost of a child, and her light blue eyes were rounder than most of her body. She was coming into her prepubescent body early. There was that familiar awkwardness with a body far ahead of her maturity.

"I'm sorry you didn't have your mother, Serenity, but I know she was doing what she needed to for your family."

Serenity was the mother-in-situ to her siblings, including Noah, from birth. This was her family in the absence of adults. As they buried their mother in February, Serenity did not cry but remained stoic, protectively shadowing the children. Now, she is losing her role as caretaker and is told to be a child she never was.

Under her breath, she angrily noted, "She was home every other third week and here for two to three days. She loved those people more than she did us."

Serenity walked toward the side road, kicking a stone or three. "We never saw her, Pele. Never! All the time she had for me was yet another baby to babysit!" She started to weep openly. Pele walked up to her and pulled Serenity into her embrace. She hugged her tightly, so the dear, dear child was assured of her love.

It has been nearly a year since Pele found Peka in their home. Now, Serenity has finally allowed herself to grieve. Pele stood with the child and held her for as long as it took. She planted kisses on Serenity's forehead as she hiccupped, her shoulders racked with sorrow for her parents, and her plaintive sob slowed.

"Promise me one thing, Serenity?" Pele said against the girl's temple. "Believe me when I tell you I have you now." Serenity hugged her even tighter. "And be so patient with Grace." Serenity stiffened before she laughed and hugged Pele tighter, burying her face into her new mother's midriff. Love and Noah were too young to be painful stitches to Serenity's side.

"Mama Pele?" Serenity asked as they were closer to Iolana and the girls who were running forward and then back toward them. Pele looked over at her. "Thank you for changing our names." Pele held Serenity a bit longer, wiped her blotchy, wet eyes with the front of her smock, and squeezed her tiny, thin hand.

As they came up the lower steps, Lesina called out to them as she was about fifty feet behind them. Iolana stopped and waved with Love in her arms. Pele glanced up from Grace on her back while Serenity pushed them both up the steps, laughing. They all stopped to wait on Lesina as she pulled up the rear. She had bags in her arms with some rations from town. As a surprise to the girls, Johann had sent up some brots and brioche buns for them.

"So good to see you, girls," Lesina said breathlessly. "We should probably look for something on the flat lands," she joked. Leaning over, she hugged and squeezed Iolana with Love, then Serenity and Grace. It was too tricky for Pele to turn around as Grace's thirty-five pounds were on her back. As they balanced out the loads, Serenity took the bread bag from Lesina, who beamed her gratitude. Serenity grinned at her. "You are welcome, Aunty."

Before they made it to their fence, Kiele ran from the fale, sobbing inconsolably. Pele moved Grace around to let her down safely and let her follow Iolana and the girls. Kiele shook her head and told the girls to stop.

"Pele! Lesina!" Kiele cried out. "I'm so sorry. Epe is gone! I went to give her afternoon tea, and she didn't answer. She's gone!"

Pele stopped, letting Grace slip down before she raced up the fale! Through the front lanai, she ran to Epenesa's area. There, she fell to her knees and found Epenesa in her death pose. She looked so peaceful, but as time settled, her mouth was agape, her gaze empty. Pele took her friend's freckled, veiny hand closest to her, sobbing, rocking back and forth on her haunches.

"Oh, Epe!" Pele cried into her fragile hand. "You were going to live with us forever!" She took Epenesa's still-warm hand and put her face into its palm.

Lesina came up behind Pele and held her niece as the girl wept, devastated and heartbroken as she was. She called Kiele forward and had her sit next to them. The young women cried out loud while Lesina sat with them in shock. They quietly sat there with Epenesa in the darkness.

As the women were in with Epenesa, Puni watched the kids and Iolana until they were asked for from the extension next door. When she heard Lesina recite the Lord's Prayer as the girls listened on throughout, Puni held Noah and Love, crying softly into Love's hair. She had lost her family to the pandemic, and now Epenesa's death this close was enough to put her back last December when her husband and two children died. She didn't know then how or why she was left behind. She looked at Love in her lap and Noah, who was in the bassinet. Across the mat, Iolana held Grace while Serenity sat at her side.

If this is my chosen road, so be it, she thought tearfully.

Lesina asked the girls to gather water, *ti*, plumeria, and *moso'oi* oil. To care for Epenesa, she had Pele and Kiele help her as she closed Epenesa's eyes and mouth. Lesina asked the girls to bathe Epe's weathered body as she prepared the oils. Once the girls had finished Epenesa's last bath, they sat aside as Lesina took over. She gently massaged Epenesa's skin as most of her had aged into this fragile crepe thinness. Once upon a time, Epenesa was this petite and probably a hellion in her early years.

Go well into the night, Epenesa, she whispered, her voice quivering. *Ia manuia lou malaga!* She put small sea stones on Epe's eyes. Lesina smiled, her eyes filled with tears that fell on Epenesa's body. She lovingly wiped their dowager aunt's face. While the girls rested, Lesina sat with Epe's body.

Before they brought out the *tapa* and wrapped Epenesa in its folds, Lesina called for her family to view Epenesa. They gathered around her body and said their last prayers. The children knew that in that somber moment, Epenesa was now with their parents. Lesina let them come closer to say goodbye and see Epenesa's body in repose.

Pele brought out the pupugi to fashion the funeral wrap. The five women gently lifted Epenesa onto this mammoth *ngata* that Lesina gained from a Fijian family in a barter of services. Kiele followed the outline of Epenesa's body. Puni helped tuck the corners at Epenesa's feet before they closed her into the mulberry bark, securing it under her chin, waist, and ankles.

Iolana informed La'auli early in the morning following Epenesa's passing. He called for Mataio to blow the conch to alert the village. Tala'i called upon other younger men to help fashion a stretcher after La'auli informed him.

This morning, the climb to Teuila was challenging as they balanced and lifted the stretcher over their heads. The girls guided them through the ascent as some young men had not been up to Teuila. As they took a breath, they were served tea, which they gladly accepted. If they had not walked this road this morning, strangers would not know that Teuila was tucked into the hill above, closer to the clouds than they were to Tava'esina or Samoa, for that matter.

With Mataio and Tala'i leading, the six men went to Lesina, who motioned them forward to Epenesa and gently lifted her body upon it after part of the ngata was cut and laid across the makeshift carrier. Serenity and Grace poured a basket of flowers over Epenesa. She always insisted on her *sei* every morning. Grace laid the flowers in order, plumerias over her body, with the gardenias near Epenesa's head.

"Oute alofa ia te oe, Tinā!" Grace pressed kisses to Epenesa's tapa-covered head. If she was any louder, the house was sure Epenesa would have sat up to remind Grace about her inside voice for the usual tenth round, as was the norm for Teuila Hill. All gathered stifled their laughter as it was very improper to break the solemnity of the moment. *Oh, Grace!*

Serenity came up to their Great-Grandmama, a name insisted upon by Epenesa, and sat at the Elder's head. She touched her forehead to Epe's and cried. "My love to my parents, Great-Grandmama! I'm trying my best and always watch after the kids. And that it's okay—we have a new mother and family. Can you tell them that?"

The women and children slowly followed the young pallbearers as they lifted Epenesa's body to the village. A lone kingfisher sat on a branch of the beach hibiscus tree where Teuila blended into the road down to Tava'esina. Pele didn't bother to look up to the harbinger. She already knew why he was here.

La'auli watched as the slow procession came toward his faletalimalo. His throat caught as he watched the five women and the young children follow closely behind the pallbearers. Lesina was at the center of the formation, flanked by Pele and Kiele to her right, while Iolana and Puni carried her left. Serenity had Noah on her hip while Grace stayed close to Pele, her chubby hand in her new mother's. Love was bundled on Puni's back.

The women were wrapped in feathered fine mats gathered at their waists, draped in bright floral colors under their mats, with feathered leis and flower *pale* of moso'oi and plumeria blooms. Wrapped around their arms were strings of shells, the hollow pods of the kapok trees.

La'auli called out one of his matais to walk with him to greet Lesina and the funeral procession. He walked down the steps of the *paepae* and waited for the matai to come around from the back.

Instead of the lone chief, So'o, the village men came in groups, in their best lavalavas, pandanus nut leis, bare chests, and feet, as did women in fine mats, followed by children, theirs and orphans alike. From the east, more came and joined their fellow neighbors on the road to form the receiving line. Weeping women stepped back as Lesina, with her wards and Puni, walked through accompanying Epenesa throughout the village to put her in the chapel at the end of Tava'esina. This was where she grew up with her parents and siblings, who had passed through the veil long ago. Her husband had been gone some thirty years before being spared all this sadness. Epenesa is there now with her husband, son, and daughter. She was no longer left behind here in this living with mere mortals.

As the sun splayed its rays on the horizon by three in the afternoon, villagers remained close after the burial. Grace stuck flowers in the mound over Epenesa's grave before stepping back to hold Pele's hand, looking up for approval. Pele clasped her little hand warmly. The sadness was palpable, but no one was moving. There was scattered weeping among the women while the men remained stoic but present in mind and spirit. They not only buried Epenesa but their husbands, wives, and children, whom the government undertakers took away to undisclosed internments.

"Ua so'ona olioli nei, lou loto ia Iesu. Ua Ia fa'aola ia te a'u…" The hymn sounded ethereal over the crowd gathered through the malae. *I rejoice now as my heart is with Jesus. Epenesa and all our loved ones, delight! For you are with Our Father! Your burdens of this world have been washed from you, and you will see your salvation through His benevolence!*

"La'auli, please have everyone go home and bring food. Let's have a toana'i!" Lesina said out loud. "It will help bring the village back to the center." La'auli, who looked his tender age right then, nodded in agreement. He made the arrangements with his matais.

The village came together, brought their foodstuffs, and shared with their neighbors, many of whom hadn't seen one another in months. There was a sense of relief and renewal among the villagers. Mats were spread out before

La'auli's faletalimalo as old families, none of which were intact, shared their mats and in the repast. New ones formed as orphaned children were gathered, eating as best as they could next to widowed mothers, made childless by the virulent disease.

"Lesina? You and the girls are accepted," La'auli said as he leaned over to her. He kindly noted that without their lead today, the whole village would have healed the sorely fractured boundary between the east and west. Still, it would be a greater tragedy as these massive extended families, while independent, were related and could trace their lineage back to three brothers. While religion and politics now split them, they were still *a'iga*.

La'auli leaned back against his pou and contentedly watched his village come back to the center. His cousins and their families made the journey back home from Apia's quarantine areas, and it was good to see them survive the rigors of the miles to the outer coastal areas.

The silence of Epenesa's absence was overwhelming in the weeks following her burial. While her family slept in, Pele grabbed her notebook as she found an unusual plant sprouting up the fence in the back. Christmas was a week ahead, and she was trying to gather as much as possible from her hill. A slight wind blew through, and she felt a sense of an end come over her. She had a lot to think of before they dismantled Teuila before New Year's. The impending changes were inevitable now. However, she could start anew with her family even if they went home to her parents. They had one another.

She thumbed through her book, laughing as she saw Serenity and Grace trace their hands on a page with Love's palm stamped in ochre. Noah's foot was on another. On the next page was their love letter, scribed over a torn patinaed page from Dickens' *David Copperfield*.

"Love you, Mama Pele." Serenity wrote out their names as neatly as she could. It is short, as simple as that. Pele held her book to her chest and wept. The children have been through so much this past year, and so much uncertainty faces them. Their mother's biological family would not take them in for these known reasons and ones that challenged her beliefs about such familial ties.

Grace hugged her neck as she rolled her belly against Pele's back, rocking back and forth. "I love you, Mama Pele," she exclaimed. Inside and outside of any dwelling, Grace was bound to make her presence known. Pele laughed and pulled her dear, dear girl into her lap. She mockingly groaned. "I love you more than the universe, Grace Spafford!" She tickled the tyke until she couldn't stand it anymore and ran from Pele, guffawing in that Grace-ish voice. It was a laugh that made one chuckle harder upon hearing it.

After their morning greetings, Grace wandered off to get them breakfast from Puni, who had the morning chore of breakfast rounds. Or so her little shadow proclaimed. Pele watched Grace's happy retreat before she turned a page over to scribe from her memory La'auli's oral history of Tava'esina.

After twenty minutes, Pele got up as that breakfast wasn't walking back, and now her belly was groaning the mating calls of whales between the Samoas, heard as far away as Tonga, maybe even Fiji. She heard the girls giggling out front, and it wasn't hard to conclude that her breakfast fetcher was down by the milkweed plants.

"Butterflies! There they are!" Grace hollered at her sisters. "They are here, EVERYBODY!" Serenity walked down to the fence post to see the beautiful, delicate kaleidoscope of monarchs and an unusual bright yellow one. For once, Grace's hollering call to assemble bore fruit.

Pele crossed the kitchen's threshold and leaned over to hug Puni as she dropped pancake dough into oil before moving on through the fale. Puni laughed as Grace blew over kisses, not for them but for the *pagikekes* frying up in the pot. That girl has a nose as intense as a bloodhound's sniffer as her chatter is loud.

Pele folded her newest addition into her notebook when she read a note to herself some time ago. As she read her scribbling, she felt so bad.

She rushed to find Lesina, who was with Kiele and Iolana, out in the lanai, lying about like sea cucumbers. *A fortnight ago,* Pele!

"Lesina, see! I was supposed to tell you that this palagi came to see you right before we lost Epe," Pele hurriedly told her. "John Lesoso? That name ring a bell?"

Lesina sat up and looked at Pele. "What did he want?"

"You to see him in town. He said he has been trying to find you to settle an estate," Pele recited from memory. Lesina started to cry. No one showed up to accompany John's body from the Immaculata. It was unlikely they'd show up now for his worldly possessions.

Without family, who are you in this world? She will be John's. *I will show up for you, my love.*

"Ma'am, I called on you two weeks ago, but I didn't get a response from you." He was as thin as a sandpiper, with a beak of a nose that hung over his disapproving upper lip. "I'm not sure if you Samoans intentionally show up whenever you want to, which is never on time."

"Mr. McKenzie, I understand you quite well, but the delay couldn't be helped." Lesina knew when these palagis condescended, and she couldn't take to it kindly. "Please give me Mr. Lesoso's personal effects, and I'll be out of your office." The place was nondescript. It was carved out of an old German apothecary shop in Apia, proclaiming *Mr. Henry McKenzie, Esq.* The essentials were his decor within its dark teak interior, with a few volumes of New Zealand law books on a shelf behind him.

"Ms. Spafford, wills are not that easily dispensed. There is much more to this codicil than you can hope to understand," he began.

Lesina stood as her patience was seeping out of her pores faster than the speed of sound. "Then help me understand quickly why it's so hard for me to get my friend's belongings." She stood up with her basket on her arm.

"Ma'am, please, sit down," Mr. McKenzie urged, this time with some humility. "I don't mean any offense, but this is a case I've been trying to settle for the past five months. You're a hard woman to find. As you were non-responsive then, I took time to look for other relatives of Mr. Lesoso. There are some children I cannot find."

"I haven't exactly been sitting around waiting for you. I didn't know of your existence until my niece told me yesterday of your visit to Tava'esina," Lesina said without rancor. "I understand John had a set of books he wanted me to take for my girls."

Mr. McKenzie looked down on his list and legal documents. "Yes, the books, but there is also the matter of his house here in Apia." He then turned a copy over to her. "Please read this, and if you consent to its decrees, then please sign over the line."

Lesina took his spare spectacles so she could read through the print. She didn't understand all this cloak-and-dagger business when she was merely collecting John's literature books that he had hauled in from New Zealand. Pele would love these, but more than favoring the bibliophile, Pele would share her love of books with everyone around her. As Lesina read down the page, her eyes widened. Then, before she reached the end of the page, she gently placed it back on the edge of his desk, smoothed their corners, as she sank to her knees from the Queen Anne settee with her face in her hands.

She wept for all of them. *When you've mastered this business of living, I'll let go.*

The government's surveyors were out early on Monday. Eli came up as the representative of the Church and the Monsignor. He went up to the house and greeted his womenfolk fondly. Lesina was happy to have him have breakfast with them. Kiele and Pele were out to serve vaisalo to the four workers who were out pinning the property. Five acres on this hill were secured for Lesina and her family. None of which touched the old plantation road. However, all that was built in the two and half years they were here in Samoa was enough to count as occupancy and residency.

"Now that this is your home, Lesina, you must stay here in Upolu, you know," Eli stated matter-of-factly. "You own the house in Apia as well." He slurped his coconut porridge loudly and asked Puni for another bowlful with a toothy smile that was as bad as Grace's *fa'alaka*.

"Yes, this would be a wonderful homestead," Lesina mused. There was so much on her plate now. With an unexpected windfall comes more responsibility. The dour Mr. McKenzie will remain as the attorney of record, and she will look up to him to help with these matters. He did insist that she get an accountant on retainer.

The irony of it all, Lesina said to herself.

"I hear a 'but'," Eli queried softly. Lesina had to remember that he was Sama's twin, not Pele's. These conversations with him were akin to talking to Sama.

Lesina surveyed her family. "The girls are growing up, and they have their interests. It's only fair that they choose what they'd like to pursue." Their fates were as varied as they wished and as far as possible as they could dream. *Or as nearby*, she hoped.

"Have you told them?"

"No, but I will. Christmas will be a good day." Lesina looked at Eli. "You should come for our dinner."

"Only if you have it in Apia. This is too country for me, my dear aunt." He laughed merrily at her look of disgust. "You should have it in Apia. They've opened some market parts, which would benefit the girls and kids." He had a valid argument, as the girls were stuck here at Teuila. It was time they went out to town for more than a market day.

The house was at the end of Germantown—clapboard, sitting on a decent yard over an acre, with shuttered windows. *Sugi* trees with bougainvillea were manicured, with giant avapuis grown as borders between lots. Harvest trees were in the back of the house. The mango tree was slight, but it looked like it had its first season. On the opposite side of the wooden fence, a lemon tree was overgrown and lying on its branches. It needed to be cleaned and trimmed down. This neighborhood valued its solitude, privacy, and its trimmed landscaping.

Lesina slowly walked through the four-bedroom villa and was pleasantly surprised that Mr. McKenzie was considerate and thorough in his review of these quarters. It was apparent that he had hired cleaners to pull off sheets and to deeply clean the interior several weeks ago, even before the reading of John's will. Two bedrooms were below and set facing the harbor. Two were above on the second floor, with one facing east over Apia harbor and the other on the abrupt end, facing the opposite view toward the western end of the Pacific.

She strolled to the study and found it accurate to form that John was a voracious reader. She ran her fingers over his volumes of literary greats that he shared with her, that they laughed over during her rounds and his story times. Lesina knew these stories by heart. Some were among Pele's treasures and had been read to commit to memory verbatim. Now, she told those stories to the children. Oh, how Lesina laughed with John over Dickens in the ward.

With John prominent on her mind today, she lovingly traced the aged spine of these editions. Lesina pulled out the Dickens anthology to feel her friend in her mind's eye. Turning the pages to see the illustrations, she traced the child's scribbles on the back cover. As she was about to close the edition, she found a little name on the top right of the front cover. "Property of J. Lachlan McAllister." She pulled another book, and it was the same across the shelves.

She called upon Mr. McKenzie after she went through the house. He confirmed that the house was in John's name, but the property was inherited from his father, Ronan McAllister. Additionally, he informed her that all was legally binding and in compliance with inheritance laws. However, the matter of John Lesoso's parentage was not open for discussion, nor was it to be public fodder.

Leaving the office, Lesina sent word to La'auli and the boys. They were invited to come over to town for several days and spend the holidays with them.

"Pele! Look! Where are *we* sleeping?" Grace bellowed as she ran from room-to-room downstairs. If a dinosaur was alive, its name would be Grace Spafford, and she'd trample all over Germantown.

"Inside voice, Grace! Serenity, can you please take the westward room upstairs? Put yours and your sisters' stuff in there." Pele dragged in a valise. Whatever Kiele and Iolana brought to town must include the trade pestle, mortar, and a whetting stone! They took the other room upstairs. Lesina had her own; she even called one of the girls to come down to bunk with her. No one said yes. Much giggling followed as they heard Lesina cuss them out.

After long, luxurious hot baths, the girls felt it was Wednesday on Thursday as it was indeed Christmas Eve. Pele could not remember when she felt her pores this clean.

The humidity was enough to cause her to dig deep and pray for better, to not whine about their often-frigid watering hole's shortcomings, and to be duly grateful that they had indoor plumbed water. The little girls were scrubbed clean, and seeing their clear, beautiful faces was so good for her soul.

Oh, dear Lord, thank you for the small pleasures. Thank you for my family, my sisters, and my keis.

The evening's festivities included dear La'auli and the young men. There was so much laughter over the simple fare. What they would have had back in Tava'esina now graced their Apia table. It wasn't haute couture, but no one seated here cared. The conversations flowed with such companionable ease.

"I can't imagine my life without any of you anymore," La'auli said, cracking his voice before he was done. "Whatever His plans are for each of us, I am grateful I have you all with me. Thank you to the boys and their help and love for me. They are not blood relations, but they might as well be." He dabbed the corners of his eye with his handkerchief.

"Here, here!" Lesina cried. "Thank you so much for all that you have done for us! We cannot imagine a better man." They gave him a standing ovation. La'auli sat so touched. While his family was all dressed up, he came in his Sunday best lavalava and white dress shirt, which had a hole in its crease and had seen better Sundays. "For he's a jolly good fellow!" And all joined in, laughing and celebrating La'auli's help.

Kiele laughingly reminded their love that her seamstress skills were so good that she'd sew him an emperor's suit! La'auli was so touched that as he looked at the others, *"Masalo ua tatau na fa'apopo le alaga upu e fa'apea—e lelei a le nofo le Samoa le Hawaii!"* The adage should be modified to add that the most advantageous, blessed marriages were between Samoans and Hawaiians!

The *pertinent*, jolly good fellow, this man!

As the family passed gifts of baked treats and homespun goods, a knock came at the door. Mataio ran to the door and gladly welcomed his uncles, Maifea and Lachlan. He showed them into the dining room to the family. Pele got some plates for the men and passed these over to them. Maifea gladly accepted the food while Lachlan waved it all off.

"So, how do you all enjoy the house?" Lachlan asked. "I hear it was some kind of inheritance to you, Lesina." He sat, looking askance at Lesina.

"Yes, from a friend," Lesina said as she put down her glass of water. She looked over at him with caution. "Do you have an issue or need to discuss this privately?"

Maifea reached over to Lachlan, seated next to Pele, while he was on this end with Kiele. He was uncertain about what his cousin was seething about, but none of it was good.

"Lachlan, stop." He kicked the other's ankle, which was pulled back abruptly.

"Did you know and sat there laughing at me when I last saw you, Pele?" Lachlan began to rage. "Sit atop your hill and keep your aunt's secrets?" He waved and waggled a finger at Kiele, "And you? Looking all innocent when you could have helped her do it. If my cousin weren't so smitten with you, I'd think you were just as bad as your leader over there."

Puni stood up and took the kids from the table. Iolana reached into the bassinet for Noah and quickly moved with them upstairs. Mataio pushed back his chair and came around to take La'auli out to the back lanai. He refused to go into the bedroom or to use one of the beds. Tala'i followed them as he had nowhere else to go.

"Do they know, Kiele? Do they know that you're pregnant?" Silence fell over the table. "Did Lesina offer to fix that for you? She sure helped kill mine."

All eyes turned to Kiele. Then to Maifea. Kiele began to cry softly as she stared at the wooden floor beneath her bare feet.

"Lachlan, how did you hear of this?" Maifea asked menacingly. He pushed his chair back and reached over to grab his cousin by the collar. He shoved his face into Lachlan's. "Wow, you had to drag all of us through the gutter. Do you feel like the top man here?"

Pele flushed beet-red from the roots of her hair to her toes. "You have been an asshole sometimes, but this tops all other occasions." She stood and stared him down as he lunged back. "Don't you ever speak to my aunt or sister so disrespectfully!"

"Why—are you the Queen of England's ladies-in-waiting?" he scoffed angrily. "You're bloody darkies, root around, and you drop them all over the place. Even this place? Did she tell you who owned it?" He stared at Lesina, who returned his gaze with contempt.

Pele stood up and threw her serving napkin on the table angrily. "We will always be better than you at your best, you jackanape. I knew you were all the same with your highfaluting airs and walkabouts in town. Go back to your precious, rudderless world and be the rootless lot that you are! You belong nowhere. *Maimau Samoa!*" Pele kicked back her chair, her *inoino* so intense. "*Maifea, fai lou uso ma lua o! Leai se a'ogā na oulua omai iai! Isa iā lea!*" She spoke to Maifea, who was so shamed and humbled but directed her wrath, utter disdain, and complete disappointment at the lout, Lachlan. Pele walked out into the closest room with Kiele crying on her shoulder.

Lesina wanted to scream and cry out loud. However bizarre this outburst was, she knew what he was raging about. The house was his by his moral accounting—fine! Yet, why did he think this rage was righteous? Or herald Kiele's pregnancy from the rafters as if that was his place to do so?

As if she wasn't a midwife by trade. Eventually, Kiele would have told them, but only until then—when she was good and ready to do so. Kiele was a grown woman with grown woman desires. That they love one another? It was a godsend in this age and time in Upolu.

Maifea pulled Lachlan out of his chair and threw him in the front, into the closed lanai of the house. Maifea returned, sad and angry all at once.

"Who the hell is he talking about, Maifea?"

"Ever heard of Emily Schumacher?" Maifea sighed. "I'm so sorry, Lesina. I wasn't thinking." He looked across the table for the food that now sat uneaten.

Lesina thought about the name for some time before she answered. "Wow." She slowly rose, walked out of the dining room, and joined her girls. The deadlock dropped in place.

Maifea didn't blame them.

It wasn't until high noon that Lachlan woke with a pounding headache. He sat up a while to find Maifea staring at him angrily. His cousin looked bearish and so much bigger than he is usually.

"I'm not going to belabor this, but you and I are done. Our mothers are gone, and I haven't any obligation to remain your kin." Maifea stood up, looking down at this man, sad and bitter as Lachlan was at that moment. He tried to feel something for his childhood, for his brother from their grandmother's lap, but found nothing left in him to care about this drunken mess of a man at his feet.

"What do you mean *we're* done?" Lachlan sat up and grabbed the chair behind him to help stop vertigo. "My blood is your blood, Cousin," he mumbled, then he laughed meanly. "My mother was always right about yours. Lowly people."

Maifea stopped in his tracks before he turned back, swept up this shameful pile of a man, and brought him eye-to-eye. "Fuck you, Lachlan. You're on your own even if you die in filth with your entrails splattered out in town." He dropped him to a heap on the floor of the lanai.

"You can't let me go, asshole!" Lachlan laughed and then cried. "Over what? Fucken women? They killed my child, Maifea! They took my child without even asking me!"

"It's Christmas. Get your shite and go home!" Maifea grabbed his shirt and walked out, slamming the door of a now-empty house save for Lachlan, who was still lying on the ground, a crumbled mess.

"Oh, Father, you *almost* had a grandson. I was *almost* a father," he hollered and cried his heart out. "God, why can't you hear me? Why can't *they*?"

He crawled to the chair and tried to lift himself, only to fall to the side. He remained there in that drunken stupor and didn't try again. Here he was, the son who showed up for everything his father had ever asked of him. No, it wasn't enough. Ronan kept tabs on his by-blow and loved him more than he, Lachlan, the legitimate son. Even his dear sisters were not enough to hold his fatherly interest. Maybe the grandchild would have turned his father into a kinder soul, but there is no knowing now.

He'd see his nephews from afar on the other end of the market. Mataio saw him openly, shrugged helplessly, and half waved before he moved on with his party. Tala'i didn't look even as Mataio told him of Lachlan's presence and not too far from the boys, Maifea and Kiele. If she was around, the others were also in the market. Iron butterflies fluttered at the bottom of his stomach.

Maifea turned his back when he saw him as if he had not seen Lachlan at all. This gaping distance, the agonizing silence were now bricks between the brothers.

Loudly over the market din, Maifea called out to *his* family, and they moved onward. Once again, they were passing strangers. Lachlan watched as the crowds swelled and thinned, the hawking and biddings swallowing up any trace of his family.

Lachlan had heard of Maifea's wedding back on January 26—one that they swore he would have been the best man since they were boys. His nephew was born on May 31. His secretary sent them a gift. Kiele returned a thank-you note and told him they were settled well with home and nephew. In no uncertain terms, it was to inform Lachlan that no further help was needed.

Eventually, Lachlan's secretary sent a wedding invite, but there has been no answer thus far. Two more weeks, so it's never too late. Lachlan hoped. Oh, how he hoped even after the cold encounters at the market! Since the Christmas debacle, Lesina and the girls haven't returned to Apia. Through Mr. McKenzie, John's house was put up as a rental as the influx of New Zealanders who needed homes to let was increasing.

The rents were forwarded to him, according to Lesina, "… he is better a stranger to us." Mr. McKenzie didn't deliver the message as it was not conducive to further aggravate the situation on both sides of this legal quandary. The house could not be written over to Lachlan, who didn't want it. Lesina would not come to town to use it and would not take the rent payments.

Lachlan sunk his time into his work, rebuilding his father's business from the ground up. The money was piling up; he and the government were in contractual business, and it was pretty lucrative in these post-war years. There wasn't any doubt that he would be the shipping magnate his father had never achieved in his lifetime.

Now that he was here, comfortable and professionally thriving, he found no peace. Or satisfaction—little but loneliness and listlessness were his best friends. He so missed his family!

"Oh, Lachlan, can you please pay for the rehearsal dinner reception? The vendors are asking." She came around the foyer and walked into his study. The clickety-clack walk of the socialite wife and hostess. She has done an outstanding job at it so far.

"Send the bills to the office, and I'll have someone run the checks over. How many are there?" To pile on the first ten.

"Seven at last count." A cloud passed over her face before she quickly declared, "Can you believe it? We're going to be married in three weeks!" Emily squealed. "Sad that my maid of honor died, but that can't be helped." She came up behind him and ran her hand through his hair. "My father will kill me if he finds out I slept with you before the wedding!" She threw her head back, laughing.

Lachlan pulled her hand out of his hair. "Maybe you should go home, and we'll do this after the wedding." He sat back and watched her twirl around with her new purchases for her trousseau.

"We'll go to Europe and see my relatives out there!" At the right time, she will ask not to come back. There was too much history here. People talk as if they haven't anything to do around here.

She tittered, "This is going to be the wedding of the century! We are going to open the season!"

"That'll be fine." He was tired and weary already. Emily had the energy reserves of ten men put together.

"Are you angry? Do you want me ever to go without?" She sat against the desk so that he had to face her. "You can't deny me anything, Lachlan."

"No, but I need to rest." He rubbed his shoulder and eyes.

"Look, if I were your darkie, you'd probably be all over her by now," Emily pouted angrily. "I saw that unpleasant woman that I went to see that night when I was out of my mind and asked her for an abortion. Today! How dare she share the space I breathe in, Lachlan. Can't *you* find a way to deport her and her mongrels?"

"What do you mean you saw her? *You* went to her?" Lachlan leaned forward, trying to understand her timeline.

"Well, yes. Imagine having a child when my father so disapproved of the Hansells," Emily confessed without remorse. "Now that I have you, we can have six or seven. Whatever you want, honey." The idea of fattening up with each one repulsed her. Two in rapid succession will get him off her back. He can easily afford a housegirl to raise his brats!

Lachlan looked at her in disbelief and creeping horror. "Why would your father have disapproved of the Hansells?" He didn't quite understand the correlation between Erich and Emily. Nor did he want to.

"Oh, you silly man. Did you really think that baby was yours? Don't you know how to count months?" Emily asked, exasperated. "And besides, you were so drunk off your head that you didn't even know you were so pissed poor. Poor Millicent, rest her soul, told me of a way to knock you out. You're good, love, but not *that* good that you can function pissed."

"Emily, are you telling me what you are telling me? Do you hear yourself?" Lachlan asked as his stomach turned over.

"Erich? Eh, that was our second mistake." She rolled her eyes. "But I have you now." *And you're going to give me the whole fairytale,* she muttered to herself. The irony of it all? Erich married Yvonne, dead Millicent's younger sister. With her, he is expecting his first child to live.

Lachlan wasn't remotely interested. "Lesina didn't attend to you? You told me that she did."

"Yes—I mean, no, she didn't—can you believe it? That she said no to *me*? That I was supposed to go to Mueller?" Emily retorted coldly. "Probably was for the best anyway. The right amount of money around this town can bring on miracles. But yes, I saw her earlier at the market." *Miracles and silence.*

She stood up from her perch next to him. "Oh, I know exactly what I said. That you dared to pursue that blackie that day at the market? Remember?" she reminded him. "Do you know what it's like to be talked about? As if I don't exist?" Emily stared at him. "Poor Emily! Her fiancé got the hots for the maid!" Maybe Millicent Riley was better off dead after all. It was a joke to all of them, but she didn't find it funny then. Oh, never again will this man make her a fool.

"All this because of Pele?" he said quietly. The lone woman in Samoa who'd see him castrated before she ever shared spaces with him again in this lifetime. If he died today, she wouldn't remotely mourn him. She'd light his funeral pyre.

"You were engaged to me, but you tore off after *her?* How dare you! I am a Schumacher!" She said, angry and ashamed in one fell swoop. "Second fiddle to a *boonga*. Imagine that."

Emily rolled her eyes, then leaned forward. She slowly ran a manicured finger down his forehead.

She whispered, "I've got you by your balls now, Lachlan. If you tell anyone about this, mostly my father, I will deny it all." She smiled, but no cheer reached her eyes, there was only hardness and hatred in her eyes. She did not bother to hide her feelings anymore now that she was about to marry Lachlan McCallister. As she was previously destined to do so above and beyond his dalliance with that boonga. No one is laughing at her anymore! "See you in two weeks, Jackson Lachlan McAllister. And tell your sister she is going to a group home."

She grabbed her brimmed hat and sauntered out of Lachlan's office only with a slight look back to wave. Her shoes pounded against the hardwood flooring and echoed throughout his father's spacious Queenslander. Her cackling laughter echoed throughout the empty hallways.

Emily spent a pretty penny renovating the house, erasing any signs of the old man. Lachlan didn't care much but drew a line about his sisters' bedrooms. Lachlan watched her departure from his window as his driver drove away from the house. Maybe—no, not maybe—he deserved this much spite for all the wrongs he has committed.

Gisele came in from the back room and asked him if Emily had left. He laughed, then motioned his youngest sister forward. Although she was saved, Gisele also developed scarlet fever and awoke partially deaf. They've had to readjust and find better communication methods as she was quiet and moved about throughout the house, a ghost among the living.

He hung on to her as if she was practically the last vestige of the family. Their parents were gone, and they lost Trudy as well. At fourteen, Gisele was bright and lovely even before she caught the flu.

"Do you have to marry her, Lan?" she sunk into the settee. "I don't need a sister." Gisele fiddled with the hem of their late mother's dolly. "Trudy was our sister."

"I know, honey." Lachlan pulled her into his arms. "I know."

Lolo, Lachlan's secretary, interrupted the siblings. "Sir, a lady at the door. She'd like to see you." Lachlan told Gisele to sit and wait for him as he saw the caller, probably one of the wedding vendors.

This small-statured woman stood up against the opaque glass center of the otherwise wooden door. A wide-brim hat partially covered her face. As she stared outside of the door, Lachlan stopped in his tracks. His heart started to pound in his ears.

"Kiele," Lachlan whispered in disbelief that she was even in his foyer.

She turned as she heard him say her name. "Lachlan." She fully turned around to see him with her baby securely tucked in her arms. He stood awkwardly, staring at her and then at the bundled infant.

Kiele motioned him closer with an easy, gentle smile. As he came to stand in front of her, she peeled the muslin sheet from her son's face. She motioned for him to open his arms as she handed her baby over, tucked into his left side.

"Thank you, Kiele." He gently cuddled the boy close, so moved that Kiele trusted him enough to hold her son. *"Ua malosi siou kei."* Kiele laughed at his funny face as her baby looked at him curiously, happy and content.

"I hope I've not imposed on your time and company," Kiele started as she reached up to pull off her hat. She was apologetic about her intrusion on his time, but she needed to see him now. It took so much bravery for her to come through the gate. "Meet Jackson, Lachlan."

He looked down at the nearly three-month-old baby, his oh-familiar face, the cherubic feet, and cried. Then Lachlan opened the blanket and saw his cousin all over this child. That Maifea and Kiele have named their son after him? He cried as he kissed Jackson's forehead. The baby grinned as if he knew this was his namesake.

"The thing of it is, Lachlan—my husband—misses you so much." Kiele looked to see if she could sit somewhere on the bench in his foyer. Lachlan waved her to do so. Tears sprang to her eyes. "He doesn't tell me, but I know that Maifea is hurting all over."

"I know, Kiele." Lachlan sat down next to her with Jackson still in his arms. "I've missed my brother and all of you."

"So now that I know this, I need you to come home. Maifea will probably hate that I interfered, but we've so short of time in this living," Kiele rushed. "But please come home. We haven't baptized Jackson. He says he wants to wait until Jack's year old, but I know he is waiting for you."

"I'll come home even if Maifea beats me to death." He laughed, wiping away the tears with the back of his hand. "I miss my brother, Kiele. I feel as if the breath of my soul has been silenced."

"I'd love that, Lachlan." She smiled, a little surer than when she was walking up to the house earlier. She leaned toward him as they sat there side by side. "The boys need you, too. This silence between all of you is too much."

Lachlan closed his eyes as he rubbed his temple. "Kiele, I'm so sorry for everything." He alluded to December and the Christmas dinner debacle. As Kiele looked at him, understanding his reference, he needn't have. "I don't know how to make it up to you."

She smiled shortly. "Then come home. Maifea's birthday is next month, as you know. You're only two weeks apart, so it would be nice to have you there. Stay, and we will celebrate you, too. All else is water under the bridge."

Three o'clock chimed on the clock over the sidebar credenza, and she reluctantly stood up. She reached for her hat before asking for her son. Lachlan planted kisses on Jack's forehead and his eyes and lifted a beefy foot to kiss. He laughed in wonderment at how Kiele gave birth to this baby.

Kiele laughed, "Oh, I know." She wrapped Jack a little more securely in his blanket.

Gisele came out of Lachlan's study curious about her brother's guest and saw Kiele with the baby. Lachlan grinned at his sister and called to her to come closer. Kiele showed Jackson to her, who was busy cooing and licking his lips. They all laughed.

"I can have someone take you where you're going, Kiele," Lachlan insisted, as walking about town with the baby was bound to be laborious.

"No, the boys are just around the corner. We're all waiting on Maifea to come out of Ah Yek's tool shop." The shop was around the bend from Lachlan's residence. She rolled her eyes, chuckling. "You know your uso way longer and better than I, Lachlan. You should have put a disclaimer on his back before I married him." They both laughed and secretly bonded with exasperation about Maifea's obsession with shiny tools.

Lachlan stood to the side and gently pulled Gisele forward. "This is my youngest sister."

Kiele looked at Gisele and traced the left side of the friendly girl's face affectionately.

"Make sure your brother brings you with him. I won't have him come home without you, *ua e loa*?"

Gisele giggled. "Thank you, Aunty!" Before she stepped out onto the front lanai, Kiele reached back to Lachlan and hugged him. "Please come home, but if I hear you told Maifea I was here, I'll skin you alive myself."

Lachlan laughed so hard he snorted but readily agreed. This was coming from this woman barely above his hip. Yet, he so appreciated her ferocity. It isn't as if she didn't have longer-limbed help.

"Kiele…"

She sighed, a little sad. She knew what Lachlan was asking and let it hang in the air. "In time, Lachlan. Right now, I need you to come home. One tiny step at a time."

He watched her walk out of his gate and disappear around the corner. Lachlan sank to his knees and cried for all of them—his mother, sister, aunt, cousins, all their beloveds who lost their lives, and those who barely survived in the aftermath.

Most of all, he yearned for his brother's company and fellowship.

The morning was already prolonged and humid in October. Kiele was eying the road, however. Her husband brought the extended family to the faletalimalo, and most elders were sitting by pous according to rank. She was nervous and excited for Maifea, but she was even more anxious for other reasons.

Orators, including Maifea, came together to speak to the bestowal of a title to one of the *tautua* who presently carried his family's two generations of service. The morning began in earnest as the last Elder sat down. The women started to serve tea before the discussion, *le talatālaga*, formed on the eligibility of the supplicant premised on his grandfather's allegiance to the family.

Kiele found Mataio and explained what she was waiting on. He stepped back, looking at her incredulously and with wonder. As she turned around to manage the kitchen, Mataio reached down and hugged his aunt to him close and tight. He went around the corner and cried as he bent at his waist.

Across the malae, a singular soul slowly approached the faletalimalo. While Maifea was still preoccupied with his family's discussions, Kiele came out of her corner. Her gaze found the soul as it ambled toward the *maota* from the near end of the northern approach.

She saw who it was and wept in earnest. Her heart could burst at any moment, but none could bring her closer to this moment. This was not how she imagined Lachlan would choose to come home.

His homecoming was a very public display of remorse. Lachlan had decided to enlist La'auli's help to aid his apology in the form of *ifoga,* the most redemptive public show of sincere remorse.

With his *to'oto'o* and *fue*, La'auli strolled toward Punae'e's chieftain with little help. His hair was colored with clay, his eyes clear, his mustache curled, oiled, and his steps assured. He came bare-chested, wearing a *tapa* tied together with a banana leaf stem hidden by his *fusi siapo*.

In the near distance, Lachlan walked up slowly, dressed waist down in tapa, with a *ula nifo*. He sat behind La'auli as the older man began as his advocate to their unsuspecting audience. The talatālaga was concluding when the elders looked out toward the malae. They were taken aback by who and what he was doing in the middle of the malae. Maifea watched this unfold with his fellows.

"Ua afio mai le tulāfale o Tava'esina, Maifea!" The ranking-titled men turned, as did Maifea, only to see La'auli stand out in the middle of the malae facing them. In the distance came two others. As they came closer, it became more apparent that Lachlan came with Lesina, who was holding a fine mat with her.

"Maifea, ete silafia se fa'alavelave ua tupu?" Maifea looked beyond La'auli to see Lachlan next to Lesina and lost any sense of what was happening. The men of Punae'e saw this also. They were puzzled as one sister's son was on the village green, presented by La'auli of Tava'esina, who is, by no means, a small man in stature, title, or character. This unfolded while the others stood on the steps of the faletalimalo, their mother's village.

Lachlan sat behind La'auli before Lesina covered him with the fine mat.

Kiele motioned the boys to listen with her as they were hidden from sight. Tala'i offered to translate for Kiele as what and whom La'auli was advocating for was a very public apology and supplication for forgiveness, redemption, and understanding.

"E le falala fua lau o laau! E falala ona le agi le matagi," La'auli began. Leaves do not shake on their own. They tremble because the winds are blowing.

"Change does not happen without cause. While I am a stranger to Punae'e, I am known to you and our great counties. I have seen some of you at family functions, including marriages between our children. Some have become serial funeral participants. We face your mountain ridge while enjoying the vast Pacific, the ocean of our forefathers." He paused, allowing this proclamation to settle over the house of Punae'e.

"This said—I'm here on behalf of a son of Punae'e, your nephew, and your cousin. He is one of your *fale tama*, raised here by his mother. While not my relative, he is my son. Under these adverse 1918 circumstances, Samoa finds herself reeling. We have redefined what families are."

Maifea's kinsmen turned from their in-facing semi-circle on their mats to lean forward, curious and to wonder at what had persuaded one of the most ranking orators to stand in front of them, asking for forgiveness on behalf of one of their own.

"… Considering these catastrophic changes we have gone through since the Great Pandemic of 1918, we've seen our families ripped asunder. We have lost so many fathers and sons without discrimination for age, status, or whose extended families they belong to in their living. We've widowers and widows, good and plenty, leave their children behind as they seek refuge with their own families in homes already decimated by influenza, brought to our shores by these *palagis* who say they are men of God. They have died with their families, leaving this extraordinary number of orphans. We have orphans who are still waiting for their parents, while other children, placentas themselves, are now raising infants. Our families on the shores of Tava'esina have not been spared. This, I believe, is your truth as well…"

The men looked at one another and nodded with pained affirmation. *"E sa'o lava oe le fono fetalai."* Punae'e lost more than a hundred of their population, leaving about three-hundred twenty-three at the last census they polled a week before. La'auli spoke to their truth as well.

"Amene!"

"The deadly virus came to our shores in a year, and these men's mothers and siblings have perished. Losing mothers meant losing their anchors to their village, to the customs and traditions of their family here, and to one another. In the absence of their mothers, it is easy to see how evil can take root in these circumstances. For this reason, I present my son's apology to his brother."

"Oute tula'i ma le fa'aalo'alo ma ou o'o mai ai i le agaga o le filemu. Oute tula'i atu e avea a'u ma sui o le atali'i nei, o se alo e fa'asino i se tasi o faletama o lo outou aiga. E ui ona o a'u o se tagata ese i ni si o outou, ae, e le o a'u o se tagata ese i atali'i nei ma nisi o outou ia o loo alala mai iinei. O nei alo, o tino ma a'ano o tina o se tasi o faletama o lo tatou aiga Sa Fanana ma na feola fa'atasi ma ni si o outou. E le o toe po se lilo i le fa'ama'i ua afea ai o tatou laufanua. O le tu'umalo ai o si o la tina, na motusia ai lo la ua so'otaga fa'aleaganuu, atunuu, fa'alenuu, ma lo la ua va nonofo aifa'aleuso. Sa iai fo'i ni tala tauave ma ni amioga le malofia sa tutupu i lo va feilofani.

"E moni o ia o se afatasi, a o lona loto, agaga ma lona tagata atoa, o ia lava o le Samoa.

"O le agaga e fa'anoanoa ai, o le nei au uso ua sola ma ua leai se va fealoai. Ua feupua'i ma fe'aina'i ma oo ai na manatu I la ua o la ua o ni tagata fa'aletonu. O nei mafaufauga e ona oo ai i se tulaga le lelei ma le masei.

"O a'u, ua ou tula'i atu i le loto maualalo ma ua ou fia fesoasoani ia i la ua nei, ina ia fa'alelei ma toe maua le loto alofa I lo la ua va fa'aleuso. O i la ua o le toto, a'ano ma o le aiga e tasi. Oute fa'atulou atu ai i le solivale mai foi o le maota, e talosagaina la outou fesoasoani i le toe fa'atupuina o le filemu ma loto e tasi i nei tuagane. i le agaga maualalo ma le 'ava tele e tatau ai."

Maifea looked over to Lachlan, who was under the fine mat. He remained standing behind his more senior chiefs and two other orators. The men turned to him, briefly consulting with one another, and they agreed. Maifea looked off to the side and saw his wife among the women who assembled under eves of the fale. She met his gaze steadily before she motioned him to act or to address La'auli.

Maifea walked out of the faletalimalo and stood facing La'auli.

In a booming, carefully modulated voice, *"Ae oute le'i utuia le vaitā ma le vaimoea ma mo'omo'o i ai aiga e fia o Samoa, e muamua ona fa'apoipoi liliā, pei ole fetalaiga ia fa'alaeo ua sa le pisa ua sa foi le pao! Ae ole tala sa le itulagi lea fai mai. Ee Salevaoe ta fia malolo o se ua ta li'lia i peau i lalo! Lea ua tafaata nai utumoe ae sila i sa'aga le seuga ile afio mai lena itu ole aiga."* He enunciated each word carefully, tempering the tonality of his words.

He continued, *"Ae ole faitau a Samoa fai mai afai ae malomaloa se fala ise fa'atafa gasegase a se ali'i taua ose aiga, o a toe upu, tautuana lo'u uso tu'o ofe. Ae afai o a'u e fa'atili I ai mata ole tao, tafaloa i paia ma aiga ma*

Let the love of our family prevail and let all we desire that we plan for our family's wellness be done with the clarity of passion, possible only as that of the eternal benevolence of our Savior, Our Lord.

I accept my brother's apology. We are of one blood, one family. This is our covenant forged with the blood of our mothers, our inherent soul bond to one another, and it is the way we will remain to the end of our days. Our mothers would have never wanted us to live lives torn apart by foolishness or by the maniacal acts of others.

As Our Lord is my witness, in front of our family here in Punae'e, I pledge my allegiance to remain brothers until our deaths. I will remain his bastion against evil as he is mine. He is my brother as he is my soa.

"Amene! Fa'afetai! Tausi tatou va feiloa'i, le va fealofani! Malo le onosa'i!" the Punae'e chieftain cried.

"Call the boys!" called off the side to the one of the au'aluma women. "Tell them to come! *Fa'avave mai!*" Tala'i came forward and sat next to the Elder, listening to him for the errand he was to complete for the men here. Before Tala'i could comply with the Elder's request, the bustle among the village elders stopped as in the distance; they saw men, then women strolling across the field, then onto the malae. They came with a song as they joined Lachlan, who remained covered. They settled beside, around, and in the back of Lachlan. They folded Lesina into their circle with love and respect as they did so.

La'auli took a side of his 'ie lavalava and dabbed his eyes. This was Tava'esina in their finest hour. They have come to offer their moral support for Lachlan's return to Punae'e and right the wrongs between him and Maifea. Maifea beamed with pride as he saw Lachlan's support garnered from his adopted father. He almost laughed out loud as he thought, *The village is easier to win over. If he has Lesina as his lone supporter, he has done something right.* He looked for his wife behind the faletalimalo. She smiled encouragingly, tilting her head. Maifea chuckled at her feigned look of innocence.

As the Elder urged Tala'i to go out and unveil the covered Lachlan, Maifea told his nephew to stand aside. He gave the younger his staff and whip. Maifea felt the enormous mountains of Punae'e fall off his shoulders. As he walked toward his uso, he felt so much light in his spirit and soul. His mother and aunt were probably calling them out, both jackasses, how they were disgraces to their wombs. *"I am so sorry, Mother, for all this stupidity."* He respectfully acknowledged La'auli as he stood aside when Maifea approached. La'auli waved him forward.

With love and infinite care for the fine mat, he uncovered Lachlan. The latter looked up to find that it wasn't his younger nephews who came but his very present brother.

They stood looking at one another, toe to toe, before Lachlan threw his arms around Maifea and cried off ten months of unbearable silence between them. Maifea caught Lachlan's face in his hands, touched cheek to cheek as in the customary *sogi*, and touched noses briefly—the *breath*.

Maifea pulled his slight cousin closer. His aunt's *ava'ava*. In his ear, *"Ai kae!"* One brother squeezed tightly while the other wailed, as they held each other close, then at arms' length, before Maifea continually cursed Lachlan well into their next lives. These ten months were so painful that a broken rib did not compare. These ten months were so painful that a broken rib could not compare.

Lachlan guffawed, then sobered briefly. *"Ai ma oe."* His aunt's *peva*.

As they celebrated their birthdays together, Lachlan couldn't help but wonder as he had Maifea, his family, Lesina, and her friend, Captain Parsons, over for dinner.

Lesina did not mention anything of consequence. "I've forgiven you, Lachlan. However, I cannot tell you what you wish to know," Lesina said resolutely. "It is not my place to tell you." She wasn't harsh but loyal to her niece.

Kiele, who had taken Gisele under her wings, did not speak to him about Pele. Not of her whereabouts or any news of her. It was as if Pele had died, and they had not found a way to tell him. Yet, they haven't given him reason to believe that Pele has died. He will not give up. He *could* not give up.

"I know. I don't blame her, Kiele," he answered contritely. "I hope that if you should talk to her, let her know that I'm so sorry what happened. I was out of my mind."

"If you were in your right one back then, I'd be worried, Lachlan." Kiele handed Jack over so the baby could get some of his uncle's love. Lachlan gladly sat down on the bench seat with Jack in his arms. This boy was going to weigh as much as his sire.

"Say it out loud, Uso," Maifea intoned, daring Lachlan to do so before laughing at his cousin's feeble attempt at looking horrified. "He will outweigh the nephews in two months or so." Maifea held a hand to his face. "Kiele, stop eating all that taro. It passes through your breasts as poi to my boy!" Kiele chuffed him on the shoulder before she walked off to find Lesina and Gisele, leaving her menfolk to babysit and bond.

"Stop feeding him your plate." Lachlan turned Jack, lifted him, and looked him in the eye. "Say after me, Jack—Daddy, no chop suey. Yes, more palusami! Come stay with your uncle, and you can learn how to be this good-looking!"

Maifea rolled his eyes. "Give me my son, Ichabod." Lachlan kissed Jack's forehead fondly before gently handing him over to his father.

Lachlan was outraged. "I outweigh that beanpole by two maybe five pounds, thank you." He sat back and contemplatively ran a hand across the bench's grooves.

Maifea sighed. "Have you taken care of your little issues with Emily? It would be best if you cut off that access road, Lachlan. *Ia fa'auma ina uma!*"

"Yes—I compensated her father and family. I hope she finds someone strong enough for her," Lachlan answered joylessly, thumbing the hem on his lavalava. "This close, Maifea." He shifted uncomfortably. "I know it's water under the Vaisigano, Brother, but I'm so sorry we went down this road."

Maifea bumped him on the shoulder. "*Lea ua ka lelei—ua uma ga aso le pogisa.*" We're good—those dark days are over. He laughed at Lachlan's seriousness. "I am not the person you must beg forgiveness from, Lachlan. BEG for forgiveness from, man."

"*Ioe, ua uma ga ou iloa.*" Lachlan looked at his cousin hopefully, appealing to his cousin's man-to-man sensibilities. "Can you give me a clue?"

"Look, you're going to put me in a hard place with Kiele. I've already slept outside in the umu, man." Maifea looked down at Jack. "Your mama has a temper, son. You make sure you know how to *fa'alaka.*" His son cooed. As an afterthought, "You and your uncle."

"I'm drowning here, Maifea." Lachlan shifted his lavalava. "*Fa'amolemole*—please help a drowning man.*"*

Maifea sighed. He felt sorry for his brother. "If I help you, you've got to keep me out of it if and when the wife asks you."

"Anything, Maifea."

Seeking help from Maifea was questionable at best as Lachlan stood in front of Anders a week later, waiting for the man. He came dressed in his proper 'ie lavalava, with a dress shirt, penitent and nervous. How Maifea got him into this was highly suspect, but it would have happened sometime in his quest. There was no way around this.

"Aren't you overdressed? You're here for your execution and not your induction into St. Joseph's, Uso!" Maifea chuckled over his lame joke. "I'm your moral support in case you need it."

"Thanks a lot, Judas." Lachlan felt his stomach plunge to a thousand leagues, drowning in bilious misgivings.

They walked through the doors and were welcomed before they walked to the table where two men were waiting. The first was in a suit and immaculately dressed, from his dress shoes to well-groomed hair. The other came in a cleric's black and white collar. *Great,* Lachlan thought to himself. Both are beyond his scope.

"*Malo soifua! Talofa lava!*" Sama stood up to greet them, as did Eli. "*Ua mai lenei afiafi?* We've met before, but I don't think either of you has met my twin. This is Eli." Lachlan did a doubletake at Eli.

"I know—a bit of a shock." Eli laughed at Maifea and Lachlan's surprise. "I'm here as his second. I guess this is our version of a duel." The men took turns shaking hands while Eli laughed at the discomfort of the others.

"How charitable of you, Eli." Sama retorted drily. "Please, go ahead and sit down." They were on the lanai looking out toward the harbor.

"So, what's going on? I hear Lesina won't tell you where Pele is, and you want to know. Can I ask you why?"

Lachlan took a cleansing breath. "I want to apologize to her in person."

"You can always write to her. I don't think she's up for company." Sama waved to the barman to come over so he could order some whiskey. "Did you have any other intentions?"

"I love her," Lachlan admitted quietly. "I'd like to see if she'd have me."

"I'm not the one to help you on that count, then." Eli chuckled. "She's my little sister but not her matchmaker."

Sama stared at Lachlan before he leaned forward. "You know about her temper, right?"

Lachlan smiled nervously, not sure if he should qualify this statement. He erred on the side of caution and did not affirm Sama's statement.

Sama continued diplomatically, "If you can survive Pele these last years, I think you're good enough to stay in her life until she kills you." He sat back and let the barman lay down their four whiskeys. "Write down your will and state where you want to be buried."

"I'd like to see if she'll have me first," Lachlan reiterated. "I know I haven't been the nicest person to her, and you both being her brothers. I apologize to you both as well."

Sama laughed, "Well, we are of the mind that we aren't your problem. Pele can hold her own, and you must take that up with her." He toasted to little sisters as Lachlan squirmed a bit. "Manuia!"

"You can blame the girl's temper on him. He raised her," Eli quipped jokingly.

Sama drily retorted, "But Lesina finished the job." There was a split second before all the men threw back their chairs. Lachlan spewed his whiskey—as loud laughter rang all around the table. Lachlan and Maifea were so overwhelmed by the hilarity of that statement that they couldn't stop laughing out loud.

"Look, Lachlan, and you, Maifea, you can witness this statement. You are grown enough and are a decent man from what little I know of you. I hope for your sake you are," Sama continued soberly when they restored a modicum of calm. "This is our little sister that you are trying to woo, or whatever it is you are attempting to do."

"I'd like to with your permission," Lachlan humbly agreed.

Sama looked over at Eli. "We are good. It would be best if you got past our parents. The respect is due to them."

Lachlan expelled a breath. Pele is home in Tutuila. The relief was so immense that he sighed out loud. "Pele took her family home, marched right into our parents' home, and declared that she has children now, and that was that." Eli offered.

"Again, this is our sister. The rest is now up to you," Sama declared. "But if you so much hurt her or come up short? We will personally kick your ass."

"I will help," Maifea threw in for the team. "He needs an ass-kicking to keep him in line. Then and now, now and then!"

"Eli, do you have anything more you can think of?" Sama unbuttoned his vest and took off his blazer. "*Matua vevela outou nu'u. Pei la agi mai fo'i se afā!*" The humidity was ever-present, often an indicator of a hurricane or gale-force storm was on the horizon.

Eli laughed and shook his head. "I don't think scaring this guy will do anything, so we will give you our blessings. If you succeed, I'll officiate. You must flip over to the Catholics, though." He laughed as he saw Lachlan's baleful expression.

Lachlan was relieved and thankful that these were honest men looking out for Pele. He was pleasantly surprised they were fair-minded and level-headed for being brothers. He didn't know what to expect from the meeting, but his relief was palpable. Eli called for another round.

"Maifea, I understand that you are with some folks. *Ua mai la?*" Sama looked over at Maifea curiously.

"*Lae lelei*, thank you for asking. *E kele a mea lae makou pisi iai.*"

"*A mana'omia se fesosoani*, let me know," Sama replied meaningfully. "You have support and means from some of us in Tutuila."

They settled into an easy flow of conversations as the afternoon dragged on. They occasionally watched the harbor and its light traffic. A little commerce has returned since 1918, allowing fishermen to return to sea, as well as the occasional steamer from the United States and New Zealand. Nostalgia banked here in Apia as they looked onto the harbor.

Sensing the quiet fall among his guests, Sama reached into his suit pocket behind him. He passed out cigars to the others. "Compliments of my boss, brothers. We can look forward to the next civil war between the Samoas."

Three tossed their chips behind Pele. "You're on your own, Lachlan. Enjoy the present company because none of us dare to tread where you will." The laughter was genuine, without malice. Sama leaned in, four whiskeys on, "But if you so much hurt a hair on her head, call her a *meauli* any time between now and your eternity; there is little that we won't do to pulverize you." Maifea would not have a body to bury.

"I hear you, and I understand."

"But the wedding is still on me," Eli piped in. "I hate funerals."

Book Three

I. 1921

O Amataga Ma Le Fa'ai'uga
Of Beginnings and the Ending

The climb up from the waterfall started, the caterwauling deafening as Grace chased after Iolana and Serenity. The women followed in their wake to the house as everyone had some parts of the weekly laundry in their arms. Sunshine cracked through the canopy to light their road. Mammoth tree ferns lined the ascent, making it scenic and lovely. Pele strapped the baskets to her back while she had Noah on her chest. He was such a happy baby. More importantly, he was a comfortable, clean baby. Behind them, Puni had sheets that they had changed out for the week.

"How are you, Puni?" Pele asked, laughing. "I'll hang once we get up to the house."

Puni shifted her weight from under the wet sheets. "Maybe we should all sleep naked. Our laundry is getting more unbearable by the week."

"We should go down to my parents and do this then. It is easier to spend the day with them, do the laundry, dry it, and bring it back up." Mother had a palagi washer they could use.

"Maybe, but then that will be a longer hike." Puni rolled her eyes, chuckling. "*Lava a lea.*"

"The sunshine is so needed here," Pele said appreciatively. She stepped on some of the flat rocks on the way up to help propel her forward.

Grace and Serenity were up from Mother as they boarded there for school. Her parents have loved the kids since their arrival, as they've begun to lament the idea they will get grandchildren from their children.

Before she brought them from Apia, Lesina helped her settle the adoptions. All four were officially Spaffords with Mr. McKenzie's help, and she would not have it any other way. What man in his crazy mind would now want a woman with four children? Indeed, none in the village. Her parents were getting older, so Father's rhetoric about Olo'ie calmed down. Pele was sure that he still hoped for his sons to return home, but this dream had become more fleeting as her brothers focused on their careers. *She* was here now.

Saturdays were the best day of their week as they were calm and primarily for chores, the girls, homework, and plays. Here, all the kids were settled in together, with Love and Noah enjoying the company of their older sisters. The year has passed quickly for all of them. The aroma of breakfast flittered out from the kitchen. If Puni cooked any more goodies, they would roll down this mountain.

The clotheslines were strung on the eastern face of the house. Ever-present winds came through here and helped dry their clothing and linen by sundown. As Pele strung up their sheets, Grace stayed nearby. She brought up a coconut and sat on it, her cherubic face so serious.

"Mama, let's talk." Grace sat properly, as much as she could, perched on the coconut.

"Oh, what about?"

"How about I stay home for school?"

Pele stopped pinning momentarily and came around to see her daughter as the sheets began to flow with the cleansing breeze. "Is something going on?"

"Kids make fun of us at school." Grace pounded her stick against the wood of the platform of their lanai. "Sometimes, I hear Seren cry in her sleep at Grandma's."

"What about? Is something wrong with your homework? Your clothes? Hair?" Iolana stayed with her parents to help them and watch the girls during their school days from Monday through Wednesday when a teacher from town was dispatched to the more remote areas.

"What does *kekea* mean, Mama?"

"What did they call you?" Pele felt a hard flush creep her neck. She dropped down on her haunches to Grace's face and kissed her button nose.

"They called us *kekeas*," Grace mumbled under her breath. "Is that a good thing or bad, Mama?"

"It is a *thing*, Grace, but nothing you should worry yourself over." No, not one bit. She sighed as she had been so distracted with rebuilding her parents' homestead up here that she had thought about how the girls fitted in with the locals. It was the least of her issues, but she could not have this happen. Children do not say things that their parents would not otherwise.

They went inside after she pinned the laundry and let the sunshine help. Serenity and Puni were putting down their papaya porridge. Pele grabbed their toddling Noah while Serenity helped Love sit at their bench table.

"Serenity, how are you doing at school?" Pele ventured as they sat through their meal.

"Okay, Mama. They brought in notebooks and books this week, so I'll bring my notebooks up next week when we break for Easter." Puni mouthed something over her back, miming that there was something wrong with their child. Grace looked at Pele knowingly, nodding.

"Anything else going on?"

"No, why?" Serenity scooted closer to Love to break her bread. Love took the bread and shared it with Noah, waddling around their living space with porridge on his cheek and bread between his few teeth.

"Noah, come back! You're s'posed to sit at the table!" Love went to get him before he painted the wall with yellow papaya and tapioca. Love was the family's rule enforcer with a well-lived four years of experience under her belt.

Breakfast continued with the usual noisemakers.

Pele kept the girls at home through Monday morning, sparing Iolana from walking them to the other end of the village where the schoolhouse was in one of the fales. Grace tore off, running ahead of them as she joined her little friends. Serenity hung back and stayed near Pele, kicking stones. When Pele walked them, Serenity felt so fortified. Her mama didn't give one iota about people staring.

Serenity reached over to hug her tight and close as they arrived. Pele returned every bit of her daughter's energy to her and kissed the top of her head and forehead. "You know how much I love you, right?"

"Yes, Mama," Serenity muttered. "Can you stay?"

"Anyone calls you anything you are not? You kick their asses. You don't have to keep being the better person, Seren." Pele laughed at her wide-eyed shock. I suppose that wasn't the correct advice, but it would be good if it kept bullies at bay. "No, you tell me these things, and I'll take care of it."

Grace ran back and plowed her over. "I love you, Mama! See you later?"

Pele guffawed, catching Grace in her arms to her. "You are loved, Keleise Spafford!" One more round of kisses and hugs before they walked hand in hand onto the campus.

"You are loved, Pele Spafford!" Grace chortled happily. "So much, Mama!" With her plump arms that went up in the air as far as she could stretch them.

Pele watched them as they safely clambered over the *paepae* before turning from them. She turned from them to get on her half-mile walk back to her parents' home. She passed the usual curious and mostly disapproving stares. She brought the girls down, skipping her parents in her khaki shorts and oversized white shirt with her brimmed hat as she was wont to dress while planting.

"Oh, this one with her *kekea* kids," one roared, uncaring.

"Yeah, I heard she came home with all these kids and no husband in sight."

"I bet her mother is happy about that!"

"All those Germans in Apia, right? And her mother had so many high hopes! Well, look at her now."

"Ai na alu e pa'umutu ma ka'a ma papalagi o Upolu! Isa!" one sneered as Pele passed her.

Pele stopped in her tracks. She pivoted on her boots and turned around. Three of these village hens were standing there, teletyping her faults. She chose the first one, daring her to move into her space.

She went toe-to-toe with Mrs. Holier-than-Thou, who purported that Pele was out whoring with the white men of Apia. Pele stared her down before stepping back.

"Are you the ones who called my kids *kekea*?" She asked this of the group while staring at the one in front of her.

"Well, they are, aren't they?" Another piped up.

"And you are to them, what *exactly*? Do you clothe them? Feed them? Love them when their days are horrible because of gossipmongers like you?"

"Well, they're in our kids' school! You shouldn't bring yours here!" The center hippo cried out, outraged by the association.

"A government school, which I am sure you don't pay for," Pele retorted dispassionately. "And you over there, remember me?"

The first hen did not. "Remember when I kicked your ass at school?" Pele reeled on her step to see all over them in their glories in front of her. "Still the pastor's kid, aren't you? What are you now, *wife* of one?" Pele looked her up and down, noting how plump she was this old.

Recognition finally dawned on the Wall. "Funny how these things come around full circle." Pele tipped on her heels. "I don't think it'd be a fair fight if we settled this right here, as I will exact every pound of pain you've caused my daughters."

"Look, we were kidding and didn't mean anything by it. *O kala a kamaiki.*" The Wall tried to rationalize the name-calling that the girls were albinos by their children was just innocent child's play.

"There's nothing innocent about this when you stand there and call me a whore. Was I one to your husbands?" Pele spat. "What comes out of mouths of babes are reflections of their parents, and you call yourselves god-fearing good Christians?"

She turned and left them like that, with mouths agape.

"You haven't changed, you good-for-nothing. *Maimau ou matua!*" The Wall commentated meanly. *Your parents are too good for you.*

Pele reared up and slammed a punch into the Wall's face so hard she could hear bones crack. The Wall crumbled to her fat knees in shock at the blow. "Just like old times, you are a flaming hypocrite. I feel sorry for the congregation you serve. To the end of your days, you'll never know or witness His love. Go teach yourselves the virtues of your religions before you attempt to teach my children about their father."

The third complainant reared to defend the Wall, "*Isa! Leiloga se Siamagi ga fai amio iai!*"

Pele scooted closer to this one. "Does the old man know? How can you lie that the child and the one you are carrying are his? Whom do you think you're fooling? The thing about nasty 'secrets' like yours? Eventually, they all come out, no matter how deep you hide them in the night. So, before you talk about other people's lives, ensure your flaws aren't already out there. *Vaai ou uo po'o 'o ai na fa'asalalauina ou tala.*"

It's amazing what an afternoon with her mother can be!

She pushed her way out of the village's gossip center. It wasn't until her parents' house was in sight that she sighed as she looked over her knuckles. Her mother would hear of her transgressions in about a couple of hours, if not sooner. Yet, she was beyond the usual *'oke*. The scolding about her code of dress is so disagreeable to her mother. Her usual brusque manner with guests, if there were any, came with a possibility of a suitor, many of whom were older than dirt Pele tilled, and had grandchildren.

Leata saw her daughter pass by and tried to flag her down from the kitchen window before returning to the hill. Pele didn't stop as she always did. Her parents' two dogs ran up to her, and she stopped for them. Leata tried again, but Pele didn't hear her over the howls or could be ignoring her mother. Leata knew then that something was troubling her daughter as she didn't stop for tea earlier when she came down with the girls. Leata sighed when Pele was in a mood, and she did not stop and visit on her return.

"You guys want to go up with me?" She asked the dogs. "I don't think I have anything for you, but I'll find something." *Saute*—South and *Matu*—North—were her father's dogs. Since Pele and her small family arrived, they had been on the mountain often. Her father mumbled something about loyalty and the lack thereof.

They howled and ran ahead of her. They knew the road as though it was a set map in their brain. They would have to settle themselves once they were at Pele's doorsteps as she had only two feet and would take a little longer with the bends in the road. She heard their happy howls and laughed. That race up to the house was bound to make them thirsty.

She stopped at the fallen Fijian rubber tree. Oh, how she loved the view of the Pacific from here. The miles and miles of clear, blue ocean where it meets the most translucent skies! The Y in the fallen tree offered a front stage seat that no one could ever take from her. One sock had slipped down behind her ankle. As she undid her boot, she could see a congregation of the usual suspects veer toward her parents' home. The busyness of these Lilliputians when declaring war. She felt like Gulliver if only she were as big and stepping on sand fleas was kosher.

Good luck with that, bloody sea urchins!

Her mother's exasperation will be heard, but not today. *Not today, Mother.* Pele wasn't about to regurgitate what those monsters had accused the children of being. The accusations were too vile to be repeated.

After the thirty-minute breather, she stopped at the reservoir and took a handful of water from the trickling spigot. The basin below was mossy with a dubious ecosystem, but Pele figured that if she had not died as a child, the water wouldn't kill her now. It always amazed her that folks were up here way before the turn of the century and put this water cement basin alongside this barely developed road into the hinterlands of her grandfather's property.

The sunshine was a blessed relief. The morning's chill was dissipating from the tops of the canopy. Days were always much more relaxed when the condensation seeped downward through leaves, especially this April morning. North, a chocolate poi pup, came running to the final bend in the road, howling and contorting his way back to her when they heard her head toward the house. She stopped and bent down to him so he would stop being so excited as he jumped on her. He slobbered all over her face before he ran back to South, who was sitting on Pele's steps, calm and collected as she was old school and knew that Pele would eventually get there.

It was strangely quiet at the house as she didn't hear the kids or Puni pitter-patter around. She went to the lanai to see if they were there, but no one was there either. She set the dogs down in the shade before going into the house. No babies, no Puni there.

On the table, a note was lying there, written on monogrammed paper. Who would leave one on this fancy paper on her old wooden table? She turned it around, and it was Sama's stationery.

Pele,

I've taken Puni and the kids to Father and Mother's. Please note that we will take care of the kids. Please let us know if all is well by the end of the week.

Know that I do this with so much love for you.—Sama

Pele kicked off her boots, rolled off her woolly socks, and pulled her shirttails out of her shorts as she sat at one of the benches. The hike on this roundtrip was as natural as breathing, but today, she was tired and weary from the encounter this morning. There were reasons why she volunteered to stay up here at the old cabin site.

When she first arrived before New Year's last year, her parents were not amused by what they thought was a stunt to stop her marriage prospects. It was soon apparent that, one, she wasn't kidding, and two, the children were legally adopted. After many silent spells with their erstwhile daughter, the children won her parents over. Even more so, Iolana was like the daughter that Mother should have had. This left her, the daughter Leata did have, busy with the work that was Olo'ie. So much was overgrown and buried under repeated storms and a recent hurricane. It took a massive effort to rebuild and re-plant the avapui row around the dilapidated, abandoned homestead. It took two hired villages and the whole family to put Olo'ie back in its original glories. She was so appreciative of the small grant from Lesina's windfall inheritance.

Pele stood up and leaned against the window. The sun's rays flittered over the hillside from the house to the valley below them. By now, she was already weeding through the steppe crops, which included watercress and spinach. With Puni and the kids at her parents' house, she wanted to slow down. She opened the windows to let the airflow through the house, throwing the beds outside to be aired out, which she would hang up later. As she put her hands on her hips, a massive yellow butterfly with monarchs landed on her clothesline. The breeze was slight, but her arms were lined with goosebumps. *Oh, Epe! Are you here with us?*

As the sun ducked behind the clouds and high-beamed every five minutes, she threw her boots and socks outside through the front landing. Herring cans were atop their pantry, and as Puni wasn't here, she took one for the pups. She mixed some old breadfruit with the fish before she called them back to the landing. They were given equal shares of food on the banana leaves, which they woofed down greedily.

Without the kids home, the house was eerily quiet. The canopy leaves rustled; birds squawked in formations as they flew over the house. The furtive hustle of geckos crawling across beams, feeding on flies and mosquitoes. Ripe coconuts whooshed and boomed as they dropped around the house and thumped down to the waterfalls. Some were cannon balls as they hit boulders or sliced through lower canopies above the embankment. She prayed that wandering wildlife didn't get pummeled by these missiles. The last thing she wanted to worry about was tetchy neighbors seeking their prized sow or a breeding boar when these falling coconuts killed them.

Do what, Sama? She wasn't invited to something that much was apparent. *I love you, too, Brother.* She loved that he knew when not to include her. She wasn't keen on family meetings for the sake of family meetings. There was so much to be done up here.

Her first harvest was successful as the Navy liked their greens up in Mauga-o-Ali'i, the residence of the Admiralty. All were shipped on time to town and to the Navy's sous chef, who came to check out the plantation. He also asked for tropical spinach, string beans, and Cavendish bananas, all of which her father grew in abundance. The success of that meeting was a notch under her belt. It helped that the head chef was her grandfather, who came more often now that he had more to look forward to in addition to seeing his daughter, granddaughter, and adopted great-grandchildren. Without even meaning to, she made her mother so happy.

She missed her market days with Lesina and her sisters, but this was where she belonged. This was home without worries about property issues or rent.

But do the kids? She sat on the edge of her bed, and an overwhelming sadness flowed over her. *Children will be children.* However, their environments strongly impacted their growth and what they said. When these women discovered that the girls were hers, it became an open season to call them albinos as apparently one of their parents was palagi. Neither parent was here to fend for them, but she was their mother now. Their health and wellness were her responsibilities. Sometimes, the heartaches of being an instant parent were more than she could bear. She cannot fend off the cruelties of these mean birds and their parroting offspring. While Grace was better at pushing off the hate with her usual shrug, the same could not be said for Serenity, who needed a little more time to process these moments when she missed her father more than ever.

Pele rolled over on her left side and cried. She cried for the girls, for missing Kiele and not seeing Jack, her godson, every day of his early months. As her mind went through her list, she sobbed for Epenesa, Tava'esina, and all their losses. She wept for her Serenity and lost chances to know her mother better. She sobbed for all of Samoa, all the families whose family members were not allowed to lie in final repose near their own homes or the grounds of their ancestors.

It had been so long since she last had an all-out cry that she wailed her life out hard, long, and without reservation. Her heart ached. It felt like it had fallen out of her chest and exploded after it collided with one of these barreling coconuts!

Lord, please help me find my feet. There must be a respite. Let there be quiet for my babies.

Her mind went over all her folk and wept hard for any semblance of hardship visited upon by others. She might as well weep for all her losses.

A loud pounding at the front door woke her. At first, she was so disoriented when she bolted from her bed. She was still in her shirt, a little ruffled but decent. She felt as though a falling coconut *had* hit her head-on. The sleep helped, but she was more worn out than she was before the nap.

She searched for their only clock; it was about one thirty in the afternoon—it was still Monday. Pele glanced down and realized she had left her shorts in the living lanai.

The pounding came again. Where were the dogs? She didn't recall sending them home before she lay down earlier. Her parents sent someone up to explain why she nearly knocked out the pastor's wife. The calls to her parents *'oke* never got old, and her anxiety over her father's stinging admonishments was at the top of her things to avoid. Living here on Olo'ie had its advantages.

Meanwhile, she found her shorts under her moody cats imported from Teuila Hill, basking in the sun that came through the door's glass center and the skylight above them. With visible hairballs all over its front, it was going to do.

And it was probably Puni playing messenger from her mother. The sense that she will never outgrow that anxiety of Mother's calls to see her will never go away.

She pulled the door open, and standing between the dogs was Lachlan. She slammed the door so hard the hinges whined in screaming protest. Her hair chopsticks were on the table; she dusted off the cat hair and rubbed the sleep from her eyes. *God, why?*

Pele hurriedly looked around the room to see if there was anything amiss. She shooed her cats to the bed.

The door opened with the disdain of the world in its creaks. "What are you doing on my doorstep, Mr. McAllister?"

"For a chance, if you let me." The dogs looked up at her as if apologizing for their betrayal. "And I have letters." She took them from him—from her beloveds in Apia, including a short note from La'auli.

"Thank you, Lachlan. How did you get past my parents?" Pele opened the door for him to step into her living, playroom, sewing, and weaving lanai. And Noah's canvas, be it a lump of coal or a nail, he found along his searches. She took her letters from him.

"I asked Sama and Eli if they could tell me where you went as Lesina, Kiele, and even my brother would not." Pele thanked her loves silently. Loyalty was a commodity that the dogs didn't seem to understand.

Lachlan looked around, and he was impressed. The corrugated tin was pushed up a cathedral-like height, the interior light and roomy even if it was one main room with varying uses, and the beds were discreetly tucked behind a movable barn wall. He filled the room as he stood inside.

"So, a chance at what exactly?" Pele asked impatiently. She wasn't panicked by his appearance but more worried that her parents would discover that he was up here. She gazed at him from head to his feet. He was thinner than she had ever known him to be.

"By the way, I've been here since Saturday with Sama, so please don't worry about your parents. They know I've come to see you." Pele peeked at the calm dogs and silently banished them back to her parents. She's had a year and a half to play this moment out. Then she got busy and wasn't prepared for this at all to happen today: a *little warning, Mother.*

He looked around the house and was further surprised by how much Pele had strived to make this barren skeleton a home. Plants and creepers were hung from a cross beam. Artwork from the children with varying skills was framed and hung against the rays, some closer to the doors. Feet and hands in charcoal were tucked in a notebook on the dining table. Pots were lined up against the wall by the kerosene oven. Hand-sewn quilts and a decorative mat were hung on the wall as decoration and a way to keep them until they were used. The windows were especially startling—not one was the same size or make. One was set into the roof.

"For the plants here indoors," she offered as she saw him look up at the roof with surprise and some apprehension. "It has held despite the rainstorms over this past year. The kids love looking up at the skies at night." Grace's voice rang through her mind when she shared this. A smile played up her lips.

Lachlan noted her tear-stained face, which she tried to hide but not without some coal and dirt streaks. He didn't say anything about this as he knew it was premature of him to assume he had the right to know. She was older in some ways that came with the enormous responsibilities she had now as she carried her role over the plantation and her single parenthood. This was certainly not the young teenager he first met on the steamer four years ago.

"I know we didn't part on good terms. I've no excuse for my inexcusable behavior."

"You were an uncouth, drunk monster." Pele didn't spare his feelings, looking directly at him in the eye. Time has passed since, and life has moved on here in Ta'ima. Her inoino, though, has never entirely gone away.

"I was," Lachlan echoed regretfully. "I don't know how to make it up to you, but I'd like a chance to do so."

"How much time do you have?" Pele hoped for a day because she had a harvest to pick for the Admiralty by Wednesday. She doubted if Lachlan even knew a lemon from an orange tree. She did not have hope for him and his knowledge of watercress.

"As long as it takes." He smiled at her undisguised dismay. "I gave Maifea reign over my businesses, which will give him good practice at dealing with the Kiwis."

"Lachlan, I like your determination, but I have a life and the kids here. I adopted the children, so it's not like I can hand them off to anyone else when I want to," she began.

"I know that much—Lesina was kind enough to remind me of this." He sat with his feet crossed at the ankles. "I'm not here to disrupt your life. I want to be part of it. Kids, pets, plantation, your parents."

He reached into his pocket and gave her the shillings. She smiled sadly as she took them. The anger he took these with that night was palpable.

"My brothers aren't so easily pushed over, and I'm sure Lesina shared with them what Christmas was all about."

"If I didn't first see the twins, I wouldn't be here," Lachlan admitted. "They were fast to remind me that I have a death wish if I so much blew a hair on your head out of place."

"What about your life in Apia? I have so much on my plate that I don't know how to fit you on it." Pele stood up to tuck her shirt back into her makeshift shorts from old khaki pants she found among her brother's old dresser. All tied with a belt fashioned by twine from a lausalui.

As she thought of what she had just said, a flush crept up her throat to the roots of her hair.

"You don't have to have me on a plate to have me, you know." Lachlan laughed at her mortified fidgeting.

"If I said that it was okay, you would be okay with everything that is my life?"

"I'd like to learn how to be friends and carry on from there."

"No promises I'll be the woman you want me to be."

"No—be the woman you are, and I'll adjust. You can learn to trust me again."

Pele swept her face with the back of her hand, smearing the coal against her cheek and eye. "I need time, Lachlan." She felt so overwhelmed. As if the last-ditched reason was to boot him off her mountain, "Aren't you engaged to that woman?"

"I was," Lachlan said. "I wouldn't have sought you out if I remained engaged to her."

Pele didn't want the details. Her mind was already traveling in so many directions as to why he was here. All that was Apia was behind her; he was among the best reasons why she left.

"You believed that woman over any of us, Lachlan." Pele averred, staring at him. She wasn't angry, but she had not forgotten his carte blanche belief system. "That you believed we were the monsters we were colored as by that woman whom you had no history with." *Save that you slept with her,* she said to herself. *That and that she is palagi.*

"I was so wrong. So wrong to do that to your aunt, Kiele, you—*all* of you." He replied contritely.

Pele held his gaze, openly reading his face. He was penitent, indeed, so sincerely. There was no denial or excuse in his eyes. She sighed, not wholly swayed, but she could not find any anger left over. The world she had built here did not include him by the stretch of her imagination.

"Would it comfort you if I stayed with your parents, slept outside in the umu, or anywhere you felt comfortable—safe—with?"

"Yes," Pele blurted. "I would like to set you up on the lanai outside until I can figure this out. This is going to take some time, Lachlan."

Lachlan was happy she wasn't sending him down to stay with her parents. The idea was daunting, with her father questioning Lachlan's motives and why his daughter was part of this unexpected, even harebrained proposal. Still, as her brothers were not the firing squad in Apia, they must know him well enough to let him come home to their sister here in Olo'ie. Then again, Fiso put his money on his daughter.

Pele gathered one of the homespun mattresses already sunned out and hung it on the clothesline. She beat it several times before she gave him a quick run over the lay of the land, showing him how to get down to the waterfalls below the house to bathe, clean, and wash laundry. The path was lined with tree ferns with a dense line of beach hibiscuses, some felled by hurricanes, but still, they grew from the breaks in their trunks. As they came up the trail, she taught him how to mark his way by looking up through the canopy.

The cash crops lined the steppes, so the irrigation flowed from one level to the next. There was only an eddy from which the water flowed. The freshwater eels at the mouth of the pool at the top of the watercress steppe popped up now and then, and they were to be spared at all costs. They keep the water flowing as they've done since she was a child, with her mother weeding these steppes.

As evening settled, she made a simple meal for them, which he was willing to eat cardboard as he had not eaten since he left Sama and her parents' home that morning. She had brought crayfish and snails from the river below, souped with coconut milk, and seasoned the boil with sea salt, tomatoes, and hot peppers with taro that they had from Sunday's toana'i.

All on dish, she served the meal outside on the lanai. It was one of the best meals he had eaten, and he told her so. She appreciated his gratitude and upped his culinary tastes by making them some lemongrass tea with pagikekes.

As he helped clean the humble dishes, Pele set out his bedding. "Goodnight, Lachlan," she said as she took the dishes from him. The dogs had come up onto the lanai and lay near the hammock. She mouthed, "Traitors!" at them. Miffed, they turned around and showed their backs to her.

Pele turned and found that he was already asleep. Pulling a pareo blanket, she covered him from his chin to his ankles. In through the door, which she locked, she was superbly tired when she lay down in her bed.

She woke up early the following morning as she had some weeding. She put some coffee on before she opened the house. The weather window was her rooftop, and none looked good, but she had to be on the steppes now that she was behind a day.

Lachlan was waiting on the lanai for her. Upon seeing him, she gasped. He was covered with mosquito bites from ears to ankles. He smiled, pained and aggravated.

She went back in and strained the coffee of its grounds. She found some cinnamon and dry basil, which they have used on the children.

Lachlan went into the house with her. Turning him around, with his lavalava tucked between his legs, she rubbed a poultice over his bites from his shoulder blades, trying to account for the rawest of them on his upper body.

Pele turned him around and was faced with his *malofie*. As it was then, his birthmark popped, but these horrific mosquito bites lined them. The last time she saw it wasn't exactly the happiest moment for either of them. The memory mortified her. Then, as he stood squirming, she started to laugh while sitting on her haunches with this pungent poultice of mud, coffee, basil, and cinnamon.

He looked down at her as she was in stitches. It wasn't difficult to remember and understand why she was on the floor giggling so hard. How lovely she was when she relaxed around him; if he weren't in severe pain, he'd laugh with her. They'd had some insanities together, and this had to top all of them.

Lachlan knew then that he was going to marry her as she lay there snorting, trying to stop her giggles until she saw his birthmark again, and she was onto another fit of merriment. He did not know a more inappropriate woman than Pele Spafford. This was another level of her crazy! He loved her as she tried to nurse him through this nightmare, which was not going well when she was on her back, wracked by gale-force laughter. He couldn't help but howl with her.

"Yeah, I have to admit, that was insanely mad," he said with cackling laughter. She held her stomach, wholly torn between nursing his bites and the utterly improper laughter at the silly birthmark and how she first knew of it.

"I swear, Lachlan, I didn't see anything! So much soap was in my eyes that it took a storm to wash it all out!" She gasped between bottomless giggles.

He had to let her come to him when she was ready. Lachlan didn't want this laughter to end. He loved this woman so much and would gladly spend the rest of his living days with her. Bide his time, he will. He was going to marry her.

The persnickety sun was coming out as the overcast afternoon was turning into evening. Two months had come and gone since Lachlan first came to find her. Now, he was standing with her father and brothers as they stuck bamboo poles into the sand and waited for fish to start biting. The tide was going out, and it was easier for fish to come in from over the reef. They came down to spend the weekend with her parents as Eli had come in from Apia to visit.

Their children were up and down the beach as Serenity and Grace were enjoying the respite from school. They were busy gathering hermit crabs into a basket they could hand over as bait. Sama knelt and showed them how to pull off the back ends of the hermit crabs. Flinching at the sight of lifeless crabs, Serenity was not with the chore, so she clambered up the knoll and crawled under the pareo blanket between Leata and Pele. Love sat on the other side of Leata, mesmerized by the breezes. Noah was with Puni, who was putting him to bed. Iolana was blossoming under Leata's care, so she was never far from her.

Grace stayed with Lachlan on the seashore, and it was clear that she was his shadow now. Pele seemed to have fallen by the wayside after they met him again, and it was cause for much laughter. The girls remembered him from Apia, so it was easier to acclimate to his presence now. Lachlan was patient with them, enjoying them as his children, as Pele was their mother.

The women watched the fishing competition with merriment before the men started to heat up and seriously compete for the most fish caught. It was every man for himself while they were throwing their lines out and pulling in as many as possible, some with the same bait. Grace was helping all the men with the bait basket, so there was some honesty among the fishermen!

When the count was done, as they unloaded their baskets, Fiso came out as the top fisherman while Sama took his second place with loud albeit ridiculous complaints the bait used did not match the fish count. Fano counted a couple of sea cucumbers, noting that someone had to think of their mother. Leata applauded his efforts to ingratiate himself into her good graces. The novice, Lachlan, was last, but he was superbly happy with the sizable parrot fish he pulled in from the dark waters as evening fell over them and the shore. On the contrary, Eli felt this was all beneath him as they compared their catches.

With a kerosene lamp to help them see, Grace and Serenity picked sea snails stuck all over the rocks along the beach while the men strung the fish before heading home. Along with Puni and Iolana, Pele helped clean the fish and the Samoan sea snails, which were as good if not better than the French escargot, according to Captain Parsons, during one dinner on the *Williamson.*

As they sat down for the blessing for the meal a couple of hours later, Pele sat near the children, as Lachlan had his back semi-turned toward her. "Lachlan?"

"Yes, *la'u* Pele?" He was the face of glowing innocence. The family would make out big if he and Grace were poker players.

"I know what you did," she hissed. Noah squirmed in her lap, trying to sit with Lachlan. He protested loudly when Pele held him back, his lip puckered. Sighing, Pele let him toddle over to Lachlan. Love came and sat in her lap while Grace scooted over to Pele's knee. Serenity had chosen to sit with Leata on the other side with her grandfather, Fiso.

"Fa'akai vae, pi'ilima, ma aua le pisa." Love said to Grace firmly. The house was already quiet, so Grace did as she was told before glaring at Love. Pele's hand rubbed her back meaningfully with a firmer reminder of their mother's '*hands to self*' before Grace bowed her head and closed her eyes over her folded arms and properly crossed legs as Love asked her to do so. Ordered her, Grace thought, peeved. *Rules were all that mattered to that girl! I will order you to stop being so bossy after Grandpa's Amene!*

Pele leaned slightly and whispered, "You are such a crook!" Lachlan's eyes went wide with hurt. Pele clapped a hand over her mouth as loud, irrepressible giggles nearly escaped. He mouthed something back to her over Noah's nodding head.

Sama turned around and stared at them meaningfully. Lachlan chuckled with his straight face looking forward. For emphasis, he hugged Noah closer.

Pele could not contain herself anymore and whispered to him, giggling haplessly, flushed from her toes to her roots. "Yes, Lachlan McAllister!"

Lachlan closed his eyes, and he motioned to her that she ought to as her father was saying the prayer. The prayer went on for an eternity, and even he began to fidget. He wanted to holler his *Amene!*

He longed to grab Pele and love her. Yet, he knew that they had an eternity to do so. Evening prayers for the family with everyone here at home were rare, so it is imperative that he learned patience. Lachlan knew that Pele's menfolk were probably not as keen on him if they witnessed him loving on Pele, their daughter and sister, so openly. They both had to behave momentarily. No, *he* had to, as much to his irritation, Pele was blissfully asleep while holding both girls to her with that schoolmarm posture of hers.

Two hours later, he and Grace were worn down to the marrow when the Amens finally echoed throughout.

Standing before him was his wife, Peletumuaotamali'i Leatalua Spafford, now McAllister, a very appropriately dressed woman. This was their last day of the wedding, and she wore a monumental dress of tapa and its adornments presented by Gisele as his sister was standing in for their mother and womenfolk. Some of the women Tava'esina were also representing La'auli as his extended family. Maifea brought his father and their mothers' extended families of Punae'e. This was as Pele's father and her uncles answered for her side. The dowry exchange went on as respects were paid to both families was immense.

The affair lasted four days as the serving persons were buried under an extraordinary number of fine mats, the flowing currencies of the islands. Fiso also opted to answer the exchange with the *mea sa*, whereby the dignitaries on Lachlan's side responded with unique fine mats to save this occasion.

Lesina and her mother were by her side, as were the girls. Her aunt beamed at how much Pele had grown up in her absence. With the pomp and circumstance of a titled wedding, Leata took the lead as the mother to present her daughter to the world.

While they waited for the ceremonies and the speeches carried out by the orators to conclude for the afternoon, Pele caught Lesina's hand and tucked it into her palm. "I love you, Lesina," she murmured gratefully, much like the ten-year-old waif whom her aunt rescued once upon a time here in Olo'ie. Lesina blinked back tears.

Being Maifea's wife, Kiele now sat on the groom's side, but the women were inseparable. The sisters spent much time reflecting on life since Basilica and the pandemic. They cried about anything and everything. Maifea passed them on his way to the congregation of men and blew them kisses. "Stop talking about me!" with a cheeky wink at his wife and Pele, now his sister-in-law.

"You are a beautiful bride, Pele." Lachlan pulled the sash by which the dress was held and helped her unravel and open the tapa so she could step out of it. To keep the exterior from rubbing her skin raw, she wore a tied-on lavalava to cover her breasts. Her hair was wrapped and pinned where moso'oi and plumerias were tucked above her head. She had never spent so much time being a pampered woman until her wedding.

Tiredly, she undid her hair while Lachlan got a towel to wipe the coconut oil off her limbs and arms. She laid back on their marriage bed, and without much ado, she curled up, tucked her feet under her, and slept.

The exquisite pressure was building, and she could not help but move toward it. It was incredibly persistent, pain and bliss all at once. She turned to her side in her sleep as a finger tenderly caressed her spine. Passionate kisses followed down the curvature of her back, raining, nibbling the skin between her ribs, his breath warm against the valley between her hip and pelvic bone. Sleep was pulling her so deep into the vortex that she fought through this highly sound sleep and woke up.

"Lachlan!" He didn't stop wreaking havoc on her senses and her body. "Please…"

"Follow me, Pele." He pushed her onto her back. "I want you to know this about loving you with my body." He took her hand and moved it down to his stiff shaft, letting her feel his veins. She held him while he pressed against her rhythmically. He rubbed her, knowing her burgeoning desires, and burned her innocence between crescendos. She was so ready to explode that she slipped down, her legs over his buttocks, arching into him.

"Lachlan, please love me!" He pulled her hips and plunged into her incredible warmth, allowing himself a moment to get her to make room for him. "Lachlan!"

"Come to me, honey!" He urged tenderly.

Pele cried out as she did, gripping his shoulder to her as he took her to heights that she never knew, as he ardently suckled each nipple tenderly as she held him. His onslaught was tantalizingly slow, painful, overwhelming, and excruciatingly loving. She wailed as her body instinctively responded to him as he exacted total bliss from her core. She cried into his neck as she lost all control. Lachlan held her as he plummeted and poured the totality of his love into her until he cried in relief, completely drained and sated. She was his wife in all manners and ways important.

Lachlan rolled, pulling her atop him, with her tresses wildly covering her face. He wouldn't let her go, staying inside her, letting her rest for a moment.

He would teach her how to love him and to receive his love for the rest of their lives. Maybe this will all get old, but today was not that day. Lachlan came around the table and held her to him. He nuzzled his nose in her soft hair that was already pinned up for the day. She giggled and slapped him on his flank. The man was supposed to be dressed and ready to go into town, but he was still in his lavalava. Lachlan pulled her favorite sticks out of her hair, watching her bun fall into the wild tresses surrounding her exquisite face. While pinning her against the table side, he dropped his lavalava and pressed into her.

"Lachlan." She had a hundred and one things to do; the most important of these was to prepare this man for his run into town. A hand reached around, unbuttoned his oversized shirt from her body, and slipped one side off.

"Look at my precious wife." He stood back to marvel at the sight of her blossoming body.

He tenderly felt each of her engorged breasts, her nipples erect for him. *"Oka se manaia ma matuā e aulelei!"* Pele blushed to the roots of her hair. Lachlan laughed as he tried to kiss her, and she slapped him on the flank again.

"Come! What's the worst that could happen? We can't get any more pregnant!" he cajoled, his voice full of aching love and yearning. If he could have, he would have married this woman the moment they set foot in Apia.

He sank to his knees to kiss her distended belly. "I love your mother. So, so much!" He rubbed his nose across her abdomen and rained kisses to and from her belly button. "We will have ten more, so your mother is always busy!"

As she tried to pin her hair, he unbuttoned her shorts. She pushed him forward and completely lost it when he pouted. In one swoop, he unleashed all her inhibitions as he rhythmically possessed all of them as he hiked her legs around his hips. Pele lovingly traced her husband's malofie as he waged war on her rational sensibilities.

The morning meeting with her civilized husband will have to wait. No, it was postponed indefinitely.

She stood by the window, having tea with Lachlan as he was finally dressed for the day. It was only ten o'clock, but it was late enough. The ocean spray was particularly rough this morning as the winds carried it inland. Next door was the Hawaiian plumeria that she had grown with her brothers years before. Upon one of the branches, a kingfisher was sitting with his black eyes darting around.

Her teacup fell to the ground and smashed to smithereens. "Lachlan, don't go! Tell my brother to hold off on the crew. Please," she cried out, knowing innately something very wrong had come to pass. The winds picked up and shook the sturdiest branches while the kingfisher stood fast on its perch. She wrapped her scarf around her neck and held onto her husband. He hugged her back to comfort and reassured her that he would heed her.

Later that evening, the tides whipped a crew attempting to land on their shores onto the reef line. Only one survivor of the eight-man team was found inland with the remains of the boat.

A week later, she gathered up Serenity and Grace, Puni and Iolana, leaving her little ones, Love and Noah, home with her parents. No, she corrected herself—*their* little ones.

It had been a while since she traveled, but she knew in her soul that something was amiss. Lachlan traveled with them as Pele was five months along, and besides, he *needed* to be with his wife. He also had business with Maifea to go over in person.

Eli was waiting for them at the harbor. He saw the girls huddled around Pele's abdomen, and when she stood up, he saw why they hovered over her. As the gate opened, Eli hugged the girls, then his sister. He was so happy to see her. This trip was dangerous, with the high tides flowing in and out of the harbors. However, when Pele had some burr stick in her mind, she was going to see it to its natural end. The weather was the least of her worries.

His sister was glowing and flushed from the hours at sea. Her baby helped. Eli laughed merrily as Lachlan came out from behind her with a rueful grin. Following them, Puni and Iolana were happy to put their feet back on the ground and leaned for hugs from their driver.

They traveled directly to Tava'esina as Pele insisted rather than stay in Apia with Eli. As they pulled up, Pele stepped out and saw Lesina, the boys, and Kiele, who was now about seven months along with their second child. While the children reacquainted themselves, Pele looked toward the hill and became teary-eyed as their home, Teuila Hill, was still up there. Lesina had taken up some orphaned girls and taught them the healing arts the last time she wrote to her.

She looked over at the chapel and was superbly surprised by what she saw. A home was built near its grounds. Koa trees lined its roundabout, looking more like a rectory at the Immaculata. Over the entrance of the house, "*Epenesa's House for Children.*" Kiele taught the kids here.

"How long has this been here?" she asked softly. Pele lifted her wrap against the stiff wind.

"Last year. We kept it open so that all children and orphans were welcome. Your husband's idea." The rent monies from John's house came here as arranged by Lachlan.

"He's trying, Pele."

He did this before he came to her and never told her. No one in her family bothered to tell her.

No one is talking to me, she thought gloomily. Her heart felt like it would burst out of her chest—*love, frustration, aggravation*. She was pregnant, not blind or deaf!

Lesina held her baby in her arms, her hand over Pele's growing abdomen. "I will be home for you. I have the both of you expecting, so I'll come after Kiele's delivery." Pele smiled back at her aunt, so overwhelmed. "Delivering grandbabies is becoming a constant business, you girls." Lesina chuckled.

They went to the paepae to see La'auli lying on his mat with his back to her. The men had taken to sit next to the pous, not looking up at her. It was unbearable for them to do so. Puni took Iolana with the younger girls and sat toward the middle of the faletalimalo, quietly chatting as they waited for Pele to come in and see her uncle.

He was worn around the face, his weathered eyes into their sockets. About twenty pounds lighter than he was when he came to the wedding. Those arms, once so solid and lithe, were emaciated, as was the rest of him. His hair and mustache were limp and lifeless against his face.

The advanced state of his condition so shocked her that she sank to her knees, speechless. She wailed without preempt, holding a hand over her breast, utterly devastated to the bottom of her soul! La'auli reached over to grab her free hand. "Oh, Uncle!" between howling sobs.

"If you came to *makagaga* over me, then you shouldn't have come at all," he admonished her sternly. *"Ke kagi mai fa'apenā ma le maloā ae lea nonofo mai lou aiga?"* Pele sobbed uncontrollably, holding onto his fragile hand. *"Soia—ae e alofa ia te a'u, e te le tagi fa'apenei!"*

"I am so, so sorry, Uncle. I didn't know!" Her heart was so constricted to see this beloved man full of life now on his deathbed.

"Of course, you didn't as I instructed Lesina *ma tagata uma nei aua, aua lava le fai atu ia oe! O nae o lea e fanau!"* Lesina and the whole entourage were not to tell her.

"I'm pregnant, not invisible! *Oute ofo lou le alofa ia te a'u ma leai se tala e fai atu!*" Pele beseeched him. "I could have been here earlier!"

"For what? It is a foregone conclusion, Pele," he gentled his tone. "For every life that we lose, there is one that comes anew. *Lea ua lua ma'itaga fa'atasi ma lou uso. Fai fa'alelei le lua fanau auā o tama fanau ia o Samoa. Ua lava ta ita ma matou ua matutua. Ua tele nei tausaga ua ou aulia. Fai ma outou le lumana'i o Samoa! Toe tepa tasi mai fanau nei aso ma le alofa ma le tofā mamao o latou tua'ā!*" He quietly asked her to sit closer as he wished to feel her baby. Pele slowly glided his hand over her abdomen. Tears slowly leaked out the side of his clouded eyes.

He whispered something else. Pele scooted closer to listen to him. She leaned into him again. When it was clear to her, she laughed out loud, crying, and laughed again.

"*Ioe, lea.*" She looked for Lachlan and called him nearer. "*Fai mai La'auli po'o o e soifua pea?*" Was Lachlan still alive?

The whole guesthouse roared in laughter.

"*Fai lua aiga ia mautu ma fa'aolaola ane—fesosoani leisi ia leisi ma ia e alofa siou afafafine!*" Here, he was so ill, and still, he worried about her. He wanted reassurance that they settled well, honored their vows, and raised their children as the children needed to be.

"*Ioe, Tamā!*" Lachlan lovingly supported Pele's back as she sought to sit comfortably with her protruding abdomen.

"Let me go, Pele. It's time."

La'auli died the following day with Pele and the women nearby. There was no struggle when he let go of Pele's hand an hour after she took over the watch from Lesina at five o'clock that morning.

Pele wailed hard and long now that he could not hear her and scold her for being so loud. He was ready to let go, but no one in the present company was prepared to do the same of him. *Why is life so unfair, Father?* Why couldn't their child have met him?

After the women lovingly bathed and rubbed La'auli's body with oils, the men came to prepare his body for burial in the tapa. The orators, including Maifea with Lachlan and the younger men, took up his carrier. They slowly carried him through Tava'esina to show his spirit the length of the village.

Aue ua maliliu toa ua maimau ai aupega o le taua. Manuteleina lau malaga. Alofa le Atua ia maua sou nofoaga ile lagi i lona oli'olisaga tumua. Amene.

The women, Pele in the center, Lesina and Kiele to her right, while Puni and Iolana carried her left with the children following. They were dressed in the finest fine mats the village offered. These were folded as skirts were crimped at their hips, with *pales* of the *laumaile* leaves and moso'oi, high wooden combs in their hair, and barefoot. So'o walked ahead with them as he paced the procession with utter respect for Pele, the closest to a daughter that La'auli had in this living.

The funeral procession was attended by villages near and far who came upon hearing of La'auli's passing. The respect was for a man who lived his most compassionate, constant humanity among his people. They showed up in droves to see him to his proper and final burial in the hallow grounds of Tava'esina. He will be known unto God as he was to his people.

They sang hymns and songs to honor him, as is the way of the au'alumā. To bring him home to the Lord's house in Heaven as he asked that they do.

"Help me go home, Pele." He had gently asked her earlier. *As you wish, La'auli. As you wish.*

Lo matou Tamā o ile lagi, ia faia Lou fināgalo!
Oh, the passing of warriors, their weapons of war left to waste in their absence. May you pass through with love as you go unto God and find your place in His holy Kingdom.
Our Father, who art in heaven, hallowed be thy name; thy kingdom come, thy will be done; here on earth as it is in Heaven!

Lesina stood over La'auli's gravesite; here was the fresh mound of dirt that marked their monumental loss. Sometime in the following days, So'o will come back with the boys and bring loads of sea rocks to mark this great man's grave permanently so he is not lost to history. *May he be remembered as he deserves to be,* she prayed quietly.

The early evening breeze flipped some wisps of hair across her forehead. She heard the girls walk up behind her. Grace's laughter pealed across the knoll. The men sat on the paepae in hushed conversations about Samoa's future while having their tea with their cheroots.

Kiele lovingly smiled at Maifea, who glanced over with his cheeky wink. Jack was talking his uncle's ears off as though he, at nearly two, was the paramount chief lording over his vassals. *Lord, that boy!* Lower on Jack's totem pole, her handsome nephews sat to the rear of the men, dutifully waiting on their elders and uncles. Not far from the paepae, Puni watched the girls give merry chase with other children. For once, they were just children, carefree, and love reigned over their play.

"For every life lost, one is born," Pele said more to herself than to the others. She slipped her arm around Lesina's waist. Kiele slipped her hand into Lesina's on the other side of them. Pele smiled at Iolana, pulling her younger sister closer. Iolana rested her small hand over Pele's protruding belly.

"It is taking three to make up for our La'auli," Lesina said casually. Her remark slipped over the girls, settled, before they cried out, laughing merrily in disbelief.

The sun began to sink over the horizon. Lesina strolled with the girls towards their families as they would come to close La'auli's day with evening prayers.

He looked up to the paepae and saw the men who awaited these souls, his daughters. Life wasn't always kind to them, but together, he knew that the future was in good hands. La'auli placed his arms behind the small of his back and walked from the fresh mound of dirt. He joined Epenesa, who was among those who had come for him. *Their time and work are done here.*

Tautai le Atua i le faigamalaga, ia mamao mala ma ia tau le sini o le fa'amoemoe ma ia manuteleina le folauga mo le lumana'i. Agalelei le Atua ma faamanuia i fuafuaga uma o feagai mo outou. Lou oli ma lou talosaga lea!

E le falala fua lau o la'au. E falala ona le agi mai le matagi.

The brave warrior will now rest in peace until time immortal. May the young carry the baton from their elders to their young as they steward Samoa to her future in manners most becoming unto You, our Lord God.

The winds are blowing through Samoa.

Dedication

This undertaking is ultimately for my daughters. Suppose I was asked what my greatest ambition I have accomplished was to be a good mother, albeit flawed and human. However quiet the times, how far you travel from me, you remain my heartstrings.

As a self-proclaimed citizen of the world, I am not without a home mooring. No matter how far I have traveled, lived, or how great the reasons why I extended my absences from home shores, I thank my parents for the home they carved out for us in American Samoa: Alaimalo Henry and Foini Porter, in memoriam. They had a love story that withstood the test of the US Navy, its countless deployments and transitional moves, the US Pre-Civil Rights era, and the transition back to American Samoa with family in the interest of filial piety.

How lucky can a girl be? I have an unending appreciation for my older brothers, without whom my childhood would not have been as enchanting, all-encompassing, epic, or evolved as it was. It would not have been as filled with music, play, and imagination—all essential to the best beginnings of life. Moreover, so much gratitude is also due to my sister burning the home fires, so we have a home to return to when the world becomes too much to bear. Kirstin and Nora, you are my sisters by choice. Thank you for the company and for choosing this family as your own.

The enormity and importance of friends who become family over years, who are family? My sincere love and affection for our King neighbors and cousins. You have been with us on every crazy outing as preteens to seeing through our parental funerals. Fa'afetai le fai aiga lelei, le fai uso moni. Sandra ma le aiga: fa'afetai, fa'afetai lava! O alofa i'inei, o alofa i'inā!

The gratitude, love, and hope are unfettered, genuine, and lifelong.

Acknowledgements

From working drafts to the first run of the manuscript, my ardent supporter and early fan, DWS, you are very much appreciated and prayed for, with so much hope and love. I am forever grateful for your company from the beginning to the end. I said I needed to do this. You agreed.

I am this far. You rebuffed any mention of your part in this, saying that this was about me and my fifth child. You were happy to be my sounding board, giving me breadth and space to get through good and bad days while you were amid many of your own. You are love I don't deserve.

6,528 miles to go. Maybe 25.

Kaneyo Hirata Mahe (Anchorage, Alaska), Victor Liu (Huntington Beach, California), and Donna Silupevaelelei Mailei (Apia, Samoa)—you are so valued in this undertaking. Thank you for saying yes to drafts and challenging reads. So much love for sticking around for the odd conversations about this and that, for having opinions about that and this.

My *fa'afetai tele* to my fellows of the FHS/MBHS 1987, for the unforgettable joys of old friends while I was writing Tepatasi on a parallel universe. You are thought of kindly, prayed for in mine, and hoped for the best as we travel the roads from thirteen through our shared winters. There is so much wholesomeness in friendships as solid as ours, as even writers in whatever form need their supporting cast. Fa'afetai tele lava mo fai uso aua lenei taumafai, Michelle and Mona.

My fondest and loving regards to my cousins and friends of Vaigaga, Tulāele, Fasito'outa, and Apia, who graciously hosted part of my heritage trip in March 2023.

No more remarkable is the importance of geography than to its people. When I started to write Pele's Samoa, I did so without a working knowledge of Samoa as an adult. I spent hours in the early morning lights pouring over archives and topographical sketches of Upolu (Samoa) from the 1900s. To this vibrant end, this happy intersection, for the epic crawl in eight crazy hours, coupled with animated discussions, a crash course in A'oga Samoa, at a National Geographic-documentarian-worthy tour? Fa'afetai le lava, Will.

Tepatasi was fortified and ambitious with its musical score. I must also thank the lyricists and soloists of eras gone by. In memoriam to those who peopled and scored local history and folklores by their genius musical compositions: Teaching College of Samoa (1970s–early 80s), Penina Tiafau, Golden Ali'is, Five Stars, and the Samoan musicologists of the 1970s–90s all-inclusive. My gratitude to the crooners and composers of Hawaii, Rarotonga, and Tahiti, who were also on my playlists. Moreover, my best and love to Peter Young, Gary King, and Victor Liu for the music while I was home.

Je vous remercie! Gracias a ti por la música, Gipsy Kings, Kiko & Gipsyland, Juan Gabriel, and Bolero Soul.

If I was remiss in my Samoan language skills, the fault is wholly mine. It is hoped the mishaps are minuscule and that these errors have not diminished the intent of the dialogues as they happened within *Tepatasi*. Nonetheless, the importance of being among the voices that inspire and push a Renaissance movement in Pacific literature is the keystone ambition, however imperfect my own is.

Afai ua sasi se tala, fa'amagalo le auauna ma lafo i nu'u le a'inā auā e poto le tautai ae sese le atu i 'ama!

This work of fiction was written with utter respect and love for those who lie in immortal rest at Vaimoso, Samoa.

Moreover, thank you to the Austin Macauley Publishers for your trust and belief that this work, Pele's *Tepatasi,* is worthy of a greater audience.